"Brimming with dangerous secrets, rich characters, and the hauntingly beautiful descriptions Sarah Ladd handles so well, 1800s Cornwall is brought vividly to life in this well-crafted tale that kept me glued to the pages. What a brilliant start to a new series!"

—Abigail Wilson, author of *In the Shadow of Croft Towers*

"*The Governess of Penwythe Hall* is a delightful and emotionally gripping tale that will tick all the boxes for any Regency lover: romance, history, and enough unpredictable intrigue to keep you up past your bedtime."

—Kristi Ann Hunter, author of *A Defense of Honor*

"Lovers of sweet and Christian romance alike will fall in love with Delia's strength amid the haunting backdrop of her tragic past and the Cornish coast. Throw in a handsome leading man willing to turn his life upside down for the children in Delia's charge, and you have a story you can't put down."

—Josi S. Kilpack, Whiney Award–winning author of the Mayfield Family Series

"Absolutely captivating! Once I started reading, I couldn't put down *The Governess of Penwythe Hall*. This blend of *Jane Eyre*, Jane Austen, and *Jamaica Inn* has it all. Intrigue. Danger. Poignant moments. And best of all a sweet, sweet love story. This is by far my favorite Sarah Ladd book. Don't hesitate to snatch up this title!"

—Michelle Griep, Christy Award–winning author of the Once Upon a Dickens Christmas series

"Ladd continues to write refreshing Regency romance with a spotlight on the working-class countryside life as opposed to the ballrooms and bustle of London . . . The Romeo-and-Juliet-esque romance between Kate and Henry is perfectly paced and dimensional. Gender discrimination, childhood labor, work conditions, and a rapidly changing society make this a compelling read as much as it entertains."

—RT BOOK REVIEWS, 4½ STARS, TOP PICK!
FOR THE WEAVER'S DAUGHTER

"Ladd's plots are tight with tension, drama, and well-researched historical details . . . [The Weaver's Daughter is a] sweeping tale of violence, romance, and above all, hope for the future."

—CBA MARKET

"Loyalty, love, and forgiveness all have their place in this story, which is rich with historical detail. Readers will sympathize with the characters' inner struggles as they face the difficulties that come when a way of life must transform."

—BOOKPAGE FOR THE WEAVER'S DAUGHTER

"A strong choice for fans of historical fiction, especially lovers of Elizabeth Gaskell's North and South. It will also appeal to admirers of Kristy Cambron and Tracie Peterson."

—LIBRARY JOURNAL FOR THE WEAVER'S DAUGHTER

"A gently unfolding love story set amid the turmoil of the early industrial revolution. [The Weaver's Daughter is] a story of betrayal, love, and redemption, all beautifully rendered in rural England."

—ELIZABETH CAMDEN, RITA AWARD–WINNING AUTHOR

"Once again, Ladd delights readers with a skillfully plotted, suspenseful page-turner. As always, her characters jump from the page, each one a realistic and achingly human assembly of merits, flaws, doubts, and faith. Like all superior novelists, Ladd doesn't default to pat endings, offering even her villains a potential happily-ever-after by putting her faith (not to mention the characters' and the readers') in God's abiding mercy."

—RT BOOK REVIEWS, 4 STARS, FOR A STRANGER AT FELLSWORTH

"This novel reads well and fast; its vivid imagery and likeable characters fill the pages. The well-crafted metaphors and tight sequences make for an absorbing read. Though set around the Regency period, the style is fresh and the voice genuine. The spiritual aspect of the novel does not overpower; it is woven into the plot and provides a graceful way to unite the beliefs and morals of Annabelle and Owen Locke. I want to read more in the series."

—HISTORICAL NOVELS SOCIETY FOR *A STRANGER AT FELLSWORTH*

"[*A Stranger at Fellsworth*] can easily stand on its own, but readers who enjoy this book will want to devour the trilogy."

—LIBRARY JOURNAL

"With betrayals, murders, and criminal activity disrupting the peace at Fellsworth, Ladd fills the pages with as much intrigue as romance. A well-crafted story for fans of Regency novels."

—PUBLISHERS WEEKLY FOR *A STRANGER AT FELLSWORTH*

"Beautifully written, intricately plotted, and populated by engaging and realistic characters, *The Curiosity Keeper* is Regency romantic suspense at its page-turning best. A skillful, sympathetic, and refreshingly natural author, Ladd is at the top of her game and should be an auto-buy for every reader."

—RT BOOK REVIEWS, 4½ STARS, TOP PICK!

"An engaging Regency with a richly detailed setting and an unpredictable suspenseful plot. Admirers of Sandra Orchard and Lis Wiehl who want to try a romance with a historical bent may enjoy this new series."

—LIBRARY JOURNAL ON *THE CURIOSITY KEEPER*

"Ladd's story, with its menace and cast of seedy London characters, feels more like a work of Dickens than a Regency . . . A solid outing."

—PUBLISHERS WEEKLY ON *THE CURIOSITY KEEPER*

The

GOVERNESS

of

PENWYTHE HALL

ALSO BY SARAH E. LADD

THE CORNWALL NOVELS
The Governess of Penwythe Hall
The Thief of Lanwyn Manor (available January 2020)

The Weaver's Daughter

THE TREASURES OF SURREY NOVELS
The Curiosity Keeper
Dawn at Emberwilde
A Stranger at Fellsworth

THE WHISPERS ON THE MOORS NOVELS
The Heiress of Winterwood
The Headmistress of Rosemere
A Lady at Willowgrove Hall

The
GOVERNESS
of
PENWYTHE
HALL

SARAH E. LADD

THOMAS NELSON
Since 1798

The Governess of Penwythe Hall

Published in Nashville, Tennessee, by Thomas Nelson. Thomas Nelson is a registered trademark of HarperCollins Christian Publishing, Inc.

Published in association with the Books & Such Literary Management, 52 Mission Circle, Suite 122, PMB 170, Santa Rosa, California 95409-5370, www.booksandsuch.com.

Interior design by Lori Lynch

Thomas Nelson titles may be purchased in bulk for educational, business, fundraising, or sales promotional use. For information, please email SpecialMarkets@ThomasNelson.com.

Publisher's Note: This novel is a work of fiction. Names, characters, places, and incidents are either products of the author's imagination or used fictitiously. All characters are fictional, and any similarity to people living or dead is purely coincidental.

Library of Congress Cataloging-in-Publication Data

Names: Ladd, Sarah E., author.
Title: The governess of Penwythe Hall / Sarah E. Ladd.
Description: Nashville, Tennessee : Thomas Nelson, 2019. | Series: The Cornwall novels ; 1
Identifiers: LCCN 2018050105| ISBN 9780785223160 (softcover) | ISBN 9780785223177 (epub)
Subjects: | GSAFD: Love stories. | Regency fiction. | Christian fiction.
Classification: LCC PS3612.A3565 G68 2019 | DDC 813/.6--dc23 LC record available at https://lccn.loc.gov/2018050105

Printed in the United States of America

19 20 21 22 23 MG 5 4 3 2 1

This novel is dedicated to L. E. G. in loving memory.

PROLOGUE

Winter 1808
Cornwall, Southwest England

A biting gust of Cornish wind screamed downward from the churning sky, billowing Cordelia Greythorne's jet-black traveling cape. She reached to secure the hood atop her head, and as she did, her grip on her valise slackened. The heavy bag plummeted to the snow-laden ground below.

Through a veil of tears, Delia looked to the satchel, and the sharp burning in her lungs reminded her to breathe.

With the exception of her trunk that had already been loaded onto the carriage, everything she owned—every single possession remaining in her small, forlorn world—was encased in the worn fabric bag. She had packed and repacked it, as if the bag held treasure. And now it sat waterlogged on the uneven cobblestone, a dusting of fluffy flakes gathered on the bag's wooden handle, appearing almost blue in the dawning light.

The rare snow would be gone soon. Warm air would eventually rush up from the sea, melting any bits of ice coating the harsh landscape. How odd that the weather should be so violent on her final morning, as if even the moorlands were attempting to push her away.

A fresh tear formed, and as she bent down to retrieve the valise, the coachman appeared at her side, the capes of his greatcoat flapping in the harsh gale, his shaggy gray hair whipping wildly. "May I?"

Delia pivoted to prevent him from taking it. "No, thank you." She snatched it up and clutched the soggy bag to her. "I'll keep it with me."

The coachman retreated to the carriage and resumed his post.

She knew she should share the coachman's eagerness to be about their journey and free of Greythorne House. Her life within these archaic walls had died with her husband. Nothing was here for her now, and yet her booted feet felt heavy and her tender heart refused to bid its final farewell.

She cast one last look back to the house's ornate facade. It had stood for centuries, proud and majestic, on the cliffs overlooking the English Channel, and it would continue to stand, no doubt, for centuries more. The magnificent sight of stone and iron had thrilled her upon her first arrival here three years prior, but now the heartless house was as dark as the night and as severe as the moors spreading behind it.

Movement at the entrance caught her eye. Delia turned to see Ada Greythorne, her mother-in-law, outside the door, her narrow chin tipped high and her posture erect. No cloak or shawl draped her thin shoulders. She stood, still and unprotected, in the wild elements, clad from head to toe in her lustring gown of mourning black, its delicate van-dyke hem dragging over the wet stones. Even at this distance, hatred radiated from the woman's icy eyes.

Mere weeks ago, that vicious expression had struck fear in Delia's heart. But now, numbness pushed out dread and took up residence in her soul. She'd withstood every bit of hateful gossip and defamation. No further damage could be done.

Delia turned to step toward the carriage when biting words froze her steps.

"I suppose you think you've won."

Delia looked over her shoulder. "No, Ada. I haven't. Indeed, there is nothing to win."

Ada locked eyes with Delia—a challenge boiling in their pale, empty depths. The wiry woman took two paces toward Delia and lowered her voice. "I'll allow you one last opportunity to atone, in part, for your betrayal. You will tell me where *it* is. You owe it to your husband's memory."

Delia raised an eyebrow, her will to argue dead. "I've no idea what you're talking about."

She proceeded toward the carriage, but within moments footsteps pounded the path behind her, and before Delia could react, fingernails dug into her upper arm, sharp even through her cloak.

Delia winced and whirled to face her late husband's mother.

Ada's jaw trembled with each ensuing word, and her eyes narrowed as she hissed the words. "Don't think that just because you're leaving, we'll—I'll—forget what you've done. My Robert told me the truth before he breathed his last—when you were nowhere to be found. It'll catch up with you, as sure as the sun rises and sets. Mark my words, you'll pay one day for what you've done. If you've any sense in you, you'll ne'er return to Cornwall. You've betrayed the Greythornes, and none will forget."

A thin layer of perspiration shrouded Delia's brow. She swallowed. Hard. She'd defend herself if possible, but weeks of protesting and attempting to reason had been fruitless. She ripped her arm free and resumed her walk toward the carriage.

"A curse on you, Cordelia Greythorne." The shouted words hurtled toward her like a rabid beast pouncing on prey. "May you never know a moment's peace or a day's happiness for what you've done."

With Delia's next step a tear blazed a path down her cheek. She refused the coachman's offer of assistance into the vehicle, and once inside she snatched the door closed and pressed her back against the tufted seat.

She'd heard the horrid accusations so frequently that she was almost beginning to believe them. Regardless, the truth—the ghastly, jagged truth—would always be on her side, even if no one else chose to believe it.

Delia squeezed her eyes shut as the carriage rumbled away.

She'd not look back. She wanted to remember how her home used to be, not foreboding and vile as it now stood.

Another tear fell.

How she wished things could have ended differently, but the dead were buried, and her shattered heart could endure no more.

CHAPTER I

Easten Park, Yorkshire, 1811

Death. It seemed to follow her, affecting those around her.

In the three short years since Delia's arrival at Easten Park as governess, death, an unwelcome visitor, had called far too many times. Only a few months into her time at the estate, the children's mother died. And at this moment their father, Randall Twethewey, was fighting for his life within these very walls.

A flash of lightning gleamed through the uncovered window, momentarily shedding its silver glow on Sophy, her youngest charge, who slumbered next to her, her head on Delia's lap. Thunder growled, and Delia held her breath as the child stirred but did not wake. Delia slowly released her breath. At least, for the moment, the little one seemed peaceful.

Delia glanced at the mantel clock. It was not yet four.

The night had been a long one, thick with the suffocating trepidation that hovers during uncertainty. Minutes stretched to harrowing hours, but eventually exhaustion gripped her charges and offered a reprieve from the fear. Julia and Hannah, the older girls, slept on the settee. Johnny curled up on the rug next to the waning fire. Only Liam, the oldest boy, had been permitted to remain by his father's side.

The nursery door cracked open, and Agnes, the children's maid, appeared in the doorway. The willowy woman's normally tidy hair hung in chestnut wisps about her narrow face, and her candle's flickering glow highlighted the dark shadows beneath her eyes.

"What news?" Delia whispered as the maid inched in.

Her expression tight with concern, Agnes knelt next to Delia. "'Tisn't good. Not good a'tall. Master Twethewey's dying. At least that's what's bein' said downstairs. His horse got spooked and fell when jumpin' over a hedge o' brambles in the east forest. The beast fell right atop o' Mr. Twethewey, and the weight o' it poked his ribs clear through his lung. He can breathe and whisper a little, but he can't move and is gettin' worse with each hour. The physician's here but says there's naught he can do."

Delia's vision blurred with unexpected moisture, and she brushed back Sophy's ebony hair from her face. "The poor children."

Agnes straightened and brushed her skirt. "The children are why I've come. Master Twethewey wants to see you and Mr. Simon."

Delia frowned. "Why would he want to see me?"

"My guess is he wants to talk about the children and what'll happen after . . ." Her voice faded, and Delia's blood ran cold.

Silence—and its lingering apprehension—resumed.

Agnes nudged her arm. "Go now. I'll sit with 'em. Mr. Steerhead's a-waitin' ye in Mr. Twethewey's chamber. Here, take my candle."

Delia eased Sophy away from her lap, slow and steady so as not to wake her, and then accepted the light.

Once outside the nursery, cooler air cloaked Delia as she made her way down the familiar corridor, her legs still shaky after having been seated for so long. The candle's glow cast long, bending shadows on the painted walls and the ornate carpet lining the hall. During daylight hours this passageway always seemed broad and bright, but now, in the wee hours, when lightning glinted through tall windows and death lingered in the shadows, the ambience sobered.

Delia passed her own bedchamber as she approached the main staircase and descended the wooden steps, their creaking loud in the silence. She hesitated upon arriving at the first-floor landing. Hushed voices and an eerie glow spilled from an ajar door on the left. The last time she'd been summoned to a deathbed, she'd been too late for final farewells. Would that be the case yet again?

Breathless, she steeled herself and stepped toward the master's chamber.

The air thinned as she crossed the threshold, and she lifted her hand to her nose, resisting the urge to wrinkle it at the putrid stench. The fire in the hearth raged, leaping and popping in its grate, and the heavy velvet curtains shrouded the east-facing windows, trapping in the heat and scents of wood smoke and perspiration. A strange, raspy sound emanated from behind the bed's canopy curtains, like the unearthly cries of a nightmare.

Activity swirled in the sickroom. The vicar, the physician, and Mr. Twethewey's solicitor all huddled near the bed, their heads bowed in hushed conversation.

She stepped in farther, sweeping her gaze to the left. Fourteen-year-old Liam and his tutor, Mr. Hugh Simon, sat in the shadows on a tufted bench opposite the men. The boy's shoulders slumped, and he sat motionless, elbows resting on his knees, his attention fixed firmly on the carpet.

Mr. Simon, her only equal at Easten Park and the only person she dared to call a friend, was the first to notice her arrival. He dipped his chin in acknowledgment and stood to his full height.

As he approached, his dark eyes glimmered in the candlelight, his brows drawn together in a familiar manner.

Often she thought she knew him so well that she could read his mind from his expression. Perhaps it was the lateness of the hour or the dire nature of their situation, but the firm set of his jaw gave nothing away. A lock of sable hair fell over his forehead, and an uncustomary scruff shadowed his square jaw.

Unable to wait for him to speak, she placed her candle on a

nearby table and leaned toward him, knitting her fingers before her in impatient anticipation. "How's Liam faring?"

"He's not moved a muscle in hours." Mr. Simon glanced back at Liam before he folded his arms over his broad chest. "He's not eaten, not said a word. He merely sits there."

"Perhaps we should insist he go to his chamber and rest."

Mr. Simon shrugged a shoulder. "Liam's not a child. He thinks he needs to be here, and I've no right to tell him otherwise."

A protest hovered on Delia's tongue, but how could she argue? This could very well be the boy's last day with his father. Motherly affection squeezed her heart as her sights fell on the boy once again, and she feared what dawn might bring.

The group of men at the bedside dispersed, and Mr. Steerhead, Mr. Twethewey's solicitor and friend, approached them. Delia gaped as the older man drew close and the candlelight illuminated his features.

Edwin Steerhead was a decided man—strict in his appearance and disciplined in his behavior. But at this hour, his thinning hair was wild and hanging free of its queue. He wore no coat, and his damp linen sleeves were rolled up to his elbows. White stubble framed his drooping jowl, and his normally florid complexion was nearly as pale as the cream silk of his embroidered waistcoat.

"Prepare yourself, Mrs. Greythorne," Mr. Steerhead whispered as he leaned close, his iron-gray eyes bloodshot and his fetid breath hot on her face. "He's not long for this world. He's weak, as you'll soon see, but he wanted to speak with you both, together, about the children. He's altered his will and named a new guardian. Instead of Mrs. Twethewey's sister in London, they will go to Mr. Twethewey's brother, Jac, in Cornwall. This is very sudden, you know. And unexpected. But he's in his right mind, there's no denying that, and he's determined."

Delia's heart thudded when Liam lifted his head, drinking in

Mr. Steerhead's words. The desire to protect him burned within her. "Perhaps Liam shouldn't hear this. Not yet. Surely there are—"

"Young William will be the master of this family shortly," Mr. Steerhead snapped, his steadfast stare direct. "It won't do to hide the truth."

Delia pressed her lips together and ripped her gaze from the boy's pallid face.

"As I was saying, Twethewey is insistent that you both accompany the children to Cornwall. It's his wish that you continue on as their educators, and he's altered the trust provisions accordingly." Mr. Steerhead stepped aside, opening a pathway to the canopied bed.

Delia hadn't realized she'd been holding her breath until a rush of perspiration gathered on her neck and black dots blinked across her vision. With hesitant steps she drew close to the bed and garnered her courage to look at Mr. Twethewey's face. Just the previous morning she'd encountered him as he prepared for the hunting excursion. His sapphire eyes had been vibrant, his round face ruddy and bright, his expression revealing his usual jovial demeanor. But now his closed eyes seemed sunken, and sweat plastered his jet-black hair to his sallow brow.

Horrified tears stung her eyes as his chest stuttered and jerked with each labored breath.

Mr. Steerhead pushed past them and rested a hand on Mr. Twethewey's forearm. "The governess is here. And the tutor."

Mr. Twethewey's eyes fluttered open, then widened as they fixed on her. "The children," he gasped. "They'll go to Cornwall when I'm gone. Penwythe Hall. They'll know no one. They need you. Don't leave them."

They need you.

The words struck her. The desperation in his voice haunted her. She glanced toward Mr. Simon. His stoic face remained unchanged. She swallowed and looked back at the dying man.

He gasped a deep breath, then with sudden energy he grasped her hand in his clammy one. "You must go with them. Protect them. Promise!"

At the touch she jumped. He pressed her hand harder with each breath. Her throat parched, she scratched out, "Of course we will, Mr. Twethewey. Of course."

He opened his mouth to speak again, but instead airy coughs racked his body. He dropped her hand, and the horrid sound of a choking man gagging for air quickly followed.

Someone grabbed her by the crook of the arm and jerked her backward. The physician nudged past, pushing her into Mr. Simon.

The men behind her whispered. To her left Liam let out a cry, and suddenly the chamber was alive with activity. People rushed to and fro, and yet for Delia, time slowed. Even as Mr. Simon ushered her from the room, she could barely tear her gaze from the scene unfolding before her—of a man fighting for life with the injury determined to take it.

CHAPTER 2

Penwythe Hall, Cornwall

Richard Colliver pinched the pink apple blossom between his thick fingers and plucked it from the willowy branch. He held the tiny flower to his bulbous nose, inhaled loudly, and then released the bloom, dropping it to the ground. "This is a risky venture you've undertaken, Twethewey. I'm not sure what to make of it."

Jac Twethewey propped his fists on his hips and squinted upward as the bright afternoon sunlight filtered through the flittering leaves overhead. All around him, the early-blooming apple trees danced in the April warmth, oblivious to the somber nature of the conversation occurring beneath their boughs. "Once we're past the danger of frost, all will be well."

"Always the optimist, are you?" Colliver gave his gray head a sharp shake and continued down the shady row, leaning heavily on his ornately carved walking stick with each step. "Apples. They're an unpredictable lot. One bad storm or a bout with disease could ruin the entire season. Financially it would take years to recover from a mishap."

"That's true for any crop." Jac fell into slow steps next to the older man. "Besides, this orchard's been here for years, well before my uncle died. It's been neglected, sure enough, but it's got solid bones. With attention and proper care there's no reason it shouldn't flourish."

"May I ask, what happens if this master plan of yours fails? What will come of Penwythe Hall then?" Colliver seemed determined to uncover fault with Jac's plan. "Word has it you've cleared the grain fields and converted them to orchards. Risky, say I, to put so much effort behind one revenue source."

Jac touched the blossom on a nearby branch and paused to examine the intricate petals but did not pluck it. The muscles in his shoulders tensed, in spite of himself.

"I've always known you to be impulsive." Colliver's raspy voice was unpleasant and harsh against the birdsong coming up from the vale. "I remember that fact well enough from when you were a boy. You and your brother would ride like wild things across the moors on those fat little ponies of yours. Be that as it may, I've never taken you for a gambling man, willing to risk your livelihood and the livelihood of countless others on a whim."

Jac bit back the sharp retort itching to be spoken.

Converting his grain field had been a weighty decision. Yes, failure would ruin not only him but also his tenants and all who relied on Penwythe land for a living. It was a gamble in the truest sense, but despite the risk, he needed Colliver to see the strategy in his efforts—and support them.

Jac forced his fingers through his thick, curling hair and brushed it to the side. "Change was necessary. That soil was depleted. Besides, we've other resources. This orchard is mature and will be fruitful. The others will be too, in their time."

"In their time?" Colliver huffed, his bushy brows rising in obvious disapproval. "And how long will that be?"

Jac hesitated, knowing his timeline sounded grim. "It will take at least three years before the newest orchard bears fruit, five years before steady growth. But don't forget, several other orchards exist on Penwythe's property, all at different stages of maturity."

Colliver tapped his walking stick against a nearby trunk. "And what's this I hear of a cider press? I was at the Harpe and Lute the other day. Your venture was on the tongue of every farmer there."

Jac was not used to explaining himself, but if he wanted Colliver to see his vision and invest accordingly, transparency was vital. Jac once again fell into step behind Colliver as he traversed down the grassy path between the rows. "The grain barn in the north meadow is to be converted to a cider mill. A granite crusher will arrive in the coming weeks, along with a press, which is currently being built in Devon."

Colliver clicked his tongue. "That all sounds very expensive."

"It is, but worth the investment."

"Worth the investment, eh?" Colliver stopped suddenly. He retrieved a handkerchief from his linen coat, lifted his beaver hat, and wiped the perspiration gathering on his wrinkled brow. When he turned back to Jac, the sarcasm vanished from his expression, and he pressed his lips together before he spoke.

"I have considered your offer to join you financially in this venture. You're a man of integrity. There's no doubt about that, so I'll be frank. Rumors are ripe, Twethewey. I consider myself above the idle prattle of small-minded men, but such talk can't be ignored. I've heard Penwythe is in dire financial straits and falls deeper every day."

Jac widened his stance. The rumors had started even before his uncle died, and now five years later he could only imagine what Colliver had heard. He chose his words with care. "I'll not deny we've had our fair share to overcome, but that's why change is necessary. My hand's been forced."

The salt-scented air blowing from the sea to the north rustled Colliver's gray hair and brought the leaves to life on their stems, dancing and twirling in the breeze. "Your uncle was a great man, one of the finest in Cornwall, I'd wager, but he had little concern with preparing for the future. I wasn't surprised when he left Penwythe to you and not Randall, not in the least, but in doing so he left you with a terrible mess on your hands." He raised a bushy brow and eyed Jac. "How old are you? Thirty?"

Jac swallowed. He didn't like the direction this conversation was taking. "Two and thirty."

A deep chuckle rumbled from Colliver's throat. "Such a young man still. God willing, you've many years ahead. I suppose you've time for risks and gambling with outcomes."

Heat crept up the back of Jac's neck. His jaw twitched. His defenses were rising, as they always did when this topic surfaced.

"I like you, Twethewey. I always have. But my tolerance for such ventures is much lower than it would have been when I was your age."

A thousand retorts darted through Jac's mind, but he pressed his lips shut. He wanted Colliver's approval. Nay, he needed it.

Colliver replaced his hat and adjusted the brim. "And what if you change your mind next summer, when the apples do not bear quickly enough and you've not enough harvest? What then? Like I said, it's the impulsiveness of your nature that makes me skittish. You can't control the growing of things any more than you can control the clouds in the heavens or the tides of the sea. And if your plan fails, well, I've seen too many well-intentioned plans fall by the wayside—and great sums of money with them."

"The orchard and plans for the cider barn were calculated decisions. It isn't as much of a gamble as you suggest. We—Andrews and I—examined the numbers numerous times. We even engaged the assistance of an expert from Devon. Penwythe is in my blood. I'd do nothing to jeopardize it, nor the livelihood of those who depend upon it."

"Be that as it may, I can only respond to what I know and what I can see with my own eyes, and right now, all I see is row after row of fruitless trees." He stared at Jac for several moments, and then he shook his head with a little chuckle.

The pretentious sound grated on Jac's nerves. He did not see this—any of this—as a laughing matter. "Just a few months and I'll prove to you that the orchards will be profitable."

Colliver nodded and tilted his head to the side. "Prove that the orchards here can turn a profit. Then, and only then, will I consider coming alongside you and supporting this endeavor financially—for a portion of the proceeds, obviously."

Colliver plucked another blossom, studied it intently, then tossed it to the ground. He stepped backward and examined Jac down the bridge of his pudgy nose. "Come to dinner tonight. I know my family would like to see you. Bring your aunt as well. My wife fancies her company. I'll be watching you—and your little project—with interest."

He turned to leave but paused. The corner of his lip twitched. "But if you and I are ever to venture into business together, I suggest you give a care to your appearance. I'll not invest my money with a man who appears like a common vagabond, regardless of how earnest you are."

Jac chuckled at the conversation's amiable turn. He'd been laboring alongside his workers all day, and as a result, mud spattered his boots and buckskin breeches. No, he didn't look the part of a landowner, but perhaps he appeared like a man who was doing whatever necessary to meet his goals. "Never could just stand by and watch another man work. I hate being idle."

"You come by that honestly, I say." Colliver's broad mouth cracked into a smile. Gone was the talk of facts and figures. "Your uncle would spend hours in that garden of his, never content to be still, refusing to let anyone else—not even the servants—tend it."

Without another word Colliver leaned on his walking stick and lumbered back down the petal-covered path toward Penwythe Hall.

Jac ran his hand down his linen waistcoat and brushed off a piece of grass that clung to his side. He couldn't remember where he'd shed his coat earlier, and now dirt and dust darkened the once-fine fabric, and his shirtsleeves clung to his arms, dampened with perspiration.

Refocusing his attention, he rubbed the back of his neck and stared down the orchard row. The scent of apple blossoms intermingled with that of the sea—an intoxicating blend, one that felt like the past and future colliding. He lifted his gaze to the sapphire sky, searching its wispy clouds as if the answer to his problem were hidden within.

Oh yes, his plans were grand: Orchards. Much-needed repairs to Penwythe Hall. Expansion to the south. Impatience for it all to fall into place surged within him.

He knelt and dragged his fingers over a section of damp, freshly turned soil where a new tree replaced one that had died. He lifted a handful and sifted it through his fingers before he stood to his full height once again. The stones had already been cast, and every last farthing he possessed had been committed to these orchards.

With renewed determination he returned to the road. There was work to be done, and plenty of it. Now there was even less margin for error. There could be no turning back.

CHAPTER 3

A steady rain pattered against the tall leaded windows in the study, and Delia tightened the black mourning shawl about her shoulders to ward off the bitter chill. A headache throbbed, and she pressed the back of her hand to her lips to stifle a yawn.

Neither she, nor anyone else at Easten Park, had slept in the time since Mr. Twethewey's death two days prior, but even as exhaustion threatened to take hold, she deliberately straightened her shoulders. Her distraught charges deserved to know what would happen in the coming days. Mr. Steerhead had been quiet on the matter, and she needed answers.

Next to her, Mr. Simon occupied the wingback chair. His foot tapped an even beat against the chair's leg, and he leaned heavily with his elbow on the chair's arm, staring at an indeterminate point on the wall. His clean-shaven jaw twitched. The twinkle that normally glimmered in his dark-brown eyes was absent.

The sudden jerking of the door snapped them both to attention.

Mr. Steerhead stormed in, accompanied by the sharp scents of brandy and tobacco. His wrinkled white cravat hung loose, and his hair, the color of which blurred somewhere between brown and gray, escaped his queue in frizzed locks. As a frequent guest at Easten House, he easily made himself at home in the room, and he dropped to the late Mr. Twethewey's chair behind the desk with a huff.

"That undertaker is a greedy snake." Mr. Steerhead pointed at them as he spoke through gritted teeth, jabbing his finger forward with every syllable. "If he thinks he is going to play on our grief to get one more farthing over our agreed-upon amount, he's got another thing coming."

Muttering, Mr. Steerhead forced his focus to the desktop and shuffled through the stack of papers, his motions frantic, as if searching for something of great import. "If there had been any other undertaker within a reasonable distance, I should throw this one from the premises. That's what I'd do."

Delia and Mr. Simon exchanged glances.

With no other family members in the vicinity, the arrangements for Mr. Twethewey's funeral had been assumed by Mr. Steerhead—a task the man clearly loathed.

Delia, ignoring his boisterous bluster, leaned forward, determined to address the job at hand. "Have the burial arrangements been made?"

"The burial?" Mr. Steerhead jerked his head up and stilled his hands, almost as if he had forgotten her presence. "The funeral will be the day after tomorrow. Of course I'd prefer to wait until Sunday, but the coffin has been purchased, the hearse and horses have been arranged, and the bearers have all been notified. I see no cause for delay, especially with the distress the children are under. Mr. Twethewey had very few relations in the area, and his business associates won't want to make the journey north from London, especially with the dreadful weather. This insufferable rain has made the roads nigh impassable."

After the onslaught of words, an abrupt silence prevailed. Mr. Steerhead removed his wire spectacles from the bridge of his hawkish nose and rubbed his forehead with his bony fingers for several moments. "It's dreadful business to arrange a funeral for a friend in such a manner."

Delia smoothed the black muslin of her skirt, ignoring the pinch in her stomach. She could relate to the emotion—the oppressive sensation of loss and dread, of sorrow and numbness. She forced the unwanted thoughts away. "Will Mr. Jac Twethewey be attending?"

Mr. Steerhead shrugged an angular shoulder. "I wrote to him, but I doubt he's received the missive. At any rate, the brothers weren't on the best of terms. I doubt he'll be pleased with Mr. Twethewey's decision to send the children to Penwythe Hall."

Delia's posture slackened. She'd hoped the children would be able to see their uncle prior to traveling to Cornwall, if for no other reason than to ease their minds.

But it was not to be.

Mr. Steerhead cleared his throat. "Of course, the young ladies will not attend the burial, but the undertaker has arranged for new black coats and gloves for the boys. At least that is one thing that mouse of a man has done efficiently. Mr. Simon, you will speak with him and see the boys are adequately prepared."

Mr. Simon nodded.

"In the meantime, you both must prepare the children to depart for Penwythe the morning following the funeral."

"The morning after?" Delia's posture straightened once again. "So quickly? It seems almost cruel to uproot them so soon."

"On the contrary." Mr. Steerhead absently retrieved his pocket watch from his waistcoat, popped it open, squinted as he lifted the face to the light, then snapped it shut. "The sooner they settle in a new environment, the better. Besides, I've had the good fortune to find a tenant to lease Easten Park, but they require immediate occupancy. Such an arrangement will provide income during this time, which is always desirable in circumstances such as these. You only need pack what the children will require for the next several weeks. The staff will remain behind and can pack the remaining items and send them forthwith."

Delia's head swam with the details she'd just received.

Income? He was really concerned about income at a time like this?

She opened her mouth to speak, but Mr. Steerhead retrieved a portfolio from the top drawer of the desk, pulled two large packets from it, and extended one toward her and the other toward Mr. Simon.

Without awaiting instruction Mr. Simon accepted and opened his missive. Curious, Delia lifted her head to see over his arm and spied bank notes folded inside the paper. Mr. Simon's eyes widened. "What's this?"

"Mr. Twethewey instructed me to give these to you. He intended it as incentive that you'd make good on your word to accompany the children to Penwythe. He feared you'd not be willing to travel so far."

Mr. Simon cleared his throat and glanced toward Delia.

She did not open her letter but lowered it to her lap and leaned forward, eager for as much information as she could glean. "What can you tell us about Penwythe Hall, Mr. Steerhead?"

He rested his elbows on the arms of his chair and folded his hands over his midsection. "Penwythe Hall is the seat of an estate on the north coast of Cornwall, quite close to the sea and north of the moors. It's an ancient place—been there for hundreds of years, I'd guess—but sadly it's fallen into disrepair over the last couple of decades."

"So you've been there?" she clarified.

"Ah, yes." He lifted his pointed chin. "A number of times. At one point our Mr. Twethewey was set to inherit the place, so I accompanied him there on many visits in anticipation of that."

"I remember that." Mr. Simon brushed a wayward piece of lint from his trousers, as if only paying half attention to the details. "Caused quite a stir, if I recall correctly."

"You do." Mr. Steerhead turned his full attention to Delia.

"This all happened before you arrived, but Mr. Simon was here. Mr. Twethewey and his brother, Jac, were raised by their uncle, William Angrove, at Penwythe Hall after the death of their parents. When their uncle died, it was expected that he would will the estate and all the associated holdings to Randall. When the will was read, however, Mr. Angrove left the estate in its entirety to Jac, the younger brother. It caused quite a rift between the two."

Delia frowned. "But if the property was not entailed, would Mr. Angrove not be free to leave the property to whomever he chose?"

"Indeed, but for years Mr. Angrove assured Randall that the property would come to him. Randall, in turn, endeavored to establish his business to ensure a financial future for the property. But in the end, it was not to be. Randall believed Jac influenced the uncle in his last days to change the will. Of course, his brother denied such accusations. To my knowledge, after the will was read they never again spoke."

Mr. Simon shifted in his chair, as if finally taking interest. "If there was such bad blood between them, why did Mr. Twethewey name him as guardian?"

Mr. Steerhead stood, moved to the side table, and lifted the brandy decanter. "Mrs. Twethewey's sister, Mrs. Lambourne, is an exemplary woman, but her husband has made questionable investments, especially as of late. Randall was a wealthy man, and now his children are wealthy. At least Liam is. The world would love nothing more than to take advantage of young people in such a state."

"And he thought Mrs. Lambourne would do that?"

"Not so much Mrs. Lambourne, but her husband. Randall said he believed Jac to be the lesser of two evils. He went so far as to revise the trust so Jac could not access the children's funds. He'll receive an annuity to see to the children's necessities and comforts, but the girls' dowry and Liam's fortune cannot be touched without my approval and consent."

Commotion out in the corridor drew their attention, and Delia turned. The undertaker, a tall, sinewy man with wan, sunken cheeks, stood in the doorway.

Mr. Steerhead's face reddened, but his eyes didn't leave the newcomer. "I must go. You two ready the children as discussed." Within moments he fled the space, the undertaker on his heels, leaving Delia alone with Mr. Simon.

She stood and prepared to leave the chamber, but the curious expression on Mr. Simon's face made her pause. "You look satisfied."

He tilted his dark head to the side and tapped the papers against his hand. "I'd be lying if I said this didn't ease the burden of relocating to Cornwall. It's a godforsaken part of the country. I can't say I have the least desire to travel there."

She looked to the seal on her letter but did not open it. The meaning and intention behind it settled on her like a heavy cloak. "Poor Mr. Twethewey. He was desperate to make sure his children are cared for and comfortable."

"There was nothing poor about Mr. Twethewey." Mr. Simon's lips curved in what could only be interpreted as amusement. He tucked the packet inside his coat and stood, the whites of his eyes flashing bright in the room darkened by the clouds outside the window. "He wanted us to do what he wanted us to do. Nothing more. At the end of the day, we are all just trying to protect our own future and that of those we love. Are we not?"

His words struck her as odd.

Under normal circumstances, Mr. Simon was a man ruled by emotion and empathy, but in this moment, indifference tinged his words. She gathered her black skirts and preceded Mr. Simon to the cool paneled corridor. "My goodness. You sound like an opportunist."

A throaty chuckle emanated. "I've never claimed to be a saint, Mrs. Greythorne, but neither am I an opportunist, merely practical." Mr. Simon fell into step with her, and they traversed the wide corridor. He angled his head toward her, as if taking her into his confidence. "None of us could have prevented this unfortunate occurrence. It's sad but a reality. I know you worry for them, but they're not the first children to lose their parents. I lost my father when I was no older than Johnny, and both of your parents are dead. We survived, and I daresay the experience has shaped both of us. The children must continue to live life, to thrive, and we will do what we can to assist them."

They continued in silence for several paces before they made their way through a narrow doorway toward the main foyer. "I've no doubt you'll do exceptionally well in Cornwall. After all, you'll be able to see your family."

She forced a smile and nodded as a thread of discomfort tightened within her at the mention of family. Yes, her sister and brother still lived in a small village not terribly far from Penwythe Hall, but her mother-in-law's image—and the echo of her stark warning—burned brightest in her mind.

"And how long has it been since you have seen your family?"

"Three years."

"See there, that should give you some comfort. Besides, we'll still work side by side, and as far as I'm concerned, that is the best incentive for staying on."

Delia warmed at his words of solidarity and his affectionate smile. Her relationship with Mr. Simon was a complicated one—one she did not fully understand. At times his manner was cool and aloof; at others she imagined that their relationship could blossom beyond mere friendship. After years of working by his side, she had learned to adjust to his swinging moods and varied sentiments, but in this moment, under these circumstances, she was grateful for his companionship.

Most governesses did not have the luxury of having an equal in the household as she did in Mr. Simon. She was no servant, but neither was she on the same footing with the family. Mr. Simon was the only other individual of her station, and she found great comfort and camaraderie in that. And despite everything else, at least their comradeship would continue.

She slowed her steps as they passed the downstairs drawing room. The two French doors stood ajar, and she glimpsed the coffin atop a table, with Mr. Twethewey's body lying in wait within. Black baize draped the walls, furniture, and even the window, blocking out all traces of the afternoon's gray light. Gold candlelight flickered and danced in the ebony space, making the room seem alive instead of what it was. The tall professional watcher who'd been hired to sit with Mr. Twethewey's body paced behind the table, the thud of his heels striking the polished floor.

Delia shivered at the sight and hurried to rejoin Mr. Simon, who had continued on without her. Oblivious to the scene she'd just witnessed, Mr. Simon gave a little laugh. "This is turning into quite a production. Seven souls are going to descend upon Penwythe Hall in a matter of days. I can only imagine Mr. Jac Twethewey's reaction."

"Surely he will welcome us. Mr. Steerhead said Penwythe Hall is quite large. Besides, I am sure the late Mr. Twethewey has made it worth his brother's while."

"You give the dearly departed a great deal of credit. You weren't here when this rift occurred between the two brothers. True, I didn't know all the details, but it wasn't a pleasant time—that I can say with certainty."

They continued to the second floor of Easten Park, on which the nursery and schoolroom were located. As he turned to enter the schoolroom, Mr. Simon paused. "You still look upset." He nudged her arm playfully. "Don't look so glum. You always tell the children to seek out adventure. Consider this an adventure of your own."

She offered a smile and swallowed the discomfort of the fearful memory of her in-laws before she continued down the hallway.

Adventure would be just what the children needed, but *she* wanted nothing more than peace.

She looked down at the packet in her hand. There was money in it. She knew without even opening it. Money was always a step toward security, and did she not have dreams for the future, to one day open her own school for young ladies? After all, the children would not need a governess forever. At some point she would be alone again, searching for her place in the world.

Even so, the money within this packet seemed like blood money—a man's final, desperate attempt to care for his children—and an ominous chill raced down her spine.

Only a few years prior she'd witnessed firsthand how far a family would go to protect its own, and now she was teetering on the edge of that old world. How she wished their journey would take them north, even farther away from her past, instead of hurling her headlong toward it.

Cornwall.

It was in her blood, and she feared she'd never escape its hold.

With a sigh she tucked the letter beneath her arm and headed toward her chamber. She did not know what the future held, but at least she would not be alone.

CHAPTER 4

"A re we really going to leave Easten Park?"

Delia paused in packing her valise and glanced over her shoulder at the three ebony-clad young ladies—Julia, Hannah, and Sophy—sitting atop her bed.

Under normal circumstances, her charges were not permitted inside her personal chambers, but now their father was dead. Life as they knew it—and the rules that governed it—was forever altered. Nothing was normal, and nothing would be so for a very long time.

Delia forced cheer to her voice as she turned to retrieve a long-sleeved gown of charcoal linen from her wardrobe and smoothed the ivory lace lining the neckline. "Yes. We'll leave at dawn's light. Mr. Steerhead has hired a bigger carriage for the ride. In two days' time we'll be in Cornwall."

"I've never been to Cornwall." Hannah sulked as she leaned her nut-brown curls back against the pillows on Delia's bed. "I think it's terrible that we have to go so far away from everyone we know."

"Cornwall is a lovely place," Delia said, finding it increasingly difficult to keep her tone buoyant. "Do you not recall the story we read of the mermaids near the coast? Mr. Steerhead told me Penwythe Hall is a little more than a mile from the sea. Won't you like to see the sea?"

The girls stared at her with blank expressions.

In the silence guilt descended.

Of course they were not eager to see the sea, nor anything else besides the home they knew and loved.

Delia cleared her throat and placed a pair of white silk stockings in her valise before sitting next to the girls. She covered Hannah's small hand with her own. "I know you miss your father and are sad to leave, and 'tis normal to feel that way. But for now, it's best that we approach this situation positively. Your father loved you very much, and it was his desire that your uncle Jac care for you. So that's what we shall do. I'll be with you every step and will not leave you for a second."

"I remember Uncle Jac." Julia crossed her arms over her chest. Her scowl transformed her normally cheerful countenance to one quite dark. "He's a horrid man. Why would Father send us there?"

Delia shot the oldest girl a warning glance. "I think we should all reserve judgment until we meet him for ourselves. That is what I intend to do, and I urge you to do the same."

Julia pinched her lips together and glared as she moved from the bed and dropped to the wingback chair in the corner.

Hannah's sudden, high-pitched cry pierced the afternoon calm. "Sophy, don't do that! It's not yours!"

Delia whirled around to see the six-year-old child on her tiptoes, her hand in a box atop the chest of drawers. At the reprimand Sophy whirled around and tucked both hands behind her back. The box lid slammed shut. Her amber eyes were wide. "I was only looking."

Delia rose from the bed and moved toward the box. "You may see inside. Here, I'll help you." She lifted the box decorated with white and pink shells and polished gray stones and lowered it to the girl's level.

At the invitation Hannah jumped from the bed in a flurry of jet-black muslin and joined them.

Delia tipped open the lid and lifted a coral necklace from the velvet-lined interior.

"Oh, how lovely!" Hannah cooed. She took it in her small hands and held it up, letting the necklace dangle between them. "Why do you never wear it?"

Delia smiled. "A governess hardly has need of such things."

"I think you should wear it every day. It's too pretty to hide away." Sophy, eager to see what else lay inside the perceived treasure box, pushed forward to pull out another trinket and held it up. "I like this one."

The afternoon light gleamed from the pendant's silver rim. Delia's heart squeezed in a familiar ache at the sight. She took the item from the child and tenderly ran her finger over the hair woven into the setting.

"What's that?" Sophy leaned heavily against Delia's side.

Delia slid her free arm around the child and drew a breath. "It's a mourning pendant."

"Whose hair is that?" Hannah leaned forward.

Delia tightened her fingers around the trinket and, for just a moment, allowed the memory to slip to the forefront. Chubby fists. Dimpled cheek. Fuzzy hair so blonde it appeared white. A tiny soul gone far too soon.

Maria.

Her Maria.

Heat flushed her, as it usually did when she thought of her greatest loss, and with her other hand she smoothed the chain. "This is a lock of my daughter's hair."

She'd told the girls little snippets about her daughter, and they'd always been curious about Delia's life before she came to live with them—about her late husband and daughter, her childhood in Whitecross, her own siblings—but Delia found it easier not to speak of it, for speaking of it always unleashed a flood of emotions: regret, loss, fear.

The girls remained silent as they looked over Delia's shoulder, as if they were bound together in the grief of loss.

With a sharp intake of breath, Delia curled her fingers over the tiny trinket. She returned the pendant to the box, closed the lid, and smiled down at the children. "We are fortunate to have each other, are we not?"

Solemn gazes and wide eyes met her, but the words were true. They had to find comfort—and strength—in that. She would never give up on the girls, not as long as she had power to care for them, and if she were honest, the girls filled a void in her heart that, were it to be vacated, would leave a terrible scar.

She nudged Hannah with her elbow in an attempt to jolt her from her sadness. "You'd best pay a last visit to the library and make sure you have the stories you want. The carriage ride will be a long one. Perhaps you can read to us."

Hannah's eyes brightened, and she grabbed Sophy's arm. Together the girls raced for the door, their slippers padding over the carpeted floor.

After several quiet moments, Julia stood from the chair, her narrow brows furrowed in disapproval. "I don't think you should do that."

Delia returned her attention to the valise. "Do what?"

"Build their excitement. You'll only give them false hope, and then they'll be disappointed."

Delia lowered a linen chemise and turned. "And how do you know they'll be disappointed?"

"You've never met Uncle Jac. I have." Julia's brilliant blue eyes, so like those of her late father's, held Delia's gaze in a silent challenge.

Julia was no longer a child, like her two younger sisters. She was trapped between the realities of adulthood and the blissfulness of childhood. Their father's death was hard on the younger two, but it was hard in a different way for the oldest sister. At just twelve years of age, she'd been forced to learn to deal with far too much.

Delia took her time returning the treasure box to the wardrobe. She was in no hurry to fill the silence in the room with words. She folded more stockings and placed them in her satchel, making sure the bag was cinched shut before she spoke.

"You're older than your sisters, Julia. You have the benefit of time. I'll not pretend you are a child. We cannot change things, and your father believed this to be the best solution for you and your siblings. You know he loved you and wanted the best."

"Then why would he send us there? To live with *him?*" Tears brimmed in Julia's eyes, making them appear even more vibrant. "He should have sent us to Aunt Beatrice. She loves us. Uncle Jac will hate us, just like he hated Father."

Delia placed her bag on the bed and moved next to Julia. "I'm sure he had a good reason for making the decision he did. He probably knew something you did not."

Julia's lip trembled, and she looked to the patterned rug beneath her feet.

When the girl did not pull away from her touch, Delia wrapped her arm around the girl's shoulders and squeezed. "I am proud of you, Julia."

"Proud?" She squinted up at Delia. "Why?"

"Because you care about your sisters and want to protect them from pain. But you must know it's all right to be sad yourself. Don't try to solve everything. Not in this moment, at least. Sophy and Hannah know very little of your uncle or what happened between him and your father. I think it best that it stays that way. They are too young to fully understand. Please try to stay optimistic. If for no other reason than to help them with this transition."

After several moments, Julia's tense shoulder eased, but her smile did not return. Instead, she stepped toward the door, paused in the threshold, and turned. "I will. For them. But I still don't think any good will come of this."

CHAPTER 5

"That's it, isn't it?" Sophy's excited voice rose above the clatter of carriage wheels as they rumbled over the uneven road. "Penwythe Hall!"

Ensuing chatter and giddy giggles filled the carriage, and Delia could not deny her own mounting excitement as she ducked her head to see through the window.

"Ladies, please sit back. There will be plenty of time to see your new surroundings."

Delia's words fell unheard as the girls pressed against the window, eagerly arching their necks to see through the panes.

With a sigh Delia leaned back against the tufted seat. There was no use attempting to contain their enthusiasm, for they were as tired of traveling as she. The drive, which was supposed to take but two days, had stretched into three. Heavy rain resulted in rutted roads, making for a damp, jolting drive, and two sleepless nights in carriage inns had drained them all of energy and patience. To escalate the frustration, the carriage carrying the boys and men broke a wheel several miles back. With thunder growling and more rain threatening, it was decided that the girls and Delia would travel ahead.

"I wonder what Uncle Jac will look like." Sophy pressed her freckled nose against the window. "I bet he looks like Papa."

"He'd be handsome then." Hannah arched her neck to see past her younger sister. "Do you think he'll like us?"

"Why wouldn't he like us?" Sophy nearly toppled from the seat as the carriage hit a rut; instead, she fell against her sister.

Julia shook her head, her expression cautious. "He probably doesn't even want us to come."

"Of course he does." Delia's quick response resounded. "I'm sure he is very eager to see all of you."

The carriage rounded a bend and jostled through the open main iron gates, and Delia's breath caught at the sight of Penwythe Hall. The massive structure of weathered stone and blackened iron rose several stories into the churning pewter sky. Dutch gables capped large paned windows, and numerous squat chimneys disappeared into low-hanging clouds and fog.

She squinted to see more clearly in evening's fading light, and her awe for the home quickly gave way to an alarming realization.

All was silent—too silent for a house expecting guests. No light winked from the darkened windows. No sounds came from the lawns or outbuildings.

The property appeared empty.

"It looks like no one's here," Julia stated as she leaned forward once the carriage drew to a complete halt at the front entrance, showing her first bit of interest. "Maybe he's not expecting us after all."

"I am certain he is." Delia settled her black bonnet atop her head and secured the dark satin ribbons beneath her chin. "You girls stay here. I'll return shortly."

One of the carriage footmen opened the door, lowered the steps, and assisted Delia down. A sharp breeze whipped around the corner, chilly and damp, rustling the leaves of the silver elms at the house's edge and disturbing the boxwood underneath the leaded windows. She stilled the bonnet ribbons as they fluttered in the gusts, instructed the driver to wait for her instruction, and turned.

She lifted her eyes to the grand entrance, shadowed and dark in the day's fading light. A low Tudor-arched stone doorway, blackened by years of weather and exposure to the elements, framed and protected a closed wooden door. Above it, paned windows stretched upward two more stories, topped by ornately carved stonework and a slate roof.

In a home this size someone should be here to greet them—a butler, footman, anyone.

But she saw no signs of life.

Nerves churned within her as she considered her next action, and she chewed her lower lip. Perhaps she should wait for Mr. Steerhead and Mr. Simon. They would know what to do. But there was no telling how long the other carriage would be, and judging by the fortitude of the wind tugging at her skirt, the weather was intensifying. The last thing she needed was for the girls to fall ill from being caught in the rain.

She spied a door knocker in the shape of a lion's head. As she approached it, a muffled voice sounded from her left, followed by a burst of masculine laughter.

Delia whirled around. Two men, clad in linen trousers, country felt hats, and mud-splattered boots, rounded the west corner of the house. The taller one, with blond hair and a dark coat, was talking, and the other man, with no coat, a light-green waistcoat, black hair, and a shovel slung over his shoulder, was laughing. Neither noticed her.

Behind her, one of the horses whinnied and stomped its hoof against the cobbled drive. The man with black hair paused, looked at the drive, and motioned for the other man to stop.

Then he looked at her.

A damp breeze swept in afresh, rustling the shadowed ivy climbing the house's facade.

They stared at each other for several seconds.

Delia sniffed. At this rate they'd never be shown inside.

She approached the men and straightened her posture to her

tallest height. "I'm looking for Mr. Jac Twethewey," she blurted. "Is he at home, please?"

The men exchanged glances. The taller man—the one with hair the color of sand and in need of a shave—nodded, amusement dancing in his hazel eyes. "He is."

Growing frustrated at the cavalier attitude, she pursed her lips. "Would you be so kind as to notify him that his nieces have arrived?"

The other man jerked. His face tightened. "Nieces?"

Delia huffed at the impertinence. Servants at Easten Park never would have been permitted to speak to guests in such a daft manner. She lifted her chin in an air of authority and straightened her shoulders. "I'd prefer to speak directly with Mr. Twethewey on this matter, if you please."

The man with dark hair handed his shovel to the other man and stepped toward her. "You *are* speaking with Jac Twethewey. How may I be of service?"

CHAPTER 6

Confusion and frustration mounting, Jac looked back to the carriage. This time he noticed three small, very white faces peering at him from the window.

He sobered at the sight. Heat gathered beneath his collar, and a knot cinched in his chest.

Surely this woman was mistaken. She had to be.

Those children in the carriage were not his nieces. 'Twould be impossible.

He turned his attention back to the petite lady in front of him. Her gray eyes, which moments before had met his with such directness, were now downcast and her cheeks flushed crimson.

He could not fault her for mistaking him for a field hand. He'd spent the afternoon in the north orchard overseeing and assisting the men as they dug new irrigation ditches down to the pond, and his clothes, face, and hands bore the dusty evidence.

But whatever the reason for her abrupt greeting, he cared not.

She'd spoken of his nieces.

His only nieces were Randall's children, and anything regarding Randall was not a topic to take lightly.

"My nieces reside in Yorkshire," he divulged, almost defensively. "There's no reason they'd be here."

The woman's delicate brows drew together. "Did you not receive Mr. Steerhead's letter?"

The familiar name ignited unpleasant memories. "Edwin Steerhead?"

"Y-yes. Mr. Edwin Steerhead. Mr. Twethewey's solicitor wrote to you, informing you of . . ." Her words faded to uncomfortable silence.

"Miss, I received no letter."

As the situation's reality trickled through his consciousness, the blood pounded in his ears, and he clutched at the bits of information, trying to make sense of them. Something was wrong—inconceivably wrong. There was no way his brother would send his children to Penwythe Hall. Unless . . .

The need for information descended upon him fervently. "Why are they here?"

The young woman again met his gaze directly. "Randall Twethewey is dead."

Jac's blood ran cold.

His breath lodged in his lungs.

The woman continued, her voice sounding very far away. "He named you guardian of his children. I—um, we—thought you knew."

"There m-must be some m-mistake," Jac stammered as speech returned. "A mistake."

"I'm afraid there's no mistake." She knitted her gloved fingers together before her. "He was buried four days ago."

Stunned, he stared at her hands as her long fingers gripped, released, and gripped each other again before he looked at her face. "And who are you?"

"I'm Mrs. Cordelia Greythorne. I am your nieces' governess."

The steady drizzle had given way to heavier, cooler raindrops, and the wind whipped about, whistling through the branches, the briskness of which snapped him from his trance.

"Your nephews are with Mr. Steerhead. Their carriage broke a wheel a few miles back, but they should follow shortly. Mr. Steerhead will be able to give you more information than I. I'm . . ." Her shoulders fell. "I'm sorry to be the one to tell you."

He blinked as the rain poured down on him. It fell in sheets now, and Jac had almost forgotten that Andrews was with them until his steward nudged his arm and murmured, "Perhaps we should go inside. It's raining and the children . . ."

Jac looked back to the carriage.

Yes, the children.

The small faces were still there peering through the rain-blurred windows. Their eerily pale expressions were made even more so by the evening's gray light.

He swallowed.

Hard.

Jac was first to arrive at the carriage door. He opened it, and one by one, he took a little hand and helped each girl to the drive. Only the littlest one paused to regard him with wide, curious eyes before she scurried toward their governess. Within moments they disappeared through the arched doorway.

Jac and Andrews followed them inside, where the housekeeper had no doubt heard the commotion and met them in the entrance hall. Her light eyes were popped wide, and the tight silver curls framing her face shook excitedly. "What's this?"

"We have guests, Mrs. Bishop." Jac kept his voice low. Controlled. He swiped the rainwater from his arms and removed his soaked hat, quickly sorting out in his mind what needed to be done. "These are my nieces and their governess. My nephews will be following. Please see that the fires are lit and the guest rooms are prepared. Also, have tea sent to the drawing room."

"The guest rooms?" She gaped at him, her voice barely above a whisper. "But those haven't been opened in nigh a year. They will require a great deal of work."

Several others of the staff had gathered beyond the corridor's edge and peered at them. "We'll make do. See that the bedding is changed."

Objections wrote themselves on Mrs. Bishop's face as surely as if they had been spoken, but her thin lips pressed to a tight line. She bobbed her head in compliance and disappeared through the corridor.

He turned back, steeling himself for the sight that met him.

Three young girls clad in damp ebony garb regarded him soberly, silently, their wide eyes assessing his every move. They stood in a row next to their governess, and the youngest, who had only been an infant when he and Randall fell out, clung to her governess's hand, her tiny knuckles white.

He'd heard that their mother died a couple of years back, and now they were here. Motherless. Fatherless. And apparently under his guardianship.

The gnawing ache within his chest intensified.

The governess, as if sensing his discomfort, stepped forward. "Mr. Twethewey, may I present your nieces: Julia, Hannah, and Sophia."

He swallowed hard.

Julia, Hannah, and Sophia.

His past had returned to haunt him, for each one, in her own way, was a smaller, younger, feminine version of his brother.

Julia, with the startling blue eyes framed in black lashes. He remembered her, how she had laughed and played on Easten Park's front lawn on his last and only visit to the estate. Now she appeared a young woman.

Hannah, with a slight Twethewey cleft in her chin and freckles splattered on the bridge of her nose.

Sophia, with coal-black hair hanging loose and wild, and her chin tilted upward, tiny but confident.

He managed to bow. "Ladies, welcome to Penwythe Hall."

The girls all dropped a slow, practiced curtsy but remained silent.

"Let's go through to the drawing room." His voice sounded strained even to his own ears. "I believe a fire has been started there, and you can warm yourselves while the chambers are being prepared."

He led the way from the entrance hall through the great hall to the drawing room, cognizant of the patter of small feet behind him, unanswered questions mounting in his mind. The drawn curtains and the sound of the rain pelting the east windows presented an ominous ambience. The fire was just beginning to take hold, and a maid was lighting candles in the room's corners.

He extended an arm, bidding the children to come in and be seated on the sofa. The two eldest did as he bid, but the youngest stepped quite close to him, her pointed chin tilted up, her curious amber eyes latched onto him. "Are you my uncle then?"

Mrs. Greythorne stepped forward to draw the child back from him, but he held up his hand. "It's all right."

He knelt to be at her eye level. "Yes, I'm your uncle. My name's Jac. And you are Sophia, am I correct?"

"Sophy," she corrected before she tilted her head to the side, studying him. Her eyes narrowed. "You don't look like my papa. I thought brothers always looked alike."

"Really? You don't think we look alike?" He pressed his lips together in contemplation. "Everyone always told us we looked the same when we were children."

"My brothers look alike," she stated matter-of-factly. "Have you seen them?"

He shifted uncomfortably. "Not in a very long time."

The little girl stepped to the window, lifted the curtain, and peered into the black night, then returned her focus to him. "Mrs. Greythorne said we are close to the sea now. Is that true?"

Taken aback by the sudden change of topic, he stammered, "Uh, yes. Very close."

Her small face brightened, and her smile revealed a missing tooth in front. "Can we go there tomorrow?"

The governess stepped forward once again and put her hands on the child's shoulders. "Sophy, there is a great deal to work out before then."

But the child pulled free, eyes fixed on him in expectation, awaiting his answer.

He faltered. "I don't know."

Rumblings from the front courtyard both caught his attention and released him from the conversation, and he stepped to the south window and lifted the curtain. Night had descended quickly, ushered in by the thick clouds and driving winds, and darkness shrouded the lawns. The ladies' carriage had already been taken around to the coach house, but another carriage now stood in its stead. Two youths stood near the horses, and a thin, wiry man stepped next to them.

Jac's focus narrowed.

Edwin Steerhead.

CHAPTER 7

E motions, ripe and hot, ripped through Jac, each one more intense
than the last.

His brother was dead.

His nieces and nephews were now entrusted to his care.

He'd barely had time to process the news, and now Edwin
Steerhead, with his stark countenance and arrogant expression, was
standing in his study.

Jac tugged at his neckcloth and jabbed at the fire with the poker,
buying time to make sense of what was happening. He garnered his
self-discipline, forced his temper to remain in check, and turned to
face the man.

Steerhead was exactly as he remembered him. The years had
seemed to have little effect on his appearance. If anything had
changed, his waistcoat seemed finer. The leather of his boots richer.
Jac had heard the rumors of his brother's financial success, and it
appeared that success extended to those he worked with as well.

If Steerhead was uncomfortable with the idea of interacting
with Jac again, he gave no indication. He nestled back in the emerald
wingback chair, retrieved his carved snuffbox from his breast pocket,
and inhaled deeply. Smug, he lifted his hawk-like nose and surveyed
the cluttered room before he returned the snuffbox to its place. "I
never thought I would see the inside of these walls again."

"And yet here you are." Jac did not apologize for his cold tone.

He leaned with his back against the oak mantelpiece, bracing himself for the conversation ahead.

Steerhead chuckled, gave a sniff, and crossed one long leg over the other. "I am judging by your reception that you didn't receive my letter."

"Your assumption would be correct."

After a pensive pause, Steerhead stood and crossed the large room to the side table to retrieve the brandy decanter. "I do hate to be the bearer of bad news."

Jac tossed another log on the fire and brushed the debris off his palms. It would be no use to prolong this conversation. Bluntness was best. "How did Randall die?"

"A riding accident." The explanation came in a rush, followed by the swish of brandy swirling into the glass. "He was hunting. His horse stumbled as he jumped a fence. Randall fell off and his horse fell across his torso. I did write to you."

Jac's stomach tightened at the nonchalant delivery describing his brother's death, and unexpected tears burned his eyes. Refusing to show emotion, he blinked them away. "And you did not think it odd that I failed to respond?"

"No. There hasn't been time." Steerhead studied the painting above the side table with feigned interest. "Besides, you and Randall were not exactly on friendly terms. I would have suspected your lack of response was intentional."

"He was still my brother." Jac clenched his jaw. Engaging in a battle at this time would not be fruitful. "Why did you bring his children here?"

Steerhead's bushy eyebrows rose. "He named you as guardian."

Jac scoffed. "Randall hadn't spoken one word to me in five years, and even before that his opinion of me was not high. You expect me to believe that he named me guardian of his children?"

"You are correct; his opinion of you was not high." Steerhead returned to the chair, retrieved a leather portfolio, and pulled a stack of papers from within. "His decision was a surprise to me as well. But I must say that even though he was dying, he was very lucid, and since I was present at the time, I could not doubt his competency."

Jac accepted the outstretched document. With a frown he angled the papers toward the firelight. He scanned them, unable to read the words fast enough. Clearly his brother had amassed much more than Jac realized to require such a lengthy will.

"You'll find the part you're looking for at the top of the second page."

Jac cast a sideways glance at Steerhead before he turned to the page.

And yet there it was. He read the paragraph. Read it again.

In the event of Randall's death, he, Jac Twethewey, was to assume guardianship of all five children until each one reached the age of majority.

Jac's face grew hot; his ears burned.

He could only stare at the foreign handwriting.

It had been one thing to hear the terms from Steerhead's mouth. It was another thing entirely to see them written in ink. He leafed through the pages until the last, noting his brother's signature, recent date, and binding seal.

Steerhead cleared his throat. "I can see this is a shock, but a man with property and holdings such as yours should have no problem caring for such a flock. You are, after all, their closest living relative now."

Jac stiffened. At the rate things were progressing, he feared he'd not have enough money to see him to the end of the year, let alone if he were to add several more mouths. A thought brightened him. "His wife had family, did she not?"

"You're correct." Steerhead nodded. "Originally, his wife's sister and husband were appointed as guardians. But when faced with death, Randall changed his mind. If I recall correctly, I believe the expression he used was 'the lesser of two evils.'"

If the words were intended to sting, Jac felt none of it.

Steerhead took the stack of papers from Jac, licked the tip of his forefinger, and leafed through the pages until he found the one he sought. "The details are explicit. You'll receive this amount per annum for each child while they are minors. This should more than amply cover their needs and care." He pointed to another line. "This is the amount for each girl's dowry. The oldest boy will inherit property upon his twenty-first birthday. It's currently held in trust until that time. A small separate trust has been set up for the younger boy. Financially they shouldn't be a burden."

The numbers blurred and swam before him. The children were going to stay with him. He was responsible. He could barely think beyond that fact. He swallowed, trying to focus on what the man was saying.

"In an effort to prevent you from sending them to boarding schools, which your brother was adamantly against, Randall made arrangements to retain both the governess and the tutor to oversee the children's education. Fortunately for you, they've both agreed to stay on, and I will be in touch with them regularly. They are employed by the trust, and their compensation will come from the trust—from me."

Jac thought of the woman clad in black who had mistaken him for a hired hand. He had only briefly seen the tutor—a man with dark hair and eyes.

"As you can see, we are dealing with a large sum of money. But he said that even though he did not agree with everything regarding Penwythe Hall, at the end of the day you were one to be trusted. As he requested, I will continue to oversee this trust until the last money is distributed."

The thought of being tied to Steerhead for at least another decade did not bode well. Jac forced his fingers through his hair and tugged at his dirty waistcoat.

"Randall had his faults," Steerhead continued. "There is no disloyalty in that statement, I believe, for he would admit it himself. Who among us does not? But if there was one thing he was determined to be successful at, it was the care of his children."

Moisture gathered on the palms of Jac's hands, and his coat suddenly felt too tight. Too binding.

Steerhead sobered. "I am not a man given to emotion. If I recollect correctly, neither are you. But you know as well as I do how the evildoers in the world would prey on these children, privileged and not without resources, without you. You're their blood. It's your responsibility to see they are looked after."

As much as it pained him to admit it, Steerhead was right. Jac and Randall had once been in a similar situation. What if their aunt and uncle had not taken them in after their mother died?

Was this fate's way of coming back around? What was done for him, he must do for another?

From the distance a childlike voice echoed, then footsteps followed.

Jac did not know what the future held, but he knew that things could not possibly continue as they had been.

After a quick meal of cheese, bread, and cold meat in the kitchen, Delia and the girls were ushered to an upstairs bedchamber. They'd not seen Mr. Twethewey again since Mrs. Bishop escorted them to the kitchen, nor did Delia anticipate they'd see him again before morning.

A fire had been lit in the room's grate, and scattered candles illuminated the square bedchamber. As promised, their trunks had been delivered and now stood at the foot of the bed.

At one time the room must have been quite grand. A canopied bed with faded crimson curtains was anchored on the north wall. A thick brown-and-gray rug covered the planked wooden floor, and an elaborately carved mahogany wardrobe stood adjacent to the bed. A compact writing desk was positioned neatly between the curtained windows, and a sitting area with two chairs and a settee flanked the fire. Despite the chamber's tired elegance, a layer of dust and the stale air spoke to its disuse.

Delia ushered the girls to the sitting area. "Come now, let's find your nightclothes. You'll be much more comfortable."

"Are we all really going to sleep in this room?" Sophy gaped at the space.

Trying to steer the conversation in a more positive direction, Delia knelt by the trunk and unfastened the latch. "Mrs. Bishop said that no other rooms were prepared, but tomorrow we'll be given new chambers. Now, where did we put your hairbrushes?"

Delia's efforts were distracted when Hannah, easily the most sensitive of the three girls, dropped to the chair and stared at the fire. "Julia was right. He doesn't even want us here. He barely spoke with us."

"Oh no, Hannah. Don't think that. He was caught off guard by our arrival, that's all." Delia forced cheerfulness to her tone. "I'm sure that in the morning things will seem quite different."

Sophy, oblivious to her sister's concerns, removed the satin ribbon securing her hair and shook out the damp locks. "This room is scary."

Delia followed her gaze. The firelight cast long, moving shadows on the ceiling's chipped plasterwork and reflected on the intimidating carving of a deer on the wardrobe. "We just need more light." She spied another candle on the desk and lit it. "There."

Delia assisted the girls out of their traveling dresses and into their nightclothes and then began to unpack the first trunk, sorting out gowns and underthings for the next day. She was hesitant to unpack too much since their accommodations would likely change, but after two days of travel, the wrinkles in the fabric would be set, and she doubted there would be time for ironing.

As she shook out the first gown, she disrupted the dust in the room, and it swirled about her. Lifting her hand to her nose to prevent a sneeze, she moved to the closest window. The long brass handle squeaked in protest as she turned it, and the ancient hinges groaned as she pushed the pane outward.

"What are you doing?" Julia cried out, pausing in her task of brushing her curly black hair. "It's storming! Rain will come in."

"Ah, but it is so musty in here." Delia pulled back the curtain, allowing the cool breeze to curl in further. "We need the fresh air."

Delia turned back to the window. And fresh the air was. She inhaled deeply.

The sea was just over a mile from Penwythe Hall, but she could have sworn she tasted sea salt on the air. The accompanying scent, whether real or imagined, stirred an ache within her. Memories, like strikes of summer lightning, flashed and blinded. She forced the invasive, uncomfortable thoughts to the back of her mind and returned her attention to the task of readying the girls for a night's rest.

Before long her charges, clad in dry nightclothes and with freshly braided hair, nestled in the clean bedding. Sleep came quickly for them, undoubtedly a gentle reprieve from the day's uncertainties. A maid had taken their wet things down to the kitchen to dry, and now all was quiet and still, save for the fire popping in the grate and the wind billowing the crimson curtains at the window.

Delia, too, in an effort to ward off the day's plaguing chill, exchanged her damp traveling gown and cloak for a fresh chemise and a flannel nightdress.

With the girls slumbering, all was finally quiet.

After extinguishing all the candles save for one, she pulled one of the sitting area chairs next to the open window and perched very close to the ledge, angling herself to be out of the wetness but close enough to drink in the rain's delicious scent. She let loose her hair, setting aside pin after pin, and began to methodically brush the long, straight strands, the steadiness and habit of each stroke bringing about a fragile sense of familiarity, calm, and normalcy.

Never again had she thought she would see Cornwall's gorse and heather on the open moorland or drink in the salty scent of the sea air. Her marriage—and the privileged yet strained life that accompanied it—seemed a million miles away, as if it had happened in a dream, nay, a nightmare.

The nostalgic sensation stirring within her was more bittersweet than she expected, for she did have happy memories here. It was on these moors that she first gave her heart to another and first held her baby in her arms.

But it was also the site of her greatest tragedies.

Her beloved babe was now in the graveyard, and she'd never again feel her husband's embrace.

The pain of reality outweighed the joys of the memories. Her mother-in-law's warning rang in her ears as boldly as if it had just been spoken the previous day.

"If you've any sense in you, you'll ne'er return to Cornwall. You've betrayed the Greythornes, and none will forget."

The Greythornes would have no idea that she had returned to Cornwall. Penwythe Hall was nearly twenty miles from Greythorne House and twenty-five miles from her brother's home in Whitecross. She was a simple governess now. No longer was she regarded as the vicar's daughter or Robert Greythorne's wife. Who would care she was here? Furthermore, how would the Greythornes ever learn of her return?

And yet her heart was uneasy.

At times she could throw herself into her work and forget about it momentarily, but the thoughts would invade her mind at the oddest times. She'd fixate on them, as if not giving them the attention they demanded ultimately led her to succumb to them. The longer she was away, the stronger the fear grew.

She had something the Greythornes wanted—and she doubted their desire for it would diminish with time.

CHAPTER 8

Morning dawned fair and serene over Penwythe Hall, a sharp contrast to the storm that raged all the midnight hours. Ethereal mists hovered over the gardens and the low-lying spaces, and the sunlight glistened on the dewy lanes and stretched long over the verdant lawns. Distant seabirds welcomed the weather's change with their chirpy song, and the breeze raced through the budding trees, weaving a melody of its own.

Despite the tranquility that had descended, Jac was anything but at ease.

He'd never retired for the night.

It had been too odd to return to his own chambers, knowing that so many strangers slumbered on the other side of the walls and just down the corridor. Instead, he passed the sluggish hours in his study, accompanied only by his hunting dog, Cadwur, and wrestled with the truth.

Randall.

Dead.

He couldn't believe it.

And yet there were five reasons he must believe it, and they were all asleep upstairs.

At dawn he'd moved to his bedchamber to wash, don fresh clothing, and attempt to remove the dirt from under his nails that the previous day in the fields had afforded. He shaved the shadow of a beard and washed and combed his hair.

As the sun crept higher in the azure sky, familiar morning sounds pervaded the house. Servants' footsteps padded on the carpeted walkways, silver clinked from the morning room, and voices echoed on the lawn as workers called to each other. Soon the house would be fully alive and ready for the new day.

When would the children wake?

Dozens of questions and concerns had surfaced as night stretched to morning, and he was determined to address Steerhead regarding them before he saw the children again. He made his way down through the entrance hall to his study, where Andrews was waiting for him.

"Been looking everywhere for you," the steward blurted before Jac crossed the threshold. "Steerhead's leaving."

"What?"

Andrews nodded, his hazel eyes wide. "He's ordered the carriage in the north courtyard. Said he's leaving immediately."

Frowning, Jac stepped to the east window, jerked the handle, and pushed the pane open. He leaned over the sill and looked northward. Four horses stood at the ready, tethered to the second carriage that had arrived the previous night. Jac muttered and yanked the window closed.

There was far too much to discuss for Steerhead to leave now. Jac rushed from his study and emerged into the north courtyard.

Mr. Steerhead was already inside the vehicle. The carriage groaned into motion, and the harnesses creaked as the horses strained against them.

Jac sprinted across the broad courtyard, and once he caught up with the carriage, he trotted alongside and pounded on the side to get the driver's attention. When it stopped, he pulled open the door.

Steerhead leaned forward, annoyance twisting his face. "Well now, what's this?"

"Where are you going?" Jac's breath heaved from the run, and he held the door ajar.

"London, of course. You're not the only business I must tend to on your brother's behalf."

Steerhead moved to close the door, but Jac held it firm. "There's more to discuss before you scurry away."

Steerhead chuckled with a shrug. "My good man, I can't imagine what. I've delivered the children, communicated the will's terms, and lined your pockets with enough money to keep the children in abundant luxury for months. My obligation has been met. Now, if you'll let go of the door, I'm expected in London."

A strange sense of panic trickled through Jac, slow at first, then hot and searing. He wasn't ready to be left with the children. Not yet.

But Steerhead was right. The children were under his care now. What else could be done?

Hesitantly, and unwilling to concede, Jac released the door and stepped back.

"Best of luck to you, Twethewey." Steerhead's expression grew smug, and he snatched the door shut, then knocked on the roof of the carriage. Before Jac could respond, the carriage rumbled away into the morning's low-hanging mist.

Jac stared at the retreating carriage and only looked away when Andrews stepped to his side. "I've never liked that old goat."

They stood in silence until the carriage disappeared down the lane and curved at the north orchard's edge. All was still again, frustratingly still, before Andrews broke the silence. "Have you sent word to your aunt about this?"

Aunt Charlotte.

The woman who'd raised both Randall and him.

The woman who'd nursed their wounds, taught them right from

wrong, and provided safety when their young worlds were forever altered.

Yes, Jac had thought of her. In truth, it had been one of the most painful points of this entire scenario. Someone would have to tell her, and he was the one to do it.

"I'll go to her yet this morning." Jac sniffed.

Andrews fell into step with Jac as they walked back toward Penwythe Hall. "Mrs. Bishop should have breakfast laid in the morning room before long. The governess told her the children take their breakfast at eight o'clock."

Jac looked to the sun, now vibrant and glowing in the eastern sky. It had to be nearing that hour. "Very good. Reiterate the need for the staff to heed the tutor's and governess's requests regarding the nursery and schoolroom, will you? Do whatever necessary to see they're comfortable and have what they need."

He left Andrews in the entrance hall and made his way to the morning room, his movements growing slower with each step. A foreign sensation pulsed in his chest as he approached the familiar space now filled with the sounds of youthful chatter. The thought of the five souls on the other side of those walls drummed up long-suppressed feelings within him.

Regret. Guilt. Sadness.

He and Randall had argued. Fought. They'd clashed on many fronts to the point their once-solid relationship crumbled.

Now Randall was dead.

Nothing they'd argued about mattered anymore.

The morning room was as bright and cheery as any day, but the chamber that had seemed so large when he dined alone now seemed far too small a space. The boys had pulled a bench up to the table, and the chairs were so close they touched one another.

Upon his entrance the children stood, their efforts not to overturn the crowded chairs as they did so evident.

His confident steps slowed. How different they looked by daylight. The children continued to remain standing in silence, an act of respect he remembered from his own boyhood.

His gaze fell on the eldest boy, who could almost be mistaken for a man, so broad were his shoulders. The sight was like a punch to the gut. He was the perfect likeness of his father, from the thick shock of black hair, to the unmistakable shade of blue of his eyes, to the cleft in his chin. It was all there.

He realized they were waiting for him to speak. He cleared his throat. "Good morning."

"Good morning, Uncle." Their voices rang in flat unison before they were once again seated.

They resumed their breakfast but remained silent. His chair's legs scraped noisily against the wooden floor as Jac pulled it out to sit. Almost instantly the footman was at his elbow to pour him a cup of coffee.

The little girl sitting next to him kept staring at him with curious, bright eyes.

Uncomfortable with the silence and the girl's scrutiny, he cleared his throat again, then sipped the steaming coffee and set the cup back on the linen tablecloth. Jac lifted his gaze to the other adults present. He'd spoken only with the governess and was briefly introduced to the tutor. What were their names? Simon and Greyhouse? Greythorne?

The previous night the governess's bonnet had hidden most of her features, and he'd been far too distracted by the events to even take much notice of her. But today sunlight filled the room, bouncing from the pale-blue walls and illuminating the occupants, giving him a new opportunity to see them.

The governess was an attractive woman. Her straight, dark hair was confined in a tidy chignon at the base of her neck. Even from the distance spanning the table, he could make out long lashes framing gray eyes, a gently sloping nose, and dimples whenever she spoke or changed expressions. She possessed an uncommon air, as if completely comfortable in this new situation that was anything but.

The tutor was seated next to her, a newspaper folded across his arm. In contrast to the governess's collected air, his tidy appearance— dark-green coat, immaculately tied cravat, cleanly shaven jaw—could not mask his annoyance.

Regardless of his impressions, Jac would have to rely on them in the coming days, for he knew nothing about children or what was needed to make them feel at home.

The silence—the deafening silence—had to be broken. "I trust you all slept well?"

A chorus of soft "yes, sirs" echoed around the table.

He looked up to see the governess watching him. Her expression communicated that she understood how awkward this must be for him. Or perhaps that was merely what he wanted to see.

"Children"—she lowered her napkin, her voice gentle—"your uncle is very kind to open his lovely home to you. Are you not grateful?"

They nodded but no one smiled.

"I am sorry you had to share chambers," he managed. "Had we known of your impending arrival, we'd have prepared. But there is an entire upper level in the west wing, and you are welcome to it. Your father and I stayed there when we were children, and it's being prepared as we speak."

His words were yet again met with silence.

He cleared his throat. "Of course the rooms will need to be cleaned and arranged to suit your needs, but you're welcome to venture up there. There's a library, a schoolroom, a handful of bed-chambers, and a small parlor."

"My father's room?" asked Julia.

He almost breathed a sigh of relief when one of them spoke. "Yes. The last door at the hall's north end."

The children exchanged glances, and gradually they began to speak with each other again. He even heard a giggle.

Jac focused his attention back on the tutor and governess. "I will be absent for some of the morning, but instruct the staff on how you'd like the rooms arranged. Also let them know what items need to be purchased. They'll be awaiting your instruction."

"Of course." Mr. Simon's gaze was direct. A little too direct—and confident—given the circumstances.

"Where are you going to be today?" Sophy asked, her bright eyes wide and still fixed on him.

He looked at her, amusement eclipsing his uneasiness. Already he'd noticed that she did not shy away from conversation. Jac liked that about her. "I'm actually going to visit a relative of yours."

"We don't have any other relatives here." Hannah shook her head, lowering her bread to the plate. "Father said the only family we had was you and Aunt Beatrice and her family."

"Oh, but you do. You might not remember, but my aunt Charlotte, your great-aunt, lives in a cottage here on the Penwythe property. I'm going to tell her of your arrival. I'm sure she will want to come by and meet you all."

"I've met her before." Liam nearly interrupted Jac's last words. The youth looked fully at Jac for the first time since he entered the morning room. "She visited us once when Mother was alive. It was a long time ago, though."

A vague memory of the older woman going to visit Randall shortly after her husband's death in an attempt to smooth the rift surfaced. It had been unsuccessful, but apparently it had left an impression on Liam.

"I stand corrected." Jac smiled. But the boy did not return it.

Jac stood from the table and straightened his waistcoat. "I'll be off then, but in the meantime, just let Mrs. Bishop or Andrews know if you have any questions."

CHAPTER 9

The sun was already high in the blue Cornish sky when Jac traveled the path from Penwythe House to Fairehold Cottage.

This particular day should have been spent in the north orchard, assessing the drainage and overseeing the ditch digging, but the work would have to continue without him. A somber task awaited him, and the sooner it was completed, the better.

When he arrived at the whitewashed gate marking the cottage's entrance, he pushed it open, noting the need for a groundskeeper to repair a broken hinge, and wove through the tulips and hyacinth—their symmetry and vitality a testament to his aunt's careful tending.

He bypassed the main entrance and entered through the kitchen door, where he found his aunt sitting poker-straight in the breakfast room, alone, bread and jelly before her, tea in hand.

She looked up as he entered and lifted her chin to study him more closely. "You've shaved since yesterday. Good. The master of an estate should never be seen with the scruff I saw on you yesterday."

"I was busy," he teased, knowing how it irked her when he was less than presentable.

"A proper valet would ensure you never left the house in such a state. What happened to your valet, again?"

"Aunt Charlotte, you know there are no funds for a valet now." He rested his hand on her shoulder and plopped a kiss atop her white mobcap. "Besides, why would I need a valet when I have Andrews?"

"Bah." She snorted at his attempt at a joke, but she covered his hand with her own. "Now sit down. You're earlier than normal today."

"Yes, but I knew you'd be up." He followed her bidding and sat next to her. Alis, her maid, placed a cup of tea in front of him before he was even fully seated.

"Will you eat?" Aunt Charlotte asked, resuming her breakfast.

"No, I've eaten, but look at what I've brought you." He glanced back to the door to make sure Alis had rounded the threshold before he reached into his satchel and pulled out a bundle. "Cook made these this morning and insisted I bring you one."

Amused, Aunt Charlotte chuckled as she beheld the bundle of tarts. "Don't let Alis see these. You know how it vexes her when food is sent. She thinks the cook at Penwythe judges her cooking and finds it wanting."

He pressed his finger to his lips. "I'll not tell a soul."

As silence descended once again, Jac sobered in light of the grim news he was about to deliver. He cleared his throat and leaned his elbows on the table. "As a matter of fact, I do have news."

She cut her pale-blue eyes in his direction. "I could tell by the manner in which you are chewing your lip. Has old man Tallack made another bid for the north meadow? I do wish—"

"It's about Randall," Jac interrupted, the sudden need not to draw this conversation out any longer taking over.

She snapped her mouth shut. Her rheumy eyes widened, and she assessed her withered hands folded primly before her. "Now there's a name I've not heard pass your lips in quite some time."

His heart pounded more intently with each passing second. He did not want to share this news. Not at all. He reached over and placed his hand on hers. "He's dead, Aunt."

Her sparse eyebrows jumped. She drew a slow, shuddering breath, and for several moments she said nothing. She stared at the white cloth covering the table for what seemed like minutes, and then whispered, "A great loss indeed."

He gave her silence to digest the news he'd just delivered.

Moisture filled her eyes, but after a deep breath she straightened her shoulders. Always proper. Always controlled. "What happened to him? Did he take ill?"

Jac swallowed, finding the words more difficult to say than he thought he would. "No. Not ill. He was injured in a riding accident."

"I see."

He gave a slow nod. "Apparently he lived for two days after the incident, but he had significant internal injuries."

She lifted her teacup with a shaky hand and held it before her. Jac thought the steaming liquid would spill, but it didn't.

She returned the dainty cup to the saucer, tea untouched.

They sat in silence for several moments, the weight of regret pushing on him now more than ever.

How many times had Aunt Charlotte urged him to make this right with his only brother?

How many times did he deny her?

"And his children?" Her question pulled him from his dark thoughts. "What is to become of them now? Do you know?"

"As a matter of fact, I do." Jac drew a deep breath, trying to bring energy back to his tone. "That is the other part of my news. They are here."

"What?" She jerked, causing her pearl-drop earbobs to swing excitedly. Her hand flew to her mouth. The color that had drained now flooded her high cheeks. "Here?"

"Yes, all five of them. At Penwythe Hall. They arrived late last night. It appears that despite the disagreements, Randall decided I should be the guardian for his children."

The corner of her lip quirked, and she tapped her head, as if thinking of a great secret. "Deep down, your brother knew your worth, just as you knew his."

"Worthy or not, there are now seven more people living at Penwythe."

"Seven?" She gaped. "Why so many?"

"A governess and a tutor came with them."

"Heavens," she exclaimed. "Penwythe is a large house. It was never meant to be empty. It needs life in it."

Jac huffed, straightening his coat's broadcloth sleeve. "Large, yes, but it's hardly prepared to house seven more people in its current state. It needs repairs. And a great deal of them. You know better than anyone the strain the recent years have put on the old place."

"And yet it's always survived." An expression of peaceful pride settled over her, and she looked to the window.

He wished he could share her optimism.

"Come," she said suddenly, swiping a tear from the corner of her eye. In a shaky rustle of emerald taffeta, she rose to her feet, pushing against the table for support, the weight causing the china and egg-cup atop it to tremble. "Take me on a walk through my garden before you take your leave. I need air."

He jumped from his chair and rushed around to assist her. He offered his arm, and once she was steady, he retrieved her heavily ruffled bonnet from the hook, waited as she placed it atop her silver curls, and then led her from the breakfast room out into the morning sunshine.

"When do I get to see my great-nieces and -nephews?"

"You are welcome anytime at Penwythe, Aunt. You know that. You need never wait for an invitation. Say the word and I will send the carriage 'round."

"Ah, today's not the day. If they only arrived last night, they're meeting enough new people and must get settled." She paused at the budding pink camellias and tenderly touched the fragrant petals before she continued down the brick path. "What is their disposition? Surely this is quite an adjustment."

He recalled their somber expressions at the breakfast table—Liam's hard stare and Sophy's curious glances. "They are in mourning and quite somber, so I don't think it's fair to judge them quite yet."

"Will they accompany you to church tomorrow?"

He looked to the east as he considered her question. "I have not spoken with their governess about it, but I assume so. If they are to live here, then they'd best be acclimated as soon as possible."

"Quite right. Children are far better at adjusting to these things than adults are. 'Tis best to set expectations right away. Ah, but it will be good to have children at Penwythe once again. Have Mrs. Bishop set out a picnic on the front terrace tomorrow, and I will spend time with them then."

As Aunt Charlotte stood from her blooms, Jac assisted her on the uneven brick path. He smiled at her, a practiced, calm smile he'd learned to employ when apprehensive.

"Don't fret, Jac." She patted her withered hand against his cheek and met his gaze. "Time reveals all, heals all. Don't lose heart. God's ways are not ours. Have I not learned that myself, time and time over? I recall very well taking in my own sweet nephews. As you will remember, it was not always easy, but oh, where would I be today without my Jac? All will work together for good, my boy. All will work together for good."

CHAPTER 10

"A ren't you coming?" Delia paused in the doorway to the library. "Mr. Twethewey asked for the children to come down to the drawing room to meet visitors—a family called the Collivers, I believe."

"I heard." Mr. Simon did not look up from his stack of books. "You take them. I'll stay here and finish this."

Delia tilted her head to the side, pressed her lips together, and watched her friend and colleague as he reached for another book.

Managing the children's emotions throughout the past couple of days had been difficult, and Mr. Simon's inexplicable dour mood added to the challenge. Her every effort toward positivity and cheerfulness seemed thwarted by his blatant pessimism, and now his refusal to assist in this matter teetered on rudeness.

She wiped the dust and dirt from her hands, untied her apron, and shrugged it from her shoulders. She'd manage on her own.

Despite the fact that her cheeks already ached from forced smiles, she feigned enthusiasm and sought the children, who were gathered in the small parlor. "Your uncle has requested that you join him in the drawing room. He has guests to whom he would like to introduce you."

Groans circled the tiny space.

Delia ignored the grunts of protest and helped Sophy to her feet. "Come on now. Your uncle has been nothing but gracious; we owe him this much. His neighbors are our neighbors now. Come. Let's move quickly."

She urged them all to their feet and guided them down two flights of stairs. Voices grew louder as they approached the drawing room, and with quick, practiced movements she straightened ribbons, smoothed hair, and brushed dirt from gowns and sleeves as they neared the door. After a morning of selecting chambers, organizing furniture, and cleaning spaces, their appearance was far from pristine, but nothing could be done about that now.

They paused at the entrance, and she examined the children's faces, each a unique mixture of trepidation and interest, and lowered her head to look them each directly in the eyes. "Remember your manners. And be polite. Everything will be fine."

After patting her own hair and straightening her gown, Delia entered the sunlit room before the children.

She'd not been in this room during daylight hours yet. What had appeared dark and almost sinister last night was now bright and inviting. Tall windows lined the west wall, broken by two sets of painted French doors that opened to a terrace. A large pianoforte was positioned in the far corner, and paintings of all sizes adorned the emerald walls. The large marble fireplace stood opposite the windows, and two settees and several chairs formed a sitting space around the fire, where Mr. Twethewey and two guests now sat.

Mr. Twethewey stood as they entered and stepped forward. His dark, curling hair was brushed to the side, and his clean-shaven jaw boasted the same square shape as his brother's. Instead of the workman's attire he wore upon their first meeting, a fine coat of dark-gray broadcloth hugged his athletic torso, and a crisp white cravat made his skin seem quite tanned.

He motioned for them to come closer. "Come in."

Delia ushered the children nearer.

"Children, may I present Mr. and Mrs. Colliver. The Collivers are our nearest neighbors and great family friends. Their estate, Bowden Manor, borders Penwythe Hall to the north." Mr. Twethewey pivoted toward his guests. "May I present Liam, Julia, Hannah, Johnny, and Sophia. Excuse me, Sophy. And this is Mrs. Greythorne. Their governess. Where is the tutor?"

Delia found her voice. "He remained upstairs to instruct the staff on how to arrange the rooms."

Mrs. Colliver shook her head, her auburn hair swaying about her face. "What lovely children you all are. I knew your mother and your aunt. Quite well, as a matter of fact. We grew up together. I see that look of surprise on your face, Miss Hannah. Did you not know that your mother grew up not terribly far from here?"

"I did not know it was so close," Hannah said, exchanging glances with Julia.

"Why, yes." Mrs. Colliver's face brightened. "It is an hour by carriage ride, but what is that when such great friends were to be visited? I daresay your mother was much younger than I, but that hardly mattered. Your aunt and I were much closer in age. In fact, I still communicate with her often. Just this winter I spent a great deal of time with her and her daughters in London, and I received a letter from her only last month."

Delia did not miss how for the first time in days, Julia's face brightened.

Mrs. Colliver reached her hands to Sophy. "Now come here. I am eager to learn all about you. Oh, it does break my heart to see children dressed in mourning black."

Sophy cast Delia a glance before allowing Mrs. Colliver to lead her to the settee and being seated. The other children followed her, and Delia stood at the door, observing so as not to intrude on the family scene.

Once the children were settled, Mrs. Colliver leaned low, her sickly sweet scent of hyacinth encircling them. "Tell me all about yourselves. What are you all fond of? Surely there is something you like to do. We must find activities here to make you happy."

Hannah straightened. "I like to sing, and Julia plays the pianoforte."

From the simple question and answer, a polite, easy conversation flowed between the woman and children—with one exception.

Liam's face flushed red, and a storm brewed in his icy blue eyes.

Mrs. Colliver's high-pitched prattle pulled Delia back to the conversation. "What lovely children. Of course Julia must play for us right now, and, Hannah, you will sing. A concert is just what we all need." She waved her hand toward the pianoforte. "I doubt that instrument's been played in years, and it will be good to hear music within these walls again."

As bid, Julia took her seat at the pianoforte, a pretty pink flushing her cheeks—the first glimpse of a return of Julia's normal countenance since before the accident. She pushed her long, dark curls over her shoulder and arranged her black muslin gown, and Hannah stood in front of her, hands folded demurely. Julia began to play, and as Hannah sang, a clear, haunting tone exuded from her, one that seemed much more mature than her tiny body would suggest.

Delia's heart swelled with motherly pride as she watched the girls. How many afternoons had they spent rehearsing that very song? A strange sensation tightened her heart as the strains reached her ears.

If this song was bringing about such melancholy feelings for her, how much stronger would those feelings be for the children? She looked to their faces. Sophy and Johnny seemed comfortable enough, but Liam's jaw twitched yet again.

As the girls sang, Delia inched forward slightly until she was just behind Liam. She placed a hand on his shoulder, intending to be a comfort, but he jerked his shoulder free and stomped toward the room's exit.

The music slammed to a stop.

Delia opened her mouth to speak, but Mr. Twethewey's firm voice beat her to it. "Young man. You've not been dismissed."

The boy paid him no heed. He was nearly to the door.

"Liam! Stop."

At Mr. Twethewey's raised tone, Liam's feet halted. His shoulders rose, and his fists clenched at his sides. After several uneasy moments, he turned. Contempt darkened his young face, and his brows narrowed with more intensity than she thought him capable of.

Delia's breath caught. Her instinct screamed for her to get involved. But she waited.

The guardian's steady, deep voice echoed from the painted walls. "I don't know how things were handled at Easten Park, but in Penwythe Hall young men wait to be dismissed."

"I don't need to do what you say." Liam's tight words slid through gritted teeth, his stormy stare fixed firmly on his uncle. "You are not my father."

———◆———

Jac returned the boy's heated glare. The surprising force behind the youth's outburst caught him off guard. Jac stepped forward, his focus steady. "No, I'm not your father, but I'll not tolerate disrespect, and I doubt he would have either."

"What do you know of my father and what he would have done?" Liam's shout cracked, and moisture glistened in his eyes.

Heat rose above Jac's cravat, but it wasn't from anger. Yes, he had a right to be outraged at the disrespectful display, but when he looked at Liam, all he could see was Randall. The sight tore at him. "You must trust me."

"Why should I trust you?" The boy hurled each word faster, angrier than the last. "I know what you did to my father. We all

66

do. I'm not a child anymore, or perhaps you can't tell. I understood what was happening then, just as I understand what you are trying to do now."

From the corner of his eye, Jac saw the governess step forward. He held out his hand to stop her. "It's all right, Mrs. Greythorne. Liam has something to say to me. Let him say it."

Liam flicked his glance over at his governess, widened his stance, and licked his lips. Jac knew this look—a look of triumph. A look of opportunity.

"You stole this from my father." Liam flung his arm to indicate the room. "All of this. Penwythe Hall. My father was older than you. It should have belonged to him. And now it should belong to me."

A jolt of frustration seared through Jac. His patience grew thin at the accusation, for he could hear Randall's voice, strong and clear, in the boy's words. "The property was not entailed, Liam. Age did not factor into my uncle's decision. Sometimes, whether we like it or not, things do not happen the way we think they should."

"We shouldn't be here." A tear escaped the boy's thick lashes, chased by a sob. "We should be with Aunt Beatrice in London."

Jac glanced over at the other children. They were all watching with eyes wide. Faces pale. None moved a muscle. He lifted his gaze to the Collivers. He'd almost forgotten they were here, and now they bore witness to an intense, personal family moment. Richard Colliver's drawn brows and Mrs. Colliver's expression of horror indicated that it would not soon be forgotten.

With crushing weight, Jac realized that this arrangement would be much more challenging than he'd originally anticipated. He'd foolishly assumed that he'd provide a roof over their heads and see that they were protected and cared for and all would be well, but already, raging emotions were pouring through the cracks of the plan.

Wanting to put the children at ease, Jac softened his tone. "Just like my uncle had reasons for leaving Penwythe to me instead of your father, your father had a reason for sending you here. I don't know why, but I do promise I'll do my part to make this transition smooth. I can't do that alone, though. It will take all of us working together." Jac turned to face the rest of the children. "Do we need to discuss anything else? It will be a lot easier for us to move forward if we speak plainly."

"Can we go to the sea tomorrow?" Sophy chirped, as if no argument had just transpired.

"What?" Jac blinked, taken aback at the jarring change of topic. "Um, not tomorrow."

"When?" she persisted.

"Soon." Jac nodded to Liam. "You may be excused."

The youth turned on his heel, his boots smacking against the polished floor with each step.

For several moments no one moved.

Then Mrs. Greythorne stepped forward with haste. "Please excuse him, Mr. Twethewey. It's been a—"

"No excuses are necessary, Mrs. Greythorne, but if you would be so kind, please return the children to their tasks and then join me in my study. And bring Mr. Simon with you."

CHAPTER 11

Delia chewed her lower lip as she paced Mr. Twethewey's study. Nearly an hour had lapsed since Liam's outburst, but her heart pattered as if it had been just moments ago.

Mr. Simon leaned his hip against the side table against the far wall, a nonchalant smirk creasing his face. "I don't know why you look so nervous. You're prancing about as if you've done something wrong."

Delia cast him a glance of annoyance before turning and pacing the narrow space once more, her pale-gray muslin skirt swishing with each step. "You weren't there. If only you'd heard Liam. I've never seen him so angry."

She paused at the small looking glass hanging on the dark wall, brushed a speck of dust from her shoulder, and smoothed a wayward lock of dark hair into place. Curiously, her eyes drifted to the reflection of the room behind her—the private quarters of the man who was now very influential in her life, whether she wanted him to be or not.

"Will you stop fussing about with your hair? It looks fine." Mr. Simon glanced up from the newspaper he was holding. "And don't fret about Liam. It'll be forgotten in no time. He's just unsettled. Aren't we all?"

"This was more than unsettled." Delia turned from the looking glass, frustrated that Mr. Simon regarded his pupil's behavior with so little interest. "It was anger, raw and real."

Mr. Simon shrugged and raised his hand, as if declaring inno-cence. "He's a child. His anger will subside. This situation is new for him. It will take getting used to, 'tis all."

"Will you take this seriously?" She narrowed her gaze. "If this arrangement is to be successful, the children must develop a good relationship with their uncle. Furthermore, it's imperative that both you and I have a good working relationship with Mr. Twethewey."

"Why? He can't dismiss us from our positions. Only Mr. Steerhead can do that." He took one look at her and sighed. "You're reading too much into this. Besides, I can't imagine Mr. Twethewey is terribly interested in having much of a relationship with the children or us anyway. I spoke with the butler, and from what I can gather, his sights are fixed firmly on the success of his orchards and cider press and very little else. Mark my words. The master will keep to his business and leave us with the children. 'Tis the way these men usually operate."

A booming voice sounded from the door. "The way what men usually operate?"

Delia whirled around as the door to the study creaked open. Mr. Twethewey stood in the threshold, his expression cool, his brows raised in question.

Her heart pounded, and she stifled an inward groan. Not only had Liam shouted at him, but now she and Mr. Simon had been caught discussing his personal affairs.

Mr. Twethewey strode past them to his desk, leaving the scent of sandalwood in his wake.

Mr. Simon returned the newspaper he'd been reading back to the side table and straightened. "Forgive us for speaking so plainly about your personal business, but we are all coming to terms with our new arrangement. The children—especially Liam—seem to be having a hard time grappling with it."

"Clearly."

Feeling the need to defend Liam's behavior, Delia stepped forward.

"Be that as it may, allow me to assure you, Mr. Twethewey, that the children are not prone to such outbursts."

"I'm not angry about the outburst. In fact, I understand. Liam seems a passionate boy, like his father was." Mr. Twethewey did not look at her. Instead, he picked up a piece of paper and read it, his eyes never straying in their direction. His expression remained stoic and alarmingly indifferent.

She needed to make him understand. She gripped the back of the chair in front of her. "He is, but there is a great deal of his mother in him too. They are all quite different, the children, that is, one to the next."

Mr. Twethewey moved and stood next to the window, the light from which fell upon his black hair and broad shoulders. For the first time she noticed shadowed circles beneath his eyes. She was struck by how much younger he looked than his brother. Yes, with his cleft chin and vibrant blue eyes, he did resemble Randall Twethewey, but he possessed none of the fine lines around his mouth or eyes.

Mr. Twethewey motioned for them to be seated. Delia did as she was bid, her nerves twisting within her. Dozens of questions swirled in her mind. Why was his manner so aloof? Was he grieving his brother? Or was he merely disinterested? She folded her hands in her lap. His disposition—and the reasons behind it—was not her concern.

Finally Mr. Twethewey turned from the window and clasped his hands behind his back. "I'll be frank. I, regrettably, know very little about my nieces and nephews. As I told Liam earlier, I don't know why Randall chose to send the children here. I'm as surprised as anyone. No doubt you have heard the story of our past, and if not, there are many who'd willingly share it with you. I'll not dredge up the details. The children are here now and they are welcome, but to make this arrangement work, I need your help."

Her breath hitched a little as she released it. "Of course. Mr.

Simon and I will do whatever's necessary to ensure the children adjust as well as possible. Won't we, Mr. Simon?"

He only nodded.

"I will ask you to keep me abreast of how they are doing—if they need anything. Want for anything. Mrs. Bishop and Mr. Andrews are at your disposal and will see to whatever you require. The children may make themselves at home here. The grounds, the stables, everything is theirs to explore."

"I know Sophy is eager to see the sea," she said with a little laugh, hoping to lighten the mood.

He did not smile but merely offered a curt nod. "Yes, she has mentioned that several times. It's about a mile from here. Not a long walk, but it can be a bit tricky at times. The road leading north from the walled garden will take you right to it. I'd rather the children wait for me to accompany them the first trip, and it would be best to take a carriage. The terrain changes quickly once you are past the orchards, and it becomes rocky and a bit dangerous."

The mantel clock struck the hour, and he glanced at his pocket watch, as if mistrusting the chime. "I must be going. I know the children are in mourning and have had a busy few days, but I think it important that they come to church tomorrow and at least see the village."

"Of course."

"It's about a twenty-minute walk, so please have them dressed accordingly." Mr. Twethewey reached for a satchel slung over the desk chair, preparing to quit the chamber.

She started, a bit surprised. That was it? All he was going to say? No reprimand for what had happened with Liam? She wasn't sure what she had thought the conversation would entail, but this couldn't really be it.

More needed to be said, and she couldn't allow this opportunity to pass without saying it, especially if Mr. Simon was going to remain so silent. She stood abruptly. "Mr. Twethewey?"

He stopped and lifted his face. His blue eyes were startling, the intensity of which threatened to make her forget what she was going to say. "Yes, Miss Greythorne?"

"It's Mrs. Greythorne, actually." She lifted her chin with an intake of breath. "Might I make a recommendation?"

"My apologies, *Mrs.* Greythorne." He lowered the satchel to the desk. "What is it?"

"The children. They are such good children, and normally so happy. They loved their father very much. They adored him, really, and this has all been rather heartbreaking." At the risk of rambling, she rushed her words to make her point. "I do hope you will spend time with them, sir. Endeavor to know them. This must be a shock to your routine as well as theirs, but all children are frightened of the unknown. Perhaps becoming better acquainted with you would ease the transition—for all of you."

At first he did not respond, leaving her to wonder if she had overstepped her bounds.

Something flashed in his eyes, but his expression gave no hint as to what. He was a difficult man to read. Was he ever going to respond to her?

He diverted his gaze, picked up the satchel again, and hoisted it over his shoulder. "Thank you, Mrs. Greythorne. I shall bear that in mind."

Mr. Simon's pace as he stomped from the study through the entrance hall matched the impatience tightening his face. Delia nearly had to jog to keep up with him.

"Will you slow down?" she hissed, careful not to be heard by the servants polishing the adjacent staircase banister.

He did not slow his steps.

"I don't understand why you're so out of sorts."

"I don't like him." Mr. Simon's voice boomed. "I don't like anything about this."

Delia gritted her teeth, forcing her words to remain low. "Nobody *likes* what has happened, but give it time. You'll adjust. We all will. It's not even been a day."

"Doesn't matter."

"You'd better make the best of it." She scurried to match his stride, wishing she could make him stop. "The children will look to you, to us, to know how to handle this."

From the corner of her eye, Delia spied Mrs. Bishop at the corridor's edge and slowed her steps. "You go ahead. I'll be up in a few moments."

As Delia left Mr. Simon's side and approached Mrs. Bishop, the older woman's posture straightened. She said something to the maid by her side before shooing the girl away and giving Delia her full attention. "Mrs. Greythorne. Is there something you need?"

"As a matter of fact, there is." Delia's voice faltered as she organized her thoughts, shifting her mind from the frustrating previous conversation and forcing herself to calm down. Normally she had little trouble giving instructions to staff, given her elevated position as a governess and prior to that mistress of her own household. But the woman's pinched expression gave Delia reason to pause.

She did not imagine the woman—or any of the staff—was pleased with suddenly being tasked with the cleaning of an entire wing or tending to a great number of guests, and yet if she were to follow Mr. Twethewey's directions, she needed to set a precedent right away. "The girls are in need of new gowns, so I'm in need of a reliable seamstress. Is there someone in the village you would recommend?"

Mrs. Bishop's gaze fell to assess Delia's simple gray gown before she folded her hands primly before her. "I'm afraid you would be disappointed by the seamstresses in Braewyn. I am sure no one would be up to the standards of the mantua makers the young ladies are used to."

Delia stiffened her spine at the cool, unhelpful nature of Mrs. Bishop's tone. She'd hoped that she might be able to find an ally in the housekeeper, but the narrowness of her gaze and the firm set of her thin lips told her otherwise.

Delia lifted her chin. "Perhaps I should ask Mr. Twethewey? Surely Mrs. Colliver, the guest he entertained earlier today, would have need of a new gown every now and again. Someone has to make them."

If she had considered it longer, Delia might have chosen a different tactic. She had no desire to make enemies, but what choice did she have? If she didn't exert her authority, she might never get the name of a seamstress—or worse yet, she might be seen as weak.

Mrs. Bishop's nostrils flared, and her weathered cheeks reddened. "Mr. Twethewey is a very busy man, Mrs. Greythorne. No need to trouble him with such a detail. I will write to a seamstress who might be able to help you."

Delia inclined her head in approval. "Thank you. Please make arrangements for her to come here as soon as possible. And to bring fabric samples, appropriate for both full and half mourning."

With that, Delia turned and made her way back to the entrance hall. She'd not realized her pulse was racing until she arrived at the second floor of the west wing. After confirming that the girls were still reading in the library, she withdrew to her new bedchamber and closed the door behind her, finally allowing herself to fully inhale and exhale.

Silence surrounded her. She leaned back against the door, closed her eyes, and took several calming breaths. Two streams of afternoon light filtered through the tall, paned windows and landed on the muslin of her gown, the warmth comforting after the chilly interaction with the new master.

She opened her eyes. She'd not really had time alone yet to assess her new quarters. They were certainly not as fine as her private rooms at Easten Park, which had been spacious and airy. But this chamber, with its low ceilings and faded plaster walls, possessed a charm of its own. A green oblong rug had been brought from another room and now covered the planked floor. A small fireplace with a surprisingly ornate mantelpiece stood on the west wall, and at the north end, a short wooden door connected her chamber to a small sitting room. A canopied bed had been cleaned for her that very day, and a writing desk had been relocated from the library.

She stepped closer to one of her windows—her favorite part of the chamber—and looked down to the walled garden below. It was still waking from its winter slumber, but even in its current state there was evidence of grandeur. At some point someone had taken great pride in the intricate layout and the color scheme. Despite its overgrown appearance, it was peaceful. Serene. She'd experienced precious little peace in the past week, and her soul craved it.

The garden's large pink-and-red rhododendrons swayed in the breeze, and a smattering of bluebells carpeted the earth under a copse of elm trees. The flowers were a familiar sight, for the Greythorne House gardens had boasted much of the same flora.

The simple memory snapped her solace.

It would be easy to lose herself in the busy details of everyday life while caring for the children. She could throw herself into their education and their relationship with their uncle and pretend that all was well. Yes, she could try to forget, but every time she saw rhododendrons or bluebells, she would be reminded that she was back in Cornwall, and not far from where she started.

Feeling anxious, she moved to her desk. She needed to write to her brother and sister to let them know of her whereabouts. They'd been the one part of Cornwall she had held on to. She'd never told them the specific details leading up to her departure, but they'd never asked. Regardless, she smoothed a piece of paper and dipped her quill in the inkwell.

A bird in flight outside the window caught her attention, and she gazed toward it. Despite the warmth of the sunlight, she shivered. It did not matter that she was in a new home and surrounded by new people.

She was not free from her past, and she doubted she ever would be.

CHAPTER 12

Dusk's purple light and long shadows were pushing out the day's brightness as Jac walked along the path from the stables to Penwythe Hall. The previous evening's rain had settled the dust and sliced the mounting humidity, and now the evening could not be lovelier. How odd that merely twenty-four hours prior all was normal, and in one single instant—the arrival of a carriage and the delivery of shocking news—his life changed.

He glanced up toward the west wing. The windows, which had been closed for years, now stood open. The breeze caught white curtains, blowing them inside and then drawing them out again as if on a whim. He had little desire to step foot in those forgotten chambers—where memories haunted every room and lurked in the shadows. They were thick with memories of another time—happy times, free of blame. Free of guilt.

With Cadwur at his side, he moved to the wing's side entrance, the very door from which Randall and he would escape when their old tutor dozed off during summer's long afternoons. He lifted the latch and pushed the old wooden door open. Immediately he was met with a spiral staircase that was so narrow Cadwur had to go ahead of him for they'd not both fit walking side by side.

Higher and higher he climbed, passing the first-floor landing that would lead to his own chamber in the west wing, upward to the second-floor landing. Before even reaching it he was met with the scent of musty disuse. A cool wind whipped in from open windows, and the day's last light falling on the abandoned space made it seem almost frozen in time.

He listened, expecting to hear voices, or at the very least movement, but none came. His own footfalls and the click of Cadwur's toenails were the only sounds in the cool corridor. Up ahead, the door to the schoolroom was open, and he approached it.

Inside, Mrs. Greythorne stood atop a stool, facing away from him, at the bookshelf. Her dark hair, which earlier had been in a tidy chignon, was still bound at her neck, but long russet wisps hung down to her trim waist and swayed with her motion. A striped apron protected her gray gown, and her sleeves were rolled up to her elbows, exposing her forearms' fair skin.

He cleared his throat to gain her attention.

She turned, discarded the pile of books in her arm on the shelf, and stepped down from the stool. "Mr. Twethewey. I didn't see you there." She wiped her hands against each other before she faced him fully.

Almost as an afterthought, he removed his hat and held it in his hands. Cadwur circled him before he sat next to his boot. "I've come to see how things are progressing."

She drew a deep breath and looked around her at the pile of books. "This will suit our needs quite well, I think."

He spied the cobwebs in the corner of the paneled ceiling. "I fear it's in quite a state."

"It is nothing that a little bit of work can't fix, and I think it is good for the children to have an activity."

"Where are they now?"

"Mr. Andrews took them down to the stables. The boys were getting restless after being indoors all day."

A pang of guilt stabbed Jac. As their uncle he should have been the one to take them, not Andrews. He cleared his throat. "Are they getting settled?"

"Yes, quite nicely. I'd be happy to show you the arrangements, if you'd like." She led the way back into the hall. This wing was one long corridor. Along one side were the common rooms—the library, the parlor, the schoolroom, and the vestibule and landing area for the main oak staircase that led to the lower floors. On the other side were the sleeping chambers—four in all.

As they made their way down the hall, Mrs. Greythorne said, "The boys will share the end chamber. It is large and big enough for two, and they're fond of it since it was their father's. Julia will have this smaller one, and the two younger girls will share the one next to it because it connects to the chamber I will be using."

"And Mr. Simon?"

"Your staff has been kind enough to find him a chamber on the floor below."

He walked in silence next to her, their footsteps clicking on the planked floor. Light flooded in from the windows, spilling through the bedchambers and tumbling into the corridor. He exhaled quietly—perhaps the first time he had allowed the tension in his shoulders to ease since the children arrived and he learned about his brother. And yet overwhelming sadness rushed him as he walked this hall where he and his brother used to play, learn, and live.

In contrast to his restless spirit, the lady to his left seemed at ease. Her movements were graceful and her expression calm, almost as if she were the one who had lived her entire life here, untouched by death or hardship.

They approached the library entrance, and she paused and turned. "This entire situation must be very difficult for you."

His eyes met hers, and he was struck by the color of them. Gray, pure and colorless, like the sea just before a storm.

He looked down the hallway. Now was not the time for noticing pretty eyes. He weighed his response, wary of revealing too much. "It is. It's been years since we spoke, but Randall was still my brother."

"Whether death is imminent or comes suddenly, one can never be prepared for it. I am very sorry."

He looked at her again, expecting to see that her attention had moved on to something else after she shared her condolences, but her intent gaze was still fixed on him, her narrow brows drawn together with concern. She was a stranger to him, but something about her demeanor made him feel as if he'd been acquainted with her for much longer than one day. Honesty and sincerity radiated from her.

Rightly or wrongly, he judged people quickly. Sometimes his judgments were right, other times not. Mr. Colliver had called him impulsive that day out in the orchard. He was not the first person to do so, but in that moment, he decided she was trustworthy.

He cleared his throat and refocused his attention. "Can you share the specifics of what happened to Randall? Steerhead told me very little."

She lowered her head and the softness in her expression darkened.

Fearing that he'd overstepped his bounds, he prepared to retract the request, but then she lifted her gaze to him once more.

"It was a fine day," she began, brushing a lock of hair from her pale face. "The children were ecstatic to have your brother home at Easten Park. He traveled a great deal, you see, and the majority of his time was spent in London. But he came home for Easter and had remained there a few weeks.

"He was due to depart the following day when the accident happened. They were hunting, and he jumped a fence that he'd landed a thousand times before. Something spooked his horse, a rabbit or mouse or something, and the horse twisted while in the air, causing its hoof to come down unevenly. And from there the horse lost its balance, and who can really be certain of the events then? From what I was told, Mr. Twethewey fell to the side, and the horse fell atop him."

Jac folded his arms over his chest and stared to the window at the end of the corridor, where he could glimpse rolling hills and vibrant blue sky.

He did not see the scenery, however.

He could not dislodge the vision of a young Randall from his mind, nor the mental image of the horse falling, angular and heavy. He wanted to leave this corridor, forget this conversation, and yet his more practical side needed to know more. "Who was with him when it happened?"

"He was with Mr. Steerhead, two associates who were visiting from London, and Liam and Johnny."

"The boys were there?" His stomach tightened. "I didn't know."

She bit her lip, then nodded, her gray eyes finally meeting his.

Hungry for more information, he forged ahead. "Steerhead said he was conscious long enough to revise his will."

"Indeed. Initially it was thought Mr. Twethewey would recover, but after several hours his condition declined."

"Did you speak with him after the accident?"

She nodded. "I did. Mr. Simon and I were called to his bedside, where he asked us to stay with the children after he was gone."

"And how long have you been with the family?"

"Three years. Mr. Simon has been with them even longer. Six years, I believe. He arrived when Liam was eight years of age."

"I remember Mr. Simon. I met him once when visiting Easten Park, but that was many years ago." He cleared his throat, pushing the memory away. "And are you from Yorkshire, Mrs. Greythorne?"

She shook her head. "No, sir. As a matter of fact, I am from Cornwall."

"Cornwall? I thought your accent was familiar."

"Yes, my father was a vicar in a small village about twenty-five miles south of here."

He paused, waiting for her to share more. He expected her to speak of her husband, but she pressed her lips together and looked to the ground. It was clear she did not want to speak on the topic further, and it would not be proper to ask her to do so.

"I see," he responded. "Perhaps in returning home, the relocation to Cornwall might bring brightness."

At his words the conversation they'd been enjoying fell flat. The hall felt too narrow, the air too thin. He prided himself on his evenness of nature, but in this quiet moment, he felt his composure slipping.

With a quick bow he bid her good evening and then retreated back down the corridor to the winding staircase with Cadwur on his heels. He might be able to leave the west wing and the things associated with it, but the memories, he was sure, would haunt him for days to come.

"The terrain changes quickly and becomes quite rocky and dangerous."

Delia lay awake in her new chamber, staring, as best she could in the darkness, at the silk canopy above her bed. Thoughts, wild and rampant, raced through her mind, keeping sleep at bay.

She'd thought of so many things as she tried to sleep: Of Liam's outburst. Of Mr. Simon's foul mood. Of the girls' excitement over their new chambers. Of her late husband and Maria. Of her mother-in-law's warning. Of her sister's illness. But at that moment Mr. Twethewey's description of the coast held her mind captive.

Delia had grown up close to the sea, and it had always been one of her favorite places to visit, but it really became a part of her life once she married Robert. Greythorne Hall overlooked the southern coast, and Robert often would take her sailing when the weather was fine. Some of her happiest memories were of the long afternoons spent picnicking on the shore.

If she'd had an inkling that the sea would ultimately play a role in her husband's demise, she doubted she would have found such happiness there. She had not thought about how it would feel to see the sea again, with its crashing waves and unmistakable salt scent, now but a short walk away.

With a sigh she rolled over and retrieved the watch brooch from the small table beside her bed and squinted to see its white face in the faint moonlight. She groaned. Dawn would arrive soon, and with it activity would resume. Her mind was not yet ready for the day's commotion.

After several more minutes of tossing and turning, she sat up and swung her legs over the side. It was useless to try to resume slumber. Shaking free of the blankets, she stood and pulled her shawl from the foot of the bed. She wrapped it around her shoulders as she strode to the window and thrust it open. It was spring, but the early morning was chilly. The faintest hint of sunshine was just beginning to lighten the cloud-heavy sky. The invigorating air awoke her senses and an idea formed.

With sudden energy Delia dressed as best she could. At Easten Park, Agnes, the children's maid, had always helped her prepare for the day. Here she had no such assistance. Delia donned her heaviest boots and cloak, and before considering the wisdom of her plan, she exited her chamber into the darkened corridor. She scurried down the servants' winding staircase and made her way to the first floor and out to the terrace.

Perhaps it was the thrill of the unexpected or the freedom of being completely alone for a while, but a strange excitement soared through her as the fresh air enveloped her, billowing her cloak and whipping her hair around her face.

She stepped toward the garden—the very one she could see from her window, with its rhododendrons and bluebells. She held her cloak tightly and made her way along the winding path to the door on the other side, then pushed open the gate.

Above her, the sun was creeping across the heavens, pushing out the blackness with silvery light. Swatches of blue stretched farther and farther into the west, and behind her, faded pink-and-orange ribbons splayed across the sky.

Mr. Twethewey was right. As she moved past the garden, the shadowed terrain shifted from the manicured lawns to orchards and then to open moorland. Wild and beautiful, it was waking with the morning sun. After a short walk she thought she could hear it—the sound of waves crashing and tumbling. It beckoned her, calling her like a lullaby, as strongly as if the voices from her past were once again vocal and vibrant.

The breeze grew even stronger the closer she drew, and the salty scent of sea air, faint at first, intensified. Her hair whipped around her face, but she cared not. The road ended at a cliff, and she eased to the edge that dropped sharply to the sandy shore below. White seabirds stretched their wings and soared overhead, their abrupt call muted only by the crashing waves.

The cool sea air reached the part of her heart she'd been purposely shuttering since the morning she left Greythorne Hall. Her breath caught at the beauty before her in spite of herself.

Blue as far as she could see.

How it reminded her of how she and Robert would walk along a similar coastline, hand in hand, planning their future. Yet the sight brought with it more somber memories. Robert would disappear for hours upon end at such a beach, racing to outrun his fears and guilt. Ultimately, it was a shoreline much like this one where his body had washed ashore, battered and barely alive.

She shivered. The memory of the night he had died rushed to the forefront, as it did so often, demanding that she remember it in gruesome detail.

A lump formed in her throat.

That fateful night all those years ago, winter's frost filled the air with the harsh scent of wood smoke and fish, stamping out any trace of the sea air that now seemed so beguiling.

From the very day she left Greythorne, she had done her best to bury those emotions—not to linger on them. Like it or not, the truth would not be ignored: Robert had been a smuggler.

For the first couple years of their marriage, she'd tried to deny it, but in time he ceased all effort to hide his true profession from her. He, along with his brothers and family, controlled the stretch of beach that bordered Greythorne property. Nothing escaped their iron grip, and even the local law could not infiltrate the tightly bound smuggling ring. The Greythornes owned their own boats, the land, and the local businesses. No one would dare speak out against them. They were too powerful. Too dangerous. It was for this reason she still regarded her mother-in-law's warning with fear and trepidation. Years had passed, but she'd be a fool not to take such a threat seriously.

A seabird squawked close to her, jarring her from her reflection. The sky was fading from vibrant pink to blue, and it would be time for the children to rise soon.

She retreated down the cliff, back the way she came. The winds that had come so strongly off the sea weakened as moorland gave way once again to orchards and then to the verdant lawn. The sea air's salty tang was soon masked by the scent of apple trees and freshly cut grass, but the dormant memories had been revived by the familiar scene, and she doubted they would leave her in peace.

CHAPTER 13

Delia made up her mind almost instantly upon meeting Mrs. Angrove that she liked her. She had first met the older lady that Sunday morning on their way to church. As Mr. Twethewey promised, they walked to church, but Delia was surprised when their walk took them past Fairehold Cottage.

Their pace slowed considerably, but the spunky lady refused a carriage, determined to walk to the village church. She had rejected Mr. Twethewey's arm and offer of assistance as they walked and insisted upon Liam helping her. Now church was over, and the family picnicked on the lawn.

Delia relaxed back into her chair, tipped her face upward to the emerald canopy of branches and leaves, and allowed the gentle breeze to wash over her face. The afternoon was a fine one. Sunlight danced and bounced through the fluttering leaves, casting lacy patterns on the picnickers below.

Mrs. Angrove's airy voice broke Delia's reverie. "Mrs. Greythorne, you look quite lost in thought."

Delia jerked her head up, surprised at first and then giving a little laugh, lifting her hand to still the wisps of hair blowing across her face. "Forgive me."

Mrs. Angrove gave her head a sharp shake as she poured herself another cup of tea. "You look far too serious for a young woman on such a fine day, but I can only imagine what thoughts would be in your head after this week's events. My, what a trying time. 'Tis a true wonder you can keep a thought in your head at all. And yet"—she raised her gaze to the lawn, where the children played in the sun— "it is good to hear children at Penwythe Hall again, laughing and running. Do you not agree, Jac?"

Delia had almost forgotten he was there, for he'd been so quiet since church.

He sat opposite her at the table. Snippets of sunlight glistened on his hatless black hair, highlighting its tendency to curl when blown about by the breeze. He leaned forward with his elbows on the table and watched the children on the front courtyard's wide green lawn. "It is."

Mrs. Angrove sighed once more as she locked her sights on the children, like a mother hen content to have her chicks about her. "I can recall how you and Randall would chase each other in that same manner. Such happy memories."

In an effort to learn more about the family, Delia leaned forward. "Mr. Twethewey told me that this picnic was your idea. That was very kind. It is a treat for them."

"But the pleasure is mine! Nothing makes one feel younger than being around young people." Her eyes beamed, then her forehead furrowed. "My dear, the name Greythorne—it is very familiar. Are your people from the area?"

Delia pivoted toward the older woman, dabbing her mouth with her napkin to buy herself a bit more time to respond. This was what she had feared, sharing details of her life. What if word were to get back to her in-laws? And yet she could not refuse to answer such a simple question. "My late husband's family is rather extensive, and they hail from Morrisea, a fishing village about twenty miles south of here. I believe some of his cousins live up this way, if I'm not mistaken."

Mrs. Angrove's eyes twinkled. "Do you still have family here?"

Delia glanced up to see Mr. Twethewey staring at her. She lowered her gaze to her hands. "I do. My brother and his family live in Whitecross. My sister lives with him."

There.

She'd said it.

She'd opened the door to sharing about her past life. Words said would linger; none could be taken back.

"How happy for you then." Mrs. Angrove added sugar to her tea, oblivious to the turmoil churning within Delia. "Surely you can plan a visit."

She glanced up. Mr. Twethewey was still looking at her, his entrancing, intense blue eyes fixed firmly on her, as if he were trying to put together the pieces of her story, as if he knew there was more she was not saying.

Then, in a sudden burst of energy, he straightened in his chair. "Are the children fond of bowling?"

"Bowling?" Delia frowned. "I don't think they've ever played it."

He gave a laugh, cracking his fierce countenance. "How's that possible? Randall and I played it all the time when we were young. Right over there." He pointed to the bowling green at the east end of the main house. "Surely he must have taught them."

Delia shook her head. "Not that I can recall. Your brother preferred hunting. Or reading."

Mr. Twethewey huffed in disbelief, stood, and wiped bits of grass from his coat. He whistled sharply to capture the children's attention and then motioned for them to draw near. "Who would like to bowl over on the bowling green?"

"What's that?" Sophy wrinkled her freckled nose. Her black ribbon had come loose, and her dark hair now hung wild down her back.

"It's a game." He gestured for them to follow him to the bowling green, which ran parallel to the front courtyard.

"What sort of game?" Johnny fell into step with his uncle.

"A very fun one. Come, I'll show you."

All the children, even Liam, followed him toward the balls set up on the opposite side of the lawn, and soon they were out of earshot. From her chair, Delia watched as Mr. Twethewey retrieved a wooden ball from the edge. Sophy danced along excitedly beside him, and Delia laughed as Mr. Twethewey teased Johnny by handing him the ball, then lifting it high so Johnny had to jump to retrieve it.

An expression of motherly pride descended upon Mrs. Angrove, and her lips formed a half smile. "It's good to see him like this. To see them all like this."

They sat in silence for a few moments, and Delia studied the older woman. A gown of deep-lavender silk hugged her willowy frame, and a fussy shawl of white lace was tied about her shoulders. Her silver hair was nearly white. Laugh lines crinkled around her eyes and mouth with each expression, and her light eyes were sharp. She seemed to be the sort of woman who observed everything and missed nothing.

"How long have you lived here, Mrs. Angrove?"

"A lifetime, my dear," she exclaimed with a smile, lifting her eyes heavenward. "I came here with my husband, William, when I was a bonny young bride and probably about your age." She studied Delia. "What is your age?"

Delia straightened her shoulders. "Six and twenty."

"Ah, no, then, I was much younger. I married two days after my eighteenth birthday and was transported here the day after. I spent many happy years in that house."

Delia followed the woman's gaze up to Penwythe Hall's paned windows and curved Dutch gables and tried to imagine it at another time.

"My husband had such a passion for this home, this land." Mrs. Angrove didn't take her focus from the building. "It was already ancient when we arrived and needed repairs even then. But William did not care to spend his time and money in repairs. Oh no, not him. His true love was the gardens."

"I can see the walled garden from my chamber window. It's beautiful and so intricate. I thought someone had to have spent a great deal of time on it."

"Ah, the primrose garden," Mrs. Angrove whispered wistfully. "That is what everyone always called it, for in the spring the entire west end would come alive in yellow and pink. It was his pride and joy."

"Such a lovely thought."

"Lovely, yes, but lovely does not keep the debts paid or the creditors at bay." Amusement sparkled in her vivid eyes before they sobered once again. "Now there are no funds to keep it as it used to be. I fear Jac inherited quite a burden when my husband's solicitor handed him the keys to Penwythe Hall."

For a moment Delia thought the topic would drop, but then, with her next breath, Mrs. Angrove tilted her head to the side. "My husband was a dreamer, Mrs. Greythorne. His head was always in the clouds and his hands always in the dirt. He was determined to make these gardens the finest in all of Cornwall. Everything you see was his vision. Even the garden at the cottage where I now live was his playground."

Delia surveyed the lawn with a fresh eye. Flowers, like jewels, bent and swayed in the early spring sun. Color was everywhere. "What a noble endeavor."

"Indeed. Beauty is always a noble endeavor, especially when it showcases God's handiwork. William had the passion of an artist's soul, but he did not have a mind for numbers." She shook her head. "No, no. He could not be bothered with sums and figures and matters of business. He was so obsessed with the gardens that the business of Penwythe simply did not matter to him. The fields and orchards were neglected. The outbuildings fell into disrepair. Beauty, valuable as it is, does not provide an income. Unfortunately,

William neglected the legacy that would be required to sustain the estate for future generations."

Delia looked back to Mr. Twethewey. He was laughing. It was the first time since her arrival she'd seen him act so freely. She recalled how Mr. Simon said the rumor was that he was consumed with his orchards. Perhaps there were more burdens on Mr. Twethewey's shoulders than the surprise addition of five children.

Mrs. Angrove paused her story to eat a jam tart, then wiped her thin lips with a napkin. "Toward the end of his life, my husband began to see the error of his ways. Impending death often brings clarity, I have found. Randall had such a mind for numbers, but by that time he'd been gone from the property for so long that William feared he'd sell it to avoid losing more money. But Jac was different. He'd never left the property except to go to university. It had become part of his blood, just like it had for William. Fortunately for us all, Jac has more practicality than his uncle ever possessed. Randall had an eye for business and profit, and Jac has an eye for people and the land. The brothers are very different people, driven by very different things."

Delia found herself intrigued. "What sort of things?"

"Randall was driven by success."

"And Mr. Jac Twethewey?"

"Oh, security." Her voice was firm with certainty. "He finds rest in knowing that everything will be well for years to come. I'm sure you've heard about the orchards. Orchards do not provide for one year, or even five. If tended properly, they can provide for decades. That's the kind of overseer Penwythe Hall needs, and William saw that in Jac."

Delia looked toward the bowling green. Mr. Twethewey had removed his coat and now stood with his hand on Julia's shoulder, helping her line up her ball. He stepped back as she rolled it across the lawn and then clapped as the ball bounced into her siblings' balls, knocking them out of the way.

Mrs. Angrove sighed happily at the sight. "*That* is why Randall sent them here. I know it. The children need that influence in their lives. Death is sad, but for those who remain behind, there is life yet to be lived. And I hope this family can embrace it to the fullest."

Mrs. Angrove's eyes popped wide. "Speaking of living life, has anyone spoken to you about the Frost Ball yet?"

Delia frowned and shook her head. "No, they have not."

"Frost is a hazardous thing to those who make their living off the land, so once we are safely past the danger of it, folks from all around come together and celebrate. For decades hundreds of people have descended upon Penwythe grounds to forget their troubles."

"What a lovely gesture."

"It is, but it is an expensive one. I was afraid that with the financial struggles we would have to forgo it this year, but somehow Jac has found a way to manage it."

"I know the children are in mourning, but I do hope they will participate. I think it's important for them to feel at home here."

"My sentiments exactly! Then it's settled." Contented, the older woman looked out over the grounds.

Delia followed her lead and turned her attention back to the children and their new guardian. Mr. Twethewey tousled Johnny's hair and his dog circled them all, causing Hannah to laugh.

For a few moments Delia felt her shoulders ease. If the children could laugh after what they had been through, then she could too.

CHAPTER 14

Jac held his arm steady as his aunt leaned on it for support, and he slowed his steps to match her slower ones as he walked her back to her cottage from the picnic.

Despite her physical exhaustion, her eyes were bright and her tone buoyant. "Who would have thought but a week ago that Penwythe Hall would be so changed in such a short amount of time?"

He listened to her chatter as they traversed the dusty lane—about Julia's maturity for one so young. About Johnny's amusing sense of humor. About Liam and how much he resembled his father.

And then her commentary turned to the governess.

"What a lovely lady Mrs. Greythorne is. Do you not think so?"

A cool wind rushed in from the direction of the sea, and he lifted his face to enjoy the breeze. Yes, she was lovely. And his opinion of her increased with each interaction. Even so, he couldn't help but notice how she had diverted her gaze when they spoke about her past. "Did you not think her manner a bit odd when she spoke of her family? It seemed as if she didn't want to speak of them."

"Do not be so suspicious." She swatted at his arm. "It isn't attractive."

"I don't mean to be suspicious, Aunt. Only observant."

"It is completely respectable if a person desires to keep bits of herself private. Not every detail of life need be an open book. But give her time. Maybe she will share with us, maybe she won't. If there is one thing your uncle taught me, it is that people are not brought into our lives haphazardly. That is hardly ever the case."

"Be that as it may, the children are my concern. Not her."

Aunt Charlotte gave a little laugh. "Oh, Jac. You've much to learn, I fear. *She* is the influence behind those children. She's teaching them. Molding them. Randall entrusted her completely with their formation. It's dangerous to hand over such a great task, and yet he trusted her with such a responsibility."

"And what of Mr. Simon? He was entrusted with their care as well."

"His absence speaks volumes. Can you not see it? Oh, you are a man, and I should not be surprised if you would turn a blind eye to such things. Mrs. Greythorne is raising those children, make no mistake. If you want a good relationship with the children, then you need a good relationship with her. Fortunately for you, she's a lovely person. And oh, such a pretty young thing."

He raised his eyebrow and did not miss the twinkle in her eye. "She is the governess, Aunt," he clarified with pointed tone. "Nothing more."

She huffed. "In case you haven't noticed, there's hardly an abundance of young ladies in the area. Do you never give a care for your future? For the legacy you will leave in life? You are well into the third decade of existence. Don't wait too long to realize there's more to life than orchards and trees. Like I said, people come into our lives for a reason. Do not dismiss it lightly."

Jac sniffed, pretending her words did not affect him.

But they did.

Yes, he wanted a wife. A family. Who wouldn't? But the timing wasn't right. Not yet. Penwythe Hall was struggling, and he did not feel right asking a woman to come alongside him to save a ship that might sink. Furthermore, his aunt was right. There were not very many women in the area, and none who had caught his eye. Perhaps he would feel differently if someone did, but for the time being, it was best that he focus on his orchards.

He deposited Aunt Charlotte safely and cozily in Fairehold Cottage under the care of Alis, then headed back to Penwythe Hall.

He'd expected to arrive back to find that the children had retreated to the house. Clouds had gathered, dark and thick, as they tended to do this time of day, settling a chill shadow over the countryside. He quickened his steps through the overgrown garden and was surprised to hear giggles and laughter when he emerged on the other side.

He smiled. After his awkward exchange with Liam the previous day, he'd been wary about spending time with them, but Jac had enjoyed the afternoon with the children more than he'd anticipated.

The children took notice of his return as he rounded the low rock wall separating the front lawn from the main road. Johnny ran toward him, the wind catching his dark hair and his small chest rising and falling with exertion. "Uncle Jac! Do you want to bowl again? I've been practicing while you were gone."

"Me too!" chimed Sophy, scurrying behind her brother, her cheeks flushing pink. "I've gotten ever so much better. I can best you now, I know it. You should see!"

He rested his hand on Johnny's shoulder as the boy walked by his side.

"Tomorrow, yes? Look at the sky over there." Jac pointed toward the north. "See how the clouds look like they are coming at us in a straight line, and feel how cool the air has become? That means rain is coming."

"Maybe tomorrow we could go to the sea." Sophy hopped next to him in excitement.

He laughed at the child's insistence. "You have my word, Princess Sophy, I will take you to the sea. Not tomorrow. But soon."

As the children ran back to their siblings, Jac looked to the oak tree where they had picnicked. The footmen had come down to carry the table and chairs back to the safety of the house, and as they hoisted the chairs over their shoulders, Mrs. Greythorne stood beneath the branches, Hannah at her side.

He slowed his pace as he walked toward her.

Greythorne.

His aunt had been right when she recognized the name. He knew it from somewhere. But where?

It could be from anything—a tenant, a visitor, a guest at one of Colliver's hunting parties. It nagged at him.

A fresh gust of wind whistled through the knobby branches, and Mrs. Greythorne pressed her bonnet against her head. Ribbons fluttered past her face, and Hannah raced ahead toward her sisters. As Mrs. Greythorne took notice of him, she collected her skirt in her hand and smiled. "Mr. Twethewey. We were just going back inside. I fear the rain is almost upon us. I trust your aunt is home and well."

He fell into step next to her, a casual, comfortable stroll. "Yes. She tires easily, but she's pleased the children are here."

"They so enjoyed the bowling green today. What a wonderful idea to share it with them."

He paused to allow her space to move in front of him as they crossed through the main gate. Her scent of lavender mingled with the scent of the lawn's freshly cut grass and rain riding in on the wind—an intoxicating blend.

With the children hurrying to the house, they were alone as they walked through the entry. Shadows reflected from the south-facing paned windows, moving and shifting, making the house seem almost alive. He adjusted his gait to match her daintier pace, enjoying this time alone with her probably more than he should. His aunt's words of legacy and her charm rattled noisily in his mind. He was used to being alone with the servants, but she was different.

Servant or governess, she was beautiful. The more he was in her company, the more he became aware of it.

He cleared his throat, forcing his mind to more appropriate topics. "Surely by now you've heard that one of our initiatives is to establish a cider barn before harvest. In a couple of days the new granite stone for the crusher is due to arrive, weather pending, of course. It will be an important addition to Penwythe. I know Liam and Johnny have schoolwork to tend to, but given the significance, I think they should witness it."

Her face brightened. "That is a wonderful idea! Anything that will foster a sense of belonging would be beneficial."

"My thoughts precisely, especially given yesterday's conversation with Liam."

She lifted her hand to still a long lock of russet hair that had blown free. "Liam is such a vibrant boy, and he's so clever. His father's death has been hard on him, and he doesn't know how to manage the pain of loss. Please do not judge him based on his actions. It was grief talking."

Grief talking.

She stopped suddenly and turned to him. She was close enough he could make out the subtle specks in her gray eyes and notice the dimples next to her mouth when she spoke.

She met his gaze directly. "Liam—all of the children, really— want to know someone is in control and will protect them. It's a basic desire for everyone. You've been kind to allow the children to live in Penwythe Hall, but walls alone do not make children feel safe. People do. It is as simple and as complicated as that. And even though Liam is fourteen, he is still very much a boy with a great deal of growing up to do."

He watched her as she walked ahead, posture straight, shoulders back, her skirt swaying with each step. Everything about her exuded kindness and confidence—an uncommon combination. The recent days' uncertainty had jaded all, but her determination to foster tranquility had a soothing effect on those around her.

Yes, he liked her—and his curiosity about her was growing.

———◆———

Later that night, Jac rode out to the south orchard with Cadwur loping contentedly at his side.

It was lovely out. The light pattering of rain had stopped, and twilight's purples and pinks intermingled across the sky. All was quiet and still, save for the rustle of the leaves through the shadows. The pink-and-white apple blossoms that had ornamented the branches had nearly all fallen—their colorful remains carpeting the ground under his horse's hooves.

Jac rode down the rows, pausing every so often to pull a limb closer, examining the tiny clusters where the blossoms had been. Before much longer those clusters would turn into fruit.

He then studied the ground. As planned, three angled trenches had been dug across the rows to encourage the rainwater to drain to the valley's lowest point, where a pond had been established to catch overflow. For days the projects had seemed nothing more than a muddy mess, but now that the workers had cleared out the debris, he could see the fruit of their labor. Some leaves had wilted in sections of the orchard from too much water, but the new irrigation system would alleviate waterlogged soil. It had to. He looked down to the pond at the south end. Already it was full.

Optimism surged.

A horse's steps drew his attention, and he lifted his gaze to the orchard's west edge to see Andrews approaching. "Are the hedges all in?" Jac called out as the steward drew near.

Andrews nodded, pulling his horse's reins to the left and ducking to miss a branch. "Yes. The workmen finished planting them last night. They seem small, though. I doubt they will do much to dissuade the winds. At least this year."

Jac surveyed the hedgerows along the north. Andrews was right. The bushes were small, much smaller than he would have liked. If moisture did not threaten the new trees, the angry north and west winds would. "It'll be at least a full season before we know if this is effective."

Andrews shifted his weight in the saddle as he looked toward the west. "Willows were planted in some of the wettest areas, in hopes the water would be drawn to them. At least we needn't fear a drought."

The steward's voice ceased, and Jac glanced over to see what had captured his attention. On the far side of the hedgerow, Mrs. Greythorne led the girls across the verdant meadowland between the orchard and the moors. Now clad in dark gray, she was only just taller than Julia, who followed closely behind, and the two little ones ran alongside. They stopped, and Mrs. Greythorne knelt to pick something from the grassy carpet and extend it for the girls to see.

Jac could not decide what to make of them. At times it seemed natural that the children should be here. They were, after all, an extension of Randall. There were other moments, however, when he'd be immersed in activity and almost forget about their presence, and then he'd catch them out of the corner of his eye and shock would strike all over again.

Jac nodded toward the ladies. "What do you think of Randall's children being here?"

Andrews cocked his head to the side. "It's not really my place to say, is it?"

"But I'm asking you." Jac sobered. "You've been here at Penwythe nearly as long as I."

Andrews's eyes narrowed, and his countenance grew somber.

Jac recognized that look—the look of a man loath to say what was really on his mind. He prepared himself for the worst. "Let's have it."

Andrews lowered his reins to his side and leaned toward Jac. "It's not so much the children that concern me, but Mrs. Greythorne. Talk around the village is that some of the folks aren't happy about her presence here."

"What?" Jac scoffed, swatting a bug away from his face. "That's absurd. What could she have possibly done to draw censure from anyone?"

Andrews shrugged. "It's not so much what she's done, but what her husband did."

Andrews's statement coupled with her unwillingness to speak of her family at the picnic added to the mystery. "But he's dead. Surely he can't be a problem."

Jac urged his horse forward as if to dismiss the conversation, but Andrews circled around so the animals traversed the narrow row side by side. "The vicar called earlier today. Some of the parishioners voiced concerns about her to him. Do you recall several years back when the excise men raided a merchant ship bound for Plymouth? Nasty business. They attacked the boat while it was still at sea, and seven of the men aboard were either killed or died from injuries. One of the men was from over in Wentin Bay. You remember, right?"

Jac tensed. Yes, he remembered. It was one of the largest successful free-trader raids that he could recall in Cornwall.

"Another one of the men killed was Robert Greythorne."

"Mrs. Greythorne's husband?" Jac blurted out as the pieces slammed together in his mind.

Andrews nodded. "The very one. The villagers have long memories, and now every tongue between here and Bowden Manor is wagging."

Jac looked up to the silver clouds, gleaming brilliantly as the sun's descending light reflected on what he had just heard. *Smuggling* was a bitter word, especially in a coastal town like theirs. It had been an increasingly difficult battle to fight, and the excise men chose that particular campaign to set a harsh example. The shock of it sent tremors all throughout the heart of Cornwall. Locals sympathized with the men who had been killed, claiming they were about their honest business. The other side believed the smugglers to be the lowest conniving lot. There were no winners or losers in that situation, just a sad end, and no resolution, for free trading continued to this day. From what he could remember, those who were tried were ultimately freed, but even so, the tales were that they were released only because of threats and blackmail.

"Are you sure about this? That Robert Greythorne was indeed her husband?" Jac asked.

"Aye, very sure. His family is in a town called Morrisea, which is not that far away, and his brothers are still rumored to be involved in the activity. The Greythorne clan is a wealthy lot. They're impenetrable. Folks are concerned that Mrs. Greythorne's presence here might draw the attention of her in-laws or, worse yet, the excise men."

"That's ridiculous. She's a governess. She's no time for anything else."

"But the staff is talking—everyone from the chambermaids to the stableboys. Apparently Mrs. Greythorne writes a great deal of letters marked for the south of Cornwall. I forget the name of the town they are addressed to. Even Mrs. Bishop commented about it just this morning."

Jac set his jaw firmly. "Randall wouldn't have hired a smuggler. Besides, if she were involved, she'd have been jailed."

Andrews nodded. "I agree, but you know how folks are, especially after the smuggling in Wentin Bay a couple years back. Powerful families can wield their power, even from as far away as Morrisea."

Jac looked back toward Mrs. Greythorne and his nieces. She was farther away now, her delicate form merely a silhouette against the green backdrop. "As far as I'm concerned, it's naught but gossip."

Andrews shrugged. "Thought you'd want to know what's being said, 'tis all."

"The solution is a simple one." Jac set his jaw. "I'll speak with her about it as soon as possible."

It sounded like a simple task, and yet he knew it would not be. Miss Greythorne, with her colorless gray eyes and disarming dimples, was proving to be quite a mystery.

CHAPTER 15

J ac returned Mr. Simon's stare with a glare of his own. The man had been a pain to deal with since the first day of his arrival, and today of all days Jac was in little humor for his haughty antics. His gaze did not waver. "As I said, Mr. Simon, the granite wheel is being delivered to the cider barn this morning. I think the boys should see it."

Johnny hopped up from his schoolroom chair and spun around to face his tutor, barely able to contain his excitement. "Can we go now?"

Mr. Simon frowned and stepped forward, placing his hand on Johnny's shoulder, then gently guided the boy back down in his chair. "Surely, Mr. Twethewey, you don't intend for them to miss their studies, especially in light of all that has happened. We've worked hard to keep on a schedule."

Jac gathered his patience. He would not be challenged, not in his own home. "Of course. But *in light of all that has happened*, this is an important day for Penwythe Hall and those who depend upon it. As masters of Penwythe Hall, they must attend."

The boys exchanged glances, as if unsure whom to obey.

Mr. Simon held firm to Johnny's shoulder. "Schedule and structure are paramount. Besides, these young men must prepare for a more management-focused future and not concern themselves with mere menial details."

Jac stiffened. "This *menial detail* is a vital investment and will affect Penwythe Hall's future profitability for years to come. We may be in the country, but I assure you, business can be—and is—conducted here."

Mr. Simon lifted his hands, as if surrendering. "You're their guardian. If you believe this to be the best use of their time, then I'll not interfere."

Jac sucked in a deep breath. He could see why Randall chose this man to oversee the boys' education—Randall never would have been interested in the installation of a granite wheel, only in the revenue it would generate. "I'll have them back by this afternoon."

"You are welcome to accompany us," Jac added as the boys closed their books and quietly moved from their table. "The day is fine, and it really is a sight."

The tutor snorted. "Thank you, no."

"Suit yourself. Good morning, Mr. Simon."

Jac led the silent boys down the back staircase and through the great hall. They turned and made their way through the entrance hall, which ran the entire depth of the house from the main entrance to the sun-drenched back courtyard. Johnny ran ahead, his enthusiastic footfalls sending up bits of mud from last night's rain. His excitement, however, was cut short when the groom met them in the courtyard, leading two saddled ponies.

Johnny stopped short and whirled around, his wild eyes seeking Liam's. He inched backward from the animals until he was quite close to his brother.

Jac closed the space and patted the pony's neck. "Don't you ride, Johnny?"

The boy did not respond. His face paled.

Liam put his arm around his brother. "He doesn't want to get on the pony. He's scared of it because . . ."

And then it struck Jac—Randall had died in a riding accident.

He cringed at the groom's unknowing misstep and his own insensitivity. Of course the boy was hesitant to ride. Jac should have thought of that.

The groom huffed. "Afraid, are you, boy? Six or sixty, doesn't matter none. It doesn't do for a man to be afraid of a horse."

The groom, oblivious to Liam's explanation, circled the pony in front of Johnny so he could mount. Johnny scooted backward.

"No matter." Jac lightened his tone. "You don't have to ride alone. You can ride with me."

"No." Liam took a sudden step forward, blocking the space between Johnny and Jac. "He'll ride with me." Without another word Liam angled his brother toward the larger pony and assisted the small boy into the saddle. "Don't worry, Johnny. We'll go slow."

Jac sobered as he watched Liam's behavior. It sparked memories of how Randall, who was nearly seven years his senior, had tended to him, especially when they'd first arrived at Penwythe. The memory, normally a pleasant one, tasted bitter in light of the week's events. He was eager for the memory to fade and the day to resume its task.

Once the boys were settled on the pony and the stable hand had brought Jac's horse to him, the small group made their way down the muddy road leading from the stable, past the orchard valley, Cadwur trotting alongside them.

"Why is the cider barn so far away from the stable?" Johnny asked after several minutes of riding.

"It has to be. Hopefully, once it is all ready, many people will come to use it. All the tenants here have at least a few apple trees, if not their own small orchard, and hopefully they'll pay to use our crusher to make their cider instead of going to the next town. Be that as it may, we want to keep them away from the main house. The lot of 'em could get noisy." He smiled down at Johnny, who was leaning to the side to see around the grove.

They rode on. The road curved at the orchard's edge, leading to a tall stone outbuilding with several small timbered windows. It was an unassuming structure, with walls of thick dark-gray stone and a thatched roof. On any other day this was a quiet space, disturbed only by the sheep in the neighboring meadow or the larks nesting in its hand-hewn rafters, but today laborers in broad country hats gathered in the courtyard, and a large wagon drawn by oxen stood at the ready. On the wagon's bed, thick ropes secured a large stone wheel, nearly half as tall as a man, in place.

As they approached the site, Jac's chest swelled with pride and optimism for what lay ahead. This was what they'd all been working toward—the key to the future of cider making in Braewyn. The stone would crush apples and prepare them for the press. This addition could swing Penwythe's fortune in their favor.

Johnny's expression brightened at the commotion, and he wiggled in the saddle to get a better view. Liam, however, remained reserved. His lack of enthusiasm flattened his voice. "This is it?"

"Ah, it's what this will become." Jac smiled and nodded for the boys to follow. "Come on."

Once at the building's small courtyard, Jac dismounted, helped Johnny down, and waited as Liam slid from the saddle. They secured their mounts and entered the building. It was much cooler inside. The wide barn doors stood ajar, shedding light on a large granite ring—the apple crusher—which had been installed the previous week, the side of which came up to Jac's knee. The ring had a wide groove in the top of it, and in the middle, packed straw was nestled around a large wooden pole sticking upward.

"It looks like a big round water trough." Johnny frowned.

"Does it?" Jac stepped closer and knelt next to him. "Now the big wheel from the wagon will be lowered into this groove. When the apples are ready, we'll put them in the groove and a horse will pull this wheel around and crush the apples to prepare them for the press. Once pressed, the cider will be stored in the barrels over there."

"Where's the press?" Johnny looked around the large, empty barn.

"It hasn't been delivered yet."

Johnny tilted his head, his focus clearly still on the crusher in front of him. "How are they going to get that wheel into the ring?"

"Oxen." Jac nodded to the thick wooden beam crossing the vaulted roof. "We'll harness them to it, and then, using the beam, they'll lift the wheel and lower it into position."

They returned to the courtyard to watch the workers wrestle the wheel from the wagon to the ground. The morning was warm, and last night's rain had done little to still the dust and dirt swirling with the breeze's whim. Grunts echoed as the men wrestled the stone, trying to finesse the stubborn mass.

Jac glanced around. Many familiar faces were in the courtyard watching the spectacle—tenants, workers, local businessmen. Even the vicar was present.

But one man in particular caught his eye.

"There you are, Twethewey," Colliver called, lifting his walking stick to gain Jac's attention. "Quite a hullabaloo here today. I had to come and see it for myself." His tone suggested he found amusement with the situation. Jac didn't like it.

Colliver folded his arms over his chest. "So this is the crusher you've been speaking of. I'd like to say that I share your optimism on the potential, but it seems impossible that this barn, this equipment, will yield the desired result."

"Braewyn's well overdue for a cider mill."

"The people can always make their own cider in the comfort of their homes and barns."

"Yes, but this is faster. It'll save time. And money."

"Well then, I'm eager for you to prove me wrong." The man's hard eyes glittered.

It was difficult to tell if he was joking or not, but Jac was in no mood for jests. "This is only part of it, Colliver."

"I know, I know, the orchards." He waved a dismissive hand. "Anyway, I wish you luck with your endeavor, Twethewey. I really do. The folks in this area could use some success, at any measure." Colliver pivoted and bowed toward the boys in mock formality. "Good day, gentlemen. And what do you think of this?"

Johnny stepped closer to Jac, trepidation radiating from his young form. "I like the oxen."

A loud, low laugh rumbled from Colliver. "Of all this, the oxen draw your fancy?"

The boys shook the older man's hand before Colliver returned his attention to Jac. He nodded toward the cider barn. "I'm off, then. I've business of my own to tend to. I'll see you next at the Frost Ball. The ladies in my home have been talking of nothing else. I do believe that a new gown or two has been requested for the occasion." Colliver took his leave.

After several moments of watching the men work, Johnny squinted as he looked up at Jac. "What's the Frost Ball?"

"It's a soiree hosted at Penwythe Hall every year, after the danger of frost has passed. It means that our crops, and in our case, the orchards, can no longer be damaged by frost."

"Can I go?"

Jac chuckled at the boy's enthusiasm. It was refreshing—and encouraging. He ruffled his hair. "The ball is for adults, but the village children always picnic on the lawn the day before. You can attend that if you like."

Liam stepped forward, his icy glare directed at his little brother. "We can't go. We're in mourning. You know that, Johnny. Why would we want to go to a dumb party when Father just died?" The sudden anger in Liam's young face made him appear much older than his years, and much more forceful.

Jac could only stare. Surely the tutor and governess couldn't object to a bit of frivolity, even if they were in mourning.

A commotion interrupted their conversation. The granite wheel scraped off the wagon bed and crashed to the ground, flinging up dirt and spewing dust and hay into the humid air. A long pole was threaded through the stone's middle to serve as an axel, and workmen assumed positions on either side to help the massive wheel roll steadily. With shouts and grunts the workers harnessed it to the oxen to be pulled into the barn.

Jac watched the spectacle, his hand on Johnny's shoulder, until footsteps pounding behind him snatched his attention. He pivoted to see Liam's lanky form sprinting toward the horses tied on the other side of the road.

The sight alarmed Jac. He gripped Johnny's shoulder. "I want you to stay far away from that stone. Understand? Go to Mr. Andrews over there by the door and don't move."

Johnny looked back at his brother, confusion darkening his small face, but he obeyed and ran to Mr. Andrews.

Once certain Johnny was nowhere near the stone, Jac jogged after Liam, who was jerking at his pony's reins, trying to free them.

"What are you doing?" Jac stomped over the long grass, confused at the sudden change in demeanor.

"I don't want to be here," shouted the lad, his voice tight.

"That's fine, but it's no reason for you to run away like that." Jac shifted and watched as a fat tear ran down the boy's cheek.

The sight took Jac aback. He reached out to still the boy's jerky movements.

But Liam ripped his arm free. "You can't make me stay here! I don't care about the stupid stone, or the stupid crusher, or the stupid Frost Ball." His movements were growing increasingly more frantic. His breath hitched in his throat.

Shocked, Jac considered his words as Liam returned his attention to the pony. He'd thought the outbursts were behind them and that Liam had already said his piece.

Jac spoke low. "That's fine. You don't have to be at the cider barn or go to the Frost Ball. But you do have to be respectful."

When Liam couldn't untie the reins, he dropped them and forced his full attention on Jac. "Respectful?" Redness flushed his cheeks. "I don't care about anything to do with Penwythe Hall."

"Your father wanted you here. Surely that counts for something."

"Not to me. You didn't see him. He was dying. He wasn't right. Mr. Steerhead shouldn't have let him change his will."

"I understand your frustration, I do. I—"

"How could you understand?" Liam's voice cracked. Then his eyes narrowed. "I hate you for what you did to my father." The boy stomped farther toward the forest lining the far side of the road leading to the village.

Jac couldn't allow Liam to walk into an unfamiliar forest. He jogged to catch up with him, but when he reached him, Liam whirled around, anger oozing from his expression. He pulled back his fist and, seemingly with every ounce of force his body possessed, punched Jac in the chest.

Stunned at the suddenness of the attack, Jac stumbled backward to keep his footing. But Liam punched him again and again, each strike faster than the last.

Jac grabbed the boy's upper arms and held him at arm's length, letting him wriggle and punch until his energy wore out.

The sight pained him.

Grief was fueling the outburst, not anger. Not anger at him, anyway.

Perspiration dotted Liam's brow. His hair clung in sweaty clumps to his forehead, and tears pooled in his blue eyes, adding to their vibrancy. "You're a thief. You stole this property from my father, and that's like stealing money. You knew he was working hard to provide for us and our future, and you didn't care. So why should you care about us now? As soon as I'm of age, I'm leaving and taking my sisters and brother with me. I hate you!"

With a fresh burst of energy, the boy swung his arm out again. This time Jac pulled the lad toward him and embraced him. Tightly. Preventing him from flailing.

Liam was no longer the adolescent on the verge of adulthood; he was a boy grieving the loss of his father.

At first Liam stood firm, but moment by moment, his muscles loosened until he was sobbing against Jac's shoulder.

Jac, not knowing what to do, remained silent and still while Liam cried, allowing him time and space to release the raw emotion pummeling him.

At length, Liam pulled away, and Jac dropped his arms to his sides. The boy who had been so tough moments before was now sheepish. He dragged his sleeve across his nose and wouldn't look at Jac.

Jac nodded toward a fallen log on the forest's edge. They sat in silence for several moments, Liam's chest still heaving, the sound of shouting and calling echoing from the distant courtyard.

"You don't have to like me, Liam. But you must accept that your father wanted you all to be here. There's no getting around it. I don't know what your father told you about the will, but there are two sides to every story. One day, when you're ready, I'll tell you my side. You're not a child, and you deserve to know the facts and to determine your own opinion on things." Cautiously, Jac draped his arm around the boy's shoulder. But Liam didn't pull away.

Jac looked from the canopy of the trees above him to the cider barn in the distance. Like Liam, Jac wished he knew for sure why his brother had sent the children to him, but he owed Randall something. And just like he would not give up on his plans for the orchards, he would not give up on the children who had been entrusted to his care.

Chapter 16

Delia stopped short as she turned the corner to the library. Mr. Simon was standing alone by the window, looking down at the grounds. His broad back and sable hair created a strong silhouette against the day's brightness.

"What are you doing?" She breezed into the room and stepped to the shelf.

He did not turn to face her. "I don't know what Mr. Twethewey was thinking sending his children here." His flat tone held no amusement, and his gaze didn't leave the window. "He must've been out of his wits when he made that decision."

Shocked at the sudden vehemence in his voice, Delia slowed her movements as she sifted through the books and then returned a wayward tome to the shelf. "Oh, I don't know. I'm rather pleased with how the children are settling in. It's only been a little more than a week and already they seem to be adjusting. I thought it would take them much longer."

He scoffed, finally looking away from the window, and tilted his head patronizingly. "You're joking."

"No, I'm not." She walked along the shelf, reading the titles as she did so. "I think they seem quite happy, especially Sophy and Johnny."

"Do you know where *he's* taken Johnny and Liam? To watch the crusher go in the cider barn, like common laborers, as if it's some great feat."

"But that's the industry here, is it not? Agriculture and things of that sort? Mrs. Angrove said that people here make their living by the sea, the land, or the mines."

"Yes, but they are a gentleman's sons, not common farmhands."

"This isn't London, Mr. Simon." She raised her voice, sensing her opinions were falling upon deaf ears. "It's good for them to be exposed to different ways of life, especially since they live here now."

"Why are you coming to the man's defense?" Mr. Simon huffed. "That's not what Mr. Twethewey wanted for them, and you know it."

Delia winced, weary of this conversation yet again. "Perhaps their uncle's trying to get to know the children. Give him time. I think he's a good man and has the children's best interests at heart."

"A good man?" Mr. Simon squawked, jabbing a thick finger for emphasis. "Don't forget what he did. He stole an estate from his brother. Good men just don't do that."

"Now you sound like Mr. Steerhead," she teased, attempting to lighten the mood. "We will never know what happened, not really, and ultimately it's none of our business."

Mr. Simon's gaze narrowed. "Jac Twethewey is a scoundrel. It'll all be evident in the end, as such things always are, and it'll be the children who suffer."

Delia gaped, unsure how to respond to the outburst. Mr. Simon was prone to extreme opinions and had a vocal temper, but this seemed odd, even for him. Perhaps he knew something she didn't. It would not be the first time the males at Easten Park had kept details from her.

After several seconds, his brow rose, as if an idea had just formed, and he folded his arms across his chest. "I don't believe it. You're actually content here."

Delia tucked a book under her arm, avoiding eye contact. "I'm happy to have a roof over my head, and to be needed. Isn't that all any woman in my position needs?"

He snorted. "You're much more complacent than I."

"I'm not complacent. I just think you are overreacting to the entire situation."

"Then you have a frustratingly small view of the world." He snatched his satchel and stuffed his book inside. "There's far more to experience in this world than staring at rows of apple trees and celebrating cider barns."

She sobered. His rant had taken a personal turn, and she rotated to face him fully. "I'm a widow, as you well know, and I have but three options in life, Mr. Simon. My first option is to stay where I am and be content about it. Secondly, I could return to my brother's house, but with my ill sister and his rather large family, I would be nothing more than a burden. That I could not bear. And third . . ."

He raised his eyebrows in a silent question.

She drew a deep breath. It would not do to speak of such a matter with a man, even if that man was a friend. And yet she felt compelled to say it out loud, even if just to remind herself of the truth. "Third, I could remarry. But since I never leave the premises and rarely meet anyone new, that's hardly a viable option. As a man, you have broader options, but as far as I'm concerned, yes, I am resolved to be happy here, and I suggest you do the same."

He stepped past her to gather papers on the far table. "Be that as it may, I've written to Mr. Steerhead about my concerns. Surely Mr. Twethewey gave him some guidance in what to do if this situation did not go well."

"My advice, if you are looking for it, is to just let the situation stabilize. You might be surprised."

The door creaked open, and a maid appeared in the doorway.

Delia forced a smile and smoothed the gray muslin of her sleeve. "Yes, what is it?"

The maid cast a sheepish glance at Mr. Simon before she entered farther. "The footman asked me to give these to you. I've one for each of you." She extended both her hands with a letter gripped in each one.

Mr. Simon snatched his letter from her hand and muttered a word of gratitude as he brushed past them to the corridor.

Delia accepted her letter and gave the maid a reassuring smile. "Thank you."

The maid bobbed a curtsy, and then Delia read the writing on the outside of her missive. She smiled at the familiar script in spite of the tension that had gathered in her shoulders. It was always good to hear from her sister. She tucked the letter in her apron and saved it for later.

———⚬———

Delia leaned down to assess the hurried scrawl of her youngest pupil's handwriting. They'd been working together for months to improve Sophy's penmanship, and satisfaction mingled with pride as Delia studied the splotches of wayward ink marring the paper. "Very nice, Sophy."

Sophy beamed and angled her paper so her sister could see. "Look, Hannah!"

With a smile Delia stepped around the table to where Hannah and Julia were sitting, and she glanced over their shoulders as they worked on their paintings.

A deep male voice broke the silence. "Excuse me, ladies. I've no wish to intrude."

Delia glanced up to see Mr. Andrews in the threshold. She straightened, surprised. She had only interacted with him in passing, such as when he would collect the boys to visit the stable. "Mr. Andrews."

"I'm looking for Mr. Simon. Is he here?"

"No, he's not. He and the boys have gone with Mr. Twethewey to the fishing ponds."

"Mrs. Greythorne, might I speak with you, then? In private?" He waited in the doorway until she joined him in the corridor. "Mr. Twethewey wanted to set up riding lessons for the boys. The groom wants them at the stable tomorrow morning at nine o'clock sharp."

Delia frowned. "Did he mean for both boys? I thought Mr. Twethewey was aware of Johnny's fear of horses."

"He thinks it is best for the boy to face his fears. Don't worry, the groom has taught many children to ride, Mr. Twethewey included." He leaned forward with a playful smile, as if taking her into his confidence. "Even so, I do not think Mr. Simon agrees with the decision."

She gave a little laugh and tucked a loose strand of hair behind her ear. "Mr. Simon has his own decided opinions, that is safe to say. But he's well intentioned."

"Would you like for me to arrange lessons for the young ladies as well? Mr. Twethewey didn't know if they could ride."

"Oh," she exclaimed, taken aback by the sentiment. She glanced at her charges bent over their paintings and studies, then observed the blue sky through the window. How pleasant it would be for them to be out riding in the fresh air instead of cooped up inside. "Their father never was in favor of ladies riding. He preferred them engaging in more feminine pursuits."

As if sensing her hesitation, he continued. "You're from Cornwall, are you not, Mrs. Greythorne? Surely you must know how important it is for everyone to know how to ride a horse, especially in the country. Even so, Mr. Twethewey wanted to leave the decision up to you."

She winced at the comment. She'd barely spoken with Mr. Andrews, and yet he knew such a personal detail about her. Like a bolt of lightning, fear struck her core, as if at any moment her in-laws would learn of her location.

She drew a deep breath and straightened her shoulders. "Thank you, Mr. Andrews. It's a fine idea."

"I couldn't agree more. Besides, you'll not find a better instructor than Giggs." He nodded toward Julia and Hannah. "I see the young ladies are painting. Were you aware that Mrs. Angrove is a celebrated artist?"

"Mrs. Angrove? No, I had no idea."

"Her paintings hang all throughout Penwythe. That one, for example." His hat was in his hand, and he pointed to a painting with it.

Delia stepped closer to the painting of a flower to admire the intricate strokes of pink, white, and green. "She painted this?"

"Oh yes. Old Mr. Angrove grew the flowers and she painted them."

Delia smiled, recalling Mrs. Angrove's words of love for her husband, as her eyes fell to a series of smaller gilt-framed paintings on the wall lining the corridor. She stepped from painting to painting. She'd seen them dozens of times, but now that she knew the artist, a new appreciation formed.

She'd almost forgotten Mr. Andrews was still there until he asked, "Do you intend to attend the Frost Ball, Mrs. Greythorne?"

She lifted her head at the common question. The Frost Ball seemed to be on everyone's lips. Besides Mrs. Angrove at the picnic, no one had mentioned it to her personally, yet she often heard the servants planning for it. "I am a governess, Mr. Andrews. My place is with the children."

"Even so, it would be a shame for you to miss it."

It was then she met his eyes. They were kind and warm—a trait she had missed in their previous interactions. She liked the way he spoke with her. Friendly, easy, unforced. As steward, he was no servant. He held a position of responsibility, and that position demanded respect. He was not on equal terms with the servants, nor was he on equal terms with the owner. Like her. How nice it would be to have a friend in him or, at the very least, an ally.

He stepped forward. "Well, if you do decide to attend, you must save a dance for me. I'll be counting on it."

She flushed under his forwardness, but there was also almost playfulness in his nature. "Very well, Mr. Andrews." She stood in the hallway as he retreated, watching as his shadow disappeared around the corner.

A man—a handsome one—had just asked her to dance.

A strange flutter jumped in her heart.

She had not danced since before Robert died. There had been a time in her life when a country dance would set her heart reeling. But now . . .

Her heart fluttered again and a smile toyed with the corners of her lips. The wayward lock of hair slipped again, and she tucked it behind her ear. It was folly, she supposed, that the mere request could make her feel young again, but maybe, just maybe, this was a harbinger of a different life that awaited her. Perhaps the move to Cornwall was not all bad. The new situation might bring new opportunities—if only she could escape the fear of her mother-in-law's warning.

CHAPTER 17

Delia chewed her lip as she traversed the path to Fairehold Cottage, mentally practicing what she wanted to say. Her conversation with Mr. Andrews had lingered in her thoughts and had sparked a plan. She was determined to make this transition a smooth one, for the children's sake. What better way to do so than to enlist the help of the children's great-aunt?

Delia probably should have discussed her idea with Mr. Twethewey, but he'd been absent all day, and she didn't want to delay. In her left hand she clutched Sophy's small one. In her right she carried one of Mrs. Angrove's small paintings, wrapped in a cloth tied with a ribbon.

Once at the cottage door, Delia rapped her knuckles against it.

The aged maid eyed her curiously once the door was open. Instead of being shown to the parlor, the maid ushered them to the back garden, and as they rounded the corner, Delia drew in her breath at the sight.

Wild and free, the garden boasted an explosion of color and living things. Butterflies added dots of floating color to the sky above, and the hum of hovering bees blended with the rustling leaves, creating music, soft and soothing. Upon closer inspection, the garden was not a haphazard collection of plants but a deliberate pattern of rhododendrons, magnolias, and roses. The mosaic stood in vibrant pink and purple contrast to the greenery around it. A sweet, familiar fragrance hung in the air.

A giant tabby cat slinked from the low boxwoods. It stopped at the sight of them on the brick path, as if frozen solid, its large gold eyes fixed on them in alarm.

"A cat!" Sophy immediately attempted to step toward it.

Delia held her hand firmly. "You don't know that cat. It might not be friendly."

"La, that's naught but ol' Cyrus," the maid interjected in amusement, hands propped on her hips. "He'll not hurt the little girl none. I'll fetch Mrs. Angrove."

Delia released Sophy's hand as the maid retreated, and the child fell to her knees next to the cat.

After several minutes Mrs. Angrove appeared in the doorway. A worried expression darkened her face, and her gaze shifted from Sophy to Delia. "My dear Mrs. Greythorne, I do hope nothing is amiss."

"Of course not!" Delia stepped toward Mrs. Angrove and offered her the steadiness of her arm. "We only came to pay a call."

Mrs. Angrove's look of apprehension melted to one of relief. "Oh. Well then."

Delia guided her toward the table, noting the tidy nature of Mrs. Angrove's hair. Not a single silver strand was out of place, and her gown of green silk was neat and pressed. As subtly as she could, Delia motioned to Sophy to come and greet her aunt, and she stepped back to allow the girl room. "I hope we are not intruding, Mrs. Angrove."

The older lady chuckled and accepted a kiss on her cheek from her great-niece. "My goodness, Mrs. Greythorne. At my age I will take any and all visitors. I am happy not to be forgotten."

The words struck a chord in Delia's heart. Was Mrs. Angrove lonely?

Mr. Twethewey said he visited here every day, but Delia glanced around the area. Trees were her only neighbors, the flowers her only housemates.

The cat trotted forward at the sound of its owner's voice, and Sophy reached down to pet his back as he passed.

"Ah there, I see you've become acquainted with Cyrus."

Sophy knelt once more, and the cat curled against her. "She's pretty."

"Well, *she* is a *he*"—Mrs. Angrove's voice danced with humor—"and he is very happy for anyone who will pet him."

Mrs. Angrove sat at the table and turned back to Delia. "So tell me, why have you come to call?"

The directness of the question might have unnerved some, but Delia found her frankness refreshing. Delia said nothing but joined her at the table and unwrapped the painting.

"What have you there?" Mrs. Angrove accepted the framed piece and angled it to get a better look. A smile crept across her face, evidence of a memory budding to life. "Where did you find this?"

"In the west wing. Mr. Andrews told me you painted it."

"So I did. Many years ago."

"It is quite beautiful work."

"You flatter me." She chuckled. "As I said, my husband was fond of the gardens, and if I wanted to be in his company, I had to find a way to enjoy spending time in the gardens as much as he did. I couldn't bear digging in the dirt, no, so I brought a paintbrush with me. He dug and I painted."

"You are quite the artist."

"I *was* quite the artist." She placed the painting on the table and leaned back in her chair. "I've not painted since my husband died."

They sat in silence for several moments, watching Sophy dangle a flower above the cat and then giggle as he batted it with his paw.

Mrs. Angrove broke the silence. "I told you that after my husband died I didn't want to live at Penwythe Hall because it held too many memories. That was true, but there was another reason. When we first lived at Penwythe, William's mother lived here, in this very cottage. He created this garden—everything you see—just for her.

It was small, but he spent so much time here tending it for her. I feel closer to him here than anywhere."

The maid brought out the tea, and Delia waited until the beverages were poured and the cakes laid out before she proceeded. "I must confess that I came here for a selfish reason. I hope you'll forgive me."

Mrs. Angrove's pale-blue eyes sparkled as sharp as her wit. "Oh? A selfish reason that requires forgiveness. Sounds intriguing."

Delia smiled and lowered her teacup to the table. "It is about your art. While at Easten Park, an art master would instruct the girls when he was making his rounds. He'd stay with us for a few days each month, and the girls always enjoyed it. Would you be willing to teach them what you know about painting?"

Mrs. Angrove waved a dismissive hand. "Oh, my dear, I've nothing to teach."

"But surely there are some skills you could impart. Besides, I know they would enjoy spending time with you. I've been attempting to teach them about the flora and fauna of the area, and this would be a wonderful way to teach them botany and other such knowledge."

Mrs. Angrove looked at her more closely. "Painting is a feeling. An extension of who you are. I must say that you're quite confident in your role and quite decided in your goals for the girls. You must care for them very much."

"I do. And I hope it wasn't presumptuous to come to you directly. Mr. Twethewey said to make myself at home, and at Easten Park I would have no problem pursuing a new instructor." Realizing what she had said, she straightened. "Oh, not that I think of you only as an instructor. I just meant—"

Mrs. Angrove threw back her head and laughed heartily. "I like you, Mrs. Greythorne. I like you a great deal. This is what Penwythe needs—a woman to keep things moving. Men get lost in gardens and orchards and the sea and the like. But you see it as I do. People, ah, people. That is where the true success lies."

Mrs. Angrove turned to observe Sophy, who was seated on a small tuft of grass amidst the lilies. The cat nestled in her lap, and she dangled a long piece of grass for the cat to play with. Mrs. Angrove's gaze softened in the way a mother's gaze would when she looked at her child. "I would like very much to spend time with the girls. Bring them to the garden early in the morning. The light is the most pleasant then. I will ask Jac to find my paints and palettes."

Satisfaction, warm and rewarding, spread through Delia. This was what the children needed—to start building foundations and friendships. To start a new way of life with new goals and new passions. She never wanted them to forget their life at Easten Park, but there were opportunities here—opportunities for happiness and growth, if they would but accept them.

———•———

Jac was late. Normally his visits to his aunt were much earlier in the day, but he'd lost track of time. He glanced heavenward and increased his pace. The afternoon sun was starting its descent.

His aunt would be upset.

She was lonely, he knew. Few neighbors matched her social status, and as such, she had few visitors. Occasionally the vicar and his wife would call, and a handful of spinsters in town would take tea with Aunt Charlotte, but for the most part, she spent her time in isolation, alone with her memories at Fairehold Cottage. Hopefully now that the children were at Penwythe, they might visit her.

He quickened his steps until he was at the cottage gate. Soft, feminine chatter and a child's laughter rose above the leaves' soft rustle.

He bypassed the front entrance and followed the brick path back to the garden, where he found his aunt and Mrs. Greythorne seated at a small table and Sophy lounging on the lawn.

"Uncle Jac!" Sophy jumped up and ran toward him, her dark

hair windblown and her cheeks flushed with the day's warmth. She bumped into him, grabbed his hand, and pulled him toward her. "Guess what? Aunt Charlotte has a cat, and he likes me. He likes to eat catnip; it makes him do the silliest things. Aunt says catnip is like magic and puts cats in a trance. Can you imagine?"

He smiled at the amazement in her face.

"The catnip makes a lovely tea, but Cyrus here likes to eat the leaves," Aunt Charlotte said. "I'm glad you could make it today. I was wondering where you were."

"I'm sorry I'm late." He kissed his aunt on the cheek and bowed toward Mrs. Greythorne. "What a pleasant surprise to find you here."

"Yes." Mrs. Greythorne turned her face toward him. "Mr. Andrews told me that your aunt is quite the artist. The girls had an art instructor at Easten Park, and I thought in light of the transition, Mrs. Angrove might be willing to share her knowledge with the girls."

"Excellent idea." He sat at the table and snuck another glance toward the governess. She was lovely in her gray gown and with her russet hair gathered at the nape of her neck.

He'd noticed the interest in Andrews's eyes when he'd watched the governess from the orchard a few evenings prior, and now to hear that he sought her out during the daytime hours was disconcerting. "So Andrews suggested that you come here?"

"Well, he didn't suggest it exactly; he merely told me of your aunt's talent. I do hope it was all right to bring Sophy here."

The conversation took its normal turn. His aunt was eager for news of the progress with the granite crusher, and he shared updates on the drainage ditches in the north orchard and the new pond. He told her of the new hedgerows that replaced the overgrown brambles and told Sophy of the family of rabbits that had made a home there.

Before long, an hour had passed, and the clock inside chimed the hour.

Mrs. Greythorne straightened. "Sophy and I had best be returning to the other girls. By now they should be done with their needlework, and Sophy still needs to see to her reading."

Behind him, Sophy groaned. "I don't want to leave."

"Then you must come and visit Cyrus and me tomorrow," Aunt Charlotte suggested. "We get very lonely out here, don't we, Cyrus? You will be just the remedy he needs."

Sophy smiled and jumped to her feet, swiping the grass and leaves from her black skirt. Then, with all the impulsiveness of youth, Sophy scurried to her great-aunt and planted a kiss on her cheek.

As Sophy turned to depart, Jac noticed leaves clutched in her hand. "What are those for?"

"It's catnip. For the cats in the kitchen. Do you think they'll like it?"

He laughed. The thought of Mrs. Bishop dealing with cats and catnip was amusing. "They'll adore it. I'll accompany you back, if you don't mind. It's getting late and I'm expecting a call from Colliver."

They said their good-byes, and as they exited the garden, Jac fell into step beside Mrs. Greythorne as Sophy ran ahead.

He was alone with her.

They'd spent the better part of an hour in each other's company, and during that time he'd thought of little else than the rumors regarding Mrs. Greythorne's husband. He needed to discuss them with her, for the sake of the children's security.

Though the words felt thick on his tongue, he managed to keep his tone light. "There is something I wanted to talk with you about. And it is of a rather personal nature, but I still feel it warrants discussion."

She glanced upward. "Of course."

"Apparently something is causing quite a commotion in town."

"Oh? And what's that?"

"Your name."

CHAPTER 18

Delia's heart raced within her chest. Suddenly the linen of her high-necked gray gown felt far too warm for such a spring day and her straw bonnet seemed too heavy.

My name.

His simple statement erased the calmness she'd enjoyed just moments before.

"My name?" She gave a little laugh, doing her best to hide the concern in her voice.

"Yes, your surname. Greythorne. It's brought to mind an event in the past."

She knew exactly to what he was referring—the raid near Bran Cove.

After her husband—and the others—died that night, the story spread far and wide throughout Cornwall, had meant, no doubt, to be a deterrent to any who would consider choosing the same path. She shouldn't be surprised that someone would recognize it.

She stole a sideways glance at him. He looked so calm. So collected. The topic did not have the same effect on him. Why would it? To him, it was just a story—a faraway tale of fateful events.

"Apparently several years ago a band of Greythornes was believed to be at the heart of a smuggling ring on the south coast. One or maybe more of them were killed in a specific raid, and this is what the villagers remember. Living so close to the sea, the locals here are very sensitive to the dangers of free traders. Our little town has been burned by the effects of it, and they are wary."

She held her breath, waiting for him to say something else, but he remained silent.

She wished it were easier to find fault with him, but he had been kind to her since their arrival, and he'd been attentive to the children. To her surprise, she cared what this man thought of her. She did not want to lie to him, nor did she wish to deceive him. But she was no fool. She was not about to place her trust in someone she had known for such a short time.

"I'm not suggesting you were in any way involved, but I wanted to make you aware of the rumor."

How surprised he'd be to know the extent to which she was acquainted with the events of that night. She had a choice in this moment. She could tell him the whole truth and be done with it, or she could allow this misperception to continue.

Delia managed to mutter, "Thank you for letting me know."

They continued down the path, their silence broken only by the seabirds that had found their way inland and Sophy's excited chatter over the flowers growing at the tree line. The secret Delia wanted to hide from could not be outrun. It kept cutting her off at every turn. The secret festered within her like a painful, raw wound that could not be healed.

Mr. Randall Twethewey may have overlooked her past to allow her to be governess to his children, but she was now living under Jac Twethewey's roof. Even though her compensation came from the trust, he had the power to oust her from her position—a position she dearly loved and desperately needed.

———•———

Hours later, night fell and her charges slumbered in their beds, giving Delia the privacy, at last, to read her letter from her sister.

She had pulled one of the more comfortable wingback chairs from the sitting room into her bedchamber and positioned it next to the hearth. After lighting two candles, she wrapped a warm woolen shawl around her shoulders, tucked her legs up to her chest, and leaned her head against the chair's back. Once settled, she slid her finger under the wax seal to pop it open, wishing she could talk to Elizabeth face-to-face instead of through letters.

Oh, how she missed her sister.

Not only that, how she missed the aspects of her life that had been closed off to her all these years since her departure from Greythorne House. Now simply being in Cornwall made her crave her childhood home even more.

She unfolded the letter and angled it toward the candlelight. The faint handwriting was much weaker than in her last letter, much shakier. Delia had pretended not to notice the decline in her sister's penmanship. Delia rarely received a letter from her brother, but even those had increased and he'd become more vocal about his concern for Elizabeth.

Delia pushed the thought away and squinted to see her sister's pale writing.

My dear Delia,

Words cannot describe my shock at hearing of Mr. Twethewey's death. What terrible news! It is nothing short of horrific to have a life taken from one so young. I have not been at ease ever since, for I keep thinking of those poor children and how devastated they must be.

Delia read on, reveling in the contents about her brother's children, her brother's most recent sermon, and a little about villagers whom Delia would remember from their childhood. The letters were much the same, but the constancy and familiarity of them made them comforting.

The time has come to end this letter, dear Sister, as I always do. If there is anything pleasant to come out of this horrible business of death, at least it has brought you back to Cornwall. I do hope you will visit. Everyone here would so like to see you, and I think you will be surprised at both how much has changed and how much has remained the same. I need not tell you how often I think of you. You are in my prayers, dearest Sister, today and every day. I hope you are finding your peace and your place.

At this, tears blurred her vision and Delia lowered the letter. If she could, she would take the burden of illness from her sister. Elizabeth had never been well, never known freedom of health and vitality of life. Even so, Delia refused to confront her sister's mortality. Her husband's and daughter's mortalities. Her own mortality and her role in the larger scheme of life.

Her sister was praying for her. She knew it. Elizabeth's faith had always been stronger than hers. Perhaps if Delia had leaned on her faith more, the realities of the past few years would have been different.

She angled her head so she could see out the window to the slice of night sky and white stars. A gentle gossamer cloud floated over the moon, the light of which limned the cloud in a silver glow.

Why she had not prayed more, she didn't know. Fear seemed to be the dictating force in her life, especially since the loss of her family. Perhaps that was why. Fear knew no bounds and came in so many forms: Fear of what the future held. Fear of more loss. Fear of opening her heart and finding pain. Fear that if she did pray, her words would not be heard.

Her heart nudged her to let a prayer pass her lips, and then she folded the letter, trying not to think about the delicacy of life and the fact that at any moment, life could change.

CHAPTER 19

"There it is!" Sophy squealed, nearly falling over Delia's lap as she lunged from the carriage seat toward the window. "Can you believe it? Julia, it's the sea!"

Delia pressed her back against the seat, allowing Hannah a better view out the window.

"Careful, Sophy." Delia laughed as the carriage wheel shifted in a rut on the sandy road. "You'll tear your gown again."

Delia should be more forceful and demand that the young lady behave demurely, but the child's joy was so refreshing. Even Julia, who'd been the most reluctant to embrace a new life at Penwythe, strained to see out the window, a smile tempting her lips.

Through the window Delia glimpsed a bright azure sea with gently rolling waves meeting the shore. The scent of salt air and the cry of seabirds beckoned them to abandon the carriage's confines and step into the serenity.

The carriage rolled to a stop, and within several moments the door flew open and Mr. Twethewey appeared in the space.

"We're here!" Sophy cried. Before he could say anything, she leapt toward him from the carriage step. He caught her, laughing, and set her down in the shifting seagrass.

"Well now." Mr. Twethewey knelt next to her, the wind catching his cravat and his dark hair. He pointed a finger out toward the water, taking several moments to give it a long look. "There it is. The sea. What do you think of it?"

Sophy flung her arms around him. "It's wonderful!"

Delia waited for Hannah, Julia, and Mrs. Angrove to exit before she put her own gloved hand on the door frame to help guide herself out. She'd expected that Mr. Twethewey would have gone on ahead with the children and his aunt, but he stood there waiting for her. A grin on his face, he extended his hand toward her. "Are you coming, Mrs. Greythorne?"

She looked to his bare hand and hesitated. It was strong. Steady. She doubted he felt fear. Not for anything. Mr. Twethewey knew very little about children and governesses—about the rules that governed their interactions. He was considerate, yes, but she was not his equal, and yet he had a tendency to treat her as if she were. Ever since their walk home from Fairehold Cottage, she'd been keenly aware of Mr. Twethewey—not only of his role as guardian of the children and, as such, her employer, but as a man.

Her guard was slipping, and he'd occupied many more of her thoughts than was wise.

She lifted her chin, smiled her gratitude, and placed her hand in his as she stepped down. At the touch, fire radiated. Once her feet were on the sandy ground, she dropped her hand quickly and looked out to the sea.

Yes, there were many things she feared, and rightfully so. But one thing she knew with absolute certainty—allowing Mr. Twethewey to affect her heart would be the most dangerous move yet.

Jac walked along the bluff's edge, where it dropped to the beach, and paused. Laughter rang out even louder than the crashing waves. The children—all five of them—were near the shore, playing with Cadwur.

A bit closer, Mrs. Greythorne and Aunt Charlotte sat on a blanket in the far bluff's shade, watching the children, and Mr. Simon sat on a nearby rock, a book held up to his face.

Jac huffed at the sight. The man irritated him. Simon did his best to avoid any sort of interaction, and on such a day, to ignore the children and even the beauty around them seemed a waste.

Jac made his way down the short, sandy cliff and inhaled the salt air. He discarded his coat on a nearby rock and propped his fists on his hips as he looked out to sea. The wind rushed in, billowing the linen sleeves of his shirt and fluttering his cravat.

It was good to be here. He could not recall the last time he was at the sea for the sake of enjoyment. Usually he only came down this way when something odd was reported or when a fishing ship lost its way.

The children were running barefoot on the beach, laughing. Liam splashed Hannah, and then Johnny chased after Julia. Sophy was collecting shells. Somehow, over the course of the last couple of weeks, these children were no longer strangers. Their thick-walled defenses were starting to fall. Even Julia's stern facade was crumbling, and the angry lines on Liam's face were softening.

Cadwur loped toward him, flinging up bits of sand and interrupting his thoughts. Sophy chased him, clutching her basket of shells in her hand. Cadwur stopped in front of Jac and nudged his hand. Sophy dropped to her knees next to Cadwur. Sand covered her forehead, her hair, and her black gown. Her bonnet had been discarded, and wisps of dark hair flew before her face.

"So, Princess Sophy." Jac dipped in a dramatic bow before he sat on a large stone and rested his elbows on his knees. "Now that you've had time to explore, what do you think of the sea?"

"It's big." She smiled, breathless, and stared out over the ocean. "Is it always so windy?"

"Always." He nodded.

She swiped the hair from her face. "Why?"

He chuckled at the question. He watched the waves roll up and crash on the shoreline, watched the clouds sail across the blue expanse of sky. "Because that is how God created it."

The answer seemed to satisfy her, and she tucked her hand in his, pulling him up to walk toward the surf. "Papa told us about how he found a turtle on the beach once."

Jac laughed at the memory. "I remember that turtle. See the rock over there, the one that juts out beyond that cliff? That is where we discovered it."

"Can we find one?" She hopped at his side.

Jac clicked his tongue and held out his hand to carry her basket for her. "Oh no. It doesn't work that way. You see, the turtles find you, not the other way around."

Her face fell. "Papa always said that one day he would bring us to the sea, but he was always too busy." Her words slowed. "And now he never will."

The melancholy in her voice reverberated more loudly than the waves crashing on the rocks. She looked down to her feet and picked up a shell. "He's dead, and my mother is dead too."

He felt as if he should say or do something to ease her sadness, but he had no idea what it was. Instead, he picked up another shell and added it to her basket.

"What if you die?" She turned to face him fully, her eyes wide with childlike honesty. "What will happen? Would we go to Aunt Charlotte's?"

He studied her amber eyes. The smattering of freckles on the bridge of her nose. She just wanted reassurance. It was what Mrs. Greythorne had said about Liam. Sophy wanted to feel safe too.

A protective feeling came over him, and he wanted to shield them from any more pain. "I'm not going to die, Sophy."

"But people don't know when they're going to die. So many people die. Mrs. Greythorne's husband is dead. And her baby."

He winced. "Her baby?"

"Yes. Maria was her name. Mrs. Greythorne wears her hair around her neck. Not every day, but sometimes." Sophy reached down for another shell and added it to her collection. Johnny called to her, and she grabbed the basket from Jac's hand and ran toward the surf.

Still stunned over the information he'd just learned, he looked back to the governess. She'd never said anything about having a child. It was none of his business, of course, and yet his heart ached at the sadness of it.

He studied her profile from his safe distance—the gentle slope of her nose, the delicate arch of her neck. She was the reason this transition had gone so smoothly. She was as helpful as Mr. Simon was frustrating. Instead of keeping the children hidden away on the second floor or in the garden, she'd made every effort to insert them into daily life at Penwythe. She found ways to make sure they interacted and encouraged Jac to spend time with them. Even this beach picnic had been her idea, and she'd not taken no for an answer.

As he approached her, she moved to stand, no doubt out of respect, but he motioned for her to stay where she was. He knelt to the blanket next to her. "The children seem to be enjoying themselves."

She nodded. "I am so happy to see them smiling."

"And what about you? Are you enjoying yourself?"

Her gaze did not shift its focus from the shore. "I'd almost forgotten how enchanting the sound of the sea on the beach is."

He lowered his gaze from her face to the black pendant around her neck. It had to be the necklace to which Sophy had referred. Maria. Her daughter.

He cleared his throat as if to dislodge the thought from his mind. "How does a young lady from Cornwall become a governess all the way in Yorkshire?"

"It is quite simple, really." She adjusted her position to face him. "After my husband died, I could not stay at his family's home. My own parents were dead, and my brother was already caring for my sister, who is ill, so I needed to find another situation. My aunt was at one time a housekeeper for Mrs. Twethewey, and it was on her recommendation that I was given the position. That was three years ago, and I have been there ever since."

He looked over to Mr. Simon, who dug in the basket and pulled out a piece of bread. "He doesn't seem to enjoy the beach."

She smirked. "Mr. Simon is more comfortable indoors."

"And what do you know of Mr. Simon?"

Mrs. Greythorne turned back to face him. "He's from Yorkshire. His father owns a mill in the north, but I believe his brother runs it now. Mr. Simon had wanted to become a physician, but his father fell ill and he was needed at home, so he never completed his formal education. But he's a brilliant man and has studied with some of the brightest minds in London. Your brother handpicked him."

"The brightest minds of London, eh?" Jac huffed, unimpressed. "No wonder he finds Cornwall so dull."

"Pay him no mind. He can be quite abrupt, I'll admit. But he is not at all like he seems." Her voice trembled. "He'll adjust."

Did she really believe the words to be true?

Above, seabirds swooped low, cawing to one another. She lifted her face to watch them, and for several moments silence hovered. Then she snapped her gaze to him.

He'd been caught staring.

"I wanted to thank you, Mr. Twethewey, for coming here with the children today. I know you're quite busy, but it means a great deal to them."

"They have been through quite an ordeal, haven't they?"

"My heart never broke so much for another until I saw their grief the day their mother died, and now, with their father gone . . ." Her voice trailed off. "Don't give up on them. They are loving children, but they are grieving. And they're lost. They need time, like anyone after such a loss." Mrs. Greythorne held his gaze for several moments.

The intensity and earnestness in her expression refused to allow him to look away. "I will not give up on them, Mrs. Greythorne. You have my word."

CHAPTER 20

"Tell me about your husband, Mrs. Greythorne." Mrs. Angrove shifted on the blanket to face Delia. "What sort of man was he? Tall? Short? Clever? Brave?"

Delia stiffened. The afternoon at the sea had been passing pleasantly, but Mrs. Angrove's question cast a long shadow over the day's festivities. For it was a difficult one to answer. Robert was not a simple man, but a man with many sides and moods.

When she did not respond promptly, Mrs. Angrove prodded further. "What was his profession? Perhaps we should start there."

Delia's tongue felt thick in her mouth. It had been years since she spoke of Robert in any depth, but she could not avoid answering this time. "His family owned an estate, as well as several small businesses. He was sort of a jack-of-all-trades, I suppose. Mostly he helped run the inn."

"Ah, an innkeeper."

Delia's stomach tightened. That wasn't the truth. Not really. He did none of an innkeeper's duties, but he did see that their smuggled hauls passed through the tunnels beneath the inn to the outlying sheds and barns, to be picked up by the next runner.

"And how did you meet your young man?"

This question was much easier to answer. "His hometown was a couple of miles away from mine. He came to buy a horse from the livery. A chance meeting in the courtyard and I was smitten." That part of their life together she could remember with a genuine smile.

Mrs. Angrove chuckled. "Ah, young love. Is there anything more splendid?"

Yes, it had been splendid, but Delia did not allow herself to savor the memory. It was dangerous—painful—to fall back into those thoughts . . . It would lead to questioning every decision and wondering how things could have been different. "It was a brief courtship. We were married shortly thereafter."

"How lovely. Your family must have supported the match."

She smiled to mask the feelings churning. At the time her father had only recently died, and it was her brother, Horace, who gave the union his blessing. In her heart, she could not help but blame him for allowing her to take such a problematic path. She had been blissfully unaware of the Greythornes' reputation. Why would a sheltered vicar's daughter know anything about smuggling and danger? But Horace had known, and yet he made no objection.

In truth, a warning might not have deterred her young, tender heart, but the fact that he withheld truths hurt her still, and over the years bitterness festered. Had he intervened, so much heartbreak and fear might have been avoided.

She glanced around. The peaceful day was closing in on her. The waves suddenly began to seem harsh, the sun glaring. Instead of playful chatter, the seabirds overhead cried ominous calls of warning. The memories, which she usually kept under tight rein, were opening the door to fear.

She forced her attention back to the shore where the children were playing, reminding herself that the fear, those years of uncertainty, were done now. They had left a crippling blight on her heart, but her reality was different; she had to recognize that.

There was one aspect of her union with Robert, however, that had been beautiful. She lifted her hand to the pendant around her neck.

Maria.

Delia did not speak of her often, but there was a gentleness to Mrs. Angrove, something about her that made her seem like a safe place. The words were out of her mouth before she fully checked them against propriety. "We had a daughter."

"Oh?" Mrs. Angrove whirled around, the wind blowing her silver hair about her narrow face. "A daughter?"

"Yes. Maria was her name, named for my mother." Delia removed her pendant and extended it toward Mrs. Angrove. "She died of a fever, but how I loved her. Love her still."

"Oh, my dear. I am sorry to hear it." Her faded brows drew together, and she placed her wrinkled hand over Delia's.

Delia did not want pity, but it felt good, at least for a moment, to verbalize the pain that accompanied her through each day. She looked to Sophy running along the beach with Cadwur. "If Maria had lived, she would have been Sophy's age." Delia's throat tightened. Was that what her blonde-haired daughter would have looked like running happily along the sandy shore, carefree and spirited?

The squeeze of Mrs. Angrove's hand brought her back to the conversation. "I always regretted not having children of my own. Of course, Randall and Jac were my joy from the moment they arrived at Penwythe, but such a situation is different. And you're young. You've a full life ahead of you. You'll marry again, I've no doubt, and more children will come."

The words were meant to be an encouragement, she knew. But Delia shook her head. She'd been wounded, deeply so, and even though the scars had healed and her skin had grown tougher, the part of her heart that could trust was forever broken. "One never knows the future, I suppose, but I've no intention of marrying again. For now, my life is these children."

Mrs. Angrove followed her gaze to the shore. "Children do not stay children forever. Surely you must think about what comes after."

At this thought she formed a genuine smile. "I have hopes, one day, of opening a school for young ladies."

"Oh!" Mrs. Angrove exclaimed. "A school?"

"Yes, I'll never be idle, far too stubborn for that, and I feel quite fulfilled in educating others."

"That is all very noble, but do you not wish for peace and rest?"

Delia almost could have laughed. With the memories that churned daily in her mind and the fear she still harbored of her in-laws, she doubted peace or rest would ever be fully hers. No, it was best to keep her mind active, lest it roam free and get lost in the fear.

———◆———

Several days after the picnic, Jac sat at his desk in his cluttered study. Night had fallen. Candles winked in the crowded space, casting long shadows over the newspapers, inkwells, and quills scattered atop the inlay surface. He'd been away from this room for days, and in his absence letters and bills had piled up. He sighed and picked up a letter, absently tapping it against the desk's edge.

Since his day at the beach, the cider press had been delivered ahead of schedule. He'd spent every free hour working out at the cider barn, overseeing the men as the press was installed and the barrel racks were hung. Even as he sat here, completely still, skittish energy raced through him.

Success was near. He sensed it as surely as he could sense a storm rolling in from the sea. Hunger for it had pushed him to dedicate every waking hour to his cause. Even the new irrigation trenches and pond seemed to be improving the saturation issue in the north orchard. The ground was dry to the touch, and the apples were growing, and before long it would be time to thin the fruit.

With the apple crusher and large press installed, they were close to being a fully operational orchard and cider barn, and yet so many things could hamper their progress. Yes, the apple trees and blossoms had survived the late-spring frosts, which had been one of his biggest concerns, but now a new lot of threats loomed. A weather disaster. Insects. Disease. He shoved his fingers through his hair and expelled his breath. He'd go mad if he considered all the ways his plan could fail, so he needed to focus on what he could control.

It was the flaw his uncle always warned him about—the need for control.

He recalled one summer when a drought nearly destroyed the primrose garden. He'd helped his uncle and the staff transport water from other parts of the estate and water each plant. *"You can't control nature, boy,"* Uncle William had said. *"Try as you might, it can't be done. The same God who makes the waves crash on the shore with such vengeance is the one who lets rain fall on these delicate roses, so gentle as not to hurt a single petal. Magnificent, isn't it? And humbling. I love these flowers, but there isn't a thing I can do to make them grow. God does it. I just take care of them."*

At the time Jac had dismissed his uncle's comments as nothing more than sentiment. But now as he found himself grappling with the nature his uncle had spoken of, the truth in the words hit hard, and he'd give anything for one more conversation with the man.

With renewed focus, Jac returned his attention to the letters piled before him. He reached for the next one and was about to pop the wax seal when movement at the door caught his eye.

Whispers echoed and feet shuffled, and he looked up to see his three nieces, all in a row, filling the door frame. They were dressed in nightclothes, each with a wrap around her shoulders. Cadwur stood from his spot on the rug beneath the window and nudged Julia's hand with his nose, his tail thumping. Julia's dark hair fell over her shoulder as she bent to pat his head.

"Good evening, ladies." Jac lowered the letter. "To what do I owe this pleasure?"

The sisters exchanged glances, and then Sophy nudged Hannah closer. Hannah stumbled in.

He laughed at their uncharacteristic sheepishness. After leaning back in his chair, he folded his arms across his chest. "What's this about? Does Mrs. Greythorne know you're here?"

They stared at each other in silence for several seconds, and then Hannah lowered her hands from behind her back. Clutched in her tiny fingers was a haphazard display of cut rhododendrons and camellias. She stepped forward and extended it to him, and the earthy scent of wood and petals circled the space.

"Are those for me?" He straightened, surprised at the sudden offering.

Hannah rounded the desk and placed them in front of him on the desk. "Mrs. Greythorne said I shouldn't pick them because they would die, but I wanted you to see them. I—we—didn't want you to miss them."

Jac wasn't sure he'd ever received flowers from anyone, and yet the simple gesture warmed him. He stood from the desk, crossed the room to the side table, and retrieved an empty decanter. "Well, they're very beautiful. Let's put them in here."

Sophy and Julia stepped in farther, and Hannah leaned on his desk with her elbow and watched as he placed the flowers in the glass. "Thank you for taking us to the sea."

"You're most welcome." He moved the makeshift vase to his desk and placed it on the corner. "There, now I shall see them whenever I am working."

Hannah smiled and stepped back to her sisters. "My papa liked flowers too. I made him bouquets whenever he was home. If there were flowers blooming, anyway."

He looked to the child, realizing how little he knew of them—of their life before they came to Penwythe. A pang of guilt stabbed. He should have known more about his brother's life.

"You must miss your father very much." The words slipped out before he had a chance to really check them.

Sophy nodded. "Do you miss him too?"

The innocent question struck him. Yes, he missed his brother. He missed the relationship they could have had. If only they hadn't been so stubborn.

The children's presence had revived the happy memories of Randall, before arguments of rights and money and inheritance came into play. They'd been friends, and they'd been close. How many times since the children's arrival had he replayed the arguments in his head? He tried to pinpoint the exact moment their relationship snapped but couldn't. And what pained him more was the regret of not making things right with him before he died. "I do miss him."

Vigor renewed, Sophy climbed onto one of the chairs opposite the desk. "Can I come to the Frost Ball?"

He gave a little laugh at the child's uncanny way of saying exactly what was on her mind. "The Frost Ball is for adults and will be after your bedtime."

"But one of the maids said that everyone can come. I'm part of everyone."

It was impossible to argue with her logic. He threw his hands up in the air playfully, as a man who had just been defeated. "It's fine with me, but you should ask Mrs. Greythorne."

"But you're our guardian," Hannah reasoned. "That's kind of like being our papa. You get to decide."

"It's nothing like being our papa," Julia shot back, her expression darkening, her sharp words popping the congenial bubble encasing the conversation.

Jac stiffened. "No, no. Not like your father. I would never take your father's place. I think being a guardian means that I take care of you."

"Oh." Sophy seemed satisfied, and she moved to the floor where she petted Cadwur.

Mrs. Greythorne appeared in the doorway, exasperation flushing her cheeks and widening her eyes. "Girls, what are you doing here? I left the room for but a few minutes and you disappeared!"

"We forgot to give Uncle the flowers we picked for him." Julia gestured to the vase.

Mrs. Greythorne bustled into the space, placed her hand on Hannah's shoulder, and took Sophy's hand. "I am sure he likes them very much, but he's working. We don't want to disturb him."

"They're fine, Mrs. Greythorne." Jac chuckled, leaning against the corner of his desk. "I'd take a visit from them over correspondence and ledgers any day."

Sophy beamed at the words and turned her face toward Mrs. Greythorne. "Uncle Jac said we could go to the Frost Ball."

Mrs. Greythorne bent down to Sophy's level. "Well then, I am sure the Frost Ball will be lovely, but right now, you all need to prepare for bed." She turned to him. "Good night, Mr. Twethewey. Will we see you at breakfast?"

He didn't understand the effect this woman had on him. His words felt jumbled. His mind, scattered. "Y-yes."

Mrs. Greythorne nodded with a curtsy, then nudged the girls to do the same, and as quickly as the crew had appeared, they disappeared in the corridor.

Mrs. Greythorne.

A rather unexpected dilemma flickered within him, and he needed to squelch it before it fanned into flame. He was thinking of Mrs. Greythorne far too frequently as of late. True, he found her steadiness and calmness comforting, but it was more than that. It was the pert slope of her nose, the quickness in her eyes, the entrancing curve of her mouth.

He needed to distance himself from her, and that would be difficult given their arrangement.

Andrews's reference to the rumor raced through his mind. She had an entire life beyond what he knew. A child. A husband. And not just any husband, but a man rumored to have been involved in free trading. And yet whenever he thought of Mrs. Greythorne, he wanted to protect her. There was no answer to his growing predicament, but he had to be careful. Too much was at stake, and he could not risk an error.

CHAPTER 21

While everyone else seemed to anticipate the Frost Ball, Delia had been dreading it.

Mr. Twethewey had been forthright with her regarding the rumors, and in the days since, she'd heard whispers and noticed stares cast in her direction. Now hundreds of people were gathered on Penwythe's grounds—hundreds of people who no doubt thought they knew all about her husband and what he'd done.

Despite Mr. Andrews's offer to dance, she'd made up her mind not to venture from her chamber for the duration of the night. In all likelihood, no one would say anything to her directly, but it was the stares she dreaded and the ensuing discomfort she feared.

When the night of the event arrived, Delia sat in her small chamber in the west wing, a single lantern burning on top of her writing table. The clock on the mantel struck the midnight hour. On the floor below dancers and guests celebrated.

Through her open window, strains of happy music and chatter danced on the breeze. Voices from the lawn and primrose garden wafted on the air, and she abandoned the letter she had been writing and moved to the window to look to the darkened grounds below. The rain had stopped, and the guests had spilled out onto the shadowed grounds. Torches had been placed around the lawn, making it seem more like a fairy land.

In spite of her reservations, the sights and sounds sparked

memories of happier times when she and her brother would attend balls, and then when she would attend them with Robert. How she'd loved dancing.

A knock on her sitting room door sounded. Delia froze.

Almost immediately the door opened and Mrs. Angrove appeared, clad in a gown of violet satin with a black-lace overlay. It was not unusual for the older woman to be elegantly dressed, but the lace and piping trimming the gown and the pearls adorning her slender neck elevated her appearance.

"Mrs. Angrove! Why, you look lovely!"

"Well, it is the Frost Ball, after all." Without waiting for an invitation, Mrs. Angrove stepped into the chamber. The scent of lily of the valley flooded the narrow room upon her arrival, and the rustle of her skirt echoed from the low ceiling. She stepped to the window and looked down to the torchlit grounds. "I'd forgotten what a splendid view there is from this wing."

When Mrs. Angrove turned back around, her eyes twinkled and a playful smile quirked the corners of her lips. "You should be downstairs."

Delia returned her quill to the table. "Someone must sit with the children. Their father never wanted them to be left alone, especially if visitors were in the house."

Mrs. Angrove lifted her chin but did not respond. She approached the desk, lifted a vase of flowers, inhaled the scent, and then lowered it. "I've been thinking of what you said when we were at the shore the other day, and I've decided that I simply don't agree with you."

Delia gave a little laugh at the odd statement. "Oh really?"

"Indeed. You said that you didn't intend to marry ever again. I believe that would be a mistake."

Delia sobered at the personal comment.

Mrs. Angrove lifted her chin. "Perhaps you think it none of my business, but I've lived a long time, and I've seen more than most. Closing your heart off to love—in whatever form—is never a good idea."

"I appreciate your concern, but I—"

"There is life to live, Mrs. Greythorne. Vibrant, beautiful life. I'm so grateful you are dedicated to the children, but tonight a ball is taking place at this very home, and I think it's imperative for you to attend." Without asking permission Mrs. Angrove stepped to Delia's wardrobe and opened it. "Why, look at all of these gowns! Half of them I've never seen you in."

Delia approached the wardrobe. She was not used to others touching her things, let alone rummaging through her personal items. "I—uh—"

Mrs. Angrove pulled down a pale-lilac gown and shook it out.

Delia's breath caught in her throat. She'd not worn that particular gown in years, not since a dinner at Greythorne Hall a month before Robert died.

"Why, this is lovely! A bit outdated, I fear, but still it is far and away beyond what most of the townswomen are wearing. Why, you would be the belle of the ball in this."

Delia nerves twisted as Mrs. Angrove pulled two more gowns from the wardrobe and splayed them across the bed. "Now, there's no time to waste. If you will give no thought to your future happiness, then I must. Think of it. Every man for miles is in attendance tonight. *For miles*, my dear. If you've truly hope of capturing a man's attention, you need to shed that dark garb you've been wearing. Trust me, no one else is wearing black downstairs. This is a celebration. If for nothing else, amuse me."

Delia stared at the gowns. How could she make Mrs. Angrove understand? If word of her presence here were to get back to her in-laws, it could be disastrous.

"Don't worry about the children. Alis has come with me, and she is in the parlor down the corridor awaiting my instruction." With a decisive nod Mrs. Angrove selected the lilac gown and returned the others to the wardrobe. "Now, turn."

Delia opened her mouth to protest, but her objection went unnoticed. Mrs. Angrove might be overstepping her boundaries, but she was still the children's aunt, and while not her employer, she was a person of great import.

Before long, Mrs. Angrove's maid had been summoned and helped Delia from her black gown. The new gown slipped over her stays and petticoat, and Alis fastened the row of tiny buttons down her back.

Delia turned to the small looking glass hanging on the wall. Gone was the confident governess. A ghost of her former self stared back at her—the timid, complacent wife and brokenhearted mother. She wanted to rip the dress from her body, discarding with it the accompanying memories.

But Mrs. Angrove's eyes were fixed on her, oblivious to the emotion stirred within Delia. "You are a beauty, Mrs. Greythorne. That color does wonders for your complexion."

Without invitation Alis tugged at the comb in Delia's hair, releasing her locks over her shoulder, and then twisted it back up atop her head and pulled a few wisps down around her cheeks. "If we had more time we would do something more elegant, but this will do."

Delia tore her gaze from the mirror and accepted the fan that Mrs. Angrove extended in her direction. Stunned, Delia smoothed a trembling hand over her hair. In a matter of minutes she'd gone from determined to sit the night out in her chamber to being dressed for a ball, and she was not comfortable with it in the least.

She consoled herself with the notion that she need only make an appearance to satisfy Mrs. Angrove, then return to her chamber at the first opportunity.

The dark coolness of the west wing's second floor did little to calm her heated nerves as Delia made her way down the main staircase.

She never would have guessed that so many people could fit into the great hall and entrance hall, and yet a sea of people swarmed at the foot of the staircase. She lifted her gaze to see even more guests lining the open balconies to the long gallery and minstrels' gallery on the floor above. Through the threshold to the great hall she spied couples dancing to the jaunty strains floating on the air.

As her foot tapped the flagstones of the main floor, she could feel sets of eyes burning holes in her.

Panic twisted within her.

Surely they all knew who she was—who her husband had been.

She bit her lip and lifted to the tips of her toes to see above the shifting crowd. She was pretty certain Mr. Simon was down here, and at the moment she needed a familiar face.

Lively music wafted down from the minstrels' gallery, showering its spirited energy onto the guests below. Candlelight from sconces and candelabras flickered, painting the room in a cheery, happy glow. She scanned the room. Mr. Simon was not difficult to spot. He stood nearly a head taller than the others in attendance, and he was against the wall.

She skirted her way along the great hall's plaster wall, weaving in and out of the chairs. He noticed her coming, and he lifted his nearly empty glass in greeting. "So you did decide to come down after all," he said as she drew near.

"Alis is with the children. Mrs. Angrove all but insisted I come down."

"And glad I am that she did." He folded his arms across his chest as she stepped next to him.

She arched her neck to the side, following his gaze to the throng of people in attendance. "See, Mr. Simon, you judge the country too harshly. You think it void of society and activity. Yes, it is different from London, but it has its charms."

"Charms?" He huffed. "Call it what you will, Mrs. Greythorne."

He laughed in spite of himself, and it was a pleasant sound. Perhaps he felt more comfortable in such a social situation. Or perhaps it was the glass of spirits in his hand. But did it even matter? She was glimpsing her old friend, and maybe this was a turning point where he would shed his gloomy disposition and exchange it for the one more in line with the Mr. Simon she knew and liked.

He leaned close to be heard over the music. "I beg your forgiveness, because I'm about to take the liberty to tell you how lovely you look tonight."

It was a girlish response, a foolish one, but a flush crept up her face. She waved him off. "Mr. Simon. Really."

"What? You think I can't notice such a thing? The one person I see daily, who has been clad in mourning garb for every day that I can recall, steps out in something different? Well, it would be shameful for me not to notice. I do hope you will continue this trend, Mrs. Greythorne. It doesn't do for such a young woman to be draped in black. What exactly is that color?"

She flushed again. It was ridiculous—Mr. Simon speaking of colors and gowns. Yet it brought a smile to her lips. "I believe the color is called lilac."

"Ah, like the flower." He set his now-empty glass on the table against the wall and extended his arm. "Will you dance, Mrs. Greythorne?"

She laughed and turned to survey the couples gathering. "With you? You never dance."

"Well, you've never seen me dance, but that does not mean I don't know how. Tonight I may make an exception. Besides, who else will dance with me? I know no one, and everyone here looks at me as if I were a monster or had two heads."

"Perhaps it is because of the sour expression you've been wearing as of late. I rather prefer this version of you."

The caller summoned the dancers, and a smile quirked at the corner of his mouth. She looked around at the guests again. No one stared at her, and the tension in her back eased at the realization. Maybe she had overreacted, letting her fears get the better of her. She might be wise to consider the truth in Mrs. Angrove's statements.

She forced her breathing to slow. A dance—a moment to slip back in time to a different place—could not be harmful. Could it?

She placed her gloved hand in his and allowed him to lead her to the crowded dance floor. With each step, with each turn and curtsy, with each clap and smile, her fear subsided. The dance lasted nearly half an hour, and by the end she was hot. Breathless. While Mr. Simon left her to find beverages, she stood with her shoulder against the wall, facing the new set of dancers lining up.

A throat cleared behind her, and then a finger tapped her shoulder. She felt a tug on her arm.

Peaceful and flushed, she whirled around expecting Mr. Simon.

But at the sight that met her, her blood slowed in her veins. Breath fled her lungs. She could not move.

Thomas Greythorne, Robert's older brother, stood before her plain as day, with hair so blond it appeared almost white in the candlelight. Eyes so black they appeared evil, frightening. It was like looking at a ghost, a harsher, darker version than the original.

Thomas smiled, flashing his white teeth against tanned skin.

The room swirled, the thick air pressing in on her. The music's incessant beat drummed in her brain. Fearing she might faint, Delia regained composure by sheer strength of determination and lifted her chin.

"Thomas." His name tasted sour on her tongue. "What are you doing here?"

"Is that any way to greet your brother?" The words slid from his lips as unaffected as if they had just spoken the previous day instead of three years ago.

Her stomach turned. This monster was not her brother. No brother would treat a sister the way she had been treated.

She glanced around to see if anyone had taken notice of the newcomer, but the festivities continued, heedless of the horror that had just entered.

She swallowed. Hard. Anger was trickling in, pushing out the fear that had gathered.

There was no need for pretense—to pretend that her association with the family had not ended abruptly. "How did you know I was here?"

"Word travels, Sister." The appellation dripped from his lips, rich with cynicism and odd amusement. "You didn't think we could forget you, did you? You are, after all, family. Why, you didn't even say good-bye before you left."

She forced herself to meet his gaze confidently and fully—the only way to address a Greythorne. "Your mother requested I leave quietly. And so I did."

"But now you're back, and so close to Greythorne House."

She drew a deep breath, hoping it would steady her nerves. It did not. "I'm here for my charges. Nothing more."

"So you've no intention to visit your family?" He inched closer, the scent of brandy overbearing. "To visit us?"

She pressed her lips together and looked out as the music resumed and the dancers started to move in their sets. "Your mother made it very clear I was no longer welcome."

He chuckled calmly, as if the conversation were the most casual in the world. "Can you blame her? You betrayed us."

"I did no such thing."

He looked around. "So this is where you find yourself. Taking care of someone else's children in someone else's home."

She faced him. "Surely there is a reason for your visit, Thomas."

He shrugged. "You always were a perceptive thing, weren't you? A bit too observant and eager for your own good."

The words evoked memories, bright and flashing, from the recesses of her mind.

He leaned closer. His whisper was close enough to brush the wisps about her face. "You know why I'm here."

She did know. Yet she refused to step backward. "I don't know what you are talking about."

He laughed, louder this time, as if she'd just said something charming, and then fixed his devilishly dark eyes on her. He leaned close again. "Oh, you have always been good at your lies, with those wide eyes and innocent expressions. No wonder my brother fell so quickly for your charms. But the rest of the family isn't so easily swayed."

Her breath grew jagged. The word *family* coming from him was a word to be despised—so dark and ugly it could only be spoken in a whisper.

She flinched.

"Come now, you look like you are almost frightened."

She straightened her shoulders and lifted her chin. "Of course I'm not frightened."

He glared down at her, his amusement gone. "Perhaps you should be."

CHAPTER 22

"At least Randall had the good sense to retain a pretty governess." Jac jerked his head to the approaching voice that rose above the music and dancers' clapping. Jacob Colliver was now at his elbow, beverage in hand, round face flushed from the heat generated from the energetic, crowded room.

Jac turned toward him. "At least Randall had the good sense to retain a governess at all, for we all know I'd have had no idea how to handle five children."

Colliver nodded to the east wall, and then Jac saw her—Mrs. Greythorne. She had said she did not plan to attend the Frost Ball, and yet here she was dressed in a gown of pale purple, speaking—nay, laughing—with Mr. Simon.

Jac never thought he would feel jealous of the dour Mr. Simon, but as he watched Mrs. Greythorne smile up at him, comfortable and relaxed, a string of envy pulled within him.

"Pretty, yes." Colliver took a full glass from a passing servant before returning his attention to Jac. "But is she really the sort of influence you want on young people who bear the Twethewey name?"

Jac stiffened. There was no use pretending he'd not heard the rumor. It was running rampant now. He'd overheard two men speaking of it when he went to meet a tenant at the public house, and already this evening he'd been asked about her twice. "I assume you're referring to her late husband."

"What else?"

Jac looked directly at Mrs. Greythorne. Her dark hair fell in soft wisps about her face, and deep dimples graced her cheek when she smiled.

"A smuggler's bride, Twethewey," Colliver blurted unceremoniously. "Under Penwythe Hall's roof. Your uncle would be horrified."

Heat pricked up Jac's neck at the judgment, and perspiration gathered at his temples as he turned back to Colliver. "Oh, I'm not so sure." He was not so willing to buy into the rumor. Not quite yet.

Colliver scoffed, leaning heavily on his walking stick. "I must say I'm surprised. You're being very nonchalant about what goes on within these walls, especially when you're on the cusp of such vital changes. Impulsive. Like I've told you before, Twethewey, you act quickly. Make decisions rashly. It makes people nervous." He pinned Jac with his rheumy stare, then tapped the side of his nose and continued on his way to the billiards room.

The dance ended, and the next set of dancers was lining up along the wall in preparation to step into position. He'd lost sight of Mrs. Greythorne and searched for the flash of lavender but did not see it. Frowning, he scanned the room for Simon and, due to his height, found him quickly. But Mrs. Greythorne was not at his side.

Curious, Jac put down his glass and made his way across the great hall, and finally he spied a gown of lavender against the wall. Her back was to him, and she was speaking with a man.

The couple shifted, and he glimpsed Mrs. Greythorne's face. Worry creased her smooth brow and flattened her lips. The customary flush on her cheeks was absent, and she wrung her hands before her. The stranger now faced him. He was a large, tanned man with thick white-blond hair. He stood nearly a foot over her petite form and was speaking to her closely, as if well acquainted. She was new to the country—no man should be speaking to her so intimately.

After pausing to allow groups of people to pass this way and that, Jac approached them. Not once did Mrs. Greythorne nor the large man speaking with her look in his direction. They were locked in some sort of conversation where the rest of the world did not seem to matter.

This was not the conversation of strangers encountering each other for the first time at a country ball. Whatever this was, Jac was not comfortable with it.

He drew quite near, and the man turned first—a tall man, nearly Jac's own height. Mrs. Greythorne immediately followed suit, lifting her pointed chin toward him, her gray eyes wide. "Mr. Twethewey." A slight tremor shook her voice. She stepped back and dropped her hands, which had been clenched before her.

Jac returned his focus to the man. "I don't believe we have had the pleasure."

"Name's Thomas Greythorne."

Jac lifted his brow. "Greythorne?"

Mrs. Greythorne stepped forward, her expression odd. "This is my brother-in-law, my late husband's brother."

Andrews's and Colliver's words of warning rushed him. When he'd spoken to Mrs. Greythorne about the rumor, she neither confirmed nor denied the accusation. He hadn't really noticed at the time, but now that he thought back to their conversation when they were walking home from Fairehold Cottage, he realized her comments had been limited. How could he not have noticed?

The expression on the man's face eased. "Penwythe Hall is an impressive place, Mr. Twethewey. You are to be congratulated on its appearance. I've heard of its gardens, even as far away as Morrisea. It does live up to its reputation."

The false flattery annoyed Jac. "Mrs. Greythorne failed to mention you'd be attending the Frost Ball."

His light eyebrows rose. "I was under the impression that it was open to all. My apologies if I've come uninvited."

Jac's jaw twitched. It was not his place to intervene in her family matters, and yet her tightened expression and the pallor of her cheeks awoke something protective in him. He said the first thing that came to mind. "Mrs. Greythorne, I believe Sophy was looking for you. Would you check on her, please?"

Wide-eyed, Mrs. Greythorne responded quickly. "Of course."

"Will you be back down, Sister?" Greythorne called as she brushed past him. "I'll be leaving town early tomorrow. I'd like to see you again before I depart."

"I'll be back shortly." She bobbed a quick curtsy before threading back through the crowd until she disappeared through the drawing room.

Jac was not convinced. He'd never seen her quite so rattled. "Mrs. Greythorne seems quite out of sorts."

"Delia?" Greythorne asked, the use of her Christian name undoubtedly intended to reinforce the intimacy between them. "She was stunned to see me, 'tis all. I look a great deal like my late brother, her husband, you see. I think it was a bit of a shock to her. You know how women are."

Jac eyed the man. To be true, no, he did not know how women were. He could barely understand them on the best of days. But still, Jac disliked the overconfidence in his voice.

Greythorne continued. "It has been quite a while since I saw her last. I thought I'd surprise her. Perhaps I should have sent word of my coming. You see, we've not seen or heard from her since she left our home after my brother's death. We—my mother and wife—were so happy to hear she was back in Cornwall. Family is always family, after all. Perhaps now we shall see more of her. I feel responsible for her, you know. Even though my brother is dead, she is still my sister by law and by the church. But she is a stubborn one."

He spoke of her as if he knew her well. In all actuality he probably did. Jac sniffed. "Do you come this far north often?"

Greythorne nodded. "Business from time to time brings me here."

Jac tilted his head to the side and arched a brow. "And what business is that?"

"I make my living by the sea. I own several cargo ships that sail from Plymouth."

Jac listened to him speak of cargo and ships, of travels and sailors. No wonder rumors of smuggling abounded. He supposed any man who made his livelihood by the sea would be under constant suspicion of it. After nearly fifteen minutes of chatter, Greythorne popped his pocket watch and checked the hour. "It seems my sister will not be returning. What a pity."

Jac widened his stance. "I can send up one of the servants for her."

"I hate to interrupt Delia. Best leave her be. But now that she is here in Cornwall, perhaps our visits can be more frequent."

Greythorne bid Jac farewell, and his exit was as stealthy as his demeanor. Jac watched the man until he vanished through the crowd. Several moments ticked by before he was able to unclench his jaw. He slid his finger between his neck and cravat and pulled. It was too tight. Too binding.

No, Mrs. Greythorne had neither confirmed nor denied anything on that walk home from Fairehold Cottage, but it no longer mattered. He had seen the fear in her eyes. Heard the tremor in her voice. Involved or not, that man was trouble, and Jac would not allow it.

CHAPTER 23

Delia gasped for air as she rounded the corner. The interaction with Thomas had stolen her breath, and now her chest burned with shock. Once she was in the corridor's dark coolness, she pressed herself against the wall, gasping and sputtering as if she had just run a race.

She'd been a fool. She should have known better. Of course the Greythornes would find her if she came back to Cornwall. They had informants in every town and village from here to Devon.

And it was all because of what she knew about their secrets.

She gathered her courage and peeked back around the corner in the direction from which she had just come. She spied the men talking—Mr. Twethewey and Thomas.

Thomas looked so much like Robert, and that had jarred her nearly as much as his presence. But what had even greater impact was that his white-blond hair reminded her of Maria's curls. The memories cut like little knives, stabbing at her tender heart.

The men shifted, and she could no longer see Thomas's face.

Oh, how the man could spin tales and exude charm. No doubt he was working his magic on Mr. Twethewey now.

If he knew what Thomas was capable of, Mr. Twethewey would rue the day he ever allowed a Greythorne—any Greythorne—into his house.

She hurried back down the hall, her footsteps falling faster and faster until she was running. Darkness surrounded her in the west wing. She should have thought to bring a candle, but in her haste she hadn't. Perspiration dampened her skin, and her gown clung uncomfortably to her back and shoulders.

She bumped against the walls as she climbed the curved staircase. Once at the landing, Delia wiped the salty tears from her hot face and opened the door to peer in at the children, only to find Sophy asleep in her bed and Alis slumbering in the chair next to the fireplace.

She blinked. Sophy had not needed her. For whatever reason, Mr. Twethewey had lied to her about the child. Perhaps he'd seen the discomfort on her face. Or perhaps he believed the rumors, knew who Thomas was, and wanted to send him away.

She eased the door closed again and turned the latch. Music and laughter echoed from the gathering floors below. She needed to return to the ball, whether she wanted to or not. She'd not allow Thomas the smug satisfaction of believing he'd sent her running off in fear. But first she needed to compose herself, so she slipped into her own chamber.

It was mostly dark, and she preferred it that way. A faint wash of moonlight filtered through the window, and she glanced around the tiny, simple chamber that was now home. She pushed open her window, allowing the cool breeze to curl in. She gulped several breaths of fresh air. Her heartbeat began to slow. She should tell Thomas what she knew and be done with it. If she did, maybe he would leave her alone.

Even if she would not be free.

No. Then she would be an accomplice to their wrongdoing, and she would become one of them—an outlaw. And the price for that would be steep—just as steep as resisting them.

Her other option was to go to the authorities, but the Greythornes were too powerful. The magistrate of the area was their cousin, and he turned a blind eye for a cut of the profits.

She shivered as the memories cast their ghostly glow on her present. How foolish to think she would be safe in this little Penwythe refuge, with its idyllic seashores, rolling orchards, and ancient gardens. She'd lost sight of how the Greythornes would stop at nothing to get their way. She'd broken their agreement, and they'd found her. Her safety was in jeopardy. What was worse, she might be putting in danger those she held dear just by being here.

With the moonlight as her guide, she unlocked her trunk and dug through the contents, her motions frantic. She longed for comfort, for some sense that she had not always been alone. After pushing aside the letters from her sister, Delia dug to the bottom and retrieved a different stack of letters. Robert's letters of love, his declarations of adoration, felt rough and cool beneath her fingertips. The missives were from the time before Maria's death—before his life took a dark turn.

How he'd adored Maria. As their world crashed in around them, she had been the one thing to bring a smile to his face. As the situations surrounding them grew more dire, Delia had pleaded with him to relocate their small family to Scotland, to be free of his family for Maria's sake, but try as she might, Delia could not free him from the Greythornes' iron grip. Their approval meant everything to him. He needed it, craved it. In the end, Robert had believed Maria's death to be punishment for his dishonesty, and Delia could not persuade him otherwise. The spiral into recklessness and self-destruction started that horrific day and did not end until his death.

She looked back into the trunk. Just beneath the spot where his letters had been stored was Robert's linen shirt. She lifted the smooth, ivory fabric to her nose. It no longer held his scent. After he died, she'd clung to this shirt as if her own life depended on it. She'd worn it while sleeping and covered herself with it during the long afternoons.

Delia hugged it to her chest. He'd not always been harsh and wild. In fact, it was his sensitivity and carefree nature that drew her to him early in their courtship. Over the years his family's demands crushed that part of him, destroying the tenderness that had been so integral to him.

She returned the shirt to the trunk, nestling it against Maria's christening gown, and leaned back. The Greythornes had destroyed her family, but they would not destroy her.

Mr. Twethewey had given her a brief escape in that moment with his lie about Sophy, but she could not avoid Thomas. Once he sensed fear or avoidance, he would exploit it.

She stood, brushed her lilac skirt, and pinched her cheeks for color. She drew a slow breath to calm her nerves before she returned to the ball. Yes, she was scared. Terrified. And once she faced Thomas again, there would be no turning back.

———◆———

From the great hall music pounded. Shouts and laughter echoed. The night was growing late, and the guests were growing rowdy. Jac should be in the great hall or billiards room entertaining his guests. But he stood alone in the darkened drawing room, attempting to make sense of what he had just witnessed.

Mrs. Greythorne said she'd return to the ball after checking on Sophy. Surely by now she'd figured out that Sophy didn't need her. And yet minutes had stretched to nearly half an hour. Jac paced the room, pausing periodically to glance out the north door so he could see the staircase coming from the west wing.

The rumors swirling about her sickened him. Just hearing her name on Colliver's lips incited the urge to punch him.

Jac didn't believe the stories.

Perhaps because he didn't want to believe them.

But Colliver was right about one thing—the villagers were talking.

He'd seen how they cast sideways glances at her. They saw her as a threat.

When he looked at Mrs. Greythorne, he no longer saw just the governess tasked with caring for the children. He saw a lovely woman with depth and vitality of spirit. With each passing day she was creeping further into his thoughts. His consciousness. Maybe even his heart.

It was dangerous territory.

Finally she descended the stairs, and he jogged into the darkened corridor. "Mrs. Greythorne. Please. Might I speak with you?"

She stopped and turned her gray eyes on him. In the corridor's shadow, he saw that there was no laughter in them, no brightness. When he'd first glimpsed her this night with Simon, she appeared vibrant—laughing and light. But now she looked tired. Dark circles beneath her eyes replaced the rosy cheeks, and her smile, which earlier seemed easy and effortless, now appeared forced.

"Where's Thomas?" she asked, breathless. "Have you seen him?"

"He didn't think you'd come back down, so he said he was leaving. He asked me to pass along his regrets and to tell you he'd contact you soon."

He tried to interpret her shifting expression. Was she happy? Relieved? Sad?

She wrapped her arms around her waist, her shoulders drooping ever so slightly, and glanced over her shoulder as if someone might jump from the shadows.

After several moments she turned her face fully to him. "I owe you an apology."

He almost laughed at the odd statement. "Whatever for?"

"I didn't know Thomas would come here. I didn't even know he knew I was here."

"Mrs. Greythorne, this is your home." He kept his voice low. Steady. "You're welcome to visit with your family, certainly. Besides, the Frost Ball is open to all."

She squeezed her eyes shut and shook her head. "That's not what I meant."

He waited patiently. Silently.

She drew a deep breath, as if trying to organize her thoughts. "The other day, when you said the villagers suggested that my name was associated with free traders, I should've been more forthright."

He swallowed, steeling himself for what could pass her lips.

"I wasn't honest with you. Not completely. If you want me to leave, I understand. I—"

"Mrs. Greythorne." His words silenced her. "There is no need for you to go anywhere."

Her brows drew together. "But you don't understand. They—the Greythornes—can be dangerous, and they want me to—"

Upon impulse he placed his hands on her shoulders, gently, to draw her attention.

She snapped her mouth shut. Confusion clouded her expression as she looked to his hands.

He did not remove them. Instead, he bent to meet her gaze directly, refusing to let her look away. "Mrs. Greythorne. I don't know what happened with your family, and frankly, it doesn't matter to me. You belong at Penwythe Hall. I—I can't imagine it without you now."

Her eyes were wide. Her lips were pressed together firmly, and her jaw twitched, but she did not look away.

As much as he wanted to leave it at that, he knew he couldn't. "Be that as it may, I respect your privacy, but my primary concern is my nieces and nephews. I need to know they're safe and that Mr. Greythorne does not mean you—or them—harm."

Moisture formed in her eyes, and her head swung slowly from side to side. "I—I—" A tear blazed down her smooth cheek.

The urge to wrap his arms around her was strong, to comfort her until the tears stopped. But he resisted. He dropped his hands from her shoulders to retrieve a handkerchief from his waistcoat. He offered it to her, and she accepted it and wiped her cheek.

He softened his voice to barely above a whisper. "If you need help, I *will* help you, but you must be honest with me."

After several moments, she lifted her head. "I do believe that my brother-in-law may be involved in some deceptive activities. In fact, I'm certain of it. I—I don't trust him."

"You're referring to the rumors we spoke about earlier this week."

"They're true." Her voice cracked and she lowered her gaze. "I don't think the children are in danger, but I might be. I'll leave by dawn."

"I'll hear of no such thing." His words rushed out. Unchecked. Protective. "You're safe here at Penwythe Hall. I promise you that, but I thank you for telling me. We cannot fight something we are not aware of, and I'll not let you fight this alone. Besides, the children—they have lost so much, and you are their rock. They rely on you. And so do I."

CHAPTER 24

Dawn's wet, chilly wind whipped around Jac and Andrews as they traversed the open courtyard.

A raindrop plopped on Jac's cheek, then on his hand. The gray light creeping across the sky signaled an end to the long night. Even as they walked, carriages rumbled away from the courtyard, returning tired guests to their homes.

Jac wanted nothing more than a long rest. But it was not to be—for now they had a new problem to contend with.

Andrews muttered low as he walked next to him past the stables and toward Penwythe's entrance. "What a blight on the night Thomas Greythorne was."

It was true. News of Thomas Greythorne's presence at the Frost Ball spread like an uncontrollable wildfire. Jenkins, an excise man from the north, recognized him. Gossip and chatter wagged on everyone's tongues, which had been loosened by ale. "This is a predicament, Mr. Twethewey, if I can be blunt."

"I spoke with Greythorne myself," Jac added, determined to fill Andrews in on the details before they were interrupted. "It was after midnight. You were right—Mrs. Greythorne is related to him. By marriage."

Andrews slowed his steps, his eyes widening in the pale light. "What will you do about it?"

Jac stopped to face him. "What do you mean?"

"Well, she can't stay here."

"Why not?" he shot back, resuming walking. "She's given no reason to think of her as anything but decent and helpful."

"That's how women are, don't you see?" Andrews shook his head. "They seem one way, and then they change and a completely different side comes sweeping down from the blue, catching all males off guard."

Jac huffed. He'd not tell Andrews of the fear he'd seen in Mrs. Greythorne's eyes or the panic evidenced in her mannerisms. It would only add to his condemnation. No, Jac wanted to protect her. He *would* protect her. "She was in Randall's household for three years. She's the victim of circumstance, 'tis all."

Andrew snorted, his fair hair fluttering in the morning's threatening wind, and he lowered his voice. "You sure your personal feelings aren't clouding your judgment?"

"What?" Jac scoffed.

"It wouldn't be the first time a beautiful woman swayed a man's opinion. With that pretty face, large eyes, and dimples, she's the sort that could work her way into a man's emotions with the man being none the wiser." Andrews halted and tapped Jac on the arm to get him to do the same. "We've known each other a long time, haven't we? I saw something between you and Mrs. Greythorne. I don't know what, but *something*. I'm no romantic, but I can read people. And, well . . ."

"You'd best stick to estate business and leave my personal life out of it."

"Like it or not, your personal life is estate business."

As they walked along in silence for several moments, Andrews's words clanged in his head, like the echo of a pistol shot long after the bullet had been discharged.

Was he allowing his feelings for her to cloud his judgment on this matter? He'd dismissed other workers for much less than a rumor. But then again, he'd never felt this strange connectedness and inexplicable tie to a woman before. It was more than just reliance on her in regard to the children.

Andrews gripped Jac's forearm. "Look."

Jac followed his gaze down the small alley between the stable and hay barn. There stood a man. He wore a hat, but the blond hair fringing his high collar was unmistakable. It glowed white, even in the morning's low light. He was speaking with another man.

"That's him—Greythorne—isn't it?" Andrews hissed.

Anger flared within Jac, heating his face and chest. "Yes."

"I thought he left hours ago."

"So did I."

They stood in the shelter of the stable's shadow and watched. The wind carried the indecipherable whisper of their voices, then Greythorne handed a packet to the other person, who tucked it into his coat.

Andrews and Jac exchanged glances. There was no way to know what was in that packet, but a known smuggler exchanging anything on his property spelled naught but trouble. After the men shook hands, Greythorne glanced left, then right, then retreated through the narrow space and disappeared behind the stable.

The other man, a tall silhouette in the darkness, walked toward them.

Jac anchored his feet, preparing for what may come. His heart thumped as the man approached and the light illuminated his features.

Mr. Simon.

Without a thought of how to proceed or what he would say, Jac stomped toward the man.

Simon's head swiveled in his direction, then his dark eyes widened. For the first time since his arrival at Penwythe Hall, the man's stony composure fell, and he looked like an animal trapped without any hope of escape.

Jac clenched and unclenched his jaw. "In my study. Now."

"What business did you have with Thomas Greythorne?" Jac demanded even before the three men crossed the study's threshold.

Dawn's growing pewter light reached into the chamber, but outside the window the clouds churned bitterly.

Simon stood in front of the cold fireplace, his cravat askew and his dark hair tousled. He locked eyes with Jac, and a smile toyed on his lips. "Can't see what my personal business would mean to you."

Andrews shifted and leaned against the doorway, blocking the chamber's exit.

Jac crossed the small room to see Simon's eyes more clearly. "You're aware that Thomas Greythorne is Mrs. Greythorne's brother-in-law, are you not?"

Simon shrugged. "And?"

Beads of perspiration gathered on Jac's brow, despite the chilly air. "I understand that he's not to be trusted. I don't have the time nor the inclination to investigate the matter. That's not my business. But what is my business is a man in my employ who associates with a smuggler."

Simon's brow puckered, and his dark-brown eyes narrowed. "That's a lofty accusation to make about a man you don't know."

"Doesn't really matter, does it? I don't want him on my property, nor do I want my nephews' tutor having clandestine meetings with him in the alley like a villain. If you've any care for your position here, I suggest you tell me why you were lurking in the shadows when you were supposed to be caring for my nephews."

Simon's jaw twitched. "So you've taken to spying, have you, Twethewey?"

Jac stepped closer, pointed his forefinger at the flagstones beneath his feet, and glared at Simon. "This is *my* property. Everything that happens on it is subject to my scrutiny." Jac snatched the corner of the packet sticking out of Simon's coat. Before Simon could stop him, Jac bent it open. Banknotes abounded.

Jac slammed the packet back against Simon's chest. "I want you out of Penwythe Hall. Now."

"You would have me leave the boys after what has transpired with their father? For what? Because of what I do in my personal time?"

"Yes."

"You've been plotting my dismissal since the day I arrived." Simon's face reddened, his eyes narrowing to slits. "Steerhead'll hear of this."

"Tell Steerhead whatever you like. He's not master of Penwythe Hall, nor is he the children's guardian." Jac nodded to Andrews. "Mr. Simon is leaving the premises. Please see that he's escorted to his chambers to gather his things. I don't want him speaking with the boys. He's to be gone within the hour."

CHAPTER 25

He'd found her.

They'd found her.

The morning following the Frost Ball, Delia still couldn't believe it. The fears that had been swirling within her ever since her return to Cornwall were ugly and raw now, unleashed by the very man who had control over them.

She wrapped her blanket tightly around her shoulders and stepped from the bed to the window. Instead of drawing it closed, she allowed the invigorating air to rush in, and she filled her lungs with its earthy scent. A silver mist hovered over the primrose garden like a sentry standing guard.

If only protection from the Greythornes could be so easy.

She'd been a fool to return to Cornwall.

She'd tried to deny it, but the truth blazed now.

Upon Randall Twethewey's death she should have taken her meager savings, gone north, and opened a school—and left the Twetheweys in her past. But she hadn't wanted to leave the children, and now even more was at risk.

And then there was Mr. Jac Twethewey.

His expression the previous night had been difficult to discern. He'd been reassuring and calm, but he'd also spoken of concern for his household's safety. He knew enough of the truth, and he'd proven himself a clever man. He'd put the pieces together, like the puzzles he and the boys had assembled the other night.

A soft knock sounded at her door and she turned. "Yes?"

The latch clicked and the door swung on its hinges. There stood Alis. "Mr. Twethewey has asked to see you right away, Mrs. Greythorne."

She could feel the blood drain from her face.

He was going to send her away.

She should have known that his encouraging words of help had been nothing more than a hasty reaction and that ultimately he'd change his mind.

For who would want a smuggler's widow around his charges?

She nodded in response to Alis, then allowed the maid to help her don a simple tan gown of printed muslin. Alis brought fresh water to the basin, and with trembling hands Delia washed her face, cleaned her teeth, and pulled a brush through her hair.

Each second brought more certainty that she would be leaving this house—leaving her Sophy, Hannah, Julia. The boys. Tears began to form before she even completed her toilette.

Once dressed, she descended the winding staircase and made her way through the corridors and the great hall, which were still strewn with the evidence of the previous night's festivities. All was quiet, eerily so, as she approached Mr. Twethewey's study.

She drew a deep breath before she lifted her hand to knock.

The sound of shuffling papers coming from within ceased. "Enter."

Even though the hour was early, Mr. Twethewey's desk was alive with writing utensils and evidence of a breakfast eaten while working, the scent of sandalwood mingling with wood smoke.

He looked up as she entered. He'd not slept, evidenced by the fact that he still wore his dress coat of green wool. His black hair fell in a lock over his forehead in wild waves, and the scruff on his jaw gave him an almost roguish appearance.

Trying not to stare, she searched his expression for any hint as to what calamity was coming, but his lips formed a tight line, and the small lines framing his eyes were unreadable.

He motioned toward the chair in front of his desk. "Mrs. Greythorne. Please, be seated."

She did as she was bid, fidgeting with the silver pendant around her neck. They'd both let a bit of their guard down the previous evening, sharing personal thoughts and feelings in the corridor's protective shadows, but now they were back in reality, where decorum and manners must prevail.

Discomfort crept in during the ensuing silence.

She was alone with him, but she did not want to be.

She garnered her courage. This moment was uncomfortable, but it would be even more so if she did not address the topic hovering between them. "Mr. Twethewey, about what happened last night, I—"

"I did not ask you to come here to talk about last night." His curt words sliced the harsh silence. He kept his eyes focused on the stack of papers he was shuffling. Finally he placed the papers in a pile and folded his hands atop them. "I wanted to speak with you about Mr. Simon."

She winced at the unexpected name. "Mr. Simon?"

He fixed his gaze on her. "I've terminated Mr. Simon's employment. He left Penwythe this morning. He'll not be returning."

Jac tried not to stare at Mrs. Greythorne.

She'd been crying. Her red eyes and pale cheeks told the story her lips did not.

At the mention of Mr. Simon's name, her normally pristine posture stooped slightly, and she looked more like a wounded creature than the confident, controlled governess he'd encountered in the past.

"I don't understand." She blinked up at him. "What do you mean he won't be returning?"

It would not do to explain. If he told her the truth behind Simon's dismissal, she might believe herself to be the cause or, worse yet, be frightened by Thomas Greythorne's odd activity. "Just as I said, I've relieved him of his duties here. He'll not be back."

Mrs. Greythorne drew a shuddering breath, then gave a little huff. A shadow fell over her face as surely as if a cloud eclipsed the sun.

He cleared his throat. "Knowing that Randall did not want the boys sent away to school, I have already begun making inquiries for a new tutor."

The words were little compensation, he knew. She continued to remain silent and stared out the window.

In an effort to fill the awkward lull, he stood from behind his desk and sat in the chair next to her. As he drew nearer to her, a subtle pink colored her wan cheeks, and her nostrils flared. He had thought her a master at masking her emotion, but even she was beginning to crack under the strain of constant change and the shock of sudden news.

"Until a new tutor arrives, I'm at your service to help with the children as needed, and we'll see that one of the maids is relieved of all other duties so she may help you fully with their care."

She jumped to her feet, and he was unprepared for the intensity in her expression. "May I ask why he was dismissed?"

He started. It was as if she had heard nothing he said after he'd shared the initial news. He stood, matching her stance. "It had to be done."

"You know the terms of our agreement. They are exacting and clear." Her voice trembled. "Mr. Simon and I are to stay on to see to the children's education, per your brother's directive. I've seen the document myself. We are employed by the trust, not you. You had no right to discharge him."

The frankness with which she spoke to him was unlike the manner of anyone else in the house, even Mrs. Bishop. "Terms or no terms, this is my home"—Jac took great pains to keep his voice gentle—"and I'll decide who's permitted to remain under its roof."

"But what possibly could have happened?"

It would be easy to expose Mr. Simon and to censure her brother-in-law, but he had seen the simmering fear in her eyes at the Frost Ball. Yes, he could tell her the truth, but to what end? He'd already sent Mr. Simon away. Jac might regret that decision one day, but for now, Mrs. Greythorne did not need to know details.

He pushed Andrews's words to the back of his mind—words suggesting that Jac's developing feelings for the young woman before him were steering his actions. But as he let his gaze stray from her gray eyes to the dimples that formed when she bit her full lower lip to the softness of her skin, he wondered if there wasn't some truth to the statement.

"I've learned to trust my instincts on matters such as this. I have my reasons, but out of respect for the children, I'll not be sharing them. It's best forgotten and best to move on."

He could see the battle raging in her eyes—she wanted to confront him and to defend her friend. She didn't understand. He wished he could soothe her anger as he did the previous night. But he was the source of her frustration. To explain why would only cause her more pain.

She let out a little mirthless laugh. "You decided that it is best and to just move on."

"I wrote to Steerhead this morning to inform him. Like I said, we will employ another tutor. Until then, I hope things can continue on as they have. Please say nothing to the children. I'll tell them myself."

"In the meantime I must just accept it." Her words were not

those of accommodation but of challenge—a calling out of the situation he was putting her in.

"I am sorry. I know you were great friends."

She said nothing else. She spun on her heel and was out of his study without waiting to be dismissed. And he was left with the ticking of the mantel clock and Cadwur for company.

CHAPTER 26

Feeling light-headed and numb, Delia exited the study. She'd show no weakness in front of Mr. Twethewey. Not again.

Penwythe's ancient stone walls, with their portraits and tapestries, seemed to close in on her as she fled through the foyer, through the great hall, and down through the corridor and up the stairs to the west wing.

She'd heard Mr. Twethewey's words, stark and finite, and yet she could not believe them.

Mr. Simon. Her friend. Her ally. Gone.

She'd expected to be dismissed because of Thomas, but no.

She pressed the back of her hand against her cheek. It was hot. Flaming.

Delia had been strong through this entire ordeal. From the moment Randall Twethewey had arrived back at the house, unconscious and bloody, she summoned courage and strength she didn't know she possessed. Driven by the desire to be steadfast for the children, she pushed her own personal fears aside. But every new transition heaped added weight on her shoulders, and she felt her feet faltering beneath her.

Her hands shook as she entered her private chamber. She'd peeked into the children's bedchambers, and they were not there. They were likely down in the breakfast room, possibly with Mr. Twethewey, wondering where their governess and tutor were.

She reminded herself that she always had choices.

No one had ever forced her to do a single thing in her life. No one had forced her to marry Robert Greythorne. No one had forced her to become a governess. The alternatives would have led her down a different path, and every choice up until this point led her here.

She could make another choice now, to leave. The Greythornes knew she was here. There was no use hiding. She could go to her brother's. She could apply for another governess position, or even at a girls' school and gain experience for her own one day.

But then she thought of little Sophy. Of Julia blossoming into womanhood and needing a guide. Of sweet Hannah in the middle, striving to find her place. Of Johnny and his fears and Liam struggling to take on his role as the man of the family. She could never leave them—not and live with her decision. Besides, they were her family now. She loved them each as dearly as she would if they were of her blood. She was destined to stay here, and even if Mr. Twethewey tried to dismiss her as well, she would fight harder than she suspected Mr. Simon did.

She'd mistakenly assumed Mr. Twethewey was an ally, but had he not just proven otherwise? He did not think enough of her to let her in on the great secret behind her friend's dismissal.

So many people she loved and depended on were gone now. The vision of a lonely future spread before her, and she did not feel strong enough to fight it.

One searing tear fell. Then another. She fell atop her bed, clutched the blanket in her hand, and yanked it up over her head to drown out the light. She thought of her prayer a few days ago. It had felt rusty and unused, a forgotten thing cast aside. But peace, albeit slim, had settled on her at that time. Perhaps it would again. She cried a new prayer, hoping it was being heard.

———— ◆ ————

Later that morning, Jac paced the drawing room, waiting for the children. He wiped damp palms on the buckskin of his breeches. He rarely felt nervous, but as he considered what he would say to them, trepidation surged.

It was one thing to tell Mrs. Greythorne about Simon's departure. It was another thing entirely to tell the children. He tapped his foot against the floor in frustration before rising and stepping to the tall glass doors that looked out onto the primrose garden.

He'd been making such progress with them. Johnny regularly accompanied him to the orchards in the evening to check the day's activity, and Liam would ride out to check on Aunt Charlotte with him nearly every day. Even the girls had taken to him, and he thought of the flowers they had given to him before the Frost Ball. They would often sing for him or read aloud to him, sharing whatever activity Mrs. Greythorne had taught them that day.

This news would hurt them and add strain to their already wounded hearts.

The realization sickened him.

His thoughts turned to Mrs. Greythorne. The previous night he'd pledged to help her, and then this happened. The hurt and shock in her eyes would haunt him. Pain and disbelief simmered under her otherwise calm reaction to the news, making him wonder if her feelings for Mr. Simon were stronger than he'd thought.

He gripped, ungripped, and regripped the back of the chair beside him. How many times had Colliver pointed out Jac's impulsiveness? He'd dismissed Simon out of anger and without thought of how it would affect the children.

Perhaps his actions had proven Mr. Colliver correct.

The shuffling of childlike footsteps drew his attention, and he turned from the door as the children filtered in, one by one, followed by their somber governess.

"Children, come in," he said as the girls sat on the sofa and the boys leaned against the back of it. He drew in a long breath, bolstering his confidence. "I am afraid that Mr. Simon is no longer with us."

"We know." Liam's voice was flat. "All his things are gone from his room."

"Why did he leave?" Sophy's face fell, and she leaned against her sister.

Johnny swung his feet as they dangled over the sofa's edge. "Was he mad at us?"

"I told you to stop pretending to read when you were supposed to be really reading," Hannah declared. "It probably upset him."

"He didn't leave because of me!"

Jac raised his hands and stepped toward them. "He did not leave because of you."

Sophy tilted her head to the side. "Then what was it?"

"Did you make him go?" Liam crossed his arms over his chest. Maturity flashed in the young man's eyes, almost as if the youth could guess the reason.

Jac felt like a cornered animal. Even though the eyes locked on him were young, they were full of anger and frustration.

He sat in the chair opposite them, taking the time to look each one in the eye. Jac didn't want to lie, but he could not share the real reason Simon had been dismissed.

He eyed Mrs. Greythorne, who sat down on the sofa between Sophy and Julia and spoke before he could form a response. "What your uncle means to say is that Mr. Simon has moved on. Remember when Mrs. Timmons's mother became ill and she had to leave Easten Park to care for her? Mr. Simon had to leave for personal reasons, 'tis all."

Jac marveled at the manner in which she calmly delivered the news.

She smoothed Julia's hair over her shoulder. "I know this is sudden. You've dealt with a great many sudden things lately. He would have said good-bye if he could have, but sometimes life is just not that simple. Do you understand what I'm saying?"

The children nodded, and Sophy rested her head on her governess's shoulder. "But *you* will not leave us, will you?"

"Oh, Sophy." She pressed a kiss on top of the child's head. "Of course I won't leave you."

"Now," she said with energy infusing her voice, "the best thing we can do is to be positive. Everything will be all right, but it will take a little while for things to fall into place. Let's go to the garden. A few of the groundskeepers should be there, and we'll help tidy some of the garden beds."

As they stood Jac added, "Liam and Johnny, I'm headed to the orchards if you would like to come. They are thinning the fruit today, and I thought you might like to see it."

The boys looked at each other and shook their heads no. Still somber, the children filed out of the room.

Mrs. Greythorne hung behind, and he approached her. She'd comforted them in a way Jac never could. She knew what to say to ease their worries and make them comfortable. Mrs. Greythorne *was* their family, the person who held their lives together.

"Thank you for your assistance with that conversation."

The warmth in her expression cooled. "Like I told you last night, I love the children and would do anything in my power to prevent them from getting hurt." She turned on her heel and walked away.

CHAPTER 27

Night had fallen, and it was far too dark for reading. The candle's light was not strong enough to illuminate the page. Delia closed her book, set it on the writing desk before her, and rubbed her eyes.

The day had been a long one. Two weeks had passed since Mr. Simon's departure. The children had adapted as well as they could to another loss, and Mr. Twethewey had been more present than she had anticipated and taken Liam and Johnny on his daily estate activities. If any good came from Mr. Simon's departure, it was the bond forming between uncle and nephews.

Despite the progress they were making, weariness dogged Delia's heart. As each day without her friend passed, her loneliness increased. And as each day ended without word from Thomas, she reminded herself not to get lulled into a false sense of security. She had no doubt they were watching her.

She pulled the pins from her hair and let it fall down her back, and she combed her fingers through the long, straight strands before she placed the pins on her dressing table. Her reflection in the looking glass above the dressing table caught her eye.

The candle flickered on her face and she sighed.

She looked tired.

Delia was still young, and a full life still stretched before her. But she'd borne a lifetime of experiences in recent years, and they all seemed to write themselves on her face at that moment.

She pressed her fingertips against her pale cheek, then lifted her chin to view her reflection from a different angle. Robert had always called her beautiful. She never really believed him when he would praise her, but oh, how she loved hearing him say it. And now she doubted that anyone would call her beautiful again.

She raised her hands behind her neck to unclasp her necklace, but when she lifted the chain away from her skin, the chain felt unusually light.

Frowning, her fingers traveled the chain.

The pendant—Maria's pendant—was gone.

Her heart lurched.

With trembling fingers she pulled the chain free from her fichu and turned it over and over in her hand, as if by doing so the pendant would magically appear.

Panic, raw and fresh, raced through her. "No, no, no!" She patted her bodice and gown with frantic movements. After confirming it was not caught in the folds of her gown, she hungrily searched the bare wood floor, tucking her hair behind her ear as she did so to get it out of her way.

Heat rushed to her face. Dizziness swirled.

Maria's hair. Her last link to her sweet child.

Gone.

Through blinding tears she ripped through her chamber, pulling open her drawers, jerking back her bedcovers, checking the floor.

Where had she last seen it? She grasped at her recollection of the day. She'd put it on that morning with the blue dress, she was certain. She could remember touching it in the garden, but that was in the early afternoon. She'd been so many places this day—in most of Penwythe's second-floor living spaces.

Oh, why had she worn it? Why had she not kept it locked in her jewelry box and safe? She never used to wear it—ever—but wearing it had become a habit as of late.

Once she was certain it was not in her chamber, she moved to the girls' room. They were sleeping, but the moonlight through the window was bright. She searched the floor. Behind the door. Next to where she'd read them a story. It was nowhere to be found.

She returned to her own chamber, retrieved her lantern, and made her way down the corridor. The frustratingly deceiving shadows played tricks with her eyes in the night's blackness. She searched the drawing room. The long gallery. The breakfast room. The ghosts of her past were with her, searching, calling.

Oh, how she wished for sunlight. The blinding hysteria gave way to a numb dismay. It was no use looking until morning. She'd never find it. Not now. Tears blurred everything before her into a mess of charcoal grays and shifting blacks. She curled against the wall and leaned against it for support. As a tear slipped down her cheek, hopelessness settled over her like a shroud.

———◆———

It was far too late to be working, Jac knew. He dropped his quill to the desk and it clattered. His paperwork could wait until tomorrow, but even so, he had no desire to retreat to the isolation of his bedchamber.

Not tonight.

Too many thoughts swirled in his head—thoughts of the children. Of the orchard and the fact that they'd not had substantial rain for weeks. Of Mrs. Greythorne. No, he'd best stay where he was and see to his tasks, for there was no shortage of letters to respond to and ledgers to review.

He lifted the quill in front of him, preparing to continue the letter he was writing, when shuffling outside the study drew his attention. He glanced at the clock. At this late hour no one should be about, but Andrews had said that he would bring the updated tenant agreements to him to review. Perhaps it was him.

The shuffling stopped.

Curious, Jac walked to the doorway, stepped down the corridor, and peered through the foyer toward the great hall. He saw no one.

He was about to return to his desk when the shuffling resumed. It was the sound of soft footsteps on stone—clearly those of a woman. Concerned, he followed the noise through the great hall to the drawing room. A flicker of light shone through the door, and he stopped short.

Mrs. Greythorne leaned against the wall, her forehead in her hand.

The floor creaked under his heel, and her head jerked upward. She was holding a lantern in her other hand, and its flickering light illuminated her bloodshot eyes and the tears trailing down her cheeks. Her hair hung long, thick, and dark over her shoulders.

The alarm on her face propelled him forward. "Mrs. Greythorne! What's the matter?"

As he drew nearer, she stiffened, drawing herself up to a more proper posture. She wiped her face with the back of her hand, and for several moments he thought she would invent an excuse to steal away.

"I've lost my pendant."

He was not sure he heard her right. Surely a pendant would not cause such an emotional reaction. "Your pendant?"

After a shuddery breath, her hand flew to her chest where the pendant would normally lie. Her gaze scanned the floor. "Yes, my necklace. It held a piece of my daughter's hair. My husband gave it to me and I . . ." Her words trailed off as her gaze met his.

Sophy's words from the day by the seashore rushed him. "*Mrs. Greythorne wears her hair around her neck. Not every day, but sometimes.*"

This was the first time she had mentioned her daughter to him.

He fumbled for words. "Then we will find it. Where did you have it last?"

"I had it this morning. It must have broken free sometime during the day."

"You didn't leave Penwythe today, did you? It has to be here somewhere."

"It is so important to me. It—" A fat tear plopped down her cheek.

The deafening silence screamed, preventing him from hearing his own thoughts.

She was trembling. Vulnerable. In a way he'd not noticed before. The urge to protect her that he had felt the night of the Frost Ball had not subsided. It had been quieted, perhaps, with what had happened with Mr. Simon, but the sight of her tears and the pain on her face reignited the impulse. "We'll find it. It can't be far. I'll notify the house staff. You were in the gardens, correct? I will have the groundskeeper search thoroughly."

Through all the pain of the past several weeks, she had been stoic, but today her facade cracked, revealing a glimpse into the tender heart beneath.

Seeing her in this different light stole his breath. He wanted to fix what was broken, to heal what was wounded. "Don't worry. All will be well. You have my word."

CHAPTER 28

Delia had barely slept. How could she? The ghosts that had arrived as a result of the lost pendant were plaguing her, preventing sleep. The night was more like a prison instead of a reprieve from the day.

At the very first glimmer of dawn, Delia rose, dressed, and made her way down to the primrose garden. The light, even though minimal, provided enough illumination to begin her search for her lost pendant.

She started by the bank of elm trees, where she and the girls had taken the day's reading, and then moved on to the copse of elms. As she searched along the bend and around the daisies, the sense that another presence was there slowed her, pricking the tiny hairs on the back of her neck.

Then a voice gripped her.

"Mrs. Greythorne."

Delia turned to discover the source.

Mr. Simon stood on the path in the garden, just where the bricks veered around the willows.

A smile twitched his mouth as their eyes met.

He was clad in a blue broadcloth coat—one she'd never seen before—and the early-morning shadows fell across him, making his snowy cravat appear that much whiter. He was clean shaven and pristine, as always. The breeze rustled his freshly trimmed hair, and he held his hat in his hand.

"Mrs. Greythorne." The manner in which the name rolled from his tongue seemed soft and intimate.

Her task forgotten, she returned to the stone path, happiness momentarily eclipsing her distress. "Mr. Simon! What are you doing here?"

"I came to see you, of course. I thought I'd find you here for one of your early-morning walks, and here you are." His knowing grin crossed his face.

She stepped closer. "I am so relieved to see you. What on earth happened?"

He heaved a sigh and motioned with his hat to the bench. "Shall we?"

She sat on the bench and arranged her skirts around her, anticipation mounting. Finally she would have answers. Mr. Simon would keep nothing from her.

He sat next to her, and the scent of smoke and sandalwood wrapped around her, familiar and comfortable. He leaned forward, put his elbows on his knees, and angled his head to look at her. "So tell me. What've you heard?"

She shook her head and gave a shrug. "Absolutely nothing. Only that you were dismissed. I was given no reason."

"And this upset you?"

"What an odd question!" She gave a little laugh and lifted her hand to still her hair blowing across her face. "Of course it did."

"I figured as much. That's why I wanted to speak with you one last time before I leave the area. I've been staying in Wentin Bay looking for a position, but I fear it's time to move on."

Mixed emotions swirled. He'd been gone for two weeks, but the fact that he would be leaving the area permanently twisted her heart.

"In the early morning following the Frost Ball, when the carriages were departing, I happened to meet your brother-in-law near the stable."

Delia frowned, dread flooding her. "Thomas?"

"Yes. We spoke for a few moments, merely in passing, mind you. I wasn't even aware of who he was at first. I'm not entirely sure what happened, but after I spoke with Mr. Greythorne, Mr. Twethewey attacked me and demanded an explanation as to why we were speaking. He raved like a madman, claiming Mr. Greythorne was involved in illegal activity, and he accused me—*me!*—of being involved. And then he dismissed me."

Delia's heart tightened in her chest. Could this be true? Would Mr. Twethewey act so rashly, so unjustly?

She rolled her shoulders forward. If only she hadn't talked with Mr. Twethewey about her brother-in-law and confirmed the rumors. "This is my fault, then."

"Don't say that, Delia."

She stiffened her posture at the use of her Christian name and studied her hands clasped in her lap. "What will you do now?"

"A family to the west is looking for a tutor, so I have written them, but in the meantime I think I will travel back to Yorkshire. I've family there, and I long for their familiar faces. Besides, I know no one else here."

She glanced up at him again. This would be the last time she would see her friend for a very long time. "It will be so different without you here."

"Nonsense. You and the children will continue on as you have, but . . ." His eyes sought hers. "I would like to ask a favor, if it's not too much to ask."

She leapt at the opportunity to help her friend after so much perceived injustice. "Of course."

"When I was relieved of my duties, Andrews packed my things, but he failed to gather all of my belongings. I wonder if you could retrieve an item from my bedchamber. I feel terrible even asking you, but if anyone—"

"Don't give it another thought." She stood from the bench. "Of course I'll help you."

He licked his lips. "There was a loose floorboard under the left window. You might consider this odd, but I felt I needed to protect my personal belongings. I put a small leather packet with letters underneath that floorboard."

"Say no more, Mr. Simon. The house is still quiet, and I should be able to get to that area without anyone noticing. Wait here."

His gloved fingers brushed her bare ones, then gripped them softly. "Thank you."

Unsaid words hovered heavily like the morning mist, and she looked to his hand still clutching hers. She flicked her gaze upward. His soft expression met her eyes, and a shot of alarm raced through her.

She pulled her hand from his affectionate grasp. "I'll return shortly."

The halls within were still shadowed, but her feet had learned the quirks of the old staircase, leaving her mind free to contemplate the odd interaction.

She had always thought that at some point, there might be something more between the two of them than companionship. Was that what he'd meant by holding her hand?

She tried to shirk the thought and continued up the stairs, quietly so as not to alert any staff members who might be awake, and she made her way to the chamber that had been Mr. Simon's. The door creaked on its ancient hinges as she pushed it open, and she paused to make sure no one had heard her.

She stepped inside. Immediately the chamber's plainness struck her. At least hers had a small fireplace, two windows, and a settee. This room consisted of a bed, a wardrobe, a small table and chair, and little else.

With a sniff and swift feet, she set about her task. Just as Mr.

Simon had said, the plank below the window lifted easily, as did the one right next to it, revealing a small pocket of space. The worn leather was cold and stiff as she lifted the portfolio from its resting place. She looked at it for a few seconds. What could be so important to him? She knew he corresponded with several people—he was forever writing letters—but why would he hide them?

Pushing her curiosity aside, she stood, replaced the planks, and retreated from the room. Quicker and quicker she moved. Delia rounded the corner and ran into something so hard, so unmoving, that black stars darted across her vision. She bounced back off of it and the packet flew from her hands, papers showering down.

Two hands grabbed her upper arms.

Embarrassment and confusion reigned, and she immediately knelt to begin gathering the papers. "I—I— Forgive me, but—" She looked up and jumped to her feet, clutching the papers to her chest.

For there stood none other than Mr. Twethewey.

CHAPTER 29

Jac stomped across the dewy lawn, gripping the portfolio in his hand, with a red-faced Mrs. Greythorne following closely behind him. He considered himself a fairly even-tempered man, but the events of the past couple of weeks had tested the bounds of his patience.

But this—this was not to be borne.

"Tell me, Mrs. Greythorne." He turned abruptly and waited for her to catch up with him. "Did you invite Mr. Simon back to the property?"

"Of course not!" She stopped short, and the willful morning wind tousled her hair about her face. "As I told you in the stairwell, he left some personal belongings and asked me to retrieve them."

He resumed walking. "And he just happened to find you in the morning hours?"

"It's no secret I walk this time of day."

"And you don't think it odd that he didn't just come to me and ask for his things?"

"After what you did to him, is it any wonder that he sought me out instead of you?"

Just outside the primrose garden he stopped again and faced her. "What are you talking about?"

"He told me how you attacked him."

"Attacked him?" he shot back with a huff, then snapped his mouth shut.

Jac pushed the gate open and held it wide for Mrs. Greythorne to precede him. The scent of lavender that always accompanied her wafted on the cool breeze. He held his breath. He'd not have his good judgment distracted by the intoxicating allure of her scent or by the softness of the tresses that had escaped her chignon.

What was this effect she had on him?

And to think he'd been so worried about her after finding her crying in the corridor. He'd been unable to think of little else. But this—this was the last thing he expected. He'd thought that Mr. Simon was in the past. Evidently Jac was mistaken. Things were becoming clearer. He would not be made the fool. Not by her, not by Simon, not by anyone.

They walked in angry silence for several moments before Jac spotted Simon, bright and audacious as a peacock, in a bright-blue velvet coat.

Jac looked down at the leather portfolio in his hands. He doubted that the contents were the real reason behind Simon's return. It would have been just as easy for Simon to write and request the items be sent to him. Jac would bet the whole of Penwythe Hall that Simon was back to see Mrs. Greythorne. To play on her feminine sensibilities. The fact that Simon had the gall to compromise her reputation by meeting her alone in the garden made him sick.

He'd not have it.

Simon turned as they approached. His initial look of surprise was quickly eclipsed by amusement. A grin formed.

This man had the ability to set Jac's mood on fire.

He did not break his stride but stepped right up to Simon. "Thought I told you not to return."

Simon chuckled and his dark gaze shifted from Jac, to Mrs. Greythorne, and then back to Jac.

Jac held up the packet. "I understand this is what you've come for."

Simon eyed it. "It is."

"I told you never to come back here. You could have written for it."

Simon shrugged. "I'm staying over in Wentin Bay. I'd get here faster than a letter, I'd wager."

Jac thrust it toward him. "You have it, then."

With a smirk Simon took the packet, flipped it open, shuffled through the contents, and then tucked it under his arm. He lifted his gaze to look over Jac's shoulder at Mrs. Greythorne.

Jac stepped in front of him to block his view. "Your business is done here."

"So it is." Simon returned his hat to his head and tipped the brim. "Give the children my best."

"The children need nothing from you," Jac snapped.

Simon took several steps and then turned. "Farewell, Delia."

The use of her Christian name was meant to get under Jac's skin. And it worked.

Jac glared as Simon retreated back down the path to the garden's south entrance. Once Simon was out of earshot, Mrs. Greythorne stepped next to him. Her expression had not softened. If anything, her cheeks flamed pinker. Her eyes narrowed tighter. "Is it true you dismissed him because he was talking with Thomas?"

He was caught off guard by the demanding tone of her voice. He was the one who should be angry, and instead her eyes flashed as if she were the offended party.

She folded her arms tightly across her chest. The morning breeze caught long strands of her russet hair and blew them across her face. She tossed her head to return them to their place. Her unblinking gray eyes were fixed on him as she awaited a response.

She deserved an answer. "Very well." He'd tried his best to protect her. In hindsight maybe he should have told her sooner. "I saw Mr. Simon accepting money from Thomas Greythorne. Your brother-in-law has a fearful reputation, and I don't want anyone in my household accepting money from him."

"You misunderstood what you saw. Mr. Simon would never do that."

"Are you sure?"

Her mouth snapped shut, but anger waged war in her eyes. Silence hung heavy between them. They stared at each other, neither wanting to be the first to look away.

Her chin quivered slightly. "If that was the case, why did you not tell me as much?"

"Because I didn't want you to worry." He softened his tone. "I didn't want you to be afraid."

She gave a little laugh, thick with sarcasm. "Oh, you thought I couldn't handle it?"

"I know you could handle it. I wanted to . . ." He swallowed. "I wanted to protect you."

The small muscles in her jaw twitched. "I don't need your protection, and I certainly don't need you hiding truths from me. As it is, I don't believe for a second that Mr. Simon would take money from Thomas. Mr. Simon has been a trusted and dear friend for many years. How dare you say such things about him?"

He stared at her—her vibrant eyes. Her full lips. The wind toying with her hair. And a strange ache tightened in his chest.

There was no use denying it. Andrews had been right the night of the Frost Ball. He'd been letting his emotions—and affections—rule his interactions with this woman. He could feel his own argument weakening, but he'd not win this battle. He wasn't sure if he really wanted to.

He straightened his coat and looked past her. "I don't want the children to know of this visit. If he comes here again, I want to know immediately. Is that clear?"

She winced, no doubt surprised by the curtness in his tone. He'd not intended to be so sharp, but it was easier than discussing the other feelings he was experiencing.

He returned his hat to his head. There was still something he needed to do to make sure Simon was off his property for good.

———◆———

The cool morning breeze cooled Jac's hot face but did little to quench the fire boiling within him. He didn't slow his steps as he exited the primrose garden and made his way to the privacy of his study.

Morning sunshine now spilled through the east window, illuminating stacks of newspapers and books, but it was the south window that drew his attention. From it he could see the iron gate that separated Penwythe property from the road that led to the village.

Simon was still standing there, in a tall black beaver hat, next to a gray horse. He appeared to be securing the packet in his saddlebag. Jac grumbled under his breath as he watched.

Simon untied his horse and mounted. He'd said he was staying in Wentin Bay, so Jac expected him to turn right. But Simon turned his horse to the left and gave the horse a swift kick with his heel.

Jac frowned. That wasn't the direction of Braewyn or Wentin Bay. In fact, the road would eventually curve and take him south.

Uncle William had always said that intuition was one of the greatest gifts God could give a man. It guided his steps and gave him clarity during decisions. Jac's intuition screamed something was amiss. The vein in his temple throbbed. Whether he liked it or not, it was no longer only his peace and security he had to concern himself with. There were children in his care.

Something had to be done. Simon was lying about something. And Jac owed it to the children—and to Mrs. Greythorne—to find out why.

Jac bolted from the study, out the workman's entrance, and north to the stables. With quick hands he saddled his horse and led him from the stable. It didn't take long to find Simon retreating down the lane. Fortunately, the road they traveled was rife with bends and turns, which made it easy to follow at a distance. Simon's absurd blue coat made him glow like a beacon in the morning light, and the tune he was whistling made the task even easier.

The pace was frustratingly slow. Simon was in no hurry to get wherever he was going. As the distance continued to increase, Jac's suspicions grew. From what he could glimpse of Simon's mount, there was no pack with supplies. If this was the direction Simon had come from, he'd traveled quite a distance to retrieve that portfolio—and had made a great effort to speak only with Mrs. Greythorne.

As the second hour of riding passed, Jac considered turning back. He'd given little thought to what he would do if he was discovered, nor what he would do if he found out where Simon ended up. Just as he was about to turn around, Simon urged his horse into a canter. A signpost at the forked road pointed toward the village of Morrisea.

Morrisea.

That was the name of the town Thomas Greythorne had mentioned.

Simon headed that direction.

Jac stopped his horse near the forest's edge where he could observe unseen. Simon turned off the road at a building with a sign reading Hawk's Eye Inn, where he dismounted and handed the reins to a stableboy. They laughed about something, and Simon tipped his hat to a man in the square. Clearly they knew each other.

With Mr. Simon safely ensconced in the establishment, Jac turned his horse back toward Penwythe. Maybe he'd wasted an entire morning. Maybe not. But at least he knew that Simon was lying about something. At least Jac could be prepared.

CHAPTER 30

By the time Jac returned to Penwythe Hall, the morning was gone. He'd stopped at an obliging traveling inn on the way back to eat and to water and rest his horse, and it had taken more time than he'd anticipated. Now his horse was tired, and Jac was filthy from the dust and bits of mud that had been kicked up during his strange, unanticipated ride.

He urged his horse through Penwythe's main gate and down the side yard along the bowling green to the north courtyard behind the house. As he rounded the corner, a dusty black carriage came into view. Two black horses were still harnessed, and the door bore a simple, unrecognizable crest.

As he slid off his horse, he tossed the reins to a stable boy. "Who's here?"

The boy shrugged. "Two men went inside about an hour ago, and they ain't come out since."

Jac nodded his gratitude to the boy and then moved toward the heavy door to the entrance hall. Once inside, he was surprised to see Johnny leaning against the paneled wall. After Johnny saw him, the youth pushed away from the wall and ran toward him. His wide blue eyes held a mixture of impatience and pride, and his words spilled forth. "Where have you been today, Uncle Jac?"

Jac smiled as he removed his brimmed hat and set it on a side table just inside the door. He rested his hand on the boy's shoulder.

Even though interactions with Mrs. Greythorne had been tense, his relationship with the children had been growing stronger by the day. "An unexpected errand sent me away for a bit, but from the looks of you, either you've had an adventure or you've news to tell me."

Johnny fell into step next to him, and their footsteps echoed from the passageway's rounded ceiling. "Mr. Andrews took Liam and me to thin the fruit. I did a whole row by myself. Well, almost by myself, and Mr. Andrews said it was some of the finest work he'd ever seen."

"You did?" The pride in the boy's words heaped more guilt on Jac. The first time the boy showed genuine interest in the orchards, and he was not here to witness it. He looked at Johnny more closely. Evidence of the day's work had left its mark, from the pink glow of his cheeks to faint traces of dirt marring his face and hands. "And what did you think of it?"

"Andrews showed me what to do, how to find the fruit clusters and pick all but the strongest, biggest ones."

Jac nodded, recognizing the satisfaction in a job well done. "Did he explain why we have to thin them out?"

"Because the apples need room to grow, and they won't have enough room if we leave all of the apples in the cluster."

Jac nodded. "That's right."

"Can I go with you tomorrow?"

"If it's all right with Mrs. Greythorne." Jac brushed the dirt from his coat. "Thank you for stepping in today while I was gone. It's nice to know there is another man in the family I can count on."

Johnny beamed under the praise before he nodded toward the drawing room. "Who are those men?"

"Don't know." Jac sobered. Unexpected visitors were common at Penwythe, but most visitors had to do with estate business and would be shown in through the study. And if Jac or Andrews was not available, they would be asked either to wait or to return, based on the nature of their business. But these men had been shown to the drawing room.

Johnny folded his arms across his chest as he spoke, suddenly seeming much older and more mature than his age. "After I got back from the orchards, I heard Mrs. Bishop tell Mrs. Greythorne that the men wanted to speak with Mr. Simon. Why would they want to talk with our tutor? He's not even here."

Jac's jaw twitched at the mention of the name.

Would they ever be free from the nuisance of that man?

"Did they ask to speak with Mrs. Greythorne?"

"I don't think so."

He smiled and clapped his hand on Johnny's shoulder. "Good. Tell your brother and sisters to come to the bowling green in a while. We may be able to get a game of bowling in before night falls."

Johnny ran off down the corridor and then Jac turned to the drawing room. Once again, he attempted to brush the stubborn dust from his coat, and he combed his hair with his fingers.

The long rays of the hot orange sun streamed sideways through the terrace doors. It was warm in here—a room that had been closed all day, trapping the heat filtering through the wall of windows.

The sober-faced men turned to him as he entered, and Jac took immediate stock of the situation.

The first man was seated on the settee. A look of pompous annoyance wrote itself on his tight, thin features. He was clad in a close-fitting, high-collared summer coat and a bright-red waistcoat.

The other man stood next to the windows. He was leaning against the frame with his shoulder, one giant booted foot crossed over the other. Whereas the smaller man was orderly and immaculately dressed, this man's tousled hair and wrinkled broadcloth coat suggested that these two men were very different sorts.

"I hope I haven't kept you gentlemen waiting too long."

The man on the settee stood, and the man at the window straightened. "Are you Jac Twethewey?"

"I am." He motioned for them to be seated. "I apologize for my appearance. The day turned out to be a rather dusty one."

"Your appearance is of little consequence, Twethewey," the tidy man said sharply, irritation oozing from each syllable. "My name is Donald Clarke. I am a partner with Clarke & Company, the bank in London where your brother kept the trust."

Jac had not really thought about the trust since Steerhead had been here to deliver the children all those weeks ago. He'd received the money allotted for the year and did not expect anything else for months. Jac extended his hand and shook Clarke's.

Mr. Clarke nodded toward the burly man standing at the window. "This is Lucas Browning."

Clarke pulled a box of snuff from his pocket and focused his attention on the painted box. "How well are you acquainted with Edwin Steerhead?"

Jac jerked his head up. The sickening, sinking sensation that something was gravely amiss tightened in his gut. "I've been acquainted with Steerhead for years, but I don't know him well. He was my brother's solicitor. And friend. Why?"

Mr. Clarke pushed his spectacles up higher on the bridge of his nose, ignoring Jac's question. "And what do you know of your brother's business dealings?"

Jac shrugged. "Very little."

This line of questioning was beginning to feel like an inquisition, but he did not know what he could possibly be on trial for. Jac narrowed his eyes. "Why?"

"As you may or may not know, Mr. Twethewey's business partners have bought out his holdings in the business."

Jac stared at him blankly. What did this have to do with him?

"Yes. Steerhead told us that he would handle the legalities of that and see that the money was added to the trust."

"Yes, that is what was supposed to happen, but I am afraid I have news for you. Unpleasant news."

Jac frowned at the matter-of-fact statement, the muscles in his neck twitching. But he remained silent.

Mr. Clarke cast a glance to the other man before speaking. "Your brother's trust has been depleted. All of the money in it is gone."

"That's not possible," Jac retorted, heat rushing to his cheeks.

"I'm afraid it is." Clarke's monotone voice was frustratingly slow. "After completing the sale of the business holdings to the partners, Steerhead invested the money instead of putting it in the trust. We only know this quite by accident. Furthermore, all these weeks Steerhead has been systematically withdrawing money from the trust. Regularly. And often. Now the trust is nearly empty."

Jac drew a deep breath and ran his fingers through his tangled hair. "So all the children's money—the dowries, the annuities—it's all gone?"

"Yes. Unless Mr. Steerhead magically appears and replenishes the funds, which I would say is unlikely"—Clarke nodded, his voice flat with sarcasm—"it appears your brother's trust was sorely misplaced."

The air thinned. Confusion gave way to anger. Blood pounded in his ears, harder with each heartbeat, and the volume of his voice increased. "And Liam's property inheritance?"

"From what I understand, that property comes from his mother's side of the family and is not part of the trust."

Jac balled his fists at his sides as he raced to map the information he'd just received. "So you've come all this way to tell me this."

"No, I'm here to find Steerhead, actually. There are matters related to the business that he must account for that have nothing to do with the trust. Your brother had many accounts with us, and this is not the only one Steerhead is running into the ground, undoubtedly to his own benefit. It's just an unfortunate side task to inform you about the lost trust. We believe he was taking money from the trust to cover his other bad business dealings. That is, of course, an assumption. We need to speak with Steerhead to get the full picture.

"We've tracked down Steerhead's assistant, but he hasn't heard from him in two weeks. He did say that he helped Steerhead arrange travel out of the country. Do you know where Mr. Simon is or perhaps Mrs. Greythorne? We'd like to ask them a few questions about Mr. Steerhead since they received some of his last-known correspondence."

"Mr. Simon has been relieved of his duties and is no longer here, but Mrs. Greythorne is."

"I should like to speak with her. I'm not a man to be taken, and I suspect you aren't either. One way or another, the money will be recouped. I hope I can count on your assistance—for both our sakes."

Jac felt as if he was going to be sick. He couldn't have cared less about the business and Steerhead, but the children and what belonged to them were another matter.

Such an exorbitant amount of money. Gone.

The children's future and his brother's legacy vanished like a puff of smoke.

The pressure was immediate. There could be no question now. He was in charge of these young souls. He would provide for them. He'd figure out a way. Somehow.

"Can you call her, please?" Clarke's words jolted him from his thoughts. "We'd like to leave within the hour, if possible."

Jac stood and rang the bell to call a footman, dreading what could happen next.

CHAPTER 31

Delia paused outside the drawing room and smoothed the muslin of her printed gown with nervous fingers. She drew a deep, cleansing breath, willing her pulse to slow and her nerves to calm.

Her heart had jumped within her when Mrs. Bishop delivered Mr. Twethewey's request that she join him in the drawing room. Their argument that morning had left a bitter stamp on her heart, and he'd been gone ever since. She had found herself watching for him as she passed a window or traversed the corridor near his study. He'd obviously been angry with her when he left the garden, evidenced by the sharp draw of his brow and his curt tone.

It bothered her, more than she would have expected. How had she begun to care so much about this man's opinion of her?

She swept her hair from her face and pinched her cheeks for color, hoping the answers to her questions awaited her on the other side of the closed door. She lifted her hand and knocked.

Within moments Mr. Twethewey was at the door. His eyes met hers, but instead of the peaceful, kind expression she had hoped for, his face boiled with fury. "Come in, Mrs. Greythorne."

His countenance frightened her. Wild and windblown, he looked as if he were ready to break something. She pressed her lips together to collect herself as she brushed past him, his scent of horse and outdoors giving some hint as to how he had spent his day. As she stepped in farther, she was surprised to see he was not alone. Her gaze shifted from one man to the other.

Mr. Twethewey swept his hand toward the men. "Mrs. Greythorne, this is Mr. Clarke from Clarke & Company, and this is Mr. Browning, his associate."

She'd never met Mr. Clarke, but she knew the bank's name. And the tall man in the corner, with his hard eyes and massive shoulders, was nothing less than terrifying. She managed to remember to curtsy and resisted the urge to step closer to Mr. Twethewey.

"These men want to speak with you." He ushered her toward a wingback chair. "Please, be seated."

She quickly searched his eyes for some hint as to what was transpiring, but his mannerisms were devoid of any feeling. Delia swallowed and sat on the chair's edge, turning her full attention to Mr. Clarke.

The thin man cleared his throat. "You're aware that Mr. Randall Twethewey's financial assets were with our institution and that Mr. Steerhead had been named the executor of the trust, yes?"

Delia tipped her head in a slow nod, not sure what she had to do with any of this.

"You will be surprised, I'm sure, to know that the money left in care of the trustee has been liquidated."

The words were foreign to her. "I—I don't understand."

Mr. Twethewey stepped forward. "It means the trust that was meant to support the children is no more. The money is all gone."

"Gone?" She winced. Mr. Twethewey was a wealthy man. This made no sense. "Where did it go?"

The gravity of the situation took hold as she listened to Mr. Clarke explain loans and money, of trusts and wills, and her heart sank. The children she adored were now destitute.

"Since you are paid from the trust," continued Mr. Clarke, "your compensation cannot be guaranteed."

She looked up to Mr. Twethewey. His lips were pressed into a fine line. His arms were folded across his chest. His expression gave nothing away.

Mr. Clark's words jerked her back from her thoughts. "The trust is gone, and there is nothing to be done about that, unless Steerhead returns it, of course, but I must speak with Steerhead on matters regarding other business. When was the last time you heard from him?"

She tried to push what she had just heard to the side so she could focus on the question at hand. "I believe it has been nearly a month since I received my wages. I wrote to him after Mr. Simon was discharged, but I never heard a response. I did think that odd, but he is a busy man, and I—"

"But he was in communication with Mr. Simon?" Mr. Clarke interrupted.

She cast yet another glance toward Mr. Twethewey. His eyes were fixed unwaveringly on her. "I believe so."

She'd barely had time to finish her sentence before Mr. Clarke's next question rushed her. "Do you know where Mr. Simon is?"

"He—he said he was staying in Wentin Bay."

"Actually, that's not true." Mr. Twethewey stepped closer, his posture tall and confident. "I thought something seemed off earlier, so I followed him after he left this morning to the village of Morrisea and an establishment called the Hawk's Eye Inn."

Delia started.

The mention of the Hawk's Eye Inn unleashed a wave of unpleasant memories.

It was Robert's inn.

The Greythornes' inn.

The inn through which contraband would pass in the dark of night.

What on earth would Mr. Simon be doing at the Hawk's Eye Inn?

Mr. Twethewey turned back to the men. "I fear he misled Mrs. Greythorne."

Delia winced at his accusation, feeling it was meant to drive home a point with her.

The silence was heavy, thick with unsaid words and suspicions. Mr. Clarke exchanged glances with the other man and then stood. "I think we have what we need."

"What are you going to do?" Mr. Twethewey asked.

"Well, if you are certain you saw Mr. Simon at the inn, then we will visit him there. Time is of the essence, and we are talking about a great deal of money owed to us. We're on the hunt and will not rest until he answers for his actions."

Delia did not move from her chair. In fact, she did not move a muscle until Mrs. Bishop came to escort the men to their carriage and she did not say a word until she and Mr. Twethewey were alone in the drawing room.

The weight of the words spoken earlier that day hung over them, and finally Delia pushed through the awkwardness. "Did I hear you correctly? Did you say the Hawk's Eye Inn?"

"I did."

Another sickening wave washed over her. The inn was a harsh place, desolate and isolated. She was never allowed to go there, but she knew the type of men who did. And if Mr. Simon had gone there, perhaps what Mr. Twethewey had tried to tell her about Mr. Simon was true.

Her pride was difficult to swallow. Would she never be free of the past? Of the fear?

The force of the memory emboldened her. She needed to make him understand. "I know the Hawk's Eye Inn. You shouldn't go there."

He folded his arms over his chest. "Why?"

"It's a dangerous place." She stood and stepped toward him. "Promise me you'll not go there again."

He tilted his head to the side. "And how do you know this?"

She sighed. This charade could not go on further. "You know about my brother-in-law." Fearing he was not taking the warning seriously, she reached forward and clutched the sleeve of his coat. "Listen to me."

Fire radiated from their touch. He looked into her eyes, his gaze narrowed. He felt it too, she knew. She had his attention.

She did not release his sleeve. "Some of the rumors about my husband are true. Probably most of them. Greythorne House is not a mile from that inn. I lived at Greythorne House for three years and saw a great deal. My husband and his brothers spent a lot of time at that establishment, and trust me, no one goes to the Hawk's Eye Inn by accident. I can't explain what Mr. Simon was doing there, but I do know that whatever happens there is underhanded."

Their eyes locked and his jaw twitched.

She forged ahead. "Maybe you were right about Mr. Simon. I don't know why he was talking to Thomas, but nothing good can come out of a relationship with that man."

His face softened. "I think sometimes when we trust someone, we cannot fathom that they'd be capable of something less than virtuous. I dismissed Mr. Simon from his position on instinct. Perhaps I was right, perhaps not. But we can only make decisions based on the information we have at hand, and at the time I was fearful. For you."

Her heart jolted. She could not tear her gaze away from the brilliant blue eyes looking at her. Tenderness and sincerity lit them in a way she had never noticed before.

Was he telling her he cared about her?

He stepped closer. "I meant what I said earlier, in the garden, when I told you I wanted to protect you. Not because I didn't think you capable, but because . . ."

She desperately wished he would finish his sentence, but he was quiet. Given the situation, it was probably for the best.

When he did not continue, she looked down to the carpet. "Did he really take money from Thomas?"

"That's what I saw. Andrews saw it too. I didn't tell you because I didn't want you to be afraid. I thought the situation would dissipate on its own. Clearly it has not."

"Just promise me you will not go back to the Hawk's Eye Inn."

A grin lifted his cheek. "Are you saying you're concerned for me, Cordelia Greythorne?"

She lifted her brow at the use of her Christian name. How natural it sounded coming from his lips. "I'm merely saying that there are dangerous people there. The children need you. It would be safest for all of us to stay as far away from there as possible."

He stepped closer. The expression on his face captivated her. "This is not something for you to take on yourself. This is not your battle to fight. But if something should come of it, you will not be fighting it alone."

Blood raced through her ears as she stood there in the faded light. His nearness confused her senses. It jumbled her words and muddled her mind.

He leaned forward. "You are needed here. The children—they, well, they need you. I need you."

She met his gaze. Tried to decipher his meaning. "The children and their well-being mean everything to me."

"Just the children?" He tilted his head to the side and quirked an eyebrow. Then stepped closer.

Never had she thought she would feel tenderness for another man, but she could not deny that it was growing. Every action, every encounter—the good, the bad, the happy, the sad—was giving it strength. No, these feelings would not, could not be ignored. And yet, as much as her heart wanted to give in to the notion of romance, her mind would not allow it.

She stepped back. She had to remind herself of her place. Of who she was. Of who he was. Fear of the unknown trickled in, squeezing out space for hope of a romantic future. She needed to protect herself. Her voice lowered, and the space between them cooled. "I am a governess, Mr. Twethewey. My first and only concern is the children. I'm afraid anything more than that is not possible."

CHAPTER 32

Delia adjusted the small watch pinned to her bodice and looked out of the schoolroom window to the north courtyard with a sigh.

Several days had passed since Mr. Clarke had called at Penwythe, and in the days that followed, life resumed some sort of normalcy. The summer days were hot and long—too hot to spend any time of consequence out of doors. How she wished for rain to break the streak of heat that had been plaguing them, but day after day the blazing sun rose in the cloudless sky.

She'd heard Mr. Twethewey and Mr. Andrews discussing how despite their efforts to improve irrigation, no one could have foreseen this period of drought.

Liam joined her by the window and leaned with his elbow against the windowsill. The humid breeze curled through the open window, lifting his black hair. "Where's Uncle Jac? He said last night that he'd walk with us to the orchards today after our studies. And now he's not even here."

Delia placed a hand on Liam's shoulder. "I think he had to go to Plymouth to see about the cider press. But he'll be back soon."

With a sigh he pulled back from the window and sank back onto his chair.

She returned her focus out the window. She wished for Mr. Twethewey's return as well. Something had changed between them that day in the drawing room after Mr. Clarke's visit. Despite her cool ending to their conversation, she could not deny that something was blossoming—something tender and lovely—something she had not experienced since the start of her relationship with Robert.

But she was different now than she had been with Robert. She had the benefit of experience. Even so, she was cautious, reserved. She could not deny the gentle leap in her heart at the thought that any moment Mr. Twethewey's horse could appear in the courtyard, bringing him home. The anticipation was intoxicating. She had to remain disciplined in her thoughts, however, for the complications of anything actually coming of this relationship were very real. Now that the money had vanished, he was her employer. He paid her wages. She answered to him.

She sighed and returned her attention to Liam. It had been over two months since their father's death. They were all coming to terms with it in their own ways. Julia's lingering moodiness and Hannah's quietness both were unusual to their characters. Johnny and Sophy seemed fairly content, but then some random thing would trigger a memory and they'd explode with uncontrollable emotion. Liam tried his best to be strong, to be protective of his younger siblings, but despite his initial distrust of his uncle, his admiration for the man seemed to be growing.

She wished she could take their confusion upon herself, but just as they were struggling to make sense of what was happening around them, she was not sure she had things any more figured out, especially as it related to Mr. Twethewey.

A new arrival to the courtyard caught her eye. A small wagon drawn by two horses carried two men—one dressed in workman's attire and another dressed in a black coat and beaver hat. The wagon curved around the driveway and drew to a stop before the carriage house. She was about to dismiss the men as tenants and started to turn from the window, but something about the man in the tall dark hat made her pause.

She squinted to see more clearly. The man's posture and movements as he climbed down from the wagon were familiar.

Could it be? A glimmer of anticipation sparked within her.

"Children, continue reading." She stepped back from the window. "I'll be right back." She gathered her skirt in her hands and scurried down the servants' winding staircase. Once to the ground-floor landing, she flung open the servants' door and burst into the dusty courtyard, ignoring how the breeze lifted the hair at her temples.

As she beheld the approaching figure, recognition burned bright. Even beneath his hat she could see his eyes and the familiar cut of his jaw and point of his chin.

It was her brother.

All other thoughts aside, she ran toward him, disregarding all sense of decorum. Tears blurred her vision into a mess of greens and browns as she flung her arms around him. "Horace!"

He squeezed her in response and lifted her from the ground. "Delia! Look at you! I hardly recognized you." He returned her to the ground.

She stepped back, breathless, hands still clutching his arms, unable to control her smile. "What are you doing here?"

At the question, his smile faded and he removed his hat. As his expression sobered, her own smile disappeared.

Something was wrong.

"What is it?"

"You're needed at home, Delia. I've come to take you back to Whitecross with me."

She dropped her hand to the side. Conflicting emotions roiled within her as a thousand scenarios rushed her.

"Elizabeth is not well. The apothecary has done everything he can, but—" The wind carried away his words, as if it did not want her to hear the words either.

The breeze lifted his dark hair, the color so like her own, and then he wiped his brow with the back of his hand.

Delia had thought of her brother so often, but not like this, with sadness etching lines around his mouth and worry creasing his brow. He looked older than his thirty-five years, but even so, the same brown eyes were gazing back at her. They were not laughing, as they had often done when they were younger. They were the eyes of a mature man, eyes full of sorrow.

"She's dying," he said. "The apothecary said there are only a few days left. You are so close now that you're in Cornwall, and she so desperately wanted to see you again, that I . . ."

The blood pounding in Delia's head and the wind rushing in her ears swept out any hope of hearing his words.

Her head grew very light. Not Elizabeth. No.

She finished his sentence with a definitive nod. "Then we must go."

CHAPTER 33

Delia rushed into her bedchamber. The ride back to Whitecross would be a long one, and the day was already half done.

But the urgency did not end there. Elizabeth was dying.

Guilt, heavy and thick, descended upon Delia. She should have found a way to visit sooner. She'd allowed her fear of the Greythornes to prevent her from stepping foot in the home of her childhood. And now it might be too late.

Elizabeth had never been well. A fever at a very young age had weakened her heart. She was never expected to live very long, and nearly two decades later she had defied the grim prognosis. This warning flag had been raised before. Part of Delia's heart clung to the idea that this was a false alarm. But she'd seen the weary fear in her brother's eyes, and he would know. He interacted with Elizabeth on a daily basis. They lived under the same roof, after all.

Her only communication with Elizabeth was via letters, and Delia knew what her sister chose to share with her. And her brother's letters were less frequent.

She sniffed, wiped her nose with the back of her hand, and drew a deep, shuddering breath. She had to calm down enough to think so she could pack. She had no idea how long she'd be gone or when she'd be back. It seemed to be the way of life lately: Packing. Moving. Nothing consistent. Belonging nowhere. One by one, the people in her life were fading from her. She did not know if she could bear another loss.

A fresh wave of emotion threatened, and through sheer force of willpower, she retrieved her valise.

Fortunately her gown for the day simply tied in the back, and she was able to exchange it for another with relative ease. She exchanged her slippers for sturdier kidskin boots. She packed her hairbrush, toothbrush, and other daily items in her bag. She stiffened at the fact that her pendant was still missing. How she wished it was with her.

Suddenly loneliness, powerful and overwhelming, stole into the room, battling grief for the dominant position. The quiet, the stillness—it was all too much.

How she wished for strong arms to hold her. A strong support, like Robert had provided after Maria's death. Robert had been many things, but in spite of his flaws, he'd been consoling and protective. He'd held her long into that horrid night, allowing her to weep.

Her thoughts turned to Mr. Twethewey.

To Jac.

Just a few days ago he expressed a desire to protect her. She closed her eyes, imagining what it would feel like to have his strong arms around her, comforting her. How much easier it would be to face uncertainty if she knew someone was beside her. But they had not spoken of such things since that afternoon. Had he said those things merely in the emotion of the moment?

But she had spoken coolly to him. No doubt he would not repeat the sentiment.

She sniffed. Besides, he wasn't even here. For all she knew, he would not be back today, or even tomorrow. There were no strong arms to hold her now, and it would be foolish to even allow her mind to entertain the wish.

Once her things were assembled, there were only a couple of things left to do. She found Mrs. Bishop to arrange for the children's care in her absence and then sent word to Aunt Charlotte to ask her to stay at Penwythe Hall until Mr. Twethewey returned. She did everything she could think of, until one thing remained: to tell the children.

With heavy steps she climbed the stairs to the schoolroom. She opened the door to see each one bent to their tasks. The sight pulled at her heart. She did not take her position lightly. She was the one constant in their lives—the one person who had remained unchanged for several years. They relied on her, and even to be gone a day would cause them uncertainty—and that she did not want to do.

"Children." She clutched her hands before her. "I have news."

"You've changed your gown." Julia eyed the black gown with suspicion.

"Yes, I have, for I need to travel today." Delia searched for the right words. "My brother has arrived, just a little while ago. He came to tell me that my sister is very, very sick and she needs me at home."

The children exchanged uncomfortable glances. "But this is your home."

"I mean the home where I grew up in Whitecross, where my family is." Reluctance to leave them started to tighten her throat. "He's come to take me to go see her."

"You're leaving?" A frown puckered Sophy's young brow.

"Of course she's leaving." Hannah's posture slumped, and a pout darkened her features.

Johnny jumped up from his chair, letting his book fall closed. "But you are coming back, right?"

"Of course I am!" Delia forced brightness to her tone. "If one of your sisters were sick, would you not want to be with her?"

Sophy lurched forward. "Is she going to die?"

"I don't know, Sophy."

Hannah and Sophy exchanged glances. Johnny looked to the ground and collapsed back in his chair. Liam's face reddened. Julia leaned to put her arm around Johnny's shoulders.

Delia rested her hands on Sophy's shoulders and bent over to look at the child at eye level. "I will not be gone long. I promise."

Sophy's chin trembled. "Who will take care of us?"

"Your uncle will be back soon, of course. And I've asked Aunt Charlotte if she would stay at Penwythe Hall until I return. Plus Mrs. Bishop is always here. You will never be alone."

"Can we not go with you?"

"No, dearest." She could not help but smile at Johnny's enthusiasm. "I must do this alone, and you must stay and help care for your siblings."

"But that's not fair!" Hannah shot back. "You can't just leave us! You promised you wouldn't leave us!"

"I'm not leaving you," Delia countered, her tone stern. "I *will* be back."

Hannah shook her head, her long locks swaying, and she turned to face her siblings. "Don't you understand? She is paid to be nice to us. To take care of us."

Delia moved around the table, took Hannah's hand, and forced her to look in her direction. "You can write to me every day, and I shall write to you all, every single day until I return. Is that a good plan? I promise, I will only be gone as long as necessary. Now come and meet my brother. I've told him so much about each one of you. He's eager to meet you."

She chewed her lip as the children scooted back from the tables, stood, and lined up by the door. She had to leave Penwythe Hall, for her sister's sake, and she would be back, but even so the departure felt, in some ways, like a betrayal. She stepped backward to allow the children room to step through the door and into the corridor. Regardless of her reason for going, she could not deny the pain crushing her heart as she prepared to leave her young charges behind.

Dusty and hot, Jac rounded the corner of the stone fence toward Penwythe Hall. The trip to Plymouth had been unexpected but necessary. Questions had come up with the building of the cider press, but he trusted no one besides himself to oversee the project—too much was at stake. And now, as he passed through Penwythe's main gates, Jac was glad to be home.

For so many reasons.

He was surprised at how much he missed the children. They were becoming a part of him, a part of his daily life. Much more than he ever expected them to.

And then there was Mrs. Greythorne.

Cordelia.

His pulse raced at the thought of her.

Her last words to him had been cool that afternoon in the drawing room, but her eyes had told a different story. The wall she had carefully constructed around her heart to protect herself from loss and misuse was beginning to crumble. He could see it. Now that she knew the truth about Mr. Simon, she no longer seemed to hold Jac responsible for his dismissal. In fact, she seemed to regard him as an ally.

He guided his horse down the main drive, across the south courtyard and along the bowling green, but his attention was drawn as Liam raced toward him. Jac drew his horse to a halt, and Liam stopped at his side, his face flushed and his eyes wide.

"Liam! What is it?" Jac adjusted his hat's brim to guard against the early-afternoon sun.

The boy's face twisted in concern. "Mrs. Greythorne is leaving."

"What?" Jac jerked and slid from the saddle.

"Yes," Liam gasped, breathless from his run, and trotted alongside Jac as they walked to the stable. "Her brother is here, and her sister is sick and might die."

After instructing Liam to return to his siblings and leaving his weary horse with the groom, Jac hurried inside. As Liam had indicated, a man stood in the great hall with his back to him, examining a painting hanging on the wall. His hands were clasped behind his back, and he appeared to be waiting.

"Welcome to Penwythe Hall." Jac broke the silence as he stepped into the room.

The guest turned to face him, and his brows rose with interest.

"I'm Jac Twethewey." He continued into the great hall, extending his hand.

"Horace Abbott." The man's handshake was firm.

With the man's straight dark hair, round face, and dimpled cheeks, the likeness between brother and sister was unmistakable. Abbott was not a tall man, yet his broad shoulders and the intense set of his jaw commanded attention.

"My nephew tells me our governess is needed at your home."

"She is. Our younger sister is ill, and the situation is quite grave. I fear if Delia does not bid her farewells now, she may not be able to at all. She's gathering her things now."

Jac nodded, absorbing what he'd just been told and suppressing the wave of disappointment coursing through him. He didn't want her to leave, yet he'd not detain her—not when she was so badly needed. He gestured back to the entrance hall and his study beyond. "Come with me. You can wait for Mrs. Greythorne in my study."

Jac led the way down the corridor, pausing to instruct Mrs. Bishop to pack a basket of food for their journey. Once in the study, he offered Abbott a glass of port, and the men sat in the chairs flanking the mantelpiece.

"I do hope Delia's absence will not put you in a bind," Abbott said after a stretch of silence.

Jac leaned back in his chair, keeping his tone steady. "She'll be missed, of course. The children rely on her, but we can manage for a while. The most important thing is that Mrs. Greythorne is with her sister now."

"I'm glad you see it that way." Abbott shifted in his chair, and he looked down to his glass. "To be honest, I'm not sure how long her presence will be required. If I had my way, sir, she would not be returning at all."

Jac lifted his head, alarm building at the odd, confident statement. "You disapprove of your sister's profession?"

"It isn't so much that I disapprove; it's that I wish she didn't need employment at all." He took a drink of port and then adjusted his position. "I've no doubt she's an excellent governess. She's always had a way with children. Be that as it may, a woman should be with her family and not on her own in the world. Should I have had a greater say in the matter, she'd never have embarked on such an endeavor in the first place."

Footsteps sounded, and Jac stood and stepped into the passageway, a sense of melancholy and dread slowing his steps. His heart sank as their gazes met in the shadowed corridor.

Despite the oppressive heat, Mrs. Greythorne was clad in the black traveling gown she'd worn the day of her arrival. Her hair was pulled back into a tight chignon. She was pale and dark circles shadowed her eyes. She gripped Hannah's hand in one hand and Sophy's in the other. At her side Liam and Johnny both carried a bag. Julia followed them.

Upon noticing him Sophy dropped Mrs. Greythorne's hand, ran ahead, and flung her arms around him. "You're home!"

He stooped to plant a kiss on top of her head.

"Mrs. Greythorne is leaving," Johnny announced, his tone somber.

"So I've been told." Jac allowed his eyes to lock with hers. He saw so many emotions there—none of which were happy or pleasant.

Could it be that she felt the disappointment of this rushed reunion as poignantly as he did?

He offered her a bow.

She offered a weak smile in return. "You've met my brother."

He nodded, not sure what one should say at a time like this. "I understand you need to go away for a while."

"I hope this doesn't inconvenience you too much. I've already spoken with your aunt, and Mrs. Bishop, of course. I'll return as soon as I am able."

He was keenly aware of all the eyes on him. He swallowed. Hard. He had thought of little else but seeing her again, and now his chest tightened at the thought of her impending departure. "I—I wish the best for your sister."

"Thank you."

Abbott was in the doorway. He flipped his pocket watch open and then snapped it shut, his eagerness to be off written in his every feature. "Are you ready then, Delia? It will be dark by the time we get back as it is."

Moisture was beginning to pool in her eyes. She hugged the children, whispering something to each one. The girls were crying. Johnny's bright-blue eyes were red rimmed. Liam's lips were pressed to a firm line. Once she was done saying good-bye to the children, she looked at him.

He forced a smile. Someone had to be strong during this unexpected transition. "Godspeed, Mrs. Greythorne. We—we will miss you."

How inadequate the words seemed.

He would miss her.

A sinking sensation raced through him. What if Abbott had his way? The dire possibility that she could leave and never return to Penwythe flashed before him. He'd lulled himself into the belief that she would be with them as long as the children were here.

He looked to the children, still clad in mourning black, their faces as pale as their governess's. Her smile was forced. He saw it twitch and then twitch again.

"Farewell, Mr. Twethewey."

His eyes locked with hers, but his mouth felt dry and no words came to his lips. There was so much he wanted to say to her. Their conversation in the drawing room several nights ago was unfinished. He hadn't been prepared for it, and now it might be too late.

"I wish you and your family the best." His parting words felt thick and inadequate on his tongue. "Hurry home."

Home.

Yes, Penwythe was her home, and she was as much a part of it as the orchards and the children and the gardens.

They all walked together to the carriage in the courtyard. Once at the carriage Mrs. Greythorne turned her smile to the children and patted Hannah's cheek before she accepted her brother's assistance into the carriage.

From the window Mrs. Greythorne smiled at him—an ordinary smile—one he had seen so often since her arrival all those weeks ago. He wanted to capture the sight and memorize every detail.

And just like that, Mrs. Greythorne was leaving Penwythe Hall.

He put his arm around Julia's shoulders as they stood in silence, watching the vehicle retreat to the main road, heavy with the knowledge that Mrs. Greythorne's brother did not wish her to return.

Movement tweaked Jac's other hand. He looked down. Sophy slid her small hand in his and leaned her head against his forearm. "I don't want her to go."

Hannah spoke. "What if she doesn't come back?"

"She will," he stated swiftly, as much to reassure himself as her. "She said as much. Don't you believe her?"

The unanswered question lingered in the hot, dry afternoon. As the carriage rumbled down the dusty road, the sensation of loss was great indeed.

CHAPTER 34

Delia never would have dreamed that she would awaken in her childhood home, yet here she was the next morning, in the chamber she'd shared with her sister.

It was just as she remembered. One large canopied bed with four sturdy posts stood in the center of the room, draped with a plain quilted coverlet. Two windows were set in the far wall, and at the moment the heavy linen curtains were drawn to prevent light from filtering through. The darkness helped her sister sleep, no doubt, but the lack of light during the early afternoon confused Delia's senses and made her drowsy.

She sat in the hard, wooden chair she'd pulled next to the bed and watched her sister sleep. Even though Delia had been present the entire night, she still could not get used to the airy sound of Elizabeth's labored breathing.

Horace had been right to come and get her. Elizabeth needed her here.

Elizabeth had never been healthy or particularly active, but in the years of Delia's absence she'd wasted away, frail and delicate as autumn's fading leaves. Her hair, which Delia remembered as being a glossy nut brown, was dull and thin and had been cut short. Her angular cheeks were wan and hollow, and her closed eyes appeared sunken.

Despite her sister's weakness, they'd spent most of the morning talking of so many things—of Horace's children and wife. Of the sea and the orchards and the apple presses. Of Penwythe Hall and the Twethewey children. Of happy memories and whimsical childhood dreams—most of which would never come to fruition. All of these were topics they had discussed through letters, but there was something special about discussing them face-to-face.

Delia spied a book on the table's edge and decided to read by candlelight. But as she moved to pick it up, her chair creaked and Elizabeth's eyes fluttered open. She smiled faintly when her gaze fell on Delia. Her voice was barely above a whisper. "I'm so glad you are here."

"And I'm glad to be here." Delia reached forward and squeezed her sister's clammy hand.

"Tell me more about your time at Penwythe. I don't want to miss a moment."

The simple, honest statement struck a chord deep within Delia. Moments were always precious, but in the fading twilight of life, they were even more so. Delia licked her dry lips and leaned closer. "It's close to the sea. You can smell it from the gardens and orchards, and the seabirds fly far inland. On one of my first days there, I rose early and went to the shore alone. It reminded me so much of Robert and of when we were children and Father would take us to the shore. Do you remember?"

Elizabeth drew a shuddering breath. "I do. But as lovely as the sea is, I want to know about you. I expected almost with every letter that you would tell me you and Mr. Simon had formed an attachment."

A bitter mixture of sadness and anger burrowed through her at the statement. Would the situation never cease to touch her? "Mr. Simon turned out to be a different man than I thought." She told Elizabeth the details—of Mr. Simon's surprise visit in the garden and the ensuing confrontation between Mr. Simon and Mr. Twethewey.

She stopped just short of the part about his taking money from Thomas and his visit to the Hawk's Eye Inn.

"Mr. Twethewey seems to be an upstanding man. Is he handsome?" The faintest twinkle sparkled in her sister's eyes. Even in her altered state, she had not lost her sense of curiosity.

Yes, he was handsome. Her mind's eye could perfectly recall his square jaw and the slight cleft of his chin. How his blue eyes could either flash with anger or warm with affection, depending on the situation at hand, and how the lock of black hair, with its tendency to curl, would fall across his forehead, giving him a relaxed, approachable appearance. There could be no denying her attraction after all that had occurred, but how much of that could she say out loud? For once said, the words could never be taken back.

"You hesitate," Elizabeth prodded with a smile. "One day you are going to meet a man who will love you like Robert loved you. It may not be Mr. Twethewey, but it will be someone."

"I'm not sure, Elizabeth." Delia shifted in her chair, trying to relax. Elizabeth was the one person on earth who could be trusted with information regarding her heart, and yet Delia was hesitant to let her in.

"You've had so much pain, with Robert and, of course, Maria." Elizabeth rolled her head to the side to look Delia in the eye. "Don't close yourself off. There's nothing worse than loneliness, unless it is living with regrets."

Delia winced at the odd comment. "What do you mean, regrets?"

"We all have regrets." Elizabeth raised one shoulder in a little shrug. "It's a part of life. And part of dying is coming face-to-face with those regrets. We all have parts we'd like to change or erase altogether. My regret involves you."

Delia released a shocked laugh. "Me? Why?"

Elizabeth's expression sobered. "After Robert died, you should have come here, to the vicarage and what was familiar to you, not traipse off to be a governess for a family you didn't even know."

Delia waved her hand in front of her, as if to pass on the subject. "It wasn't the right time for me to come here. Besides, this house is too full as it is. I am perfectly capable of making my own way."

"Yes, you are capable, but you said it exactly. The house was too full. Because of me."

Delia blinked. "But that's hardly your fault. It couldn't be helped. I'll forever be grateful that Horace was able to provide for you."

Elizabeth lifted her hand as if requesting silence. "That's just it. He had to provide for *me*. You had just as much right to a home here as I, but you couldn't, because Horace had to care for me. All these years you have been providing for yourself, working, and I've been here."

Delia tightened her grip on her sister's hand. "My life is a fulfilling one. It really is."

"Mine has been too." Elizabeth squeezed back. "I see the look in your eye. You wonder how I can say that when I've lived half my life from this bed and the other half with the shadow of illness hovering over me."

Delia lowered her gaze.

"I don't know why God chose to give me this illness. How I wish it could have been otherwise, but if I had spent my life questioning His reasons or if I had wallowed in the fear of impending death, I would have wasted the days I'd been given. If I let myself linger on the possible dangers and pain that could lie around the corner, what sort of life would that be? Once I came to peace with this path, my fear subsided. Don't misunderstand, I mourn what I've missed—love and children and adventure—but I'm not angry about it. Mourning and anger are very different things."

Tears formed in Delia's eyes. She'd often wondered if her sister was frightened of dying. They'd never spoken of it. Despite her sister's bravery, Delia's own fears for the future rushed her.

Elizabeth gave way to a round of shallow coughs before she removed her hand. "Our struggles are different, yours and mine. You have your own battles. You've lost your husband and daughter, and I'll not pretend to deny I heard the rumors surrounding his death."

A tear slipped down her cheek. Elizabeth was the only one who knew the truth about the Greythornes' cruelty toward her—at least, she was the only one who believed it. "I can't seem to see past it," Delia confessed. "It haunts me. Plagues me. I want to be free of it. I do."

"Faith," Elizabeth said softly. "Faith is how you get past it. Faith that you will not be given a heavier burden than you can bear. Faith that there is wisdom to be gleaned from every situation. Faith that you are exactly where you need to be, even in the valleys, either for your sake or for His will. Never are we promised an easy life, but we are promised that when we rely on Him for strength, we will have what we need to face our challenges. Fear is a bitter, vile enemy—it will rob you of today's joys and steal your strength to fight for your purpose. Faith is why I don't fear tomorrow or the next day."

Delia wiped a tear, recalling all the times when fear froze her to her spot, refusing to allow her to think rationally. She saw the wisdom in Elizabeth's words, but what was more, she saw the sincerity in her sister's eyes, and the peace—true peace—that does not come from self but something more.

Elizabeth patted her hand. "There is a journey, dear Sister. You are on it. I don't know where it is going or where it will end, but if you lean on your faith, you'll arrive at a destination created just for you."

CHAPTER 35

Jac stood in his study and looked out the east window. If he angled his shoulders just right, he could glimpse the orchard through the trees lining the bowling green. Humid heat hung in a thick haze over all, and the landscape glimmered verdant in the morning sun.

They were halfway through the growing season—halfway to the first harvest—and what was more important, halfway to seeing if his plan would work out as he had hoped.

The fruit had been thinned from the branches. The grounds had been tended and turned. Barrels had been carefully crafted for the specific purpose of fermenting cider. If only it would rain. The orchards were dryer than he had ever seen them. He hadn't been that worried until he visited the north orchard. The dry leaves withered on the branches and were already falling to the ground.

His greatest concern at the beginning of the season had been waterlogged soil, and he thought he'd addressed the concern with the irrigation ditches. His uncle's words about man's inability to control nature drummed in his mind. He almost laughed out loud. He had no control, and with every change, every unexpected development, he felt what little control he did have slip from his grip. He'd thought he'd be happier at this stage of the plan, but everything seemed uncertain.

His thoughts turned to another situation that felt hopeless.

It had been over a week since Mrs. Greythorne had left.

Of course he wished for a full recovery for her sister, but selfishly he wished for her to be back at Penwythe Hall where he could see her. Speak with her. He knew the children felt the same way. Aunt Charlotte had been staying here until Mrs. Greythorne's return, but even so, a somber shadow darkened the sunlit days. She was missed, and it grew more evident by the day.

He occupied his mind by overseeing the orchard work and tending estate business by day and spending time with the children in the evening. Any task was a welcome distraction. Just earlier today he'd received word that one of his tenant's orchards was struggling with insects, so he and Andrews were going to ride out to see if anything could be done to save it.

He donned his wide-brimmed hat and shoved some papers into his satchel. He fiddled with a loose button on his summer coat—he needed to ask Mrs. Bishop to tighten it—when a light, feminine voice echoed in the corridor.

He stopped short. He could not make out the words, but even so, he didn't recognize the tone. It was not Mrs. Greythorne, nor was it one of the Collivers. What reason would any other woman have to call here at this time of day?

Jac did not have to wait long, for within moments a tap sounded at his study door. He looked up to see a tall lady filling the door frame, and his countenance sobered.

There was no denying her identity.

Beatrice Lambourne—the children's maternal aunt.

He supposed he shouldn't be surprised, for after everything that had happened since the children's arrival, nothing was normal. Not anymore.

"Well, well, Mr. Twethewey." She raised her chin high as she swept into the room. She looked down her straight nose in his direction. "We meet again. How long has it been? A decade at least."

The rustling of her taffeta gown was loud in the small chamber, and all he could do was stare at the little dog tucked in the crook of her arm.

He was used to people of all sorts coming into this chamber for one reason or another, and normally he knew just what to say, or at least how to proceed, but he was not sure what to make of the woman whose bonnet boasted an uncanny number of feathers. He stood and leaned to the left to see behind her. Surely her husband was with her, or at least a companion of some sort. But he saw none.

He cleared his throat and bowed. She was, after all, his late sister-in-law's sister. She was no stranger, not really, and a visit was entirely proper. "Mrs. Lambourne. What a surprise."

The tiny dog barked, and she patted his head with her gloved hand before looking at his coat. "Your coat is dirty."

He looked down to the dust on his shoulder and brushed it away. "My apologies. This is a working farm, Mrs. Lambourne. I have been in the fields. I wasn't expecting company."

"Working in the fields? Oh, that will not do."

The small dog barked again, the pitch of it strumming Jac's already tight nerves.

"Don't mind Oscar." She stroked his ear. "He isn't fond of strangers."

A dozen sarcastic retorts bounced in his mind, but instead he muttered, "Please, won't you be seated?" He tugged the bell pull to call for tea and waited for her to be settled in her chair, then sat opposite of her. "It has been a long time, Mrs. Lambourne. What brings you to Penwythe?"

A coy smile curved her lips, and she met his gaze directly. "Come now. Surely my visit isn't that unexpected. I believe my nieces and nephews are here, are they not?"

He shifted uncomfortably. "They are indeed."

"I'm surprised how quiet it is here. Not a child to be seen or heard? Do you have them tucked away somewhere? I assume Mrs. Greythorne is tending them."

"Actually, Mrs. Greythorne is away from Penwythe at the moment. A family illness has called her to her family's home in the south. But she should return in the near future."

"Oh?" Mrs. Lambourne shot him a sour look. "So there is no governess right now? And I heard about that business with the tutor—what was his name? That is very odd. You must be beside yourself."

He shifted, anger rising within him. How exactly did she receive her information? "I assume you're here to visit them."

"Of course I am," she said, almost with a hint of amusement in her voice. "I delayed my visit for as long as respectable. After all, I wanted to give you all time to make the best of this arrangement. But I grew concerned when I heard the reports about Randall's trust. All that money, gone. What odd business that is. I can't imagine what a shock that must have been for you."

His stomach sank. The pompous air about her was nearly as suffocating as the lily-of-the-valley scent that wafted from her. He shouldn't have been surprised that news of the lost trust would spread, especially to her, since she was family. He did not want to discuss it, though. Not with her—not with anyone. "Is your family traveling with you?"

"No. They've remained in London, for I do not intend to stay in the country long. While I am here, I need to see for myself that the children are well tended. I owe that, at the very least, to my late sister. And as you know, I am very great friends with Mrs. Colliver. She has written and tells me that the children have displayed shocking behavior."

He glared at her but pressed his lips shut. *Mrs. Colliver.* Suddenly Mrs. Lambourne's presence here made sense. She had to be referring to Liam's outburst in his early days at Penwythe.

"She also told me that you quite fancy yourself the farmer, growing apples and trees and things. I suppose every man needs a hobby."

He drew a deep breath at the insult, letting it roll off him.

She stood, the fabric of her gown rustling ridiculously loudly, and the dog in her arm growled. She ignored it and paced toward the window. "Death and dying is sad business. But it's a part of life, is it not? And neither of us is a stranger to it. Allow me to be frank, Mr. Twethewey." She turned to face him once again. "You can imagine my surprise to learn that the children were left to your guardianship. My sister had always made it clear that if anything were to happen to them, the children would come to be in my care. I'm not sure what events led to the change in Randall's decision."

"We may never know the reason for that."

"Reason or not, I have great affection for them and have seen them often over the last several years. You've not seen them since Jonathon was born, and he is quite a young man now. So how is it that your brother suddenly changed his mind and altered his will? It makes no sense."

"I asked Mr. Steerhead the same question, and he had no answer."

"Mr. Steerhead is a useless puppet," she snipped. "I'll not say something about a man behind his face that I'd not say directly to him, so I will tell you plainly. The gossip is all over the important circles of London. Randall was supremely wealthy, and now Mr. Steerhead is nowhere to be found. Mr. Steerhead stole every last farthing from Randall, mark my words, and you'll ne'er see any of it. I've also heard about your financial situation. Penwythe is barely surviving as it is, and now the girls have no dowry. And what are you going to do for them? Grow apples and hope for the best? No. No, that will not do. Not for my sister's children."

Her words pricked his pride. Some things may have been out of his control, but he could provide for the children. He was not destitute. Not yet. "Mrs. Lambourne, I understand you are concerned, but everything is under control."

"And you've dismissed Mr. Simon, and Mrs. Greythorne is nowhere to be found?" She ignored his attempt to soothe her. "Oh yes, I know. Mrs. Colliver has kept me apprised of it all. One might think you are allowing the children to run amuck, and Randall never would have approved of such negligence."

His voice grew firmer. "The children are well cared after, and like I said, we expect Mrs. Greythorne will return any day."

"Will she? Do you really think a woman in a paid position such as a governess would come running back when she has family to care for her? What woman would choose that for herself? This is all quite distressing."

He gritted his teeth. "There is no need for you to worry. I think we are doing quite well."

"Quite well?" She shook her head, her earbobs swinging with the motion. "No, no. I propose that the children come and live with me in London for now, and then they can go with us to the country for the winter. Their lifestyle will be much more in line with what they are used to."

The realization of how much he cared for the children ripped through him like a bolt of lightning through a summer sky. They had become a part of Penwythe—a part of him. He was not the same man he was even three months ago, and he never wanted to go back to being that man again.

He fixed his hard stare on her. "The children are staying here."

She opened her mouth to interrupt, but he raised his hand to silence her. "Contrary to what you may think, I do love the children, and they are happy here."

"But consider, you're a young man. Surely you wish to marry one day, to start a family of your own. That would be an adjustment. Don't flatter yourself into thinking that you will breeze through it with nary a care in the world. Think of your future wife. Do you wish to bring her into this?"

Almost as if on cue, the children's voices echoed from the front courtyard, and he glanced out the window. They were walking with Andrews, who was no doubt returning them from their riding lessons.

Mrs. Lambourne pivoted at the sound. "Ah! The children. At least now I will be able to judge their state for myself."

Without waiting for him, she, along with Oscar, swept from the study and made her way through the corridor. He quickened his steps behind her. The heavy door to the entrance hall creaked open, and the children bustled in, all light and laughter. Johnny raced ahead, his face flushed from the day's warmth, and the two younger girls were chattering with each other, each one giggling.

Julia stopped short upon seeing her aunt, and a smile lit her face. "Aunt Beatrice!" She ran to her aunt and threw her arms around her.

Jac watched the others carefully for their reactions. Hannah rushed to Mrs. Lambourne as well, but the boys lagged behind, and Sophy held Liam's hand.

"What a surprise!" exclaimed Julia. "How did you know where to find us?"

"Why, Mr. Steerhead, of course. When I heard of your father's death, I wrote to him straightaway to inquire after you." Mrs. Lambourne took Julia's hand in hers and gently led the children through the great hall to the drawing room, as authoritative and determined as if she were the lady of the home. "Oh, dears, I am so sorry for what you have endured. What a loss! How are you coping?"

Julia glanced at her brothers and sisters. "We are well. All of us. Did you bring Jane with you?"

Jac wasn't sure who Jane was, and it reminded him just how little he knew about the lives of the children entrusted to his care.

"No, she's at home with your cousins. I only came to visit your uncle, and you all, of course."

"Why did it take so long for you to come?"

At Julia's question, Jac winced. Had they been anticipating her arrival? He remained quiet, waiting for her response.

"My darling, I would have come straightaway to comfort you, but I wanted to give you time to adjust here." Mrs. Lambourne looked over to Sophy. "Sophia, come here, child."

Initially Sophy did not release Liam's hand, but after several seconds she dropped her hand to her side and inched forward. After a stiff embrace, Mrs. Lambourne held Sophy at arm's length. "But where are your mourning clothes?"

"Mrs. Greythorne said we could go to half mourning. See the shawl?" She lifted her lace shawl. "It's black."

Mrs. Lambourne tsked. "But it hasn't been long enough!" She shook her head. "Tell me, do you miss Easten Park?"

Her words hung heavy in the air. Jac held his breath.

"Well, do you?" the older woman prompted again.

The children exchanged glances. Johnny leaned against the sofa's arm. "I miss Papa."

Mrs. Lambourne deposited Oscar in Hannah's arms and lifted her brows with excitement. "Tell me, children, wouldn't you like to come with me to London?"

Hannah snapped her eyes toward Jac. "Leave Penwythe Hall?"

"Of course!" Mrs. Lambourne's loud voice filled the room. "You could always visit Penwythe Hall, of course, whenever you wanted to, but London is much more suitable."

Jac wanted to intervene—to make her stop talking about leaving Penwythe. But he remained silent. He wanted to hear their honest responses.

"But Mrs. Greythorne wouldn't know where to find us if we left," Sophy interjected.

Mrs. Lambourne gave her head a sharp shake. "My dears, if you are waiting for Mrs. Greythorne's return to bring you happiness and contentment, you should reconsider. She's an employee, nothing more. Besides, if she really wanted to be with you, she'd be your governess wherever you lived, even in London. Did you not believe your tutor to be loyal, and now where is he? No, my dears, it is best to set your sights and hopes on blood relatives."

Jac's temper simmered at the derogatory words about Mrs. Greythorne. The concern on the children's faces tore at him. Eager to offer the children solace, he said, "Mrs. Greythorne gave her word that she would be back. And she will."

"Oh, and you are a great authority on the absent Mrs. Greythorne, I see." Mrs. Lambourne laughed at her own ill-timed joke and turned toward Liam. "Tell me, has your uncle found you a new tutor?"

Liam flicked his gaze toward Jac. "Not yet. But we have been busy helping Uncle Jac."

"La, child, you are not a common field hand. You are destined for greater things, like your papa."

The words were intended to sting, but Jac would not let them. He could stand no more. He stepped closer and placed a protective arm around Hannah, then put his hand on Liam's shoulder. "Thank you for the offer for the children to join you in London, but they will be remaining at Penwythe. And the decision is final."

CHAPTER 36

Prior to leaving Penwythe Hall, Delia had packed her black mourning gowns in anticipation of the inevitable. Now, more than a week later, the dark fabric felt stiff and scratchy against her skin.

Two days had passed since Elizabeth's death—forty-eight agonizing hours. Her heart was numb, and her head throbbed from all the tears she had shed. After spending weeks in her brother's crowded house, she longed for peace and solitude. So she made her way to the garden.

Roses, wild and untended, grew in the walled yard behind the vicarage, just along the main road and opposite the church. When she'd been young, she and Elizabeth would help their mother tend these very plants on long afternoons. With its walls of ivy-covered gray stone, the garden always seemed like another world. She would often disappear in here when she was younger, and now she wanted to do so to be alone in her grief.

Delia clipped a dead stem from a rosebush that climbed the wall and added it to a pile of debris. Clearly her sister-in-law had neither the time nor the inclination to put forth any effort for the upkeep. The once-vibrant rosebushes were now thin and spindly, yet even so, brave, bold blooms clung to the stems.

She wiped her brow with her forearm and glanced up toward the sun. It was hot, even more than usual, and her black gown added to the heat, but she was not ready to go back inside.

She may have lived on this property at one time, but this modest vicarage, with its paned windows and slate roof just visible above the garden's wall to her left, was clearly no longer her home. She was fond of her brother's family, and they did make her feel welcome, but her heart ached for something familiar.

The Twethewey children entered her mind for the hundredth time. How she missed them. Each child held a tender place in her heart, and a smile crossed her lips as she recalled Sophy's insistent requests to visit the sea. Her smile faded as her thoughts turned to their uncle and the things that had been left unsaid before their last parting.

She clipped another yellow bloom and added it to her basket when the sound of a gate drew her attention. Expecting it to be one of her nieces, she stood and wiped her hand on her work apron. She turned but stopped short.

Thomas Greythorne, his fair hair vibrant from beneath his hat, stood in the gateway, and his brother, Henry, was just behind him.

Panic skittered through her. Had grief conjured a nightmare? No, they were really here. She swallowed and glanced around. She was trapped in this tiny garden.

And alone.

That sickening, sly grin crossed Thomas's face. "Your brother told me we could find you here."

Shock momentarily robbed her of speech. She stared at the brothers—alarmingly alike with their white-blond hair and piercing black eyes. They stood shoulder to shoulder, blocking her path to the garden gate.

She knew what she had to do. She could show no weakness.

Delia shifted her steely gaze from one brother to the other. "Why are you here?"

Thomas smirked. "Come now. You really must work on your hospitality skills. We heard of your sister's death, and we came to support our sister-in-law in her time of grief."

She lifted her chin, ignoring the wind whipping longs strands of hair in her face. "I fear your visit is in vain then, for I'm in no need of support." She raised the hem of her skirt and began to brush past them toward the door, but Thomas caught her by the crook of her arm, halting her. She snapped her gaze upward. "Let go of me, if you please."

The brothers exchanged amused glances, and Thomas dropped her arm.

Clearly they were not going to let her pass.

With a sharp intake of breath, she backed away from them and adjusted her gardening basket on her arm, catching a glimpse of the sunlight reflecting off the shiny metal of her gardening shears. She could use them as a weapon, if need be.

She returned her attention to her brothers-in-law. "It seems you are developing quite a habit of following me, Thomas."

"Not at all." Thomas folded his thick arms over his chest and glowered down at her. "Like I said, we've come to offer our condolences. You will understand that our mother was unable to join us. Although I must say that after all that's transpired, I am surprised to see you here. Given the circumstances around your departure, I mean."

"Of course I came back. My sister is dead." She hardened her gaze.

"So is our brother. And some would argue that you had a role to play in that."

Even after all this time, those words stung, their venom spreading through her with prickly pain.

He stepped closer to her. The scent of brandy laced his breath, and tobacco smoke clung to the linen fabric of his coat. "You never were very good at hiding your thoughts. They write themselves on your face. Like now, for instance, I can plainly see that you want us to leave. We've shown up uninvited and ruined your gardening."

She narrowed her eyes. She needed every ounce of energy she possessed not to shrink back and avert her eyes. Her chin trembled. It could not be helped.

Thomas's eyes gleamed and he shook his head. "That does sting. We are, after all, family. Be that as it may, there is one way to ensure we go away, and you know what that is, don't you, Sister? Simply tell us where *it* is, and we will be out of your life. Forever."

"I've told you repeatedly," she forced through clenched teeth, "I don't know what you're talking about."

"Well then, one of you is a liar, either you or Robert. Who is it?"

She stared at him.

He guffawed. "You've reentered our lives. Out of respect for Robert we were prepared to let you go silently into the night, but your presence here has reignited our desire to find it. After all, it belongs to us."

The full force of his vehemence radiated from his face. "Should you suddenly remember where it is, you know where we can be found." Thomas swatted his brother on the shoulder with the back of his hand, and they turned to leave. Then Thomas stopped and fixed his ebony eyes on her. "We are very patient people, but even we have our limits. We fully intend to find out where Robert hid our property, and as much as you deny it, we know you know. So you have a choice, *Mrs. Greythorne*. This can go smoothly. Or not." A grin slid over his face. "You choose. Again, I'm terribly sorry about your sister."

Delia could no longer bear the stuffiness of the room and the endless line of mourners paying their respects. She needed fresh air, open spaces, and blue sky—even if only for a few hours. There was a task she wanted—nay, needed—to do before she left the southern coast, and now her heart yearned for it.

She needed to visit Robert's and Maria's graves.

Upon her arrival at Whitecross, she had been nervous to do so, for visiting their graves would take her into the heart of Morrisea—right across from the Hawk's Eye Inn—where she might encounter her in-laws. But they knew now she was here.

At first Horace had protested her going to Morrisea, especially alone. But Delia was not used to asking permission to go anywhere or do anything, and she certainly did not need a protector. At length she persuaded him, promising that she would only be gone a short while. He finally relented and allowed her a bit of solitude.

The hot morning sun shone brightly, its brilliance mocking her melancholy mood. Even as she drove her brother's donkey cart along the well-traveled road, fear that the Greythornes may have lingered after their encounter in the garden wound its way around her heart, making her leery of the shadows lurking behind the trees lining the road and the sounds of the birds and animals nearby.

"Fear is an enemy—it will rob you of today's joys and steal your strength to fight for your purpose." Elizabeth's words whispered to her as she traversed the path.

Yes, Delia was fearful.

The weight of it was suffocating her. It was as Elizabeth said—it was robbing Delia of her joy and strength. Whether she felt like it or not, she would try to fight. She owed it to her husband and daughter to visit their resting places.

As she approached the village, Morrisea's familiar sights and scents conjured memories with poignant clarity.

Robert's passion for her, his adoration of her.

Their whirlwind romance.

Maria's birth.

Maria's death.

The searing anguish of loss.

The pain of watching Robert spiral into a completely unrecognizable person—one who would risk life and limb for monetary pursuits and the approval of his family, regardless of how it might hurt those who loved him.

She curved her cart down the winding dirt lane and turned onto High Street, careful not to look in the direction of the Hawk's Eye Inn. She did not want to see it, nor did she want to risk being seen. Mr. Twethewey had said Mr. Simon had entered that establishment, but even if he was still there, she did not want her two worlds to touch.

The graveyard was next to the ancient church that had stood there since before the village had taken root. For decades it had been the only church for miles, and families would travel from far and wide to attend services beneath its slate roof. But now villages and towns were plentiful, and the parish itself was rather small. This was her husband's family's village, and only people associated with or employed by the family remained.

She set the donkey cart brake, grabbed the small bundle of flowers she'd picked before departing, and adjusted her bonnet so it was lower over her face. Even with her vision partially obscured, her feet knew where to go. She'd traversed the tidy footpath so many times through tear-blurred eyes that she knew it by heart—four paces to the left, then twelve to the right. Turn again at the elm tree. And so she did just that and found herself at the head of a tiny grave next to a larger one.

At the sight, sharp, bitter emotions ripped at her heart, and tears that had been held at bay slipped down her cheeks.

How she missed them.

How she longed to feel her daughter in her arms once more, to feel the comfort of her husband's embrace. She was beginning to forget the sensation of both, and that realization stabbed even more.

Time was fleeting. Love was precious.

Now she had plenty of time, but what of love?

Oh, precious love.

One by one, those she held near to her heart had gone away.

She knelt at Maria's grave. Someone had left a smattering of daisies there. She added her wildflowers before she sank to a stone bench near the Greythorne family section. There she sat, staring at the markers in the shade of the grand elm. The warblers chirped in the leafy boughs overhead, and squirrels scurried in the undergrowth around the trees.

She was not sure how much time had passed as she sat there, wrapped in the fading memories, but the sun had shifted in the brilliant blue sky, and the light filtered through the elm at just the right angle that it created lacy patterns on her gown. After her tears were exhausted, she pressed her handkerchief to her face.

She needed to get home.

Her brother wouldn't be happy she had been gone so long.

She found his strictness surprising and stifling. After being the one in charge of things for so long, she found it difficult to comply with his schedules and his demand to know where she was at all times. He was being protective, she knew. He cared about her. But she was no longer a child, and she wasn't ill, like Elizabeth had been.

Drawing a deep breath, she stood, kissed the tips of two fingers, and pressed them to both headstones. The sudden urge to be free from the graveyard pressed against her. The vibrant memories were strong, and now that she was here, they tightened about her, binding her.

She turned toward the road to retrieve her cart. Almost by accident, or perhaps out of curiosity, she glanced toward the Hawk's Eye Inn.

It had not changed much in the intervening years. Not really. It was a long, narrow structure, stretching two stories into the sky, and stood free from those around it. A dusty, dry courtyard separated it from its stable and coach house. A small group of men clustered around the wooden-pole fence that divided the property from High Street, and she quickened her steps to avoid being seen.

"Mrs. Greythorne!"

Delia jumped at the deep baritone voice booming behind her, thick with a country accent and raspy with age. She hurried faster.

The voice called to her again. A shimmer of recognition dawned, and she slowed her pace.

Could it be?

Uneven footsteps lumbered behind her. "Mrs. Greythorne, is that you?"

She halted and turned. "Philip?"

An old man, clad in a shabby tan coat and with unkempt white hair, approached. A broad smile cracked his weathered face, exposing two missing teeth. "Yes, Mrs. Greythorne. 'Tis me. Philip. At your service." He clutched his hat in his wrinkled hands, and he ducked his head in a bow. "Didn't think I'd ever see you again, and it's glad I am to be doin' so."

In front of her stood one of the only people she could say she truly missed from her time at Greythorne House. "Oh, Philip." She smiled at the groundskeeper who'd been such a kind friend to her in the past. "How good it is to see you."

"I heard you was back in the area, what with your sister and all, and I never thought I'd see the day." He squinted in the bright sunlight, and Delia thought for a moment she heard emotion tremble his voice. "When I heard you was here, I thought for sure you'd be comin' to visit your husband and the little one, so I've been stoppin' by the graveyard every day, waitin'."

"Was it you, then, who put the daisies on Maria's grave?"

"Yes, ma'am. The missus took to puttin' flowers there after you left. She did it regular. She's gone now, so I do it for her. I know she'd want me to."

"Your wife is . . . ?"

Philip nodded. "Yes, miss. Two years ago this autumn. She's buried there, under the oak tree."

Genuine sorrow tugged at her as her gaze followed his pointed finger to the graveyard's north edge. Any words she could say felt inadequate, and yet she managed to utter, "I am sorry."

"I don't need to tell you the pain that comes with the loss of a spouse."

She could only nod.

A breeze swept down, rustling the leaves overhead and pushing the hot air downward. "Are you back for good then?"

She shook her head. Even though she had been here only a short time, it already seemed like a lifetime since she hugged each child and bid Mr. Twethewey farewell. "No, Philip, I am not. I'm a governess for a family north of here. I need to return soon."

"Will you be calling out at Greythorne House? I heard Mrs. Greythorne asking after you just this morning."

Delia's heart froze. She could handle seeing Thomas and Henry, but the thought of seeing Ada Greythorne again sent a chill to her very marrow. "After all that has happened, I am not sure I'm welcome at Greythorne House."

Philip did not answer. He, of all people, was well acquainted with the mighty Greythornes. He knew the truth, and like so many others, he was powerless to escape them.

They stood for several moments, their unspoken understanding filling the silence between them. At length she offered a smile. "It really was good to see you, Philip. Thank you for putting flowers on my Maria's grave."

He nodded. "Good day to you, Mrs. Greythorne."

She watched him for but a moment as he lumbered away, then glanced back at the Hawk's Eye Inn. She would need strength as potent as Elizabeth's to survive the rest of her visit, and she breathed a prayer for fortitude.

CHAPTER 37

Jac winced as the dry grass crunched beneath his boots, and he looked up, blinking against the sharp sunlight splintering through the still boughs. The leaves were not brown, not yet, but they hung limp and weak from the branch. He reached out to touch the fruit, noting its small size.

He clicked his tongue and fell into step next to Andrews.

The steward plucked a partially formed apple from the tree and held it close to examine it. "I paid a call over to the Stewarts' orchard yesterday. Trees are as dry and weak as I've ever seen 'em. Their potatoes and turnips are faring a bit better, but they need rain as badly as we do."

Crops all over the area were suffering under the unusual drought, and the Penwythe orchards were no different. "What about the Davies'?"

"I'll call out there tomorrow." Andrews peered through another branch, deeper into the tree, before he returned his attention to Jac. "Word is that they're doing well, but time'll tell, won't it?"

Jac nodded, removed his felt hat to wipe his brow, and looked up at the clear blue sky that boasted nary a cloud.

"The men are bringing buckets up from the pond and watering by hand. For now it will have to suffice, but the trees could use a nice, long soak." Sarcasm dripped from Andrews's huff. "And to think, we were worried that waterlogged soil would be a problem."

"What about having the pigs clear the dropped fruit?" Jac asked as the rotting fruit on the ground captured his attention. "Are the orchards ready for them?"

Andrews nodded. "I know you're uncomfortable with the plan, but Stewart has employed that technique to clear the grounds and dropped fruit for years. We'll work on one orchard at a time." As they walked, Andrew reached in his breast pocket and retrieved a stack of letters. "I meant to give these to you back in the study."

Jac accepted the letters in stride, and as he walked he flipped through the missives. Just as he suspected: a letter to Hannah and a letter to Johnny, written by Mrs. Greythorne's hand. True to her word, she'd written the children. Every day at least one letter arrived for one of them. The children were thrilled, and he was happy for them.

Jac knew better than to expect a letter addressed to him, although he longed for one. It would not be proper for her to write, nor for him to write her. She was, after all, his employee and an unmarried woman. The children had given him updates on her from their letters, but more than anything, he wanted to hear that she would be returning to them soon.

They approached Penwythe's servants' entrance, and Jac led the way in. Once they reached his study, Jac dropped the letters to the desk.

Andrews helped himself to a drink from the side table. "Got a letter from as far away as Devon asking when it would be all right to bring fruit to the cider barn and what the cost would be. Word is spreading. Apparently the barn north of Plymouth was getting too high and mighty and charging a hefty sum."

"Good. We'll need the business." Jac kneaded the back of his neck. "The crusher and cider barn and orchard improvements were costlier than anticipated."

When Andrews didn't comment, Jac straightened his shoulders. "What is it you're not telling me?"

With a sigh, Andrews rounded the desk and lifted the ledger from the drawer. "I was going over the ledgers just yesterday, not just for the farmwork, but for the household too. Like you instructed, we're keeping the money we've already received for the children out of it to use for future expenses. It's not ideal. With five extra bodies and the costs of a governess, the future could be in jeopardy. If the orchards don't produce well, we might not have the resources needed to prepare for next season, and then . . ." He glanced at the floor for a moment, then looked up. "It might be wise to consider selling the north meadow. Both Colliver and Tallack have been eyeing it for some time. Or perhaps you should take Mrs. Lambourne up on her offer to help care for the children."

Jac snapped his gaze toward Andrews and then nodded toward the thick ledger. "Leave it here, will you?"

With a nod Andrews returned the book to the desk and took his leave.

Jac stared at it for several seconds, gathering the will to review it. It was not an option to send the children away, but the sale of the north meadow might be worth considering. He opened the cover when something sparkly caught his attention from the corner of his eye. The sun slid in through the window, and the object winked from beneath the chair just inside the door.

The plank floor creaked beneath him as he crossed the chamber, knelt, reached under the chair, and retrieved the item. It was smooth and cool under his fingers. As he pulled it closer, his breath caught.

Mrs. Greythorne's pendant.

He smoothed his thumb over the lacquer. She'd be happy. Thrilled. Already he anticipated giving it to her and imagined how her face would brighten, how her gray eyes would sparkle, and how her smile would dimple her cheek.

But then Mrs. Lambourne's words rushed to him.

What if Mrs. Greythorne did not return? What if her brother

convinced her that her place was with his family? It had already been a couple weeks. Even if she did return, what would happen if he could not afford to pay her what she had been paid by the trust?

Questions he did not know the answers to bombarded him. The last several days with the children had proven what a large piece of his heart they were claiming, but he could not raise them alone, nor did he want to. No, he didn't want to raise them with anyone but Cordelia.

CHAPTER 38

Liam was just about to close the book he'd been studying when the door to the schoolroom flung open. Julia stood in the doorway, her blue eyes wide and her face as pale as the day Papa died.

"What's the matter?" He frowned, noting the scowl on her face. "You look as if you saw a ghost."

She didn't answer, nor did her countenance brighten. Instead, she shook her head, her curls bouncing, and stomped into the chamber. "Worse."

On the settee Sophy lifted her head from her sewing, her face forming a pout. "What could be worse than a ghost?"

Julia crossed her arms over her chest and dropped to a chair. "I was in the kitchen and overheard something I shouldn't have, and now I wish I hadn't. Mr. Andrews told Uncle that they are running out of money."

"I don't believe it." Hannah's mouth fell open. "Look how grand everything is here."

"It might be grand, but it doesn't mean that Uncle has enough money to pay for it," Liam said, standing from his chair.

Hannah leaned closer. "What else did you hear?"

"Mr. Andrews told Uncle that he thought he should send us to live with Aunt Beatrice because we are expensive and Mrs. Greythorne has to be paid. And all that costs money they don't have. That's all I heard."

"Why didn't you listen harder?" Sophy demanded. "I would have listened harder."

"Young ladies don't eavesdrop, Sophy." Julia tilted her nose upward. "Mrs. Greythorne would be appalled. You know that."

Johnny folded his forearms atop the table and rested his chin on his hands. "What if he sends us away? I don't want to go to London."

Liam stood from the table. Someone had to remain calm. For the sake of his siblings, he'd say the words that needed to be said, even if he didn't genuinely feel them. "Uncle Jac told Aunt that we are staying here. I believe him. You should too."

"But he really likes his orchards. He's been working so hard on them." Hannah's forehead furrowed. "He probably likes them more than he likes us. What if he listens to Mr. Andrews?"

Liam chewed his lip. He'd also heard the servants say as much. Money was important. It had been the item his father's world revolved around: Securing money. Saving money. Spending money. How many times had his father pulled him aside to explain a purchase or acquisition? His father had tried to instill the idea that financial security was the only kind that mattered. Maybe Uncle Jac felt the same way.

"I wish Mrs. Greythorne was here." Johnny sulked. "She'd know what to do."

Hannah cupped her chin in her hand. "What if Aunt was right? What if Mrs. Greythorne doesn't want to come back after going to her home? Maybe she only pretended she cared for us because Mr. Steerhead was paying her to."

"That's ridiculous." Julia's brows snapped together. "And I don't want to hear you say that again. Oh, this is a mess."

Hannah tilted her head thoughtfully to the side. "Perhaps we should talk to Great-Aunt Charlotte about this."

Johnny shook his head, his shaggy dark hair in need of combing. "Don't you think she would tell everything we say to Uncle Jac?"

"Maybe." Hannah shrugged. "But at least she likes us and wants us to stay. I can tell because she gave us extra scones and let us only pretend to do yesterday's reading."

"Maybe we should just ask Uncle Jac," suggested Julia with a shrug. "Then we would know for sure."

"And what if he says it's true?" Hannah's lower lip quivered. "What if he wants to send us away?"

Liam hated hearing his brother and sisters in such uncertainty. Perhaps if he had been better behaved, if he had not lashed out at his uncle on more than one occasion, he'd be more inclined for them to stay.

"No." Liam straightened his shoulders. He was the eldest. He was the man of this family now. It was up to him to put everyone's mind at ease. He may not be able to give the answers they wanted, but he knew who would be able to. "I don't care what Aunt Beatrice says. The only person we can truly count on is Mrs. Greythorne. We need her. And I will go to her."

"Liam, you can't!" Julia shot back, her voice rising.

"Why not?" He shrugged, standing as tall as he could.

Julia tilted her head to the side. "Because you are fourteen and Mrs. Greythorne said it was over twenty miles to where her brother lives. You can't travel that far alone."

"I can." He fixed his jaw. "And I will."

Julia shook her head vehemently. "I'll tell Uncle. It's dangerous, and it—"

Liam stepped around the desk to cut her off. "Do you want to go to London and be trapped inside stuffy schoolrooms all day? At least Uncle likes us. I know he does. Aunt only wants us there because she knows I have an inheritance that will come to me one day. You may not be able to see it, but I do. I'm the one who has to be concerned about these things and make sure you are always taken care of. That's why I should be the one to go."

"How do you know she just wants your inheritance?" Julia's eyes narrowed.

Fighting his reluctance to share what he knew, Liam forced confidence to his voice. "I didn't tell you this because I didn't want to scare you, but I heard the groom talking to the groundskeeper. Don't you wonder why Mr. Steerhead hasn't been here in so long? Before he died, Father put him in charge of all the money, but instead of helping us, Mr. Steerhead took it all for himself. We don't have any money. If Uncle can't afford to keep us, even if he wanted to, we might have to go to Aunt Beatrice's anyway."

"There's no money?" Sophy's eyes grew wide. "What does that mean?"

No one answered. A hush fell over the room, and they sat in silence for several moments.

Hannah twisted her face. "But Mrs. Greythorne's sister just died. You saw the letter. We can't ask her to come back."

"Why not?" Liam slammed his book shut and returned it to the shelf. "If I leave now, Uncle Jac won't even know I'm gone. Not until dinner at least."

"But how will you get there?" Hannah bleated.

"Horseback."

"No!" Johnny shouted. "It's dangerous."

"I'm a good rider. And I will stick to the main roads and go slow. I should be there by nightfall. How hard can it be? I'll ask for directions in the village."

"I don't like it." Julia's gaze bored into him.

"Well, you'll not change my mind." Liam looked around the table. "Are we all in agreement that Mrs. Greythorne needs to know?"

Glances were exchanged and sighs were heaved, but eventually reluctant nods circled the table.

Julia, on the other hand, stood firm. "I think it's a *horrible* idea.

The groom will notice if you take the horse and don't come back. He'll tell Uncle."

Liam scoffed. "They are all far too busy with the new orchard. My mind is made up."

Julia's lips twisted in a frown. She wrapped her arm around Sophy's shoulders. "Fine. If you're determined. But wait here."

The mantel clock ticked the seconds as Julia fled the room and reappeared minutes later with a small pouch. "This is all the money I have. Mind you, I don't think you should go at all. But this is for you. Just in case."

Johnny piped up. "And I will go to the kitchen and sneak some food for you to take. Even if Cook sees me, she won't think a thing of it."

"Good. I'll go down and tell the groom I want a horse for a ride. I'll leave within the half hour." Liam drew a deep breath, his pulse racing and his nerves rattling at the adventure before him. Even so, a deep pride radiated through him. His siblings needed him. And he was going to be there for them.

CHAPTER 39

If only it would rain.

Sweat dripped down Jac's forehead as he exited the cider barn. He blinked it away from his eyes and looked up to the evening sky. Even now, as the purple light of twilight fell over the parched lawns, the previously absent clouds had gathered, but they only whispered a promise of relief. Their thick canopy held the heat prisoner, allowing it neither to rise to the heavens nor to blow away.

If only the clouds would release their grip on the moisture they held within their darkening depths and let the rain flood the ground. A solid soaking would slice through the oppressive mugginess. But it hadn't rained for weeks now. The clouds' iron fists had not relented. Jac didn't think it had rained since Mrs. Greythorne left over a fortnight ago.

Mrs. Greythorne. The thought of her was plaguing him. He cut across the lawn, the dehydrated grass crunching beneath his boots. Not knowing when—or if—she'd return was haunting his waking moments and invading his dreams. The children, too, were missing her. They'd received letters from her, of course, but they had been safe, simple letters with stories of the cat in the shed or flowers in the garden. Her absence draped a listless blanket over them all, and that, coupled with the lack of rain, threatened to drive him mad.

Never had control been further from his grip. He hated it. He felt like a horse tethered and chomping at the bit, but even if he was given his head, he didn't know how to make the rain fall or convince Mrs. Greythorne to return home.

He thought of her at the oddest times. This strange mix of the Hawk's Eye Inn and Mr. Simon and the stolen trust and Mr. Steerhead swirled around him—a bitter brew, one probably better left alone—and with each day that passed, the unsettled feeling within his chest gripped tighter.

And at the center of it all was Mrs. Greythorne.

She had been another man's wife. Loved another man. Borne another man's child. Lived another life.

If she did indeed return, it would be solely for the children.

He repeated that to himself time and time again. He dared not even consider that she might regard him in any way other than as the children's guardian. Yet the glimmer of tears in her eyes the night she'd lost the pendant burned itself into his brain. He wanted to be the person to permanently erase all of her sadness, if he could.

Suddenly a sharp breeze swept from the slate roof, and something warm and wet hit his cheek. And then his hand.

He lifted his eyes to the churning sky.

Rain. Beautiful, nourishing, warm rain was falling—a balm long overdue.

Hope trickled through him, reaching to his fingers, his toes. He jogged back toward the house, and with each step the storm intensified. By the time he finally gripped the handle on the servants' door, the rain fell in sheets, and that, mixed with the evening's growing blackness, made it difficult to see where he was going.

When Jac entered the study, Andrews was already there lighting a candle with a flint. He grinned as the candle's flame leapt to life. "About time we got some rain, eh?"

Jac shook the wet coat from his shoulders and spread it over the back of a chair to dry. "Let's hope it keeps up. What are you doing?"

"Scheduling. The earliest apples should be ready in September.

The cider barn should be full throughout October and maybe even into November. After that the cider that is stored here will need to be tasted."

Jac nodded and stepped to the window. The rain appeared like a sudden squall from the sea that rushed the banks and then subsided. The wind howled and groaned, shaking the windowpanes. He looked heavenward. He'd been anticipating rain for days, and now that it was here, he should be happier. But the wind sounded different. The rain sounded hard. Suddenly a loud *plink* came from the window—like the sound of a small pebble hitting it. And then another. And another.

Alarmed, Jac jerked toward Andrew, who had jumped to his feet. *No.*

No, no, no, no!

"Hail!" Jac breathed, barely able to force his voice out above a whisper.

The men stared at each other, both knowing the implications.

It was the one thing he had dreaded. The trees had avoided insects and even survived the dry conditions, but this?

Jac raced toward the servants' door and flung it open. Rain drove into his face, and the wind smacked icy bits of moisture against his cheek and pounded the linen of his shirt. But there could be no mistaking it—perfectly formed round balls of ice pummeled the ground, then bounced up with animated vigor.

Jac stepped out into it and started to run across the lawn, but Andrews followed and grabbed his arm. "What do you think you can do for the crops? More likely you'll get knocked senseless with the hail. It might as well be rocks falling from the sky."

Andrews was right. Jac returned to the corridor and paced like an animal caged. The hailstorm seemed to last an eternity—every second, every breath that passed would spell disaster for the tender fruit still maturing on the branches. He turned his eyes toward the still-open door, watching the white ice attack.

He'd not panicked about the summer's odd situations—about the changes in his plans or the depleted trust. He'd comforted himself with the thought that he always had his orchards to fall back on. But now all of it was threatened. All of it.

Footsteps echoed down the corridor, sounding more like a stampede than children. Sophy reached him first. She lunged toward him, her face shiny with tears and eyes wide with alarm. "What is that? What is it?"

He picked up her trembling frame in his arms, and she hid her face in his shoulder. Somehow he managed to get words to pass through his dry mouth. "It's hail."

"When will it stop?" she shouted, her words nearly blotted out by the seemingly endless deluge of ice hitting the house. A window broke somewhere. And then another. The eerie tinkling of glass tumbling to the floor sounded over the pinging ice. Hannah screamed and Sophy tightened in his arms.

"I want Mrs. Greythorne!" Sophy sobbed.

He looked around at their shadowed faces. All wide eyed. All frightened, even Julia. He put an arm around Johnny and drew him close. "It will be over soon."

And just like that, the pounding stopped. The noise shifted from the sharp ping of ice on glass to the patter of rain.

Relief broke their serious expressions, and then he noticed an absence. "Where's Liam?"

The children exchanged glances, the whites of their eyes bright in the dark corridor. He was no expert on children, but he was learning, and they were up to something.

Jac knelt and returned Sophy to the floor. When they did not respond, he repeated, "Where's Liam?"

Growing frustrated, he propped his hands on his hips. "Either someone tells me now where Liam is or—"

"He went to get Mrs. Greythorne."

"What?" Perhaps one of the balls of hail had struck him on the head a bit too hard when he'd run out onto the lawn. The words sounded ridiculous, and yet the somber expression on Julia's face hinted that she was in earnest. "What do you mean, he went to get Mrs. Greythorne?"

Julia stepped closer. "We were afraid you were going to send us to live with Aunt Beatrice. We wanted her back. So he went to fetch her."

Anger shot through him, trailed by frantic concern. He whipped his head to look through the open door. It was black now. The hail had ceased, but rain still pounded the lawn. Breathless, he whirled back around. "When did he leave?"

Julia swallowed in obvious hesitation. "Late this morning."

"How did he get there?"

"A horse."

Dread sank in his stomach. The boy was a fair horseman, but the journey could be a difficult one—not to mention a long one. Liam would be riding through open moors. Through rocky terrain. Jac had to go get him.

"I want all of you to return to your chambers, is that clear?"

"Why? Where are you going?" cried Johnny, eyes wide.

"To get your brother."

CHAPTER 40

In a rush Jac flew through Penwythe. Heart pounding, pulse racing, he grabbed his oilskin coat and wide-brimmed hat and tossed a change of clothing into a satchel. He reached for his pistol, thinking how dangerous it could be to traverse Cornwall's roads at night, especially in the south. All the while his mind created horrific thoughts of what dangers could befall a fourteen-year-old boy on such a ride.

He bid the children farewell, gave them last-minute instructions to mind Mrs. Bishop and not to leave the property, and then met Andrews, who had his best horse saddled and ready for him.

"Want me to go with you?" Andrews had saddled a horse for himself.

"No. I need you to stay here and assess the damage to the orchards. Hopefully this hail was localized. We won't know for sure until the light of day."

"I'll ride with you to the main road then. We'll pass the east orchard and can check it on our way out. I've already sent Willoughs and Johnson out to assess the others as best they can in the darkness."

"What could Liam possibly have been thinking?" Jac said as he did his best to guide his horse through the puddles on the now-soft road.

"I'm sure he'll be fine. He's fourteen."

Jac shook his head. "No, he's *only* fourteen. How does he even know where he's going?"

It didn't take long to reach the east orchard. Jac slid off his horse before the animal even came to a complete stop and stumbled across the spongy ground until he reached the first tree. He grabbed the first fruit he saw and held it close to examine it.

His heart lurched.

Gash marks had sliced through the tender green skin. He turned it over in his hand.

He snatched another apple. Then another. Those, too, bore the dents and ripped flesh of hail's damage. He gripped the apples tight and then let them fall to the ground. They were useless now. They were not mature enough to pick, and with wounds like this, they would be ripe for insects and disease. They would need to be removed.

He looked down the black row. Were they all like this?

He stood in the silent night. The rain was little more than a drizzle now. The wind had calmed. The waterlogged leaves hung limply from their battered branches. The beaten fruit gathered in pockmarked balls at his feet.

But as he stared at the apples mingling with the thawing hail, his heart and thoughts turned to Liam. The boy was what was important in this moment. The apples and the orchards would have to wait until he was certain the boy was well.

After instructing Andrews to oversee the orchards, Jac took off down the south road with fresh determination pulsing through his veins.

———◆———

Night had fallen over the vicarage in Whitecross, and rain fell in soft, gentle waves against the modest home.

The melodic, soothing rain was refreshing. Weeks had passed with little more than a sprinkling, and a relentless humidity had plagued the area. Even now, Delia and her brother were seated in the low-ceilinged sitting room after the children had retired for bed, listening to the rain's rhythmic tapping. The candle's light flickered on her needlework, but she could barely concentrate on the task. Her stitches slowed as she wondered if it was raining at Penwythe Hall.

She found herself thinking of the estate a great deal. It crept through the cracks of her simplest thoughts. The vicarage gardens reminded her of Hannah and her love of flowers. The paintings on the walls brought to mind Mrs. Angrove. And so many times her heart turned to Mr. Twethewey and their unfinished conversation. Her mind had mapped out what subsequent conversations could be like. But the more time that lapsed, the more unreachable those memories seemed.

She glanced up. Round spectacles were balanced on the bridge of her brother's nose, and he had the newspaper angled close to his face. His pipe balanced between his fingers, the smoke curling up, and the candle's light flickered odd shapes on his freshly shaven cheek.

She frowned, realizing this was one of the only times that she and Horace had been alone since she arrived. When she first stepped foot in the vicarage, all focus had been on Elizabeth, and in the days after her death, an endless processional of visitors and mourners demanded attention. Now Elizabeth was buried. All things related to her were settling down, but instead of a feeling of relief, a sense of discomfort descended upon her.

When Delia looked at Horace, she glimpsed evidence of the boy he had been. He was plumper now, and his hair was thinner, but there was still that thread of somberness that had been part of his countenance since they were children. So many times over the last years she had thought of him, but instead of fond remembrances, bitterness had crept in.

He'd given his permission for her to marry Robert. He'd encouraged it. She'd been too young, too innocent to know of the rumors surrounding the Greythorne family, but he had known them. It had been her decision to marry Robert, of course, but never did he voice a concern or share what he knew about the family's reputation. The only explanation she could conjure for his silence on the matter was that he no longer wanted to be responsible for her care. Now she was independent, but her heart still hurt at the rejection she'd felt.

He looked up, and when he saw her peering at him, he lowered the newspaper. He removed his spectacles. "I'm glad we're alone now, for I'd like to speak with you."

Trepidation crept in at the weightiness of his tone. "What would you like to talk about?"

"Penwythe Hall."

She sucked in a breath and stiffened her spine. "What about it?"

"I don't think you should go back."

Ghostly silence prevailed. His words seemed to echo as if they had been shouted.

"You can live here, in Whitecross." He continued when she did not respond. "With us, of course. Your chamber is available now, and I know Mary could use your help with the children. Wouldn't you rather share your talents with your relations? Besides, we can always use help with parish responsibilities. There are so many ways you can share your gifts with others."

At his words, her chest tightened, and the beating of her heart intensified. She'd anticipated this conversation, but she was not prepared for it so soon. Though his words sounded kind, helpful even, she wondered whose best interest he had in mind.

She stared down at her hands. They looked gray and pale in the low light. Over the past weeks she'd considered what it would be like to live in Whitecross again after such a long absence, but her life was different now, *she* was different, and the vicarage was nothing like the childhood home she remembered. Independence had changed her, and after having to answer to her brother nearly every time she stepped out the door since her arrival, she knew she could never go back.

"You're awfully quiet," he said, shattering the silence. "I know it probably doesn't sound very enticing to live here, but consider, Delia. You'd never be alone. There are people here you have not met. Men here you have not met. There is a future for you here. Maybe even a family."

Her face and ears grew hot. She recalled Mrs. Angrove saying similar words, but the tone had been so different. Mr. Twethewey flashed in her thoughts. It was possible for her heart to love again, she knew. She'd felt the glimmer of it, but at the moment, Penwythe Hall seemed so far away, and her past seemed so near.

CHAPTER 41

Delia was just about to retire for the night when a faint knock sounded at the door.

Mary, who had just joined Delia and Horace in the drawing room, glanced up from her sewing, a frown marring her round face, and fixed her tired eyes on her husband. "Are you expecting someone at this late hour?"

"Not that I know of." Horace lowered his pipe. "Must be a parishioner or the like." He waved off the approaching maid and rose to answer the door himself. He disappeared into the entry hall, and the door creaked open.

A young voice echoed, "Is Mrs. Greythorne here?"

Before the sentence had been fully uttered, Delia, spurred to action by the familiar voice, jumped from her chair and ran to the door. "Liam?" she cried, breathless, as she rounded the corner, clipping her shoulder on the threshold.

Horror raced through her when she saw the boy—her Liam—standing in the door frame against the black of night. His wet clothes clung to him. No hat covered his head, and his ebony hair stuck to his forehead and temples in thick locks.

She pushed Horace aside and took Liam by the shoulders, all the while studying his face. "How did you get here? Why are you here?" She pulled him inside, ignoring the rainwater that splashed from his coat and boots to the wooden floor. She grabbed a shawl from the nearby peg and wrapped it around him. "Is it Sophy? Hannah?"

Without waiting for a response, she guided him onto the sofa, and he blinked away the rain and looked around the modest room before he fixed his attention on her. "We need you to come home. Aunt Beatrice visited, and we're afraid she is going to take us to London."

With a shaky sigh of relief, Delia lowered her shoulders.

Nothing was wrong. Not seriously.

Her tense muscles relaxed, and she dropped to a nearby chair to look him more fully in the face. Dirt smeared his wet cheek, and his wet hair was tangled. Her heart swelled with affection for this young man who had been in her care for so long. He was such a protective young man, so she was not surprised that he'd act on behalf of his siblings, but as he sat on the sofa, she saw the little boy she'd met when she first arrived at Easten Park. He was fiddling with the cuff of his soaked coat and he bit his lower lip, something he often did when he felt ill at ease.

"Tell me what happened."

Liam glanced to Mary and then up to Horace over her shoulder. He drew a deep breath and then pivoted to face her. "Aunt Beatrice wants us to live with her in London. We heard Uncle Jac and Mr. Andrews talking about money, and we are worried they will send us to live with her. We don't want to go. We didn't know what to do. So I came to find you."

Understanding began to dawn. The children were perceptive, and the thought that they might feel unwanted broke her heart. "Does your uncle know you are here?"

He shook his head slowly, looking down at the rug covering the floor.

She drew a sharp breath, and the realization that Mr. Twethewey must be beside himself with worry trickled through her. "You shouldn't have come all this way without your uncle's permission."

"I know, but the children were *scared*. And they were afraid you weren't going to come back."

She tilted her head. "Why would they think I'd not come back?"

"Aunt said the only reason you were kind to us is because Father paid you, and now that the trust is in trouble—"

"How do you know about that?"

"Everyone is talking about it. I first heard it from the groom in the stable the other day."

"Liam, did you talk to your uncle about any of this? All of it probably could have been avoided by a simple conversation. I think you'd find that he does care for you very much. All of you." She paused to take a breath. "How did you get here?"

"I rode a horse."

"All this way?" She huffed in disbelief. "The horse must be exhausted. Where is it now?"

"He's tied outside. I promise, I wouldn't have come if you weren't needed."

"Well, first thing tomorrow you must go back. I'd wager your uncle is frantic at your absence. Do you not see how dangerous this was?"

The boy bit his lip, and his eyes were red rimmed. Regret filled his face, so she softened her tone and stood. "Come, let's see to the horse and get you out of these wet things. A good night's sleep will set this all to right."

———◆———

Rain dripped from the brim of Jac's hat and slid down the back of his collar. He pounded on the vicarage door. Again. Why would no one answer? It was the midnight hours, but still, he was making enough noise to wake the dead.

The horseback ride had been difficult. Rain—precious rain—had plagued him nearly the entire way. He'd had to be very careful. Water flooded parts of the road. He was cold. Tired. But most of all, he was worried sick. He pounded on the door again and shifted his weight from foot to foot, stretching his muscles.

The door did not open.

He cupped his hands around his eyes and peered through the window next to the door. All looked dark, but this had to be the correct place. The vicarage next to the church in Whitecross.

He raised his gloved fist and pounded again. What would he do if he couldn't find Liam?

The possible scenarios of what could have happened to the boy flashed before him, twisting his stomach and squeezing his heart.

Sudden commotion sounded from behind the wooden door. He jerked his head up, and hopeful anticipation flickered.

Horace Abbott, dressed in a dressing gown and nightcap, answered the door.

"Mr. Twethewey." He blinked at him sleepily, like an owl from above his spectacles. "I thought we'd see you soon."

"I'm looking for my nephew," rushed Jac. "I believe he came here searching for Mrs. Greythorne."

The man stepped backward, rubbed his face, and opened the door farther. "Come in, Twethewey. No need for alarm. The boy is here, safe and sound."

Relief warmed within him. Liam was here. Safe.

He took a deep breath to ward off the frustration flooding him. What could the boy have been thinking?

Jac swept his hat from his head, careful not to let the rain fall to the floor, and ducked his head through the low doorway. The rooms were dark, given the lateness—or rather earliness—of the hour, but when he turned, he saw that a small cluster of people had gathered. Abbott's family, no doubt.

"My apologies." He nodded in their direction. "I didn't mean to wake you."

Footsteps sounded on the stairs behind the gathering, and another face—a much more welcome one—appeared.

Mrs. Greythorne.

At the sight of her, a peaceful calm washed over him.

She stepped purposely through the group. A long black shawl was wrapped around her shoulders, and her hair was gathered in a thick, long braid that fell in front of her shoulder. The light from her candle flickered on her smooth cheek, highlighting her dimple and her eyelashes.

Liam had been his focus for the entire ride, through the rain and dark of night. The boy's safety had been paramount. But now that he knew Liam was safe, the tension pinching Jac's shoulders eased. Her very presence was a balm, and she hadn't even said a word.

"Liam's here, isn't he?" Jac whispered as she drew near.

She nodded, her eyes wide. "He came to see me. I am sorry he worried you."

Further commotion in the hall drew his attention, and he looked up to see Liam standing there, hair mussed, white shirt untucked from his trousers. He approached cautiously, as if Jac were a snake ready to strike.

But at the sight of the boy, all frustration and anger fled.

Liam was alive and well, but his eyes were red with tears. "I'm sorry, Uncle Jac, really I am. I—"

Jac took two large steps forward and embraced the boy, mindless of his wet clothes. After several seconds he released Liam and held him at arm's length. "Don't do that again! I've never been so worried, thinking about what tragedy could have befallen you."

Liam's eyes flicked to Mrs. Greythorne and then back. "But Julia heard you. You and Mr. Andrews want to send us away."

Jac swallowed hard. He glanced up and saw all eyes fixed on

him. He did not like having his personal business on display, yet he needed to clear this up once and for all. "Listen to me, and listen well. I don't know what Julia heard. But you're not going to London. Not a single one of you. You all belong at Penwythe Hall, and that is where you'll stay."

He softened his tone. "The Twetheweys have been through a great deal the past several months, haven't we? It's not been easy, but nothing worth having ever is. You have my word, and I'll never go back on it. You and your brother and sisters will always have a home at Penwythe. Always."

CHAPTER 42

D elia lay in her bed, awake. Her two worlds had collided hopelessly, and she wasn't sure what to make of it.

The rain still pelted down, and the steady, staccato rhythm,
which initially was such a source of peace, now added to her tension.
When sleep would not come, she rose and paced her small chamber,
trying to organize the thoughts and feelings churning within her.

Mr. Twethewey was here, in the vicarage, just one floor below.
He'd not come all this way to see her, of course, but he was here
nonetheless.

After uncle and nephew had reunited, Liam returned to the cot
in the kitchen where he had bedded down for the night, and Mr.
Twethewey had accepted the invitation to sleep on the drawing
room sofa.

She imagined Mr. Twethewey was tired. Both he and Liam were.
Her carriage ride alone was unpleasant. How much worse would it
be on horseback? Despite the exhaustion Mr. Twethewey must be
feeling, she felt she knew him well enough to know that he was not
asleep.

Not here. Not now.

Mr. Twethewey had said little when he arrived, but one thing
he had said caught her attention: the children would always have a
home at Penwythe.

Perhaps it was being here in her childhood home—the place

where she first learned to dream—but oh, the sight of him after more than a fortnight of separation had awakened something in her heart. Her stomach quaked nervously, and she paced the room like a giddy schoolgirl.

The next morning, as soon as filmy light crept across the heavens, Delia rose and began her preparations for the day. She wanted to speak with Mr. Twethewey before the rest of her family woke. She dressed quickly, feeling a little foolish for taking extra care with her gown selection and how she arranged her hair. She caught a glimpse of her face in the looking glass as she prepared to leave the chamber. She looked pale. She pinched her cheeks for color and then headed downstairs.

All was quiet except for morning sounds coming from the kitchen. One of the servants had made coffee, and the smell wafted to her. She paused near the door to the drawing room and held her breath. The sound of a newspaper rustling caught her attention.

Her heart leapt within her. She went to the kitchen, assembled a tray of coffee, and bit her lower lip as she made her way to the drawing room. Mr. Twethewey looked up as she entered. He was seated on the edge of the sofa, newspaper in hand, blue eyes bright in the dawning light.

Heat rushed to her face. "I thought you'd be awake."

He chuckled but said nothing. He only pushed his fingers through his still-damp hair. He stood, the shadowed stubble on his chin and jawline making him seem approachable.

There was something comforting about his nearness. His manner was relaxed. He'd borrowed dry clothes from her brother. The fit was terrible, but even so, he was handsome.

"I thought you might need this." She set the coffee tray on the table.

"Ah, you're right." He accepted the cup she offered. "Thank you." He took a drink and returned to the sofa where he had been sitting.

"I am sorry to intrude on your family like this. I have no idea what would make Liam act in such a fashion."

"It's no intrusion. Everyone is just happy Liam is safe and sound." Delia sat on the settee opposite, under the room's front window. She took advantage of the early-morning light to study him. He wore no cravat. The corded muscles in his neck tightened with each movement. His square jaw was clenched, his eyes bright, even in the pale light.

"It could have been disastrous." He slowly rubbed the rim of the cup with his thumb. "That ride through the moors is treacherous. My horse stumbled a handful of times. I'm surprised he made it. I never could have forgiven myself if something had happened to him."

"Liam may be only fourteen, but he's resourceful." She reached for the shawl she had left on the sofa the previous evening and wrapped it around her shoulders. "You left the other children well?"

He nodded, stretching out one booted leg before him. "They are confused by everything that has happened, but they are well. And they miss you." His expression sobered. "They are not the only ones who miss your presence at Penwythe Hall."

Her eyes flashed upward, her gaze locking with his. "I—I have missed you all as well."

He surprised her by standing. He moved from his chair and sat next to her on the settee.

Her heart was wild in her chest now, beating and thudding as if she'd run a race. He smelled of rain and weather, of wildness and the moors. It was intoxicating. Suddenly after the long days of feeling restless and sad at her family home, a reviving strength surged through her—purpose and desire were intermingled.

She wished things could be different—that he was not a guardian and she was not a governess—that they had met at another time and under different circumstances. She recognized the passion in his eyes, even though it had been years since someone looked at her that way.

He felt it too. Surely he did. The inexplicable thread that bound them to each other, that grew tighter with time and experience. They'd been acquainted for over two months, but had she not established her feelings for Robert in much less time?

"I almost forgot." He stood, crossed the room, and retrieved something from the pocket of his coat. He returned to the settee and sat near her—so near she could feel the warmth radiating from him. He leaned his elbows on his knees and carefully unwrapped the item.

Her pendant.

Maria's hair.

A gasp choked from her. Her hands flew to her face, and tears blurred her vision. She took the piece from him. Her most precious keepsake. Relief mixed with gratitude, yet everything around her seemed to slow. She clutched it close to her chest. "You found it."

"It was in my study. Somehow it must have come loose from the chain."

She shook her head, unable to tear her gaze from the jewelry. "I—I don't know how to thank you."

He smiled and covered her free hand with his own warm one. "You already have." He inched closer to her.

At his closeness, talk of death and trusts and betrayal and orchards fled her mind. It was just the two of them in the cool morning shadows, basking in the warmth and glow of words both said and unsaid. His presence made her feel a strength that had been missing for some time. It made a broken part of her soul feel whole again.

She wanted him to say more, and yet she didn't. How she wanted this feeling of security and happiness and hopefulness to endure. She wanted to hear her name on his lips. His thumb rubbed the top of her hand, and in this moment she knew that, for better or for worse, their relationship would never be the same.

CHAPTER 43

Later that morning, Delia was both pleased and anxious when the Twethewey men joined the Abbott family for breakfast.

The rain continued to fall steadily, now as if to mock them, and dark storm clouds blotted the sun. The occasional strike of lightning flashed brightness into the gray room, and at distant intervals thunder rolled, deep and unsettling.

Despite the rain, the conversation was cheery inside the Abbott breakfast room. A generous basket of bread and fruit sat atop the table. Poached eggs and ham were on a platter. The Abbott children were curious about their guests, and Liam was eager to share the story of his journey. Mary was a polite and gracious hostess, but her brother's sternness was less than inviting.

Horace said very little during the meal and glowered at Mr. Twethewey as if the man had done something—or was about to do something—wrong. Mr. Twethewey didn't seem to notice. In fact, she would glance his way to find his gaze on her, warm and kind, and a thrill surged through her.

Horace drew a deep breath, the suddenness of which attracted the attention of the table. He leaned heavily on the table with his elbows and stared at Mr. Twethewey. "What are your plans from here?"

His harsh words sliced the merry tone of the breakfast, and Delia lowered her napkin.

Unfazed, Mr. Twethewey shifted in his chair. "I'd like to return to Penwythe as soon as possible. There was some storm damage and it needs to be addressed."

"Storm damage?" Delia frowned. "What happened?"

"A hailstorm just before I left. I'm still not sure how much damage was done."

Delia's stomach sank. She'd heard the workers talking about the devastating effect such a summer storm could have on the tender fruit. The beautiful apple orchards. "I had no idea."

Mr. Twethewey glanced toward the window. "We'll wait until the rain clears, and we'll need to hire a carriage. I've no wish to repeat that rocky ride on horseback. Do you, Liam?"

A strange sense of panic raced through her at the thought of them leaving.

Mr. Twethewey continued. "I've no wish to trespass on your hospitality further, Mr. Abbott. Is there a nearby inn where Liam and I can stay until arrangements can be made?"

"There's the Widow's Crest, just a town over, and then there is the Hawk's Eye Inn, but I'd not recommend it."

She jerked at the mention of the Hawk's Eye, shocked he would speak of it knowing its history as he did.

Unperturbed, Mr. Twethewey lowered his napkin to the table. "I'm sure the Widow's Crest will be suitable."

At the suggestion that the Twetheweys would be departing, Horace's demeanor brightened. "You could probably hire a carriage from there as well and be back at Penwythe within the day."

She figured that most men would bristle at her brother's tone, but a comfortable grin crossed Mr. Twethewey's lips. He looked at her. "Mrs. Greythorne, I am not sure what your plans are, but you're welcome to return with us. The children would be happy to see you, and I'd hate the thought of you making the return journey alone."

The weight of her brother's stare slammed into her. Heavy.

Expectant. She'd never given him an answer as to whether she would stay or return to Penwythe. She drew a deep breath. "Thank you, Mr. Twethewey. I—I shall let you know."

Horace stood, scraping his chair loudly against the floor and disturbing his silverware. She jerked at his sudden movement. Color flushed his round face, and he pushed his spectacles up on his nose. "Mr. Twethewey. I'd be happy to escort you personally to the Widow's Crest, but first, may I have a word? Privately."

Jac's steps slowed as he followed the vicar to a small study off of the drawing room and stepped inside. Like the rest of the house, the room was plain. The only items of significance were a large bookshelf on the far wall, a single window overlooking the garden, a large oak desk anchored in the middle of the room with two smaller chairs opposite it, and three silhouettes hanging in plain wooden frames.

Abbott nodded to the chair. "Be seated. I want to talk with you."

Jac did as he was bid. The chair groaned painfully loudly in the silent room. How on earth could a house with three children be so quiet? He looked toward his unwitting host. "Yes?"

Abbott leaned back in his chair and stared at a point on the ceiling for several seconds before he refocused on Jac. The vicar's somber expression made Jac feel almost like a child about to be scolded.

"Mr. Twethewey, my sister is a grown woman. She's a widow. A mother. She's seen more life than most women her age, and I know she's quite independent. Be that as it may, she is still my sister, my *unmarried* sister, and she has found her way back to my home. I am sure it comes as no surprise to you that I do not approve of my sister's presence at Penwythe Hall."

Jac narrowed his eyes. Abbott's words were strikingly similar to what he'd said at Penwythe Hall. Jac adjusted his position and prepared for a similar conversation. "You object to her being a governess?"

"We've been through this." He huffed in obvious annoyance, leaning forward on his elbows on the desk. "I'm not sure why your boy is traveling across Cornwall alone, nor do I wonder why you are thundering after him. But this is all quite unusual, and it does not bode well with me. I daresay it wouldn't with most people. You've managed to cast some sort of spell over my sister, and I don't think it proper."

Jac shook his head. "I am not sure what you are referring to, but I—"

Abbott lifted his hand for silence. "Out of respect for the kindness you have shown my sister up until now, I feel it right to inform you that Cordelia will not be returning to Penwythe."

The words sliced through Jac, yet he did not so much as flinch. "That's for her to decide, is it not?"

"She has a home here now. I've already told her that her place is here."

"And if she does not comply?"

The men locked eyes. Jac had no wish to go up against a man of the cloth, but he also would not be pushed around or stand idly by while the man coerced Mrs. Greythorne.

Abbott stood from the desk. "Circumstances have changed here, sadly, but they've changed nonetheless. Cordelia has endured scandal before, and no doubt once word gets out about your midnight visit here—and it will get out, for news such as this always does—she will once again be the object of town gossip. Yes, word travels fast, even here in sleepy Whitecross, and I'll not have it. I've watched the way you look at her, Twethewey. The way you speak with her. I know about men in your position, and I'll not allow her to be taken advantage of."

Jac winced, slightly taken aback. "I'm not taking advantage of her."

Abbott rounded the table. "Do you mean to tell me that you have feelings for my sister? That the flirting and long glances are sincere? I doubt it, Twethewey, for what can she give you? She has no money, no social standing."

Jac stood to match Abbott's stance. "I appreciate your concern, I do, but your sister's virtue is quite safe. And as for whether or not she returns to Penwythe, again, that is for her to decide."

"Perhaps I have not made myself clear." Abbott stepped forward. "No good can come from her presence there, and I will not see her heart broken—not again. You will leave my sister alone, and that is final."

CHAPTER 44

Delia watched Mr. Twethewey adjust Liam's stirrups and then stood back as the boy mounted the large black horse.

The rain had dwindled, and now just a humid drizzle fell. The clouds were thinning. No longer were they thick and impenetrable. Intermittent sunlight would find its way through the shallow places.

When Mr. Twethewey turned back around, the warmth that had radiated from him at breakfast was gone. Something had happened while he was speaking in private to Horace. The lack of expression on his face reminded her of her first days at Penwythe when he was indifferent. Distant.

And it tore at her.

He stepped toward his hosts and extended his hand toward Horace. "Thank you again for your hospitality. I'll not forget it."

Mr. Abbott shook Jac's hand but said nothing.

For a moment she felt a bit of panic thinking they would leave without addressing her, but then he pivoted to face her. His expression did not change. "Mrs. Greythorne, I'm going to hire a carriage and will send word regarding our plans. I anticipate, if the weather continues to brighten, that we will depart for Penwythe in the morning. My offer still stands if you should choose to return to Penwythe Hall with us. The children are eager for their schedules to return to normal. You'll hear from us soon."

She nodded, stepped toward Liam, and patted his horse's neck.

She looked up at the boy and smiled. With circles beneath his eyes, he seemed as tired as she felt. The past day had been taxing on everyone, and even his energy and youth could not spare him from the sensation. "Be safe, Liam. Listen to your uncle."

Liam lowered his voice. "Are you coming with us?"

She swallowed the lump in her throat and looked back. Mr. Twethewey's cool expression had not softened. "I'm not sure quite yet, but do not fret over it. Everything will be normal again soon."

Liam leaned down over the saddle. "I'm sorry for causing so much trouble. I didn't mean to do so."

She patted his hand and offered a smile. Oh, how her heart went out to this sweet child. "Don't give it another thought. I am honored you think me worthy of such a journey."

Mr. Twethewey mounted his horse. With a click of his tongue, the horses were set in motion toward the main road that would lead to the next village.

With the guests gone, Mary turned to enter the house. Delia moved to follow suit, but Horace caught her arm. "Be careful."

She jerked to a stop and turned to face him.

"I see the way he looks at you, and the way you look at him. Be careful, Cordelia."

She sighed but did not respond.

He dropped his hand. "You've had your fair share of tragedies in life. More than most, I reckon. You are not naive and you've always been reasonable. But even reasonable people can be taken advantage of."

"I'm not being taken advantage of here." Her attempt at a careless laugh sounded forced, even to her own ears.

"Men like Twethewey, wealthy men, prey on women in your situation. And before you disagree with me, listen. You can't have a future with a man like that. It would never be. They do not marry governesses. I know you care a great deal for those children, but I care a great deal for you. They're not your family, and they never will be. Your family is here. I want you to live here, with us. Renew your life where you can make real friendships and have a real chance for a future. It hurts me to think of you caring for someone else's family when you could possibly start one of your own."

Delia could not believe what she was hearing. "Do you really think me so incapable of managing my life? Of knowing my own feelings?"

"You've been hurt in the past, and I don't want to see you hurt again."

She stiffened as her anger intensified. If he really didn't want to hurt her, he would've shared what he knew about the Greythornes before she married into the family all those years ago.

Be that as it may, she did know one thing: this was not where her heart was.

She swallowed. "Horace, that is very generous and thoughtful of you. As much as I love you and your family, I cannot stay."

Shock slackened his jaw. "May I ask why not?"

The children flashed in her mind. Sophy. Hannah. Johnny. Julia. Liam. They all held a piece of her heart. And now Mr. Twethewey owned a piece of it too. They were worth the gamble. For what else did she have to lose?

"My life at Penwythe Hall may not seem like much to you, but it is still *my* life. I have built relationships and have a purpose. I have my own goals and my own dreams, and now they start and end there."

He gave his head a sharp shake. "Help me understand, because I cannot. Why would a woman choose to be away from her family?"

"I did not choose to leave my family after Robert died. I was sent away—you remember how it was. There is a very great difference between the two. Over the years I have adjusted and accepted it." She paused, attempting to read his face. "I do realize that I have choices now."

"Yes, you have the choice to come stay here."

"Please, Horace. I must make my own decision about this."

He tensed with irritation. "You'll do what you want. You always have. But there will come a time, Delia, when you'll need your family. Maybe not this year or the next, but I think life has taught you that everything is very uncertain. And when you realize that, you will be back here, mark my words."

She straightened her shoulders and leveled her gaze. "You are my brother, and I love you dearly, but there is much about me you just don't know. And you are making assumptions about Mr. Twethewey based on other men like him. Do you not trust my judge of character enough to know the difference?"

She didn't want to argue with Horace. They'd spent years apart, and their time together should be precious. Maybe that was why it was so hard for her to hear his opinions—or maybe his opinions were just coming too late.

The Widow's Crest was about what Jac expected. Decrepit and run-down, it offered only two rooms, and one was already let. Jac settled the payment with the innkeeper, and once inside the narrow bed-chamber, Jac dropped his satchel on the bed. Liam's footsteps fell heavy behind him.

Jac stepped to the window and lifted the thin linen curtain to stare down to the soggy courtyard below. Two ponies stood at a swollen water trough, and a broken wagon leaned against a fence separating the property from the road.

He'd not been alone very much with Liam since he'd arrived in Whitecross. At first he'd been so grateful that Liam was all right that he hadn't asked too many questions about why he'd left. But now, as emotions had settled, questions bubbled in Jac's mind.

He turned back to Liam, who had also dropped his satchel onto the bed, and his downcast eyes and silence served as a clear indicator of his discomfort with what had happened.

Jac scratched the back of his head, contemplating what to do. They needed to discuss what happened, and why. It would be easier to deal with this situation if he did not see so much of himself in the boy. Liam had acted on impulse. Time and time again, Jac had too. That was probably why part of him understood Liam's action—the need for an immediate solution and the desire to set things right as soon as possible, whatever the cost.

With a heavy sigh Jac dropped to the bed and rested his elbows on his knees. "Well, Liam, let's have it."

Liam blinked up, his brow furrowed.

When he did not respond, Jac prodded further. "Why did you run off like that?"

His answer was immediate. Rehearsed. "Julia said she thought you were going to send us to live with Aunt Beatrice."

"And you did not think that you could talk to me directly?"

Liam shrugged but said nothing.

Jac let seconds tick by, buying time to formulate his next words.

Clearly Liam—and the rest of the children—regarded their governess as more of a protector and authoritative figure than him. And that was all right. Even though they'd been with him all summer, it was still a fairly new arrangement. But if he were honest, the lack of trust twisted uncomfortably within him.

Jac squared his shoulders and stooped to meet the boy at eye level. "I'm going to make a promise to you, Liam. And I want you to listen to me well." He waited until the boy made eye contact with him before continuing. "You and your brother and sisters are my family. And I'll fight for you. I'll protect you. I'll always be on your side. But this is not a one-sided relationship. You have a part to play in this too."

His face pale, Liam looked sad. "What's my part?"

"You must trust me. You have to believe that I have your best interest at heart. You have to be brave enough to come to me when you don't like something. We're still getting to know each other, and in the meantime, you have to make the conscious decision to uphold your end of the bargain."

Liam swiped the back of his hand over his nose and sniffed. Jac thought he wasn't going to respond, but then he murmured, "I'm sorry."

"I'm sorry too."

"No," Liam said. "I mean, yes, I'm sorry for what I did yesterday, but I'm sorry for the other things too. I'm sorry for saying I hate you and for saying you stole my father's money. I know it's not true."

Jac's throat tightened. He was not one given to emotion, but in this narrow moment of time, the past, present, and future collided. Emotions shifted and grated against each other. Anger toward his brother. Sadness for his death. And now, hope for a new relationship with his children.

Jac placed his arm around the boy's shoulder and gave a good-natured squeeze. "This is behind us now, isn't it? We'll not speak of it again. You're a lucky young man that no harm came to you or your horse."

The boy sniffed again.

"I'll tell you what. You stay here. I'll make sure the horses are bedding down all right, then see what I can do about hiring a carriage. Mrs. Greythorne might be traveling with us, and if she does, I don't think she's cut out for a horseback ride that long, do you? Then we can get some supper and turn in early."

Jac grabbed his hat and headed out into the damp afternoon. What he had thought had been a disaster just might have turned into a new foundation of trust and honesty between him and his oldest nephew, and at that knowledge, fresh optimism swirled.

CHAPTER 45

Making carriage arrangements took much longer than Jac had anticipated. He was forced to go into Morrisea to find a carriage for hire—and in doing so he passed the Hawk's Eye Inn.

Mrs. Greythorne's warning stirred afresh in his mind. She'd said the entire town was run by the Greythornes, and he did not doubt it. He glanced at the faces he passed as he traversed the street, wondering what role, if any, they played in the Greythornes' work or if they'd known Delia when she'd resided here. He kept an alert eye out for Thomas Greythorne, and for Mr. Simon as well, but his visit to the livery passed without incident.

After making the necessary arrangements, Jac returned to the main street. The thought that Delia had spent so many years here was not lost on him. She'd walked this street. Attended that church. So much of her life had been here—so much of her heart. His gaze fell on the graveyard next to the church—a rather large graveyard, with ancient oaks offering shade to the graves below. He sobered. The space called to him, drawing him in like a beacon, and he stepped toward the resting place.

As soon as he entered the walled enclosure, he noticed several ornate headstones carved with images of angels and animals, all of which bore the name Greythorne. Reginald Greythorne. Jane Greythorne. Matthew Greythorne. He continued down the row, until one name stopped him in his tracks.

Robert Greythorne.

From the dates, this had to be her husband. He pivoted to the side, and then he saw it. The infant grave.

Maria Greythorne.

Fresh flowers adorned both headstones. He did not doubt for a moment that Delia had placed them there. He could only imagine the pain of loss she had endured. He recalled the tenderness that lit her eyes and softened her expression when she had accepted the pendant earlier. But even as happy as that made her, it would never bring her little daughter back. And Maria could never be replaced.

He stared at the tiny marker for several seconds. A pair of noisy birds squawked above. He raised his head, and upon doing so he noticed wild daisies growing at the fence's edge. He stepped over, gathered a handful, and placed them on the child's grave.

If he could, he would take Mrs. Greythorne's pain upon himself, but nothing could change the past. But maybe, just maybe, he could help change her future.

When Jac returned to the Widow's Crest Inn, his stomach was grumbling. Surely by now Liam should be rested and ready for a meal. But when he arrived in the courtyard, no stablehand was there to take his horse. Odd. He settled the horse on his own before he returned to his room.

He entered the inn and found it deserted. No innkeeper was at the desk, no barkeep was in the dining room, and no guests milled about. Earlier the inn had not been lively, but people had been present. Now, the stillness was eerie.

He was not a superstitious man, nor was he prone to dramatics, but something about the inn's still atmosphere and stuffy silence was unnerving. He sniffed. He'd be grateful to leave this place once and for all and return to Penwythe Hall. He was worried about the orchards and eager for life to get back to normal.

He made his way up the stairs. As he did, the hair on the back of his neck inexplicably prickled. It was too quiet. Once at his chamber's door, he retrieved his key from his waistcoat pocket, but when he put the key in the lock, it struck him—the door wasn't locked.

Alarm rushed him. He flung open the door.

Liam was nowhere to be seen.

Jac's mouth went dry. His head felt light. He spun around with jerky, desperate movements, poking his head around the bed and in the cupboard. "Liam!"

No response.

"Liam!" he repeated, louder this time.

No sounds met him, just the sound of the sign outside the window banging against the wall in the breeze.

Panic ripped through him. He quickly took inventory of what remained. Liam's satchel was on the hook on the door, right next to his. Beyond that, the room was devoid of any personal items.

"Stay calm," he muttered. "There's got to be an explanation." Jac stomped to the window and looked down into the courtyard. No one was there.

He raked his fingers through his hair and whirled around. And then he saw it—a piece of paper on the pillow. He crossed to the bed in two paces and snatched up the note.

The time has come for her to right wrongs. As long as she meets us at Turf House, the boy will be unharmed. She knows the ramifications if she fails to comply. None will stand against us. She must come alone.

Jac hungrily absorbed each word of the note. Then he read it again. Perspiration beaded on his forehead, and dampness covered his palms.

Now he fully understood the fear roiling in her eyes the night of the Frost Ball. Thinking of her living with this terror for all these years tore at his heart.

He did the first thing he could think to do: he grabbed the satchels and the note and ran down the stairs. He flew to his horse, saddled him, and jumped on his back. There was not a moment to waste.

CHAPTER 46

Delia's argument with Horace weighed heavy on her heart as she stood at her bedchamber window. She didn't want to leave him and have their final conversation be an argument, yet he would not be happy unless she changed her mind.

And that she would not do.

She turned back to her valise and assessed her belongings, but the items on the dressing table caught her attention—Elizabeth's possessions.

Horace had told her that she might have whatever personal items of Elizabeth's she would like. Part of her wanted to pretend they weren't even there. The pain associated with loss was still too raw, and experience had taught her that it would take a long time for that pain to subside—if it ever did. But as she walked around the room, her gaze fell on a leather-bound book on the small table next to the bed. Delia lifted it.

Elizabeth's *Book of Common Prayer*.

Delia lovingly ran her fingers over the book's cover and hugged it to her, and after several moments, she flipped it open. The words leapt off the page—words so familiar, so comforting. Especially after Elizabeth's words of faith, Delia knew her sister would want her to have this.

She tucked it in her valise and was about to join the family down in the drawing room when hoofbeats thundered in front of the house. She frowned and crossed back to the window. Immediately she recognized Mr. Twethewey's broad shoulders and black hair evident from beneath his hat. He'd said he would send word regarding their departure but said nothing about visiting again in person. And where was Liam?

She hurried down the narrow, paneled corridor and descended the straight staircase. By the time she stepped onto the main floor, Mr. Twethewey was pounding on the front door. Horace emerged from his study off the entry corridor, his face flushed.

He flung an arm out in Delia's direction. "What is the meaning of this?"

"I've no idea." Delia brushed past him to open the door.

Mr. Twethewey did not greet her. Instead, he stormed through the door and into Horace's study and turned abruptly. "They took Liam." He thrust a piece of paper at her as she drew nearer, and then he paced around her as she fumbled to open it.

Time slowed as she read the missive. Word by word, the meaning penetrated, deeper and deeper, as if sinking into the fabric of her being.

Her past had jeopardized the very boy who risked his life to cross the moorland and make his way to her.

Her hand flew to her mouth. "What did—? How did you—?"

Mr. Twethewey stepped quite close. So close she could feel his heat, his anger, radiating from him. "They. Took. Liam." His blue eyes scorched her. "He's gone. Whoever wrote this has him."

Delia had almost forgotten about Horace until he stomped into the study. "What's the meaning of this?"

Mr. Twethewey ignored him and pinned his sharp gaze on Delia. "Do you know what they're talking about?"

She tensed and pulled the study door closed lest anyone overhear their discussion. The very thing she had been fleeing all these years had caught up with her. The secret she was desperate to erase from her memory flared back to life. Vibrant. Haunting. Crucial.

She drew a shaky breath and locked eyes with Mr. Twethewey, and the intensity she found there almost frightened her. The less he knew—the less anyone knew—the better. "Yes, I know where they are referring to. I'll go now."

He launched forward in one great step and took her arm. "No, you aren't."

"Have you not listened to me?" she hurled, ripping her arm free of his grasp. Tears blazed in her eyes, and her voice cracked with uncontrollable emotion. "Did you not believe me when I told you how dangerous they are? I know what they want."

Over Mr. Twethewey's shoulder, she saw confusion darkening Horace's face. Her brother clenched his fists and pushed closer, like a child determined to have his way. "Delia, I demand to know what is going on."

Desperate, she turned her attention to Mr. Twethewey. A thousand words were exchanged in that single glance. With a grunt of impatience, he nodded toward Horace.

She followed his silent direction and extended the note toward Horace.

Horace angled the missive toward the light, and the color that had so quickly rushed to his face drained, leaving him pale. He lowered the note, dumbstruck. "I don't understand."

"Think, Horace," she snapped at him. "Who do you know who would expect something like this of me? Who would be capable of this?"

Horace's face fell, and he handed the note back to Mr. Twethewey.

Delia stepped nearer to her brother. "You've known all along what they are capable of. Did you really think that at some point I wouldn't find out what they were?"

Mr. Twethewey's nostrils flared. "We're wasting time. We must go after him. Who is the magistrate here?"

"It's no use." She shook her head. "The magistrate is Thomas

Greythorne's cousin. He'd sooner throw you in the gaol than help us."

"Is there no one then?"

Horace ran his fingers through his thinning hair. "There's a customs office about three miles from here. I can't make any guarantees that they'd be willing to help, but I can go there tomorrow and—"

"That will be too late," Mr. Twethewey barked, pivoting to Delia. "Do you know where this Turf House is?"

She nodded, her stomach curling at the memory of the tiny dwelling with one window, flagstone floors, and a slate roof. "It's on the moors, halfway between here and Morrisea. It's near the sea."

Mr. Twethewey's mind had to be whirling. His eyes were wild, and he scanned the room hungrily. "Do you have any weapons here? Pistols, anything?"

Horace stuttered, "Our f-father kept a pair of dueling pistols, but only because they were given to him as payment for a debt. I—I don't even know if they still fire."

"I have my traveling pistol, and those will have to do. Fetch them, will you? Along with a hunting knife if you have one." He turned back to Delia. "You need to tell me where this place is. Be specific."

She shook her head. He was asking the impossible. "Surely you know I can't describe that to you—especially when you've never seen it for yourself. The moors are nothing but rocks and crags. No road is straight. I—I have to be the one to go. Besides, they'd sooner kill you on sight than listen to you try to reason with them."

He stepped closer and set his hands on her shoulders. He stooped to look her in the eye. "There's no way I'll let you go there. It's too dangerous."

She shrugged. "But you aren't listening to me. They won't hurt me."

"You've been frightened of them since the day I met you," he retorted. "Why would you think they wouldn't hurt you?"

"Because I have something they want."

She shifted her gaze between Mr. Twethewey and her brother. Her blood rushed through her head with such force that she found it difficult even to think, but she owed Mr. Twethewey an explanation, and it was about time Horace knew the truth as well.

Mr. Twethewey's question was barely above a whisper. "What do you have?"

"Knowledge." She licked her lips and tried to organize her thoughts above the wild beating of her heart. "Robert never really spoke of his true ... *occupation* before we were married, but it wasn't long into our marriage that I knew the Greythornes—all of them— were smugglers. The night of his death, we'd been invited to his cousin's home to dine. He'd been so agitated in the days prior, and instead of taking the carriage and the main road as we normally would have, Robert took the trap and a pony. He was determined to travel through the moors, which was especially treacherous in the stormy weather.

"We rode out by the Turf House and cliffs, and all the while he muttered and scanned the horizon. He was frantic and said he was in danger. He kept repeating that he'd been betrayed and that if he died that night, I had to tell his brothers that the last haul was hidden in the crags above the sea. He was adamant about showing me the exact location so I could show his brothers, but I protested. I didn't want to know. I didn't want any part of it. But he forced me from the trap, dragged me to the cliffs, and showed me the path. It was the first time I had seen with my own eyes exactly what he was up to when he would leave the house during the midnight hours. It was a true confirmation that he was a thief. I saw the crates. Saw the cave.

"He then forced me to go back to his cousin's cottage and locked me in a room there, like a prisoner, while he went back into the night. It wasn't until the next morning I was taken to the beach, and by that time he had already died. Apparently during the night he'd gone out to sea to meet another boat coming from France to unload the shipment, but he was right—he'd been betrayed, and the excise men were waiting for them. Robert was shot while on a boat. One of his crewmen somehow pulled him to safety, but he only lived long enough to tell his brothers that I knew where the haul was. They demanded that I show them where it was."

She glanced up to see shock in Horace's expression and sadness in Mr. Twethewey's. Both men remained silent.

"I lied when they asked me where Robert had hidden the goods and told them I had no idea what they were talking about," she blurted. "I emphatically denied knowing anything, because if I told them, I'd be breaking the law. I'd become one of them. I knew they'd never kill me, not with all eyes on them after the raid. Instead, they sent me away, but part of me was always prepared for the fact that one day they'd demand answers, and that day is here."

She turned around. Horror had drained Horace's face of color. Mr. Twethewey's expression of sadness had morphed into anger. His brows were drawn, his lips set in a firm line.

She forced strength to her voice. "They want to know where Robert hid the crates. Apparently they never found them; otherwise they wouldn't need me to show them the way." She stepped forward. "I'll go and tell them what I know. They'll free Liam and it will be over."

Mr. Twethewey shook his head. "Absolutely not."

A sudden confidence surged through her, and she clutched his arm. "Nobody knows the Greythornes better than I. I lived with them and understand how they think. Furthermore, I know the moors and beaches like the back of my hand. Robert took me there often. Liam is a prisoner because of me. I'm going. You can't stop me."

Jac's expression did not crack as he stared at her. She could see it in his eyes—his mind was mapping out every possible scenario. "Well, you're not going alone."

Did he not hear her? "I told you—"

"You're not going alone, and that's final." He pivoted toward

Horace. "Go to the customs office. Get the officers, now. Tell them what she just told you, and take the note."

Delia turned her full attention on Horace. She searched her memory, calling to the forefront every detail she could remember. "Take them to the beach just above the east end of Bran Cove. Up in the rocks there is a series of caves. They are all connected, and you'll want to find the northernmost entrance. That's where the crates were stashed that night. It's hard to see, and even harder to reach. But most of all, be careful. I can't imagine there will be many men there, but you know the Greythornes' reputation."

She could see it in his eyes. Horace didn't want to go. He didn't want to get involved. Going against the Greythornes was a death sentence. She hadn't known that before she married Robert, but she knew it now. And clearly Horace knew it as well.

"A little boy's life is at stake, Horace." Her strong voice echoed in the space. "If you don't go get the customs officers, they might kill Liam. You don't want young blood on your hands."

Horace hesitated, then reached for his coat and hat from the pegs next to the door. "Very well."

Her tone softened. Their relationship might be a complicated one, but despite everything that had happened, he was still her bother. "Do you remember that birdcall Father taught us?"

He nodded.

"Listen for it. And I'll listen for yours. But be loud with it. The surf is loud against the rocks. It might be the only way for us to communicate."

With that Horace left and turned toward the stable.

She was alone with Mr. Twethewey now. He said nothing but wrapped his arms around her and hugged her to him. She pressed her cheek against his chest, feeling his strength. Even through the broadcloth of his coat she could feel the steady yet fast beat of his heart. He was as frightened as she was. How could he not be? She clung to him for several seconds. They were partners in this—the two of them against what seemed an invincible foe.

His grip on her loosened and she looked up. Despite the tense lines on his face, tenderness radiated from his eyes. "You don't have to do this, Delia. I'll go."

She saw the sincerity in his eyes. She could feel his passion, his intensity. Whatever it was that had balanced between them the past months was taking shape. Her giddy feelings of girlish infatuation were evolving into something deeper, something more central to who she was.

The expression in his eyes communicated he felt the same. He needn't say the words.

She studied him for several moments. The cleft in his chin, the stubble on his jaw. She reached out and touched her fingertips to it.

Mr. Twethewey. Her Mr. Twethewey. Her *Jac*.

She tore her gaze from his. "I have to do this. Can't you see? If I don't, I will forever be in fear. Forever chased by the ghosts of my past. No. I must go."

In the next breath he lowered his head and pressed his lips against hers. Sweet and strong, he deepened the kiss.

She could get lost in this sensation—this feeling of safety and warmth. For a few moments she gave herself over to it. The desperation she felt matched his. They were both hungry for something just out of reach.

Finally he released her, and reality slammed into them. She looked to the window. Outside, darkness was falling. Soon it would be pitch black. She was already dressed in a gown of mourning. How ironic that such a symbolic color would be what she needed to camouflage herself in the night. "Let me get my cloak and we'll be off."

As she turned to go, he gently caught her by the crook of the arm. Determination narrowed his eyes as he spoke. "Everything will be fine. This time tomorrow we will be back at Penwythe Hall. All of us. Just wait and see."

CHAPTER 47

It was always windy on the moors. The first breezy gust, cold and sharp, forced fresh life to Delia's memories, as if they'd happened yesterday instead of years ago. She glanced upward, squinting against the breeze. Thick, shifting clouds, like silken gossamer, glinted under the moon. The edges gleamed silver as the moonlight pushed through the night air.

It had been drummed into her: *"Don't go onto the moors at night. Stay to the road where the ground is even. The bogs will trap you; the stones will snap a pony's leg."*

The warnings were well founded. She'd heard enough stories of men who met their fates on the harsh terrain.

The steady rhythm of Jac's horse clomped behind her, and she looked backward. The animal's breath plumed into the night. She lifted her hand to signal him to halt. "The Turf House is just beyond that hill. I don't think you should go any farther."

"I don't like this," he whispered, pulling his horse to a stop next to her.

She lowered her cape's hood. The wind caught it afresh. It took strength to resist swaying with the force of it. "Trust me. Greythorne House is there, beyond those hills. The moors stretch out into a meadow, and it meets up with Greythorne property. Bran Cove and the sea are the other direction. There." She nodded, turned, and pointed. "See that rock there that juts to a point, and the smaller one to the left of it? There is a crevice in between those rocks. Once you go through it you'll see the cliffs and the cove below. That's where the caves are. There are dozens of them. Most of them connect, and they are narrow and difficult to navigate."

"Do you think the haul is still there?"

"I don't know."

"And you have no idea what's in it?"

"None."

"What will the Greythornes do if the haul isn't there?"

She shuddered at the thought. They would probably accuse her of keeping it for herself. To reassure herself, she nodded firmly and said, "I am sure it's still there."

Thunder grumbled, and the wind whistled down, bringing with it fresh pellets of rain. She circled the horse around. Jac was watching her. For the first time she saw fear in his eyes. His concern mimicked her own. Any kind of dealing with free traders was grave, and the Greythornes were as vile as they came.

"If you go to the cove, go on foot. Leave your horse here," she instructed. "There's a small grove of trees on the edge of the rocks over there where you can tie him."

She clicked her tongue to move her horse, but Jac reached out and stilled her reins. His hand lingered on hers, strong and re-assuring. "This goes against everything in me, to let you go in there alone. Surely we should get the magistrate or wait for the excise men. Anything."

"The excise men can't do anything until they catch them in the act of transporting goods. That's why the Greythornes have evaded them for so long, don't you see? Besides, the excise men don't know this land like the Greythornes do. I'll lead the excise men, and God willing, my in-laws will be caught. Like I said, I believe they won't hurt me, but they wouldn't think twice about hurting you. Or . . ."

She stopped short of saying Liam's name. She couldn't. Fear lodged the name in her throat.

His tone darkened. "You've a great deal of faith in the people you say will kill."

"My faith is not in them, Jac." She turned her face into the wind. The prayers that had become more constant in her life sustained her. Somehow, through all of this despair, God had spared her. She'd survived her parents. Her husband. Even her child. Like Elizabeth had said, there was a reason she was here, a purpose. Perhaps this was it—perhaps not. But no, her faith was not at the mercy of those who bore her name. It was in Someone far greater.

He inched his horse closer and placed his palm on her cheek. It felt rough yet tender against her chilled skin. He kissed her, there in the wild wind, the intensity of which rivaled the gales sweeping from the cliffs. When he straightened, he dropped his hand and pulled a pistol from the saddle. He checked it and then handed her the handle. "This is loaded."

She stared at it, noting the way the moonlight glinted off the metal. Pistols frightened her, ever since she saw one that belonged to her husband discharge in their very own drawing room. The roar had been deafening, and the look of alarm in Robert's eyes would haunt her for years to come. "I don't want it."

"But you need it." He took her hand and slid the weapon into it. "If you get into trouble, scream loudly. I'll be there."

She licked her lips. They tasted salty from the sea air. "I will. I'll be bringing them back this way when I take them to the crates. Stay clear of this path. Go up to those cliffs, but be careful. I'm sure they have watchmen out. Keep low, and listen for the birdcall." She kicked her horse, sending it along the path.

Her horse trudged up the hill, and when they crested it, she looked down to the valley. The white stone cottage was barely visible in the dark night, yet it was there, standing as it had, no doubt, for centuries. Despite its fortitude, it was anything but welcoming. She scanned the landscape. If the Greythornes were within, they'd be watching. They were probably watching her now.

She tightened her cape and urged the horse forward. There was but one window in the cottage and just two doors, one facing north and the other facing south.

As she drew closer, her mind raced to make sense of the entire situation. She didn't know who was inside and had no idea if Liam was with them. She focused on Jac's promise. This time tomorrow they'd be at Penwythe Hall, among the orchards and the flowers. The sun's warmth would brighten all, and this dark, desperate experience would be nothing more than a memory.

The cottage came into sharper focus. Heavy stone walls, strong enough to withstand the wild wind and sea air, and a slate roof harvested from the moors themselves. She slid from the saddle and tied her horse to the post just outside the door.

She whispered a prayer, then drew a breath.

Delia prepared to knock, but before she could, the door flung open. She jumped at the suddenness of it and squinted at the brightness, her heart thudding so strongly she thought surely it would give out.

The flickering light from within illuminated the silhouette of a man. Thomas Greythorne.

A throaty chuckle rumbled from his big chest. "Sister. You did come. Saw the error of your ways, did you?"

She swallowed. Showing any fear would not do. They would sniff it out. Exploit it. She had to play the part of a brave woman, even if she didn't feel it. She pushed her way past him. "What is the meaning of this, Thomas Greythor—" She cut her words short.

She blinked and looked around the room. Liam was nowhere to be found. But none other than Ada Greythorne was present and, just behind her, Hugh Simon.

Delia felt as if she'd been struck. It would have been bad enough to come face-to-face with her mother-in-law, but Mr. Simon? None of it made sense.

Scraps of Jac's warning about the man swam in her head.

The sight stole her words momentarily. She wanted to lash out at Mr. Simon and demand an explanation of what he was doing here. But instead, she drew herself up quickly. "What, Henry couldn't join us?"

Thomas laughed. "Our brother's just outside. No doubt he saw you approach. Someone has to watch out for our safety. You never know what sort of dangerous folk lurk out there on the moors."

She set her jaw and looked back to Mr. Simon, staring him dead in the eye. He blinked and his Adam's apple bobbed under the scrutiny. "Hello, Delia."

She narrowed her eyes in his direction, then let her gaze slide to Ada Greythorne. She was seated at the cottage's only table, her dainty hands folded primly before her. She was a small woman, even smaller than Delia. Her hair boasted more silver than in years past, but otherwise she was exactly as Delia remembered.

Ada's expression remained stoic, and she lifted her chin. "I always wondered if I would see you again. 'Tis a shame we had to resort to such methods."

"Where's Liam?" Delia demanded. Perspiration beaded on her forehead, and her heart's wild beating made it difficult to think clearly.

"Ah, ah. First the location, then the boy."

"But where is he?"

"He's safe. Everything else will come later."

Delia shifted her glare to Simon, standing just behind Ada. She didn't know how or why he was here, but suddenly shadowy pieces of information shifted together and formed a complete picture. Jac had seen Thomas giving him money. Surely they had been paying him for something. But what? To keep an eye on her?

"What's he doing here?" She nodded at Simon, unable to let even his name pass her lips.

"Come now, dearest," Ada said, her voice frustratingly cool. "You didn't think we would let you go all the way to Yorkshire without keeping tabs on you, now did you? After all, you are the only one alive who knows Robert's secret hiding place, and Mr. Simon was an obliging assistant. Oh, you know patience is a great virtue of mine."

Delia stared at the mastermind, the woman who directed her sons and the rest of them like puppets.

It made her sick.

Behind Ada, darkness shrouded Mr. Simon's expression. The distance was too great to read it with any certainty, but she did not care to see it, for shock stung. Betrayal burned. She'd considered him a friend, and even more, Liam trusted him. Whatever happened, however they had lured Liam away from the inn, she had no doubt that he played a role in it.

She despised him for it.

Delia licked her lips, determined to keep her wits about her. She needed to go as slowly as possible. It would take time for Horace to get to the customs office, and even more time for them to return.

"Cordelia," Ada purred, her voice smooth and low. "Show Thomas and Mr. Simon here where the shipment is. Then you can get your boy and you will leave Cornwall once and for all. But do permit me to say that if you ever venture this way again, we will not be so lenient, family or not."

Now perspiration trickled down Delia's temple, and she resisted the urge to wipe it. As she stepped toward the door, Thomas grabbed her arm, jerking her to a halt. She snapped her gaze to meet his. A sloppy grin slid over his face, and he nodded toward her skirts. "Not that we would suspect you of anything so vile, but you wouldn't by chance have a blade or pistol or the like in those skirts of yours? I can check for myself, but it would save time if you would just hand it over. I ask only as a precaution, of course."

She gritted her teeth but did not look away. It was useless to hide her weapon from him, for she had no doubt he'd find it. Without a word she reached into her pocket, retrieved the pistol, and handed it to him.

Thomas chuckled and held it up to the light. "I figured as much. No wife of Robert would venture to the cliffs without one of these."

She held his cold gaze for several seconds before finally yanking her arm away from his grip with a sniff and stomping through the door.

Once she mounted her horse, Thomas urged his horse beside her, and she eyed him. Now a pistol of his own rested on his lap, and he made no effort to hide it. "Just in case you thought you might turn that pony of yours and take off running."

Simon rode on the other side of her. She saw no pistol. She lifted her face, and their eyes met briefly. He quickly looked away.

The deceitful weasel.

She pivoted her head forward and pinched her lips together so tightly they ached. Instead of being angry, she'd throw her energy into getting Liam back. Jutting her chin upward, she urged her horse forward. He might have bested her in this instance, but she *would* win in the end.

CHAPTER 48

Jac licked his lips and wiped perspiration from his brow. He didn't want to blink. The clouds had completely eclipsed the moon, and he feared missing the sight of Delia moving across the moors.

He clenched his jaw, squinted, and scanned the landscape. She'd said they'd be coming this way. Minutes ticked past in a painfully slow cadence, and then he heard it—the call of a night bird. It was faint and barely audible above the rustling of the straw-like grasses, but it was there, soft, certain.

He couldn't tell which direction it came from. He listened harder.

There! It came from the south. By the cliffs. It had to be Abbott.

He was caught between his desire to wait for Delia—to see that she was safe—and the need to go and join the men. He had no idea if Delia and the Greythornes would have Liam with them. The thought of the boy being frightened ripped through him. If a confrontation did ensue, they'd need as many men as possible, which spurred him to join the excise men.

He led his horse to a sheltered spot near the road's edge and secured the animal. The birdcall sounded again, rising above the deafening surf and crashing waves, and then again at regular intervals, louder with each careful step toward the coast.

Jac heard them before he saw them, the echo of crunching stone and hushed whistles and voices.

Following Delia's directions, he shifted the pistol at his waist, secured his blade, and located the stone jutting to a point. As she had said, a narrow crevice was at its side, and he squeezed through.

The sight that met him stole his breath.

The sea, as far as he could see, spread into the night's blackness. The intermittent moonlight glittered on the waves, making the entire expanse seem alive. Below him, shadowed craggy rocks descended sharply to the shadowed beach.

Then the birdcall sounded again, mournful and low.

He followed it, testing his footing before putting his full weight on any rock, until he reached the sandy beach. Out of nowhere, a man's rough hand grabbed his arm and pulled him backward. Jac stumbled on the shifting ground and fought to regain his footing.

Jac jerked to face the man who'd seized him. The large man's features weren't visible in the light, but then Jac saw six additional men pressed against the stone wall, Horace amongst them. The vicar looked out of place next to the other darkly clad men, but a new respect for him simmered within Jac. Abbott had done it—he'd found the customs office and persuaded several of them to come.

One of the men motioned toward him, and Jac leaned close, hungry for details.

"Now's not the time to be timid, lads." The man's voice was gruff and low. "We'll make no move 'til we see them with cargo in their hands. Am I clear?"

The passing seconds dragged into minutes, and the minutes seemed like hours—little sections of eternity that time had forgotten.

Jac wiggled his foot impatiently. Would they even come?

Two of the customs men, dressed in black, spread out to see what they could find. Horace, Jac, and the other men stayed put.

A white spot caught Jac's eye, and he looked out to sea. He jerked. A small boat approached the shore, lapping in with the waves.

It rocked and swayed as it drew nearer, and then two men jumped out, pulled the boat to the sand, and secured it behind a rock.

The leader of the customs men leaned in. "This is it, gentlemen."

"What are they doing?" whispered Horace.

"To move the cargo from the cliffs, they need a way to get it down. They can't move it back through the rocks to the moors, so my guess is they'll take it out to sea and go to another cove with better access to land."

Jac watched intently. He'd heard of these things—the intricate plans of the free traders. They were masters of moving cargo, quietly, silently, more like phantoms in the night than men of flesh and blood.

The scrape of stone against stone pounded above him. He looked up to see a flash of black. The toe of a boot.

The customs officer lifted his finger to his lips. Whoever was above them seemed to be unaware of their presence. He raised his pistol and motioned for Jac and Horace to do the same.

Jac's hand trembled as he lifted the weapon, which now seemed to weigh twice as much. Like it or not, he'd been swept into this world of danger—driven by his desire to save the boy who depended upon him and the woman who had captured his heart. Every thump of his heartbeat was like a stab in the chest. A cloak's black fabric swished again, and then he heard a voice. A soft voice. A woman's voice.

Delia was here.

They were here.

And after tonight life would never be the same.

CHAPTER 49

Delia discarded her cloak. It was too hot. Too binding. Too dangerous and cumbersome on the cliffs. Her boots were not intended to traverse such harsh terrain, and more than once a cry had escaped her lips as her foot slipped on the wet rocks.

Adding to the difficulty of maneuvering on the uneven landscape, Thomas's thick fingers dug into her arm and squeezed with each step. She tried to jerk free, but he gripped tighter.

"How much farther is it?" he grunted through clenched teeth.

"Close."

They'd already made their way through the cliffs. A man and a boy she did not recognize were on the other side of Thomas, and Mr. Simon trailed behind them. She cast him another look of disgust. Disdain for the man who had betrayed her and Liam intensified with each step.

All around her narrow caves with walls of stone and rock jutted inward. Some were dead ends. Others opened after small gaps. She set her gaze on the one straight ahead of her as the moon flitted out from behind the clouds. The last time she had been here, Robert had been gripping her hand, refusing to release it. The memory tightened her throat. "There, that one."

"You go in first." Thomas released his hold on her, thrust his lantern in her hand, and pushed her forward.

Delia looked back at Mr. Simon. Their gazes locked. She could see it in his eyes. Shock. Dismay. Perhaps even regret. Perhaps he'd initially thought himself clever to keep an eye on her in exchange for money. Perhaps he even considered it easy income. But now the wideness of his eyes and the tightness of his mouth told another story.

He'd clearly underestimated the Greythornes. He didn't have the benefit of knowing the family's reputation before he accepted his thirty pieces of silver.

She thought of Jac's words. *"Everything will be fine. This time tomorrow we will back at Penwythe Hall. All of us."*

Once at the cave Robert had shown her all those years ago, Delia knelt low to fit through the opening. She had not actually gone inside the night he brought her, but she'd watched him enter. Now, with naught but the small lantern as her guide, she crawled through the black space. As the walls grew tighter, panic began to knock. Her skirt caught and tore on the jagged rock. But then the ceiling lifted, and she could stand once more. Her yellow lantern light flickered on two tunnels.

"Which one?" Thomas growled.

"I—I don't know. I didn't come in this far."

He shoved her to the side, slamming her against the wall, ignoring her cry of pain as a stone dug into her arm. He stomped down the path to the left. A slew of curses rang out, and then he reappeared, the lines of his face hard and ominous. He glared at Delia and pointed a thick finger at her. "This had better not be a trick or so help me, I'll kill you with my bare hands."

Without shifting his glare he pounded down the path to the right, and then laughter, low and sinister, bounced back from the hard rock. "Ah, Robert, you never did steer your brother wrong, did you?"

The shadows shifted as he reappeared with a wooden crate, as wide as his shoulders, in his hands. "Abraham, get in here. Get this to the shore."

Delia pressed her back against the wall, hoping to be invisible as the man he called Abraham carried out crate after crate. What the wooden boxes contained she did not know, nor did she know how Robert had obtained them. But she knew the truth—however he got them was illegal.

And to him, it had been worth risking his life for.

Perspiration trickled into her eye. The longer she felt trapped in the darkness, the more desperation crept in. She wanted out of here. She needed to be out of here.

She forced her mind to picture the orchards. Their overhead emerald canopies and the freedom and lightness she felt beneath their boughs. They would be there soon—all of them. Jac had promised her.

Suddenly a gunshot shattered the mental image. Loud. Clear. Unmistakable.

Her hand flew to her mouth and she stifled a scream. Distant shouts resounded, and she snapped her gaze to Thomas. He rushed her, pistol drawn. He stopped inches from her face and hissed, "Who did you tell?"

"No one," she lied, unable to look away from the hardness in his eyes. "I told no one."

He growled and grabbed a smaller crate and tossed it near the door before he clenched her arm once again. He shoved her toward the entrance.

She stumbled and fell. Stone ripped through her sleeve and flesh, deeper than before. Searing pain radiated and she scrambled to her feet. He continued to force her through the narrow space until they were clear of the jagged walls.

Salty air forced its way into her lungs, and she gasped at the freshness of it. She was free of the cave now, but danger still held her captive. Wind whipped her hair in front of her eyes, obscuring her vision. Thomas's sinewy arm wrapped around her waist from behind, fairly lifting her off her feet, and the cold metal of his pistol raked against her cheek. "I'll show you what happens to those who inform on the Greythornes."

Desperate and at his mercy, she glanced down to her right. The cliffs dropped off steeply to the shadowed beach where crates littered the sandy floor, and a boat bobbed in the water.

Another shot rang out. And then another.

Her stomach clenched. She squeezed her eyes shut, thinking she might be sick.

Thomas's grip on her tightened.

Prayer after prayer raced through her head. Safety for Jac, Horace, and Liam. Deliverance for her. Justice to be brought on the Greythornes.

A bullet fired and scraped against the stone right near her head. She screamed and lunged back, and before she knew it, Thomas yanked her back to the entrance of the cave, where Greythorne's men had been stacking the crates, undoubtedly in preparation to get them down to the beach.

He threw her farther into the cave and belted his pistol. He reached for more crates. "Get rid of this. Hide it best you can. Now! Simon, what are you waiting for?"

When she turned around, she saw Mr. Simon again. In the frenzied activity she had almost forgotten he was there. But his gaze was not fixed on her. It was fixed on Thomas behind her—as was his pistol.

"What are you doing?" Thomas bellowed, eyeing Mr. Simon's weapon. He moved to draw his own pistol, but to her surprise, Simon stepped even closer to her brother-in-law, his pistol aimed straight at Thomas's chest.

"Delia, get out of here. Now." Simon's words were low. His gaze did not leave Thomas. "Liam is at Greythorne House."

When she hesitated, he shouted, "Go!"

She lifted her tattered skirts and rushed from the cave, bouncing against the low walls and scraping her head against the low ceiling in her haste until she emerged outside. The wind caught her and disrupted her delicate balance on the uneven terrain, but without looking back she took the quickest route away.

She had to get to the top. To the moors. Back to where the land was familiar and she could find her way for help.

Higher and higher she climbed, then, from the rock above, a strong hand grabbed hers. Upon instinct she jerked to free herself. She struggled and pulled, but the hand did not let go. She looked up.

Jac.

Precious relief flooding through her, she scrambled up, leaning on him as she did so. Chest heaving, she gripped him, clinging to him as if he were the key to freedom. The moonlight shifted, and she caught sight of blood soaking her sleeve where her arm had dashed against the rock.

Jac muttered under his breath, whipped off his coat, ripped the sleeve of his own shirt, and bound her wound with quick, adept movements.

As he worked she whispered, "What's going on?"

"Shh." He made quick work of the makeshift bandage and pressed them both against the protection of the rocky wall. "The customs men are seizing the property on the beach now. How many men were with you?"

"Three. And a boy."

"Where's Greythorne?"

"In the cave still. With Mr. Simon."

Jac's eyes flicked up. "Who?"

Below them, from the direction of the caves, a shot rang out. A man's painful cry echoed.

She winced, and Jac's arm flew protectively around her. Shouts rang out again, and when all was silent, she lifted her head. Jac's face was close to hers, so close she could make out the blue of his eyes, even in the darkness. She forced the words from her dry mouth. "Liam's at Greythorne House."

"You sure?"

"I think so. Mr. Simon told me."

"And you trust him?"

"He is the one who let me go." She angled her head to see down past the cliff to the shore. "Where's Horace?"

"He's down on the beach. Are you sure there were no other men helping Greythorne?"

"I only saw them."

He moved to stand, and she clutched his arm. Jac looked down at her, and his expression softened. He pressed a kiss to her head. "Let's go get Liam."

CHAPTER 50

Jac guided Delia to the top of the cliff, gripping her hand as if her life depended upon it, still grappling with what he'd seen. They'd taken the smugglers by surprise. Clearly the Greythornes had underestimated their sister-in-law's grit.

He and Horace had waited with the excise men until several crates had been loaded to the boat. They had been the longest moments of his life, waiting until the customs men were ready to strike. Once Greythorne's men were in the boat, it was an easy ambush, for the free traders had all holstered their weapons in anticipation of a voyage. Jac had seen the rest of the men, like great black spiders, scurrying down from the cliff. Assuming that was where Delia was, Jac had made his way upward.

Now she was in his arms.

Thank God she was safe, but the nasty gash on her arm incited fresh anger. They'd injured her, and that could not be forgiven. He pressed his lips to the top of her head again, her hair wild and untethered in the wild moorland winds. There would be time for a proper reunion after they rescued Liam, for they were anything but safe.

With shots and shouts continuing to ring out on the beach below, Jac clutched Delia's hand with renewed vigor, and together they continued to climb. Once they were on flat land, they retrieved his horse, both got on its back, then blazed across the black moors.

He let her take the reins—she knew the marshland and the bogs, the rocky places and the heather. In short bursts she told him what had happened. How Simon and her mother-in-law were in the cottage. How Simon had been the one to turn a pistol on Thomas Greythorne.

Jac had no choice but to trust that Horace and the excise men would ensure the Greythornes and their men were apprehended. He had no idea if Thomas was injured, or even if he was still alive, but that didn't matter now. The thought of Liam in the custody of men this dangerous pushed him farther. Faster.

The churning clouds overhead were dissipating, and the moonlight was growing brighter, shedding an eerie white glow on the moors. The landscape flashed by them as they thundered across it, delving deeper and deeper into the meadows.

Surely this could not be the way.

But then, almost as if out of nowhere, a giant black house with squat, square chimneys rose from the barren landscape. Beyond it, the black outline of a forest appeared, and just like that, the moors had reached their end.

They dismounted at a safe distance and tethered the horse in the forest. With surprising strength and force, Delia clutched his hand in hers. She crept low along the tree line and led the way to a darkened, timbered outbuilding.

She leaned toward Jac, her breath warm against his ear. "This is the groundskeeper's lodge. He'll help us."

She tapped on the door and then jiggled the rusted handle, but it did not swing free.

After several moments, shuffling sounded from inside the old building, and then the wooden door creaked open. A stooped man with shaggy white hair and side whiskers emerged from the shadows and filled the narrow opening.

Recognition flashed on the leathery face as he beheld Delia, and he opened the door wider. "Mrs. Greythorne! What are you doing here?"

Still gripping Jac's hand, she stepped inside, brushing past the man. "I need your help, Philip."

Philip reached for a lantern on the table, presumably to light it, but Delia grabbed his hand. "No light."

He lowered his hand to his side and cast a curious glance toward Jac before he settled his focus back on Delia. Philip's gaze landed on her arm. "You're hurt, Mrs. Greythorne. Let me tend it for you."

"There isn't time." She tightened her grip on his arm, as if to capture his focus. "The Greythornes have kidnapped a boy, and I believe he's in the house. Have you seen anything? Heard anything?"

Once again, Philip eyed Jac warily in the moonlight. "No, ma'am. I ain't seen or heard nothing."

"I need to get inside the house without being seen," she persisted. "Are the doors locked for the night?"

For several moments Jac thought the old man would not respond, but then he nodded his head. "Kitchen entrance is usually unlocked, but the house seems dark. I'm not sure if anyone's about."

Delia moved to the cupboard authoritatively, shifting the contents on the narrow shelf. "Thomas took my pistol. Do you have one, any weapons at all in here?"

"'Course not." Philip shrugged. "Don't like weapons on the property. You know that."

Delia's shoulders slumped in disappointment. "It's important, Philip. Please. Do you have anything to use for protection?"

"Got me a hunting knife, and there are a few rabbit snares in the back."

Jac stepped forward, eager to make their next move and get to Liam. "Can we borrow the knife?"

Philip retrieved the knife from a cupboard and handed it to Jac.

"Don't worry, Philip." Delia patted the groundskeeper's forearm, calming him as she would one of the children. "I will explain everything eventually. Just please, stay here."

Philip's expression softened as he and Delia locked gazes, evidence of some age-old understanding between the two of them. Philip nodded and then stepped out of the path of the door. "Yell if you need me."

Jac followed Delia back into the cool night and handed her the hunting knife. A filmy mist was gathering in the low-lying areas, and in the distance an owl hooted an ominous song. He gripped the pistol in his hand and gazed ahead to Delia. How odd she looked with a blade in her hand. It appeared much too large for her small frame, and yet she exuded confidence. Her presence of mind in this situation impressed him. They crept along the base of the house, around to the back entrance.

She stopped and waited for him to join her at a closed door. She turned the handle and it gave way easily. She smiled at the success and pushed her way through.

They stepped inside to what appeared to be the servants' quarters. Faint moonlight filtered through the windows flanking the door, and to his left, a low threshold gave way to a dark and silent kitchen. To the right, a wine cellar and pantry. Their steps made little sound on the flagstones beneath their feet, and as they ventured farther in and rounded a corner, darkness completely surrounded them.

The dim corridor opened to a great hall. A muffled voice echoed from somewhere, and both Jac and Delia froze.

She lifted her finger to her lips and then pressed closer to him. "It's coming from the library. Through that doorway, to the left."

He saw it instantly. The door was slightly ajar, and warm light flickered from the room. "Do you think Liam's in there?" Jac whispered.

She shrugged. "Everything else seems quiet."

"I'll investigate." He motioned for her to stay put, then tiptoed along the wall, careful to test each foot before he put his weight on it fully, in case the floor should creak. Just outside the door, he paused to listen and readjusted his sweaty grip on the pistol. The reality—and the danger—of the situation pressed on him, full and heavy.

He had no idea what was behind that door.

Liam could be there. Or perhaps not.

There could be one armed man. There could be twenty.

There was no way to know. He licked his lips and looked back to Delia. Her eyes were wide, unblinking. She nodded encouragement.

He sidled against the door frame, keeping his head low. Heart pulsing, chest tight, he pivoted and leaned. His eyes adjusted to the light, and he saw the profile of an elderly woman sitting next to the fire.

His heart fell, and he lowered his weapon. Surely Liam was not here. They were mistaken.

He was about to pull back when movement to the left snared his eye. He shifted and his breath hitched. He saw the back of a head. Black hair. Broad shoulders. It was Liam. Desperate for details, Jac leaned in farther. It was then he saw the rope around the boy's shoulder.

Rage, molten and fluid as lava, surged through him at the sight. He motioned for Delia to join him. He nodded and pointed inside. When she was close enough, he held up one finger. "Liam's there. One woman's inside," he whispered. "Follow my lead."

And then he straightened and stepped through the door.

CHAPTER 51

Delia's every nerve, every sense pricked painfully with the injustice of the night. Men had died. She was sure of it.

Such knowledge was eerie. Ghostly. And stung more than the wound on her arm. Furthermore, Jac had just confirmed that Liam was inside the library. Her heart could not bear another loss. He'd also confirmed he was in there with one woman, and she had no doubt as to that woman's identity.

Delia breathed deeply. She had to remain strong. Just a little longer and this entire business would be complete.

Jac held up three fingers, and one by one, he lowered them until none remained. Then, with pistol drawn, he burst through the door.

She followed behind and assessed the room immediately. Liam was in the corner, tied in a chair. And by the blazing fire her mother-in-law sat in a chair. No one else was present.

Jac fixed his pistol on Ada as he spoke over his shoulder to Delia. "Cut him loose."

Delia snapped into action and rushed to the boy. Tears of relief threatened to blind her, and her fingers shook as she used Philip's blade to cut the rope.

The ticking of the clock was excruciatingly loud as her fingers made slow work, but eventually the ropes gave way and fell to the ground. Liam jumped to his feet and threw his arms around her. It was then—and only then—she turned her attention to Ada.

Jac's pistol was still pointed at Ada, and yet she sat as calmly and still as if she were simply enjoying an evening by the fire instead of holding a young boy hostage. A malevolent smile toyed with her thin lips. She lowered her book, her icy stare pinned on Delia alone. "So you've found me, have you, Cordelia?"

Their last meeting at Greythorne House rushed to the forefront of Delia's memory. She'd been so frightened, so weary then. Now the need for justice flared through her, and courage raced through her veins. It was her turn to ask questions, her turn to make demands. "How could you do this? Liam is a boy!"

Ada's ominous smile deepened, and she tilted her head to the side. "I warned Robert about you. Oh yes, time and time again, but he wouldn't listen, the stubborn fool. You always thought you were a bit too good for the Greythorne way of life, high and mighty you were. Yet you lived in our house, ate our food. You, my dear, are one of us, whether you like it or not."

Delia would not be drawn into the emotion of her words of the past. She focused on the present. She had to. Based on her words, Ada did not know about the ambush on the beach. But it did not matter. Nothing the Greythornes did would ever matter to Delia again. "I'll never be one of you."

Jac stepped forward and his sleeve brushed her arm. "Liam, get that rope. We're going to see that this woman never hurts anyone again."

As Liam scurried back to the discarded rope, Philip caught her eye. He stood in the doorway, hat in hands, a blank expression on his face.

Jac noticed him too. "Philip, have you a wagon we can borrow?"

Philip shifted his rheumy gaze from Jac, to Ada, and finally to Delia, sadness sagging his shoulders.

"Please, Philip," Delia urged. "It's important."

Before he could respond, Ada ground out, "Philip, don't you dare." The curt tone of her voice offered the first indication of fear.

Philip turned his eyes back on Delia. "I'll be right back, Mrs. Greythorne. You were always nice to me and my wife, and like I told you, I'll never forget it."

———◆———

It was dawn by the time everyone had reassembled at the vicarage in Whitecross. Delia sat on the sofa. Jac sat next to her, his arm protectively—and affectionately—around her. She leaned her head against his shoulder and nestled it against his neck. He hadn't moved a muscle since they arrived, and she hoped he never would.

Liam slept on the chair opposite her, his black hair framing his face, his chest rising and falling smoothly with each breath. She'd been proud of his strength and courage throughout the ordeal, for it was one that no child should have to endure. Horace and one of the customs officers stood near the fireplace. Mary entered the parlor, tea tray in hand.

"I can't thank you enough," the customs officer said as he accepted the steaming cup. "The Greythornes have been terrorizing the area for years, and we've been powerless to break their hold. Thanks to your tip, we finally have a true case to bring against them, not to mention evidence to support it."

Delia accepted her own cup of tea from Mary. She leaned back so her sister-in-law could hand a cup to Jac. It seemed strange now that after so much time and fear the unrest was finally behind her. So many of her questions had been answered, but one more remained. The question had plagued her since that night on the moors with Robert, and while it did not really matter, her curiosity got the better of her. "Did your men learn what was in the crates?"

The excise man rocked back on his heels. "Silver. And a great deal of it. Crate after crate of silver plates, coins, bowls, and anything and everything else you could think of. Quite a hefty bounty. No wonder they were so keen to get their hands on it."

Silver.

She stifled a huff of disbelief.

Crates of silver had been the source of Robert's fear, not to mention her own. It almost sounded silly now.

"I'm only sorry it came to this." Delia glanced down at the fresh white bandage on her arm, then at Liam to ensure that he was still sleeping, before she asked her follow-up question. "What will happen to Mr. Simon?"

"He's been injured, as you know, a knife stab to his shoulder, but he'll survive. He has his own wrongs to account for—he shot and killed Thomas Greythorne, and he lured the boy out of safety and aided in a kidnapping, so there will be an inquisition into that. We found a portfolio of missives in his possession of how he'd entered into a business arrangement with the Greythornes, and it's proven to be quite a wealth of information. Those letters alone are enough to see that he is behind bars for a good long time. If he's got a brain in his head, he'll turn king's evidence against the Greythornes for a lesser punishment."

At the mention of the portfolio, she knew what they were referring to—the very packet she had retrieved from beneath the floorboards in Mr. Simon's chamber at Penwythe Hall that morning so many weeks ago. Even so, unexpected, inexplicable sorrow trickled through her at the thought of Mr. Simon in prison. She hated him for how he had betrayed them, but in the end a strange sort of loyalty—or at least conscience—prevailed. "And Ada Greythorne?"

"She and Henry will be imprisoned. I can't see how any jury would find fault with this case. I don't care how powerful the Greythornes are. Their empire is crumbling, and no doubt it will be every man for himself—every free trader from here to Devon will want to avoid swinging from the noose. Nothin' looses a man's tongue like staring at the rope."

The bittersweet words hung somber and poignant in the air. It was then she noticed her brother's tight, colorless expression.

What a shock this must have been for her brother—the vicar—to step from his quiet, safe world into danger. Perhaps he did do it for Liam, but she knew he did it for her as well.

Despite all the tension between them, she loved her brother. "Thank you, Horace, for everything you did tonight."

Horace ignored her words of gratitude. It spite of his flaws, he was, in the end, a humble man. In true form, he changed the subject. "I suppose you're all eager to go back home to Penwythe Hall."

All? Could it be that he had finally accepted her decision?

She exchanged glances with Jac. A smile softened his expression.

Yes, home. To Penwythe. To the children, and to the life they were all building there.

Horace sighed and then nodded. "As your brother, I wish you'd stay with us here in Whitecross, but I do understand your reasons, and I can admit when I'm wrong."

At his hesitation to continue, Delia rose from her place next to Jac and approached her brother. She reached out and touched his arm but remained silent.

He patted her hand and pursed his lips before continuing, as if considering his words. "I've not always been the brother I should have been to you. I've not always acted with your best interest at heart, and for that I'll forever be ashamed. I hope you can forgive me."

Moisture stung her eyes. They'd never spoken of the fact that he'd kept the Greythornes' reputation a secret from her. And now that he had, it didn't seem to matter. "It is all behind us, Horace. All of it. Of course I forgive you."

"I want that to be different going forward," Horace added quickly, his tone brightening. "I misjudged the situation and spoke out of turn. Return to Penwythe Hall, Delia, and go with my blessing."

Delia flung her arms around him. A sense of tenderness, a sense of family, was released at the embrace. "Thank you, Brother. For everything."

CHAPTER 52

Delia and Jac walked the customs officer out of the vicarage. The first blue light of dawn was creeping over the forest to the east, and a low-lying gossamer mist still hovered over all. Jac curled his fingers around Delia's smaller ones as the officer bid his farewell and disappeared in the morning's quiet stillness.

They were alone now, and Jac preferred it that way. He did not want to return to the vicarage, where her family still gathered. With sudden energy he squeezed her hand. "Come on."

She laughed—a joyful, peaceful laugh. How long had he yearned to hear that sound? He led her to the walled garden and opened the door. She didn't resist as he led her through the gate, and once they reached the stone wall's shadow, he pulled her closer.

Clutching her hand against his chest, he whispered, "Do you trust me, Cordelia Greythorne?"

"I seem to remember you asking me that question once before." She smiled up at him, leaning closer, melting against him. "You know I do."

His gaze landed on the soft curve of her lip. He couldn't look away, even if he wanted to. Her nearness clouded his thoughts, yet there was one specific thing he needed to know. "Let me ask you this, then. Will you trust me with today, tomorrow, and every day for the rest of your life?"

She bit her lower lip in that way she was oh-so-prone to do.

Tears glimmered in her eyes, and yet she met his gaze boldly. She inched closer, so close that the hem of her skirt brushed against him and the scent of her hair intermingled with that of the roses and wrapped itself around him, intoxicating him and fueling his desire all the more.

"You could not possibly know how much you have given me," he said. "You and the children have brought happiness into my life, and I now realize how far I would go to protect it. Penwythe Hall would be nothing to me if you were not there by my side. You've become part of it, and you've forever taken up residence in my heart."

He could wait no more. He dropped her hand and wrapped his arms around her, feeling the softness of her body against his. He kissed her, her lips softer than velvet against his own, and the cares and the worries of the past several months melted away.

He brushed her dark hair from her brow, the look of happiness on her face encouraging him. "Cordelia Greythorne, *my* Cordelia Greythorne, I have to say that somewhere along the way I have fallen hopelessly in love with you, and I never want to be parted from you again. Will you consent to be my wife?"

A little giggle burst from her, and she rested her hands against his chest, her gray eyes brimming with joy. "Well, Jac Twethewey, *my* Jac Twethewey, I have fallen in love with you, and nothing could possibly make me happier than becoming your wife."

EPILOGUE

Delia clutched Sophy's hand in her own as she breathed in the scents of apples and the cool crispness of late autumn. Sophy pranced and danced as they walked together. Not since the Frost Ball had Delia seen so many people at Penwythe Hall. The cider barn's courtyard was alive with activity, and at the center stood Jac.

"Do all those people want to talk with Uncle?" Sophy asked, tilting her head as she assessed the crowd.

Pride at Jac's success swelled within Delia. He'd gambled and won. Farmers from all over had brought their apples to the cider barn, and from where she and Sophy stood, they could see the horse inside dragging the stone around the crusher. Though the hailstorm may have damaged well over half of Penwythe Hall's crop, they were still busy, day and night, crushing apples, pressing them, storing them in barrels. Even Mr. Colliver had been impressed and was eager to join Jac in future ventures. Word had spread far and wide, and now they would have enough business to keep Penwythe busy for months to come.

They'd fought so many battles, many of which seemed a distant memory. Mr. Steerhead may have stolen the children's money, but Jac had given them something far greater: A home. Family. Love. Mrs. Lambourne continued to request that her nieces and nephews live with her in London, but their desire to stay and live and thrive at Penwythe Hall warmed Delia's heart.

"Yes," Delia answered at length, a contented sigh passing her lips, "All those people want to talk to your uncle."

A sweet-scented breeze blew in, and Delia lifted her face to it. How wonderful it felt to be able to live at Penwythe free of fear of the past and fear of the future. Just months ago, paralyzing fear had ruled her thoughts, and sadness prevailed over all. She continually thought of Elizabeth and her words of faith and peace, and daily Delia found renewed strength in them.

She tenderly touched the pendant around her neck. Her past—Maria, Elizabeth, her parents, and Robert—would always be a part of her story, and she was grateful for her time with them. She would never cease mourning for those she had lost, but now her heart was opening to the possibility of happiness once more.

Delia and Sophy continued toward the courtyard, and Jac looked up as they approached. Hair wild, skin tanned from days spent in the sun, he flashed a white smile at her, excused himself from the man he was speaking with, and jogged to meet them. Sophy broke free from Delia's hold and ran to meet him. He scooped up the child in his arms.

"Well, Princess Sophy, what do you think of all these people at Penwythe Hall?"

"I want it to go back to when it was just us and we could play bowling on the bowling green." She pouted.

Jac laughed and lifted her higher, then stepped closer to Delia and wrapped his arm around her. "It will all be normal again soon enough. We've the rest of our lives to spend together, and that, God willing, will be a very long time, and we can bowl until your little heart is content."

"I bet I'll win." Sophy smiled and wriggled down. "Oh, look! There are Liam and Johnny." She took off running toward the courtyard, her peach dress fluttering behind her and her long white ribbons streaming.

They watched the little girl weave through the crowd to her brothers, who were standing with their new tutor—a man who encouraged the boys to learn as much as they could about the family business. They lingered on the scene for several moments, and then Jac turned to Delia and took her in his arms. She laughed and pressed the side of her face against his strong chest. As much as she wanted to stay here forever, she could not help but notice the curious glances in their direction. "Everyone is watching us."

He did not break his gaze. "I don't care. Do you, Mrs. Twethewey?" He pressed a kiss to her forehead.

They walked together, arm in arm, back to the courtyard. Her new family, her new neighbors, her new life swirled around her in vibrant colors. No more was she watching the tree line for danger. Instead, her focus was firmly on her present, firmly on her blessings. She looked toward Jac again, and her heart leapt within her.

Finally she had found her home.

ACKNOWLEDGMENTS

This book was an absolute joy to write! I am so grateful for those who encouraged me and worked beside me to transform this idea into a finished novel.

To my family: thank you for your unending cheers and support. You mean the world to me!

To my agent, Rachelle Gardner: your advice, guidance, and friendship are a treasure.

To my fabulous editor, Becky Monds, and to my incredible line editor, Julee Schwarzburg: thanks for rolling up your sleeves with me to polish this story. To the rest of the team at HarperCollins Christian Publishing—from marketing to sales and everyone in between: thank you for all you do!

And last but not least, to my writing friends, especially KBR and KC: thanks to each and every one of you for sharing this journey with me.

DISCUSSION QUESTIONS

1. When Delia learns that she'll be returning to Cornwall, she realizes she will have to face a past she wanted to forget. Have you ever been in a situation where you had to confront issues in your past that you would rather forget?

2. Throughout the story, Jac struggled with being impulsive. Do you think this is a positive trait or a negative one?

3. If you could give Delia one piece of advice at the beginning of the story, what would it be? What advice would you give her at the end?

4. Do you have a favorite character? If so, who is it, and what draws you to him or her? Who is your least favorite?

5. Jac was faced with the sudden and unexpected responsibility of caring for his brother's children. Can you think of a time in your life when you were tasked with a major, unexpected responsibility? How did it affect you?

6. Let's talk about Mr. Simon. Do you think he was ever a true friend to Delia? How do his actions support your opinion of him?

7. Elizabeth told Delia, "*Fear is an enemy—it will rob you of today's joys and steal your strength to fight for your purpose.*" Have you found this statement to be true?

8. Now it's your turn! What comes next for Delia and Jac? What about for the children? If you could write a sequel, what would happen?

DON'T MISS THE NEXT
CORNWALL NOVEL FROM

SARAH E. LADD!

The

THIEF

of

LANWYN
MANOR

AVAILABLE JANUARY 2020

THOMAS NELSON
Since 1798

AVAILABLE IN PRINT, E-BOOK, AND AUDIO

Kate's loyalties bind her to the past. Henry's compel him to strive for a better future. In a landscape torn between tradition and vision, can two souls find the strength to overcome their preconceptions?

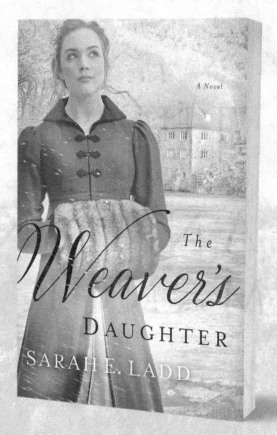

A Novel

THE *Weaver's* DAUGHTER

SARAH E. LADD

"A strong choice for fans of historical fiction, especially lovers of Elizabeth Gaskell's *North and South*."

—*Library Journal*

AVAILABLE IN PRINT, E-BOOK, AND AUDIO

THOMAS NELSON
Since 1798

DON'T MISS SARAH LADD'S TREASURES OF SURREY NOVELS!

RT Book Reviews calls Sarah Ladd a "superior novelist" and the Treasures of Surrey novels "Regency romantic suspense at its page-turning best."

THOMAS NELSON
Since 1798

AVAILABLE IN PRINT, E-BOOK, AND AUDIO

WHISPERS ON THE MOORS

JOIN AMELIA, PATIENCE, AND CECILY ON THEIR ADVENTURES IN REGENCY ENGLAND.

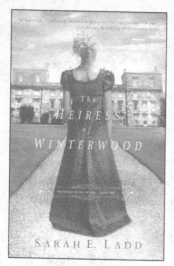

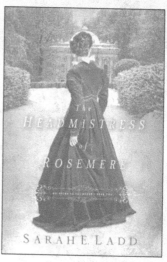

"Ladd proves yet again she's a superior novelist, creating unforgettable characters and sympathetically portraying their merits, flaws, and all-too-human struggles with doubt, hope, and faith."

— *RT Book Reviews*,
4-STAR REVIEW OF
A Lady at Willowgrove Hall

Forever Smiling Photography

Sarah E. Ladd received the 2011 Genesis Award in historical romance for *The Heiress of Winterwood*. She is a graduate of Ball State University and has more than ten years of marketing experience. Sarah lives in Indiana with her amazing family and spunky golden retriever.

Visit Sarah online at SarahLadd.com
Facebook: SarahLaddAuthor
Twitter: @SarahLaddAuthor
Pinterest: SarahLaddAuthor

Printed in the USA
CPSIA information can be obtained
at www.ICGtesting.com
CBHW010717270424
7622CB00023B/266

9 780785 223160